BOATS AGAINST
THE CURRENT

BOATS AGAINST THE CURRENT

Bevis Longstreth

ISBN-13: 9780692599686
ISBN-10: 0692599681
Library of Congress Control Number: 2015920733
Honeycomb Publishers, New York, NY

CONTENTS

1 . . . . ·1
2 . . . . ·35
3 . . . . ·73
4 . . . . ·86
5 110
6 153
7 182
8 187
9 . . . . ·209
10 . . . . ·222
11 . . . . ·233
12 . . . . ·257
13 . . . . ·264
14 . . . . ·281
15 . . . . ·289
16 . . . . ·306
17 . . . . ·314
18 . . . . ·325
19 . . . . ·347
Selected Bibliography ·359
Acknowledgments ·363
About the Author ·365

1

WITH SPRING UNFOLDING, NEW YORK City should have been a playground for young and old, like a well-tuned Steinway on which all could play rhapsodies. But Benno, along with thousands of others, was unemployed. And now, like many, he had run out of money. He couldn't afford to move out of town, and from day to day he couldn't see how he could stay. His savings and what his brother had contributed were gone. Money itself didn't mean much to him. It never had. Just a means to survival, something that was there when he needed it, an easy assumption that, without much thought, he developed growing up. His Father, Dan Murdock, cared little for money, perhaps because he had never felt the panic that comes from running dry. He taught his boys that money was nothing more than an enabler, like veins in one's body — useless except as a means of delivering life's blood where it needs to go. Dan never flaunted his wealth through lavishness. As cattleman and dirt farmer, he favored real assets — barnyard smells over the smell of money.

It was more than just running out of cash. It was fear of losing one's sense of self, one's dignity and pride. It was fear of losing control over one's life and, much worse, of giving up the fight to retrieve it. Looking around on almost any street in Manhattan, Benno could see men who had quit. In his head they formed a long line, a column of human waste. He saw himself joining these men, and it terrified him.

He lived on 21st Street, on the fifth floor of a tenement just off First Avenue. Rarely did his substandard flat have hot water. Climbing the stairs was a challenge. As cockroaches and ants scurried away, he would try to hold his breath against the ugly odors that chased him all the way to the top. Benno was gradually taking on the habits of the other tenement dwellers, a drifting, reckless, hungry crowd, smelling of unwashed skin. Aware of the drift, he struggled against it, beating against the incoming tide of forlorn hopelessness.

Hunger finally brought Benno to his knees, turning him into a petty thief, like others in the neighborhood who lacked work. Hunger hurts around the clock. One thinks of nothing else. Nighttime was bad but Benno could fall asleep on an empty stomach. Waking up in the morning was worse: first, the desperate empty feeling literally gnawing away on itself; then, the distinct odor of poverty; and finally, the realization, landing unawares like a brutal fist in the face, that the new day offered nothing but hunger.

He started begging. "Can you spare something for a cup of coffee?" "Can you spare a nickel or dime?" He tied burlap on his shoes to make them look worse than they were. As the bread and soup lines lengthened, he took to stealing. Scallions were the easiest to hide under his coat. But anything edible would do. Milk from trucks, bread from bakeries, jam and mustard from grocery stores. Even peanut butter, if he could find the smaller jars.

Benno was developing a coyote mentality. Dan had explained coyotes to the boys growing up. "They're predators. Courageous and cowardly at the same time. They'd run from you but when cornered they'd fight. They were crafty and mean. Had to be, 'cause they were no match for the wolf. And even a big dog could run them down."

Tony was Benno's landlord. Short and balding, he favored cheap undershirts and changed them once a week: the same day he shaved. In New York City, landlords were of two types: hard or soft, indifferent to their tenants' suffering or understanding and kind. With Tony, Benno got lucky. He understood Benno's predicament. Not a unique case. Knowing he couldn't find a paying tenant to take the flat, and liking the quiet sculptor from Kansas, he let the rent accumulate. "Benno!"

he would say on the first of the month. "You're gonna sell a piece, I can feel it. Your luck, she left you. Down the toilet. But, Benno, take it from me, she comes back."

Tony was practicing a common convention, and he did it well. They both knew the possibility of a sale was highly remote. But it was Depression time in the city, when even transparent denial and make-believe helped ease discourse and salve the mind.

At street level there was a candy store. Benno liked Mabel, the lady who ran the place. Soon after moving into his flat, he had taken a Hersey bar when her back was turned, stuffing it under his shirt. Unexperienced, he had failed to notice the mirror.

"Put it back, thief," she cried. Three nine-year-olds spun around to see the action. Benno looked into Mabel's dark eyes, like spotlights stripping his conscience bare. Humiliated, he looked away, only to notice youthful eyes watching him. Kids for whom, in better times, he could have served as mentor. Mortified, his pride dissolving in shame, he lifted his shirt to fetch the brown and white package. Handing it to Mabel, he said: "I'm sorry. So hungry. No work. A loser." Dizziness overcame him. He staggered forward to the counter, leaning over it for support. Before anyone could react, he regained his balance. Mabel put the candy bar back in his hand, saying, "You could use a sugar fix about now. Pay me later." She winked at the boys, and with a scolding voice said "Now listen here. Don't you kids get any big ideas." In fact, Mabel was just plain generous, especially to the local kids, giving away, it appeared, as much taffy, jelly beans and Hershey kisses as she sold.

Benno might never have discovered that the candy store was a front for a backroom bathtub gin operation, had not Stanley, his stinking, gnarled and ugly neighbor on the fifth floor, explained how the lady's huge profit margins on gin sales enabled her generosity.

Stanley praised Mabel as one street-smart, savvy dame. "Yea, she's got men. All she needs. They work for her. All kinds of ways. I hear she's got steady hot water. They say she bathes 'em. But she don't show 'em off. Keeps 'em in the backroom."

Benno caught Stanley's eye, giving him a questioning look.

"Ok, kiddo, let me tell ya what she did to a new cop who popped in, probing. Ya see, Mabel was regular in giving the Precinct's police captain a drink when he came round. Sometimes a bottle. Sometimes two. Ya get it? No one bothered her. But, then one day, this newbie patrolman comes in and starts asking questions. She knew he was working up to a pinch. So she prepared a bottle for him. He talks her into selling it to him. Then he grabs her and takes her into court. Tells the judge she sold him booze. Waves the bottle around. Before the judge, Mabel asks the cop 'how do you know it's booze?' The cop pulls the cork and takes a swig, then spits it out. It was piss. 'Case dismissed.'"

Later, in his flat, Benno reflected. He knew the cause of the dizziness. He had experienced it once before, as a kid about the age of the ones in the store, when his Father, Dan Murdock, had accused him of stealing some silver from the bureau in his Father's bedroom, where he typically left pocket change. Dan was right. He had taken some coins. He had done so with his brother, Adam. Dan suspected only Benno, who was too loyal to Adam to tell their Father the whole story. He suffered a bad licking, but not before nearly passing out from dizziness when his Father confronted him. Dan caught his son as he began to fall and lowered him roughly into a large chair in his study.

Later, when the boys were in the privacy of their bedroom, Adam took his shorter, wiry brother by both shoulders and looked him in the eye. "Why'd you take the rap?" he asked, his voice tremulous.

"Why didn't you join me?" Benno replied, knowing Adam had no answer, believing this is the way we are, the way we instinctively behave when there is no time to think things through. He felt no anger, and Adam knew it from the smile creeping across Benno's face.

Benno would sometimes walk as far as Columbus Circle to stand in line for bread and soup. Most often, though, he'd try to stem his hunger in the closest bread line outside nearby Henry Street Settlement. The best it could do was to bridge the gap between gnawing hunger and starvation. No matter how early he would arrive, a long line of men preceded him, shuffling forward, coats drawn around them with collars turned up against dawn's chill, waiting their turn for coffee and bread or a donut or soup or whatever else might be on offer. Benno never saw a woman in the line. He wondered how they managed the problem of hunger. The men never got enough for themselves, much less to take home for others. He couldn't explain it.

On the first day of May, 1935, he found himself in front of a young man of dark complexion. His face was hidden, partly by a skull cap pulled down almost to eye level and partly by a scarf wrapped around his neck and overhanded in front of his face. Benno engaged the fellow in conversation, looking, as usual, for solace. The fellowship of suffering, he called it in letters to Adam. He could even find comfort from news chronicling the fast growing number of city applicants for relief, of whom only about half were actually on the relief rolls. In early January, just before President Roosevelt promised a new Federal works program in his annual message to Congress, Benno saw a *New York Times* story reporting that three out of every four seeking relief were "urgently in need of assistance." When there are enough of us to form a voting block, he thought, help will come.

Beyond the perverse comfort of hearing another man's woes, Benno clung desperately to the notion that someday the guy right behind him might hold the key to a change of fortune. This thought could cut Benno's fertile imagination loose. Suppose the guy had the clue to hidden treasure buried in Central Park but needed someone who could read Latin to translate the message. Or he was a rich gallery owner bent on discovering exciting young sculptors who believed, naturally, they could best be found in bread lines. Or, perhaps, a scout on the prowl for a male model with that Midwestern look. Benno could no sooner turn off these daydreams than stop breathing.

"Been in town long?" Benno said.

"Just a day, believe it or not. Got off the train from St. Louis yesterday. They sent me to Henry Street. I got lucky. They found me a place to stay. And here I am. How about you?"

Benno was about to respond when the line moved. An impatient server held out the morning's fare, barking a command. Benno wheeled around and handed the server his bucket, staring at the offering of soup and a slice of bread. The guy was ladling out the greasy, watery stuff off the top of the pot. Benno knew the drill. "Please, mister, dip down there and get me some stuff from the bottom." The guy pretended not hear. Benno yelled out, "Dip down, for heaven's sake. Way down."

Benno took his bucket and stepped aside to let the young man behind him take his turn with the server, whose lip had curled. As the fellow stepped out of line in the direction of Benno, his bucket turned, spilling hot soup that burned his hand, causing him to drop the bucket. In trying to recover, his cap fell off and with it a pile of raven's black hair fell about the now distinctly revealed face of a pretty black-eyed girl.

Benno thought her a veritable sylph. In an instant, he had stepped forward and scooped up the empty bucket. Extending both arms, in one he offered this imposter his own bucket of soup and in the other, her cap. "Take it. They don't allow refills, even for accidents. Please," he implored, seeing her head shake.

"I can't do that. I don't care that much for soup anyway. Took it more for the heat. More than I bargained for." Her voice had a soft twang to it.

Benno read the deepening rose color spreading across her face. She was flustered. Not from the spill, he guessed.

"Here's an idea. There's a Horn & Hardart close by. Let's go there, sit down at a table and eat our bread. Who knows, maybe by then you'll accept a swallow or two of this slop."

She nodded. They set off. Once in the cafeteria, they took off their coats and sat down at an empty table chosen by Benno because it was as far away from the wall of caged offerings as possible. He could share his soup with this strange female, but he lacked even the nickel necessary to buy her a cup of coffee. As they began to talk, he felt edgy, anticipating the certain humiliation to come to a penniless man who had invited an attractive young woman to the Automat.

"Do you know Edward Hopper's work?" Benno asked.

"No. Should I?"

"No reason to. I thought of him because some years ago he did a haunting canvas of a woman in a Horn & Hardart. But for her, the place is empty. Nighttime with no activity outside. It's a study in loneliness. Nothing like your cheerful face."

"You an artist or something?"

"That's my ambition. I'm a sculptor. But don't tell anybody. I'm still undiscovered. When the right patron comes along, I'll reveal myself."

The bread and soup were gone. She had taken a share.

"And what's your ambition? But, hold on, we've not been introduced." Stretching his arm across the table, he offered his hand. "Benno Murdock, born and raised in Manhattan. That's the other Manhattan, in Kansas. And you?"

She took his hand in hers. Firm grip Benno noticed. "Violet Long. I lived in St. Louis until I was 14. Then we moved to the High Plains, to Dalhart in the Texas Panhandle. I've heard of your Manhattan, but I doubt you've heard of my Dalhart."

Violet didn't want to explain why she had pretended to be a man. What would she say, if he asked? It was shame, of course. But why? The line was filled with others, a vast brotherhood of need. That's the point, he thought, "brotherhood." The absence of women in that line summoned the sense of being alone, of being out of place, the other.

"And what brought you to New York?"

"Ah, that's a long story. I could try to give you a shorter version. But first, I've got to put something else in my stomach. That measly slice of bread is the only thing I've eaten since getting off the train." Examining the room, she looked confused. "This thing's new to me. What do you recommend?"

Benno saw the time to face the music had come. He'd try to delay, looking for a miracle.

"Pies are good. Let's have a look," Benno said, rising from the table and beckoning Violet to walk with him over to the wall where desserts were gathered in little glass window cases. Pies were priced at a quarter. Cherry, apple and peach appeared in separate windows.

"See anything you like?" Benno asked, thinking how good they looked, how hungry he was, how hopeless the situation.

"Oh, yes. I love pies. Could eat them all, but I'll pick apple. Which do you want? I'm buying." Fetching two quarters from her coat pocket, she handed one to Benno, then asked how it works.

"Thanks, but ... but I'm not hungry." The lie was so plain, Violet almost laughed in his face. He tried to return the quarter, but she wouldn't take it. "Come on, now, I bet you can eat a slice of pie. If not, I'll eat some and take the rest home with me. Where does the quarter go?"

"I'll show you. You drop the quarter in the slot, turn the knob, and presto, the door opens. Take out the plate, close the door and enjoy the pie, in this case my favorite."

Benno's mind cast him back, as it always did when a cherry pie was sighted, to Dr. Rachel Bernstein and her kitchen seminars in Manhattan. Here he was, virgin still, in the company of a young woman of mystery, a woman with a bit of money, yet one who stood in the early morning breadline for breakfast, a woman from Texas, where Manhattan boys believed, and Texas boys claimed, girls were born horny.

Benno wished for Adam, who always took the lead. What would he have done? Benno had lied in his youth, but not without guilt, which made him lousy at it. As he grew up, the guilt overwhelmed him. It became impossible to lie without confession, sooner or later. Adam could meet the demands of everyday life by saying what needed to be said. His formula was to do whatever caused the least harm to those involved, including himself. Often, it compelled him to lie, a skill he had mastered.

Violet got her plate of apple pie. Before returning to the table, she watched as the platform on which the plate had been resting rotated out of sight and a new one appeared, bringing another slice of pie to the window.

"Magical," Violet said.

"It's less efficient than it looks. There's an attendant back there, rotating the platforms and refilling the stations. A popular job. I know, because I've applied to Horn & Hardart more than once."

"But you're an artist. That's not the job for you."

"Even artists have to eat. Look, I haven't sold a piece for over a year. I'm behind in my rent. I need work — any kind of work. And here's a confession. I haven't even a nickel to buy you a cup of coffee. It kills me not to be offering you the pie. It's my town, my restaurant, my invitation. And you, having arrived just yesterday. I said I wasn't hungry. That was a lie. I'm down to a scallion or two and a can of sardines. Now let's hear your story."

They had returned to the table, each with a slice of pie, but were still standing when Benno finished. Violet decided to proceed as directed. Sitting opposite each other, they put fork to pie.

"My story's brief. I came to New York to escape. And to survive. Something I couldn't do at home."

They had finished, leaving not a crumb.

"I get what you've said. But there's some backing and filling left, don't you agree? Today's calendar is pretty open. If yours is too, please, let's return to where you planned your escape."

"Ok. But I bet you'd like a cup of coffee. And I want something warm to wrap my fingers around. Here's a dime. How about getting two cups while I put up my hair."

When Benno returned, Violet resumed her story. Somehow, perhaps because he was a stranger, perhaps because she had so important a story pent up inside, it felt easier to unbutton her heart to him. Quickly, she covered the years of abundant rain and great harvests, lasting until 1929.

"The town was jumping, mad with wheat money," Violet recalled. "Life was beautiful; we felt God and nature had ordained it to be that way. And to never change. Daddy would say he had the world by the tail with a downhill pull. He loved our new President. He kept newspaper clippings of Hooverisms and repeated them so often I learned some by heart." Rising from her chair, left arm across her chest, hand disappearing in coat, she raised her right arm to hammer the imaginary opponent. "I tell you Americans are nearer to the final triumph over poverty than ever before in the history of the land."

"That was just before the stock market crashed. Actually, when it happened, in Dalhart we didn't feel a thing. But gradually, the effects of that calamity moved west, causing a collapse in the price of wheat. At forty cents a bushel in 1930, a mere 1/8th the price it fetched a decade earlier, we could barely cover the cost of farming. We used savings to pay interest on the loan from First National of Dalhart. Daddy saw no option but to take on more land, plow under more grass, plant more wheat."

Benno could imagine less risky options. After all, if the price dropped below break-even, the more acreage planted, the bigger the loss. He recalled overhearing a quip by Bill White during a meal with his Father in their Manhattan home. Something about a dumb publisher who explained to his investors how the newspaper lost two cents per copy but, not to worry, he would make it up on volume.

Violet eyed Benno closely.

"You're right. The forty cent price didn't hold. By 1931, with the greatest harvest in history, the price had dropped to half what it cost us to grow. That same Summer the rains went away and the bank failed."

"Did your daddy have savings …," he trailed off as she nodded, her face fraught, a tangle of pain.

"We never questioned the safety of it all. The bank looked rock solid. Corinthian columns, for God's sake. That set it apart from all the ticky-tacky in town. Keeping our savings with First National of Dalhart gave us status. Daddy put every last cent there, 'lest we lose it under the mattress. But that's not all. Every time daddy went there, his pride grew, and with it, our family's pride, our sense of success, of belonging to a town on the move. Yes, for sure, we lost everything. But you know what? Those lost savings were an abstraction compared to the heat. Summer was a blast furnace of endless days when the thermometer broke above one ten. It's still a fire in my brain."

"Your daddy's President said some pretty dumb things. In the high flying days, he was quick to associate character with money, something I bet your daddy wouldn't accept, just as I don't. Here's something he directed at my gender, and I bet more than half of us across the land will never forget it. And never forgive him for it. He said 'If a man has not made a million dollars by the time he's forty, he is not worth much.' Imagine that, coming from our nation's leader. Imagine how it makes someone feel who hasn't even a nickel to buy coffee for a new friend."

"I came here with all the cash I could gather from family and a couple of friends, enough to last a week or so. Perhaps not. Who knows? You're helping me focus. I've got to find work. Let's save the rest of my story. I'm going back to Henry Street for advice."

"They can't give you much encouragement. I've been through the drill. First, they'll tell you that less than half the unemployed are on the relief rolls. Then they'll tell you how few work relief jobs exist out there. And those are filled by men. Only men. You're best hope may be as a transient. The Feds have a special program for them. I've been here too long to qualify, but being 'just off the boat,' you would, for sure. Ask the settlement folks. I'll tell you what. I'm going up to Central Park for the day. This is my third Spring in New York, and when I discovered the park two Mays ago, it became my temple. If you saw my flat, you'd know why. If you like, we can meet here this evening. Say 7 PM. Perhaps by then I'll be in clover."

"Who knows. Perhaps I will too. See you at 7:00."

"By the way, how old are you?"

———◆———

Violet Long was born on April 14, 1914 in St. Louis, Missouri. She had Apache blood on her mother's side, blended with French and Dutch. From her Father, a mix of Cherokee, English and Irish. By twelve she could ride ponies with the best of the boys. Good thing too, since that was the year her family heaped their belongings high on the Model T with baling wire to hold them fast, until the whole rig looked like the leaning tower of Pisa, and set off for Dalhart, a young town in Dallam County, Texas, way up in the northwest corner of the Panhandle. Founded in 1901, Dalhart believed in itself. It had grit and flex and imagined a future as THE CITY of the High Plains.

Violet's Father, Bobby, was a farmer at heart, despite having bounced around from one non-farm job to another in St. Louis, all the while dreaming of the acreage he would one day own. In 1926 he heard of the High Plains, a fabled flat land — an immensity of grass from waist-high-bluestem to short buffalo and grama. From Nebraska to Texas, from Oklahoma to Colorado, it was there for the taking under the Enlarged Homestead Act of 1909. The Government called it "the last frontier of agriculture." With the newfangled tractor combine and one-way plow, a wheat farmer could plow and plant an acre of High Plains land in three hours, compared to the 58 hours it would take with horse-drawn plow. When news of the Dalhart land rush reached him, Bobby figured he'd saved just enough to make the trip and put down a little equity on the equipment loan he would need to get the right stuff.

The move to Dalhart had other benefits. In the moist climate of St. Louis, Violet's mother Alice's asthma had grown steadily worse. As her wheezing bouts increased, the family doctor urged a move southwest, to the High Plains, where breathing was supposed to be much easier. It all became obvious when Bobby discovered that the elevation at Dalhart was 4,600 feet. "Close to a mile high and clean as a hound's tooth," he would repeat in Alice's ear, his voice a blend of pleading, urgency and excitement.

Riding wasn't Violet's only talent. She could dance and sing. Not all parents rejoice in finding their child's interests leading them down unfamiliar paths. They can become baffled and the child estranged. But the Longs embraced every skill their daughter displayed, familiar or not. They were quick to imagine a brilliant career for Violet, first as a stunt rider in the circus, then on the stage.

The family reached Dalhart in October of 1926, when its population was a little over 2,000. Three years later it had doubled in size. Less than 50 years earlier not a single human being had registered on the census as living in the four counties that comprised the far corner of Texas' northwest Panhandle.

On entering the only school in town, Violet was invited to try out for the Spring musical, *Lady, Be Good!* Picking such a recent and sophisticated musical was Dalhart's way of showing the outside world it was on top of things. Knew about the Gershwins and Astaires. Had large ambitions. To satisfy them, it would have to attract thousands upon thousands of "sodbusters," the affectionate sobriquet used to describe aspiring farmers like Bobby Long, most of whom had never before owned a piece of land.

At 12, Violet was a work in process. In profile she was thin and straight, awaiting the curves that would define her post-puberty. Her nose had advanced in size out of context. It took a parent or close observer to realize the rest of her face, even her weak chin, would catch up to compose, at the end of this awkward period, something balanced and appealing, perhaps to some delightfully so.

Violet's voice put her at the top of the list for female lead. Her nest of crow's wing hair, shoe-button eyes and dark complexion, however, were something else. At a distance her skin looked dirty, but scrubbing couldn't erase its honey-dark hue, a deep color that in certain lights, and from certain angles, was luminous, like old ivory. At school a drumbeat of whispers grew behind her back, convincing both students and teachers that she must be either "nigger" or "Mexican." The lead went to an older student, one with egg-shell skin and hair the color of straw.

Within the Long family, only Bobby suspected the school of prejudice. As a newcomer to town, he said nothing, despite a life-long tendency to call things the way he saw them, chips fall where they may. He saw no need at this stage in Violet's life to expose her to the anguish of thinking she might have been judged on skin alone. For her part, Violet felt a wound of rejection but not discrimination. She was too embarrassed to discuss it with her parents.

When Bobby saw the show on opening night, suspicion turned to conviction. Discounting heavily for his natural bias, he found nothing to redeem an obvious casting mistake. The lead's voice was a faint imitation of what Violet would have produced in audition. And now Violet knew it.

"Why didn't I get the lead?"

They were walking home after the show, Violet sandwiched between her parents.

"I guess ... well, they must have thought Peggy fitted the part better," Alice said.

"But you heard her, Mama. And that's after weeks of practice. It can't be her. It's me," Violet said, sobbing freely.

Bobby put his arm around his daughter. "What do you mean?" he asked.

"A friend warned me a few days ago. Said the low-down on me was I'm a nigger trying to pass. Said a nigger's never going to get a lead in this state. Who am I, daddy?"

"An American beauty, that's who. A girl of many talents, that's who. A white girl with nary a drop of nigger blood, that's who."

"Don't believe that friend of yours," Alice said. "Schools don't do that sort of thing. Whatever the reason, it couldn't have been your dark complexion."

Alice pulled Violet around, wrapping her in a tight embrace and catching, as she did so, Bobby's look of anguish. Gradually, as they continued on in silence, Violet's sobbing subsided despite the shock of truth that was registering in her head.

The Longs began the farmer's life in a house that Bobby built out of prairie grass sod cut into blocks and stacked one on top of another. It was located on the half section of land they could prove up and own as homesteaders, some 320 acres of flat grassland in an area of the country that, until the cattle came, had never sustained more than roving bands of prairie Indians and buffalo. With the Government's help, the plow had followed the herder in the absolute conviction that rains would follow the plow.

For $75, Bobby bought a windmill kit. Using a horse-powered drill, he pierced the great Ogallala Aquifer at 40 feet. "No better tasting water ever came out of the ground," Bobby declared as he gathered his family around the windmill to savor the crystal-clear fluid. "God's bounty," Alice declared. "Pop's bounty too," Violet added, "for didn't he pick the spot?" "Perhaps," Bobby said, "But this here city's the cause. Never felt such electricity in a place before. Let's be clear: Dalhart's what gave it to us."

The folks in Dalhart knew they were blessed. Called themselves the chosen. Convinced themselves the aquifer would never give out. "Inexhaustible" was the word in the town's promotional fliers that were scattered to the four winds in search of more sodbusting pilgrims.

Wheat was Dalhart's ticket to fame and fortune. Turkey red, the new Winter wheat, so vigorous it was hard for a farmer to fail. In 1910 the price of wheat was 80 cents a bushel, enough to get by. The Great War changed everything. The Government put a floor under wheat, guaranteeing a price of $2 a bushel. It was a simple matter of national security: grow wheat to win the war. By 1926, when the Longs arrived, the guarantee was gone, but world demand supported a price well above $1 a bushel.

With bank loan in hand, Bobby bought an International 22-26 tractor, a Case combine and a twelve-foot Grand Detour one-way plow, the most efficient tool ever invented for ripping up High Plains grass.

The Spring of 1926 had brought rain in uncommon abundance. Already there was a country club, out past the steam laundry. Farther out was a brothel, Number 126 house, to which girls from Denver and Dallas, like worker bees to the linden tree in Spring, were lured to meet the growing demands of a town on the make. There was

DeSoto's, an aspiring hotel where the doormen wore white gloves, the Felton Opera House, the Mission Theater and Herzstein's, a first-class department store. And there were two railroad lines to carry new recruits to this Mecca of the High Plains. From the East they rode the Rock Island Line. From north or south, they came on the Fort Worth & Denver.

By June of the following year, Bobby had harvested his first cash crop of wheat at a cost of only forty cents a bushel. He got $1.30. They were off and running as part of the greatest farming bonanza the country had ever seen. As Bobby plowed more sod under for wheat, the profit potential for the Longs seemed as limitless as the prospects for Dalhart. If its citizens had heard of the connection between supply and demand, it was pushed back far into the recesses of their minds like so many inconvenient truths that one assumes can always be faced later, on the remote chance that demand didn't track supply. As High Plains grass disappeared at an ever increasing clip, Dalhartians saw this phenomenon as progress, unmitigated progress. God's invitation, it was, to tear out the grass and, in its place, create an Eden of wheat. Signs around town proclaimed "NO IDLE LAND."

It took 35,000 years to develop the rich prairie cover of blue-stem, buffalo grass and grama. It took but the five years from 1924 to 1929 to plow under over 1.6 million acres of these rich grasses in the Texas Panhandle alone. One day, Violet, after watching Bobby turn over the lush grasses with his one-way plow, exclaimed "You know, daddy, Easterners might think you're leaving the soil wrong way up."

———◆———

Before setting off to Central Park, Benno checked his mailbox at the foot of the tenement stairs, a pathetic metal container covered with ages of rust that obscured the apartment number and rendered the locking mechanism immovable.

It contained a letter from Adam.

April 26, 1935 — Cambridge Mass.

"Dear Benno,

Only four weeks to go. Classes end next week. We have a week to prepare for finals; then exams, spread over two more. After that, freedom. Graduation comes in June, attendance optional. Most at law school skip the ceremonies, having already plunged into preparation for the Bar.

I have big news. As you probably know, FDR's Civil Works Administration is being replaced by something called the Works Progress Administration. Like the CWA, it will be headed up by Harry Hopkins. Last week his people came on campus looking to hire a couple of graduates as aides to the great man. I happened to be standing outside the Placement Office when the notice was posted, just a day ahead. Signed up immediately and had my choice of a time slot. "Always be first," I can remember Father instructing. "Interviewing is like going to the dentist. Best to get him while he's fresh." I still recall your response: "Apples and oranges. Aren't final impressions the most lasting?"

Well, Benno, I want you to know I followed your instincts, signing up for the last slot, at 3 PM. It turned out well. Due to the short notice, there were only eight of us for the whole day. When I arrived, they had been waiting for over an hour since the last interview ended. Far from being tired, they seemed hungry to engage. Their technique was a shock. Instead of talking about the WPA, they asked me who I would rather be, a Supreme Court Justice, Secretary of State or Leader of the House. Didn't have a clue what they were after. I said any one of these would be attractive, but if I had to choose, I'd take House Leader. And then they pounced. "Why?" Only then did I realize my choice was irrelevant. The game was to test my reasoning, to open me up. Really to see if there as any reasoning behind my choice.

I guess it worked, for I talked about being able to affect policy more from a Capitol Hill perch than in those other posts, how issues of policy appealed to me, how bothered I was by reading cases where good policy was sacrificed on the altar of <u>stare decisis.</u> The senior of the two, a Jacob Baker, left after 20 minutes, saying he had to catch a train back to Washington. The other man, John Carmody, hung around for half an hour, asking more questions — none as challenging as the first — and then telling me a bit about the job, which essentially is to clerk for Harry Hopkins, helping him, as Carmody put it, from the profound to the ridiculous, from speech-writing and advance work to travel arrangements, race track visits and dinner party seating charts. Even emptying ashtrays, since apparently the man is a chimney. Pay hasn't been set, but, Carmody opined, with a mischievous grin, that given the Hopkins style it would be reckoned at a nickel more than what would drive me away. If they only knew!

When he got up to leave, almost as an after-thought, Carmody invited me to come to Washington for an interview with Mr. Hopkins. Travel expenses covered. I was thrilled. And then I almost dropped when he mentioned I would be the only Harvard student brought down. Before getting too big a swelled head, I recalled the notice was late, allowing little time, and, in fact, the slots for the day were not all filled. That plus a lot of my classmates still longed for Hoover.

I'm like a butterfly in heat, as my torts professor liked to say. I'm trying to tamp down dreams of glory, for who knows how many others, from Yale, Columbia or wherever, received the same invitation. I take the early train tomorrow, spend the night at the Willard (where Lincoln stayed) and go to the WPA offices first thing next day. If you'll have me on your floor overnight, I plan on stopping in NYC for a quick visit on the way back. If I get this job, you need to help me figure out how to break the news to our FDR-crazed Father. If not done with care, it could finish him off.

Again, I insist you save stamp money for food. Find enclosed a self-addressed, stamped envelope, some paper and a check for

$5 bucks, all I can send right now. If I get this job, we can share the loot.

> Love from your brother,
> Adam.

Benno went to the Park, where he wrote a quick response:

Dear Adam.

What terrific news! Trouble with you is you won't accept a real compliment without turning it over in search of less complimentary explanations. Bathe in the success, as a family we've had few enough of them. The sooner you get down there, the sooner I will get a job and be able to buy a decent meal for myself. Right now my situation is almost unbearable. This morning I suffered the humiliation of inviting a young woman I met in our local breadline — let me say an attractive young woman — to Horn & Hardart, only to be forced to allow her to buy me a slice of pie because I hadn't even a nickel to my name. I know how, long ago, it seems, you begged me to reconcile with Father and regain his support, and perhaps, if things continue this way, I'll be forced to follow your advice. I've got some stuffing left but who knows how long it will last. Going back to the CWA office this afternoon. With Spring breaking forth wildly, women's skirts airy and short, blouses opening up and the city parks infused with the softness of pale green hues, all innocent of the plow, I'd swear my mind is split down the middle: one part consumed with the irresistible urge to celebrate the season, to be happy through remembrance of Springs past, to rejoice as a pagan kid again and run naked in Central Park, dancing and singing; the other consumed with hunger and my wretched unclean condition, my lack of purpose and, above all, my loss of control. Out the window it went, along with my dignity and pride, not to mention my confidence. I won't elaborate. One could drive the proverbial truck between these thoughts, so separate and remote from each other they seem.

I will expect you in a day or so. You must help me discover who I am.

Good luck with Harry!

Devotedly,

Benno

Benno mailed the letter, then turned west to Columbus Circle to check out the City's most notorious breadline. It was William Randolph Hearst's, biggest in the City, so big it made Mrs. Ogden Reid of the Herald Tribune jealous, since hers was small by comparison. Hearst used a truck to bring huge cauldrons of hot soup and piles of bread for those in line. Men, some in rags, others in suits or long coats, stood less than a foot apart all the way around the Circle and beyond, the line stretching north along Central Park West as far as Benno could see. It was the same the last time he visited this place — except for the soup, which reeked of onion and garlic. When hungry all the time, one remembers these things. Last time the soup had the gentle aroma of white bean.

——◆——

On November 9, 1933, President Roosevelt created the Civil Works Administration to provide employment to workers throughout the country. It was intended as a temporary stop-gap to get through the Winter, which turned out to be one of the harshest on record. New York City was given a quota of only 175,000. This at a time when 1.5 million men and women in the City were, as the legal test for support put it, "employable persons willing and able to work." The CWA closed down in April, 1934. A year passed before the WPA was signed into law on April 8, 1935. The programs for home relief and work relief handled by the CWA were turned over to the Works Division of the Emergency Relief Bureau until the WPA took over in the Summer of 1935, occupying the same space in the Port Authority Building on Eighth Avenue between 15th and 16th Streets that the CWA had occupied.

Turning south, Benno headed for the Port Authority. He knew the way, could probably have gotten there blindfolded, so many visits had he made in search of help. Although Benno's initial ambition in seeking CPA assistance was to find work as a sculptor, a goal that, with eloquence and passion, he had elaborated in CPA's intake form, he was bluntly told by a sympathetic CPA case worker, Hillary Zark, that to get a job he should demonstrate eagerness for any kind of work and also to apply for relief. Still on the job after the WPA takeover, Hillary greeted Benno with a broad smile. Relief had just come through. Hillary said that an investigator had gone to his room, met with Tony, inspected the premises, reviewed his file and issued a favorable report. She said his rent would be paid going forward. In addition, as living expenses, he would be paid $5.00 every other Friday, beginning immediately.

The news was a shock to Benno, whose focus was entirely on finding work. In truth, he had forgotten about the request for home relief. Now, with the rendezvous with Violet looming, a miracle of bureaucracy had plucked him from the gutter, stuffed a five dollar bill in his stained and smelly pants and promised many bi-weekly returns. In submitting to this form of kindness, Benno found solace in having been brought to his knees, then lower still by the pie incident with Violet. He accepted his destitute condition. There were other reasons to accept the handout. Hadn't he continued his art until he ran out of money for material? And tried every way imaginable to sell it? Hadn't he tried, for a year and more, to find work? Any work that paid. And, with money in hand, he could give up petty thievery. Even repay those from whom he stole. And, he told himself, the WPA relief money could be considered a loan, something he would pay back as soon as he could find something to replace it. Stuffing his mind with these ingenious rationalizations, he felt armed to face down the dreams of his Father's wrath that he knew was sure to come. And, of course, there was Violet's generosity. Yes, he would get over the shock.

As he strolled east to meet Violet, with a sense at times of floating just above the pavement, Benno's wayward mind became consumed by a different kind of hunger. It was always thus, when he walked the streets of New York, but particularly in the Spring, when women fling forth their figures through coverings at once delicate, thin and sparse. When, in his youth, did this obsession take root, this keen training of his eyes begin? He could not recall, except to connect it to the early teachings of their neighbor in Manhattan, the Freudian psychiatrist, Rachel Bernstein. Benno admired a woman's gait, particularly when all parts were set gently in motion, buttocks shifting from side to side in counterpoise to hips. Oh, but for his condition what heavenly harmony he could find on these sidewalks in the Spring.

Women didn't pay particular attention to the male form. This theory was solely a product of Benno's observation; he had taken no polls. Were women as interested in the shapes of men as men were of women, the male dress code would have evolved along much more revealing lines. Perhaps, he reasoned, women were more interested in getting inside a man's mind than stripping him of his clothing.

Imaginary savorings existed side by side with the blank slate of experience. The possibility of actually touching, except by accident, or of exploring, enveloping and being enveloped by, the female form had always been for him, beyond hope, as out of reach as a star, as remote as Zanzibar, as daunting as surmounting Popocatépetl or drinking from Lake Titicaca.

Violet had been attired in what one might call High Plains Calico, a shapeless seed sack of a dress with faded floral design. It was buttoned tight around her neck and dropped straight to her ankles. He found it far easier to apply his imagination to those passing by than to guess at what might be found under that Dalhart smock.

When Violet returned to the Horn & Hardart, Benno was waiting for her. Describing the day, Benno insisted on taking Violet to Tuscan Art, a notoriously cheap Italian restaurant, just a little hole-in-the-wall nearby, where they could get fresh bread, homemade pasta and even a glass of cheap wine.

"I don't want you splurging your new-found wealth on my account. Things change. When did you last eat there?"

"A year ago, before my money gave out. You're right, they may have slipped, like the rest of us. But they won't have raised prices, I can guarantee you that, and they're still popular. The tables are always full when I walk by."

They grabbed the last outdoor spot. Oddly, despite being in full view of passersby, they felt an aura of privacy greater than being indoors at the cavernous Horn & Hardart. "Being together and unknown feels good," Violet whispered. "Yes, the anonymity of great cities," Benno offered.

"This is my first time in an Italian restaurant. Dalhart had one, but daddy refused to go near it." Picking up the menu, Violet saw it didn't mean a whole lot to her.

"Dalhart fare was limited. Why don't you order for me."

"Ok. I'll describe and you can object. So. For the appetizer, kale salad. Raw kale chopped fine and seasoned with pine nuts, raisins, garlic, olive oil and vinegar. Then, vitello tonnato, a Northern Italian dish. Veal smothered in tuna fish sauce that's peppered with capers. We can do dessert later. How's that sound?" The bread had come, along with a small dish of olives. No butter.

"I feel better than I have since the train pulled in. You have the persuasive lilt of a food salesman. Ever worked in a restaurant?"

"I've always loved good food. And cooking it," Benno boasted, beaming the guileless smile of lingering youth, as if speaking of a lost art.

"Actually, I haven't done much cooking since leaving home."

Like thirsty lions at a watering hole too small for two, they washed the bread down with water. The waiter brought more, then took their order.

They settled down to resume what they had started at Horn & Hardart. It was that once-in-a-relationship sort of talk that occurs at the outset, when a couple explore each other's history in the context of countless future possibilities.

"You stopped your story in the middle somewhere. Was it the Summer of 1931?"

"Ah, yes, when the heat came and the rain left." Anxiety crossed her unlined face, as inescapable as the frequent dreams that disrupted her sleep or the overpowering taste upon waking that caused her to spit out, like tobacco juice, the dirt that was no longer there except in dreadful imagining.

"The irony of it all. 1931 saw the biggest wheat crop of all time and, at 50% below cost of production, the lowest price ever. Next Spring the ground was hard pan, too dry to plant. About the only thing that grew was Russian thistle, a tumbleweed that would blow across the prairie to kingdom come unless stopped by barbed-wire fence. Daddy had us store up all we could find to use as Winter feed for our cows. Imagine that."

"I know a bit about cows, at least Jerseys, which I milked as a kid, and Herefords, which I cared for in the Flint Hills. It would be a feat of alchemy for cows to turn tumbleweed into milk."

Violet smiled awkwardly. "Excuse me. Perhaps I'm telling too much? You're giving me the first chance since leaving home to speak of my life there." Benno caught a kind of desperation in her voice, a need, now that she had started, to tell the whole story.

"We were reduced to subsistence farming, just trying to stay alive. Eggs from our chickens, bacon from our last pig, vegetables in a patch of ground we kept watered as long as the well lasted. What made it bearable was daddy's belief in the rain's return. Wet follows dry from year to year. Daddy said so. 'Just wait till next year.' Everyone in Dalhart said the same thing.

"Nature proved them wrong. Each year was worse than the one before. Then the black blizzards started. It was January, 1932. We didn't know what to make of it, a dark wall climbing the sky. It moved fast across the plains, blocking the sun. At first, when it hit Dalhart, some claimed it was a sandstorm, and true enough it stung like sand. But when the sun returned, casting light on its droppings, we could see coal-colored dust coating everything. Blow your nose and out came black snot. Cough and up came black phlegm. It was like black snow, a solid wall of it, rising up to envelop the town. An oddity to remember but not to worry about.

"Daddy was wrong. By March we had suffered half a dozen of these "dusters." Although we didn't know what caused them, we sure knew when one came rolling through town. You couldn't see your hand at six inches. The dust blinded our cows' eyes and choked their lungs. They bawled. In April the wrath of God appeared. His messenger, an earth man named Bennett, came to town and gave it to us plain and simple. We had only ourselves to blame. We caused the dusters. Through 'stupendous ignorance,' he said, sounding like an Old Testament prophet, we had destroyed the land. Turned soil wrong-side up. By plowing under the sod we had sown the seeds of epic disaster. It took one thousand years to create an inch of topsoil, he said. But only minutes for the wind to sweep it away if nature's grasses had been removed. Your lives will never be the same."

"Did you believe Bennett's story?" Benno asked.

"One farmer stood up to challenge Bennett by quoting from an official agricultural bulletin that claimed 'Soil is the one resource that cannot be exhausted.' Bennett shot back, 'I didn't know so much costly misinformation could be put into a single brief sentence.' Another farmer rejected Bennett's case by laying blame on the drought. Bennett agreed that the weather quickened the pace of soil removal, but stuck to his theory. 'It's just a matter of time,' he said.

"Not many of us left that meeting convinced. It would take a while for the ugly truth to sink in. But I know some who heard Mr. Bennett that day walked away accepting his assignment of blame and adding to it the probability that God had summoned the drought to punish us for scalping the plains."

The kale arrived, smelling of cinnamon. "Let's try a glass of wine," Benno said. She nodded, enthusiastic and wound up. Cathartic, he hoped.

"Were you one of them?" Benno said, looking into Violet's flashing dark eyes, trying to read her state of mind, worried he might have probed too far.

"You were direct with me this morning. Let me confess something to you. It's not about the kale, which I have eaten before, but never as good as this. Score one for your choice of appetizer. No, it's about the wine. This is my first taste, ever. Daddy didn't drink. Nor Mama. I'd had a spoonful of beer, enough to know it's an acquired taste. They were serving beer in Dalhart, even though it was still illegal. But wine, not a sip. And here I am, having sipped half this glass, and feeling it. Had to get that off my chest."

Benno wondered at her smooth olive skin. He half expected it to be pock-marked by those black dusters. It looked like ivory.

"Now, to your question, no, not I. Hearing Mr. Bennett, I found it easier to blame the Government for getting us into this mess than either God or ourselves. But daddy walked away with the mark of sin upon him. And it started a spiraling of his mind into the depths of despond that, I'm afraid, continues today. Well, he was a believer of the Old Testament kind. The longer rain stayed away, the more blame he took on himself. By the time I left Dalhart, it had all but destroyed him. That and the dusters. He aspired to mind over matter. But matter overcame mind and was doing him in."

"I won't order a second glass. Take your time with what you have left and you'll be fine. The story's heartrending. I know that's trite. I'll say it anyway, because it's true. Those living in the East, with their own problems, don't know what's happening on the High Plains. The press has so much to cover here that Dalhart families are forgotten casualties of the depression."

"Not true, Benno. That's what's especially cruel. Let's have one more glass, please. I'll pay. It's not economic conditions that have spelled doom for us. Sure, the price of wheat has hit the skids, and that would hurt, if we could grow wheat, but the lack of rain means we can't grow anything except tumbleweed. Relentless wind and lack of grass adds up to dusters, and that's what's killing us. We're choking on our own topsoil as it blows away. Could anything be more pathetic?"

Violet began to cry.

"I misspoke. Here in New York it's easy to imagine all hardship being caused by the depression. Even at full employment and a roaring bull market, the tragedy of the High Plains would be happening." The waiter had taken away two empty appetizer plates, replacing them with larger ones on which vitello tonnato was heaped.

"I hope you have room left for this," Benno said, a broad smile covering his face, an effort to cheer her up.

"Are you kidding? Just watch. You'll be lucky if I don't lick the plate as even the more civilized of us Texans are known to do." She was smiling through tears, still running down over high cheek bones to salt her plate.

"So, you stayed until April. End of school? What made you decide to leave? What was it like living among the dusters?"

"The veal's great. Especially with wine. See, I'm sipping slowly. Let me give you some highlights of life on the Plains after the rain vanished and the dusters appeared. Grasshoppers swarmed, killing anything they could chew. Black Tarantulas appeared in bathtubs and kitchen sinks. Black Widows crawled out of corn stacks and woodsheds. Cattle began to starve. The Government came with a mercy program that paid us $16 per cow to put them out of their misery. The men had to dig huge ditches to bury them. After that, the plague of jackrabbits. These little things with long legs and ears were starving, on the move seeking food. The town organized rabbit drives, at first using shotguns, then clubs, spokes really, taken from wagon wheels. Their screaming sounded like babies crying. Only on Sundays."

"You ate them?"

"Of course. And were grateful. But oh my, the cost, especially for Dalhart's children. Somehow, we got by on rabbit stew, dried beans, canned vegetables and fruits. Occasionally some cornbread. We put up rabbit meat. After the rabbits came static electricity. It killed whatever was left in the ground, watermelons, any wheat left standing. It was amazing, a freak of nature, caused by the dusters and the bone-dry conditions. We felt black dust between our teeth. On skin it was like face powder, heavier than sand. We washed with cheap lye, which hurt as much as the dust it removed. Finally, by the Spring of this year, everyone who still had possession of his wits had given up on the idea of redeeming cycles. The rain had abandoned us, gone forever."

Their plates were cleaned. The glasses drained. The waiter cleared the table.

"Aren't you getting tired of this tale?" Violet said. Benno knew from the energy in her face that she had more to say.

"Not a bit. Don't leave me out there in Dalhart."

"Ok. We now come to my twenty-first birthday, April 14. At the start, a glorious day. Daddy and mama planned a special lunch for me, with friends from school and from the restaurant where I waited table and occasionally sang. It was Summer in April, a rolled up, unbuttoned shirt sort of day, the kind one throws open the windows for. Even in Dalhart. After 49 dusters in the last three months, 12 in the last 12 days of March, after 27 days of hard-blowing wind, you can imagine the relief that a windless, blue-bird sort of day could bring to us. Our joy, the whole town's joy, throbbed, like the beating heart of a newborn. And what a wonderful celebration we had, beginning with Spring cleaning of windows, walls and floors, followed by baths all round. The only place the black dust hadn't penetrated yet was the aquifer that gave our well a purity that was strange, in the sense that nothing else could in any way be considered pure. There followed a birthday feast and games in the bright sun. The many pleasures of the day lasted until evening. We had changed into our Sunday best for evening services, gathering outside the house. Daddy was the first to see it, coming fast out of the north, a long black line across the horizon, moving towards us. Shouting, he told us to get inside. Just above tree level, I saw huge flocks of birds and swarming insects fleeing south. To the north a wall of what looked like muddy waters surged towards us. The barbs on our fence lit up and glowed. Then everything went black. The wind scrapped and howled. The temperature must have dropped 20 degrees or more. Sitting there, on the floor of our living room, I cried, pouring out tears of rage and defiance. I had an overwhelming urge to escape. From Dalhart. From the High Plains. I'd never felt so determined. Nothing was going to stop me."

Benno tried to visualize the conditions Violet was describing but fell short. Manhattan had its Summer floods and hail big as golf balls, but they seemed like nothing compared to Dalhart's dusters.

"I learned later that my birthday was called Black Sunday, the day the great granddaddy of all dust storms laid waste to Dalhart. Our newspaper caught the mood in a screaming headline the next day: SUMMER DAY TURNED INTO NIGHTMARE."

"Did your family leave too?"

"Not yet. They cling to a sliver of faith in the future, however battered. Change is hard. Dreams die slowly. Hope kept them going, despite repeated heartbreak. Daddy and mama worked so hard to build a home on the High Plains that it was hard to surrender, even when God's brutal message seemed pretty clear. They haven't forsaken their religious roots, though these too are badly torn. But their faith has shifted to FDR, who they consider God's disciple, put in the White House to save the farmer. Daddy got very angry with a congressman just a few days before Black Sunday, when he saw this quote: 'If God can't make rain in Kansas, how can the New Deal hope to succeed?'

"But the nesters were leaving in increasing numbers. Daddy supported my decision. A surprise, for I feared he and Mama would accuse me of jumping ship."

"You were accusing yourself?"

"I sensed they hoped I might find something good in New York City, something we all could be proud of. But guilt? I tried to duck. Couldn't find the perfect excuse. It still clings to me like duster grit."

"Ouch," Benno said.

"Oh, there's something else I wanted to tell you about Dalhart. It had the truest of all true believers in a man named John McCarty. He was the town's biggest booster. Hot on the heels of Black Sunday, he announced the creation of 'the Last Man's Club,' offering membership to anyone pledging to be the Last Man to leave town. They would be Spartans, he declared, hunkering down in their dust bunkers until hell freezes over. Despite McCarty's near crazy enthusiasm for sticking it out, nesters continued to leave. Most headed west, for California. A few moved east. By the time I left, the heat was again breaking records."

Benno felt embarrassed. Watching the pain in her face, hearing the hurt in her voice as she told her story, Benno was at a loss. What words could be adequate?

"What a story. As a child of sorrow growing up, you should be heartbroken. But no, here you are, through tears telling me of Dalhart with a glow that bespeaks hope, even confidence. There's nothing broken or bowed about you. By the way, when did you last see a movie?"

Violet shook her head. "I thought so," said Benno. "Not that I've seen many. But they're cheap. And I have something to celebrate. There's a musical playing that's supposed to be fun. *Love Me Tonight.* Rodgers and Hart music, with Maurice Chevalier and Jeanette MacDonald. Rouben Mamoulian directs. Maybe you've heard of him. He's the genius who did *Porgy* on Broadway. Come on, let's go. My treat."

Benno jumped to his feet. Violet followed. Grabbing his hand, she exclaimed, "Why not! Two can starve as easily as one."

After the show, in moonlight they walked north to Central Park, where its tall oaks and sycamores were draped in pastel shades of shimmering green.

"What did you like most?" Benno asked. They had seated themselves on one of the long curving benches that lined the Park Drive.

"That film was thrilling. So many things. I'm in awe. That symphony of Parisian sounds, the traveling theme of *Isn't It Romantic* passing from Maurice's tailor shop to Jeanette's chateau, the three aunts conjuring up a man for Jeanette as the three witches conjured evil in *Macbeth,* the stag hunt, a magical tour with that delicate, bouncy air for strings keeping time with the deer's feet. I have little to compare, but it's got to be the best."

"It is, I agree. From your take, I suspect you of loving music. So do I. And those songs — *Isn't It Romantic and Love Me Tonight. Mimi.* But the background music too. It all fits like a glove with the plot. And that final scene, when Jeanette stands in front of the train, the way you and other Dalhartians challenged the dusters."

"Yeah, but there's a difference: the train stopped. Another thing about that movie: I love the make-believe stuff. Pretending to be someone else." She paused, took a bead on Benno and said: "I mean, how do I know who you really are or what you really want to be?"

"Ha-ha. That's a good one. Here I am, hanging out in the breadlines and at the Sally, but secretly rich as Croesus. Or, I'm a big shot who lost all his coconuts. In the movie the impoverished tailor pretends he's a Baron. Make-believe only goes in one direction. I don't want to be a great man, with my picture on a postage stamp. Just give me a chance to get to first base. And you?"

"Look at that moon. The same one I saw in Dalhart, but here it's beautiful, not shabby with dust. Same moon sending the same message, but received differently depending on where one sits. Or what kind of glasses one looks through. From here I want to reach for that moon and pop it into my mouth, like a perfectly round marshmallow. Let's not try to fool one another. Together let's make believe we have found work: for you, commissions to sculpt great art; for me, leading lady in a Broadway show directed, why not, by my new friend, Rouben Mamoulian."

Violet and Benno had other meals together. And early in their relationship, Violet demanded to know about Benno's early life in Manhattan.

———————◆———————

Benno's Father, Dan Murdock, was a big cheese. Ask anyone in Manhattan, Kansas, where he farmed a large spread close to town and where, far up in the Flint Hills, year after year, he birthed and tended the best Herefords in the State of Kansas. They said he had money, although no one seemed to know for sure, or whether it came from family or his ranching and farming. He didn't flaunt whatever wealth he had, but his house on Humboldt Street was large, as, selectively, was his generosity. They said he had gone to some elite college in New Jersey and then to a business school in New York City. Plenty enough education to farm, some said. Others thought it a bit much, but if pushed, might reveal a certain envy. He had an easy way with ranch and farm hands, willing to show as well as tell, to lead with his sleeves rolled up, soaking his hatband and bandana as much as the others.

He wasn't a tall man, but wiry and athletic, with eyes of corn-flower blue, so deeply etched they looked black unless, like the indigo bunting, the light was just right. He had wayward eyebrows and a gradually receding hairline. He was seldom without a pipe, the smoke from which infused his clothes. The strong smell of tobacco and the inescapable odor of horse and leather defined the man, at least for those in close quarters with him.

Everyone in town knew Dan had religion, for on that subject, beyond all others, he spoke publicly, with passionate conviction. More Old Testament than New, his God directed not just the seasons, but the rainfall and wind, the rise and fall of the Kaw, the temperature and all other natural conditions that led to success or failure in field and pasture. But Christianity couldn't contain his open and eclectic approach to faith. Somewhere along the educational path he trod, Dan became enamored of the ancient Babylonian Epic of Gilgamesh and his bosom friend, the primitive wild man, Enkidu. He was captivated by Gilgamesh's painful discovery that eternal life was beyond man's reach. He made the Epic mandatory reading for his boys. And there was more. When he began farming in Manhattan, Dan studied with admiration the Indian culture that surrounded him, which, to those willing to see, had infused the land and even the habits of the white folk. It surprised no one that he named his farm "Wyandot," for the language Iroquoian Indians brought to Kansas.

Like Job, he accepted the lot that God gave him, day by day, season by season, year by year. He saw himself as an upright, God-fearing man of courage, compassion and integrity. But he also believed that the cards God dealt him had nothing to do with divine punishment or reward. His was an impersonal God who would only punish a man for trying to tamper with the world's natural order. Yet, Dan's acceptance of God's will did not spell capitulation to fate or the forces of Nature. In Riley County, it was said, from one season to the next, that "hope sustains the farmer." For Dan, hope was involved, to be sure. But only as a topping on abiding self-confidence, gritty determination and the will to succeed, qualities that, Dan believed, God doled out equally to all at birth. Like muscles, there by the grace of God, to be developed or not — a matter of free will. Thus, poverty, to Dan, was a problem of individual character rather than social organization. It had to be that or God's will, Dan thought, and he was plumb sure God didn't come into that picture at all.

Dan's circle of friends and colleagues was wide and as varied as an appaloosa mare. In contrast, his wife, Juanita, kept mostly to those women in town who wore silk or velvet. It was from their families that guests for the Murdock dinner parties were drawn.

The Murdocks' home was located in a tree-lined residential area within easy walking distance of the Kaw River (to the east) or downtown (to the west). By 1908, Manhattan, with 10,000 residents, was the largest city in Riley County. It had a school age population of 2,680. It was a college town, with all the pretensions and advantages, real and perceived, that towns with gowns possessed. Kansas State Agricultural College got its start during the Civil War. The Land Grant Act of 1862 gave 90,000 acres of Federal land to the state for endowment of a college to teach "agriculture and the mechanic arts," the ultimate purpose being to "promote the liberal and practical education of the industrial classes."

On June 30, 1910, Juanita Murdock gave birth to fraternal twin boys. It was a difficult labor, and when nature had run its course, two lives were exchanged for one. Juanita's death came without warning. Manhattanites grieved with Dan, whose philosophy, though informed by countless lives lost in animal birthings, did nothing to equip him for such a brutal assault upon the family. He went into denial, angrily calling Juanita's death "the wrath of God." By the time of her funeral service, Dan had softened this to "God's will be done."

First out of the womb Dan named Adam and the second Benno. Until one got a feel for the character that inhabited each of Adam's and Benno's similar bodies, they could not be distinguished. Neighbors easily mistook them for identical twins. As they moved from diapers to knee pants to trim knickers with argyle stockings, their personalities formed as if within a circle, each having what the other lacked. Adam spoke early and often. Benno was late and, even after he could speak in full sentences, hardly ever got a chance to complete them, so quick was his brother to fill in the thought.

Dan, who had studied a bit of Chinese philosophy in college, was convinced that his sons were a perfect human example of *yin* and *yang*.

Adam was a rebellious extrovert, always appearing cheerful, pushing the limits, brimming with boy's ways. His pockets bulged with rubber bands, string, bottle caps and marbles, and a thick glass piece, sharp-edged and likely to cut through the pocket, which he used to scrape and polish cow horns. He picked his nose, even in public, and often ate the snot. And he liked to pass gas with a bugle-like sound, especially when people open to shock were within ear-shot.

"Father raised hogs. On Sundays the family would enjoy what, from his place at the head of the table, Father variously called "sweet swine," "swine divine," "heavenly hog" or "perfect pig." It was his favorite meat. And not just because it was his from birth to slaughter, for he raised beef cattle and plenty of chickens too."

"Why the word 'Father? Sounds like the Lord's Prayer. I wonder what he saw in hogs. Around Dalhart, they were pretty awful-smelling."

"You're right. But we didn't have any more choice in what we called him than in what he called us. He insisted. As for hogs, he admired the raw exuberance, their lust for life, their appetites, so zealous and uninhibited. Often he told us God had breathed something special into these animals. And then broken the mold."

"Not every hog farmer could get a large herd of hogs through the hot Manhattan Summer without mishap. It took exceptional skill to move a herd safely. They panicked easily and would charge about, crazed and desperate in the heat until they collapsed, often to die. As a grower of hogs, Father was in top form, year after year, and his pride seemed to flavor his taste for pork."

Benno's memories of childhood crowded his mind, piling layer upon layer, too much to relate.

2

———◆———

FRIENDS TYPICALLY ATTENDED THE MURDOCKS for Sunday luncheon, and treasured their invitations. They came directly from church. Dan's faith, like most of his other practices, had no need for intermediaries. While others were attending church inside the First Presbyterian's aged and lovely limestone building, Dan would take the boys out to the Flint Hills where, depending on the season, they would learn fly fishing for chubs or silversides, using the barbless hooks Dan favored, or watch Cactus, Dan's reliable fawn-colored stallion, earn his keep. Cactus was a quarter-horse of impressive lineage, whose services were much in demand across the Midwest. Dan declared him nature's profit center.

"Watch closely lads. This is God's transcendent treat." Uttered imploringly, with absolute conviction, these words never varied from mare to mare, whether large or small, black, bay or chestnut, eager or frightened, even though the boys didn't know exactly what he meant. There were many such visits over the years, for in Dan's mind the repeated sight of this particular act of nature's way to plant and harvest was worth more to his boys than all the words they might expect to hear in church. Or from him about sex. Dan considered his Fatherly duties with respect to "the birds and the bees" accomplished through the compelling acts of Cactus. No more need be said, he comforted himself in thinking. Nor did the boys push him. What Juanita would have thought never crossed his mind.

Dan's way of talking was to lecture, especially to his wife. From the outset of their marriage, Juanita accepted his self-confident ways, even though they were often framed more by a sense of superiority and power than by understanding, reason or compassion. He could, with what he thought to be a generous, compensatory splash of humor, put her down when she seemed not to grasp something he thought she should grasp, like knowing she would blow a fuse when the toaster and coffee maker were used at the same time, or knowing how to find the blown fuse or how to replace it. Juanita never found his style of humor refreshing. She was as wise as she was kind. As tolerant as she was forgiving. Knowing her man before she married him, she "bought the ranch," every inch of it, and her love for all that he stood for usually overwhelmed his reliably thoughtless behavior. To the boys, the loss of their mother was beyond measure. Or their imagination to fathom.

Children should learn to memorize and recite, Dan believed. "It marks a man as educated," he told the boys. "And like the Greeks, it must be learned early and practiced often. Our schools don't begin to do enough." He devised a home-study plan to teach the boys rhetorical skills. And he loved Lincoln. He had read the biographies, a collection of Lincoln's correspondence and the work of Walt Whitman. Dan often urged the boys to memorize the Gettysburg Address. To no avail. But then, in 1918, before a Sunday lunch to celebrate Dan's 55th birthday, Adam decided to try. At age 8, he had Dan's self-confidence.

Luncheon was served for twelve, not counting the boys, who ate at a separate table. Before carving, Dan raised a glass of white Burgundy, inviting all to drink to his "Swine Divine." It was October. For dessert there was apple pie made with the Murdock farm's own winesaps and vanilla ice cream made from the cream of Dan's herd of Jerseys. Arrival of the ice cream brought forth another simple toast, one the boys had heard too many times to count. "My friends, to the Jerseys and the world's richest cream!"

After dessert, just as guests were about to leave the table, Adam declared he had something to present. "It's a gift for Father."

Like Benno, Adam was dressed in the sailor costume so popular among the upper strata of American society, east to west. That it had penetrated Kansas was more attributable to Murdock connections to the east coast, where Dan had attended university, than to pretensions in Manhattan.

Adam took a firm stance before the grown-up table and began to recite. The room was still. Adults hung, tense, at Adam's words, fearful of a mistake. Could an eight-year old master such a piece of oratory? Despite struggling a bit over "dedicate," "consecrate" and "hallow," and missing some of the rhetorical rhythms that Lincoln intended, he managed to get through the whole thing. There was loud applause. Adam looked like he'd won the lottery. Dan was beside himself with surprise and pride. Relief showed on adult faces. Adam had made the whole room feel good, the way a daughter-in-law does when she births the first grandchild. Benno joined the others in applauding his brother.

Praise for Adam continued for some time, each guest feeling bound to add a personal touch to the warm feelings that rose from the table. Adam preened like a movie star. Just as Dan rose to declare the luncheon over, Benno moved toward Dan, saying softly, "Father, I know it, too."

Dan said, "What's that Benno? "

"Four score and seven years ago," Benno began hesitantly, his voice cracking, his pace and inflection uncertain. But confidence grew. By the end, he had captured the meters of the address noticeably better than his brother. Bowing at the silence that greeted him, Benno turned and almost ran from the room. Before he could disappear, applause broke the silence, following him out and lasting after he had gone, perhaps an expression of the audience's futile hope that the young orator would take another bow.

As soon as he could, Adam escaped the adults. He wanted an explanation from Benno. So did Dan. Benno had nothing to say. As with a clam pulled from deep in a sandbar or a turtle plucked from the middle of a road, there was no way to get him to open up. He congratulated his brother. There was nothing triumphant in his expression or mood. As to his performance, not a word.

———◆———

In February, 1922 Rachel Bernstein arrived in Manhattan with her family. They had traveled from Vienna, where she had studied with Sigmund Freud at his Institute, gaining a Doctorate in the newly invented field of Psychoanalysis. On receiving her application, the Institute had been reluctant, despite distinctions earned at university, to admit her. The problem was not that she was a woman. It was her looks, which some of the male staff at the Institute believed would cause her immense difficulties in treating males. She was attractive. Despite a lack of interest in fashion or learning the ways of make-up, her face proclaimed, if not beauty, character and appeal, through skin tones of light and dark, eyes that laughed through lashes long and black like her hair and a figure small and shapely. No single element in Rachel's looks was remarkable. In total, however, she exuded an earthy attractiveness that couldn't be missed even if she had tried to hide it. In the end, it was precisely this appeal that overcame the staff's reluctance to take a chance with her.

Although many Manhattanites had heard of Dr. Freud and some of his theories, no one in town knew enough to engage intelligently with Dr. Bernstein on the subject. With Rachel came her son, Aaron, an 18-year-old who went directly into the senior class at Manhattan High School, and her husband, Isaiah, a chemist turned businessman in Vienna, where he had founded a cement plant with seed capital from Osterreichische Landerbank, in the form of loans and a controlling block of stock.

It would be an exaggeration to say the Bernstein family "fled" Vienna. Certainly, in 1920, the nastiness to come, which metastasized into the horror that even Dante couldn't have imagined, while bubbling beneath the surface of middle and upper class society, was not evident in everyday life. However, it was felt, intermittently, as sudden gusts from a confusing wind by the more discerning of those against whom the hurricane would ultimately be directed.

Isaiah had made a success of the cement plant. By 1920, it had momentum, growing both revenues and net profits for three consecutive years. The board of directors consisted of the bank's President and his appointees, Aryans all, drawn from top management of the bank. At board meetings, as Isaiah was about to report on progress, the President would invariably welcome his gang to the table, referring to them as "my watchful ones, here to keep our CEO honest." Or words to like effect. Light-hearted banter, it was, and so amusing to the gang that minutes might pass before Isaiah could distract them from fawning over the chairman's cleverness.

In apparent paradox, the more successful the company became, the more its board challenged Isaiah. At first he couldn't fathom the directors' reactions to his ascending accomplishments. He was too filled with success. Rachel was not so enthralled. She warned that, perversely, his grip on the company would become weaker as he drove it to higher levels of success.

"When they think the ship can sail without you at the helm," she whispered, "you will be thrown overboard."

And so it was.

His removal came with six weeks' salary.

"It can only get worse," Rachel announced while washing for Shabbat. She urged him to look West.

The soft round hills of eastern Kansas, called Flint Hills by some, Bluestem Hills by others, were centered just outside Manhattan, and extended north along the Blue River in Pottawatomie County and south until they blended into the Osage grazing country of northern Oklahoma. It was the flinty lime rock found throughout the Hills that gave to the coarse grasses that carpet them a unique power to add bone and beef to cattle fortunate enough to graze there. In addition to seasoning these grasses to make them especially palatable and nutritious for Herefords, the limestone was quarried to make building material of highest quality, as anyone visiting KSU's campus could see. These enduring stones came from the cottonwood seam, which outcropped just beyond town near the summit of the Hills. At Dan Murdock's pasture, some ten miles beyond, this seam was the lowest of numerous limestone ledges that form benches on the bluffs.

Beyond loving Rachel and exuding pride in her mastery of a subject beyond his ken, Isaiah knew one thing: how to make cement, the essential ingredient of which was limestone. But it was not only the abundance of this material that drew the Bernsteins to Manhattan.

Country selection was easy. They saw the United States as the most promising land of "milk and honey" west of Vienna, where refuge and opportunity lay side by side.

It was more of a challenge to decide where in that huge country to settle. Seeking maximum flexibility to abandon their choice if it didn't work out, Rachel favored the East Coast, but a five- or six-day voyage by steamer back to Europe. Isaiah saw things differently. Turning Rachel's reasoning on its head, he sought a home as close to the middle of the country as possible, viewing every extra mile between the Bernsteins and the ocean an extra layer of safety. Safety from what, he could not say; yet land, he believed, offered protection.

Rachel pronounced her husband daft. "To understand this, I would have to put you on the couch for a year."

"No time for that, love. In Vienna I recall you telling me that the more irrational one's beliefs, the more freedom one has tenaciously to cling to them. Indulge me this once."

And so it was, through give and take, they settled in a house on Humboldt Street in Manhattan, Kansas, only 328 miles west of the precise center of the country. Their house was large for a family of three. It boasted an ample play area in a cellar claimed to stay dry even when, in Summer, the Kaw River ran wild down city streets. Rising two stories, it had three bathrooms and a dormered attic bedroom with ceiling fan and small windows on four sides. Just beyond the kitchen facing the ample backyard, and towering above it, was a healthy and productive sour cherry tree, identified by the seller as a Montmorency. When the Bernsteins installed themselves in February, 1922, the tree was bare but Rachel noted how robust its Winter buds appeared. Its presence had made the house irresistible, despite being a bit outside their price range. Their home in Vienna had boasted a pair of Morellos that each year provided what to Rachel was what limestone was to Isaiah, the essential to life's pleasure, the key ingredient for making her lace-work cherry pies. In this manufacture, she had a special gift disconnected from Dr. Freud's line of work, although Rachel was sure he could have found a connection if challenged. In Vienna she had taken pleasure in sharing the bounty of her craft with neighbors. But she did it not just for pleasure. What some among her targets considered proselytizing for Freud's theories was to Rachel a duty she felt keenly and was driven to perform, much as the early priests traveling east from Iona must have felt about spreading a new Gospel. She had an agenda for applying her pie-making skills in Manhattan. There she planned to do the same, thinking of it as a place-setter for gaining acceptance, making new friends and clients.

When the time for picking arrived, she would open her kitchen to neighbors, starting with the children, who she reckoned would not easily resist a well-made pie of proven European design. The first guests to try her offering were Adam and Benno, whom, as neighbors, and with one of the town's most important men for a Father, Rachel had encouraged Aaron to befriend in school and bring home. This he did through Winter and Spring. When she met them on the sidewalk in front of her house early one morning toward the end of June, they had already become well acquainted through Winter sessions of hot chocolate and cinnamon toast. Now, they were on their way to Dan's farm for a day's work. Pointing to the tree, dark with red fruit, Rachel said, "Would you come by late this afternoon for some cherry pie? It will be my first here in Manhattan and you, my first tasters. Shall we say 4 PM?"

Over warm wedges of cherry pie, the boys chatted with Aaron and his mother, whose fame as "Doctor Rachel, the pie lady" was beginning slowly to spread around town.

"Vienna's in Europe. We know that much. But where, exactly?" Adam said.

Actually, Benno knew more. Remaining silent, he saw Vienna in his mind's eye, a capital city in eastern Austria. He winced when Adam invited attention to Rachel's heavy European accent.

"But, of course, we speak German. Austria's national language. I spoke Yiddish growing up in Galicia but dropped it after moving to Vienna. At home, my parents encouraged English too, and it was taught in school."

"We will study Latin and either French or German in high school," said Adam.

"Not much need for either one out here in prairieland," said Benno.

"Don't be so hasty," said Rachel. "There's much to learn through language, whether you're in the Flint Hills of Kansas or on the Boulevards of Paris. For example, as you probably know, 'Amo' in Latin means 'I love.' And all sorts of words derive from this root. 'Aime' in French, 'Amigo' in Spanish. So. More pie?"

A second helping led to a third before Adam got around to asking the big question — one Benno had begged him to avoid.

"Father says you practice a weird medicine. It treats our minds. He said that in ancient Greece you'd be called a 'soothsayer,' in Africa, a 'witch doctor,' and in New England, just a plain old 'witch.'"

Benno looked around for a place to hide. Would she turn them into frogs? Would their Father, who, they still believed, could have both ears to the ground at once, burst in to condemn this breach of confidence? He concentrated on breathing, only to discover he couldn't remember how.

"I was hoping you'd ask what I do, besides making lace-work cherry pie," Rachel said, a delphic smile appearing below her furrowed brow. Her eyes caught theirs and held on. "I am a psychiatrist. I practice psychoanalysis, a branch of medicine originated by the second most famous man from Vienna, Sigmund Freud. He was my teacher at the University of Vienna. No need to raise your hand, the most famous was Wolfgang Amadeus Mozart. So."

After a long, studied pause, she said, "And what is this practice? Dr. Freud mapped the human mind. He did this to treat mental illness. Just as doctors dissect the human body to discover how to treat bodily illness, Dr. Freud analyzed the mind, looking for clues to how it works, or doesn't work."

"Yes, but from the outside, right?" Adam said.

"Yes, and that's an important difference you've put your finger on. It makes the job harder. It's likely the reason no one had tried to build a medical discipline around psychiatry before Dr. Freud.

"Now, what do you Manhattanites call someone who steals off into the forest and returns with a basket full of strange things to eat — things like wild mushrooms, toadstools and fungi? Things that most of us think will kill us. Someone, according to Humboldt Street gossip, who is actually indoctrinating his twin sons to follow in his footsteps? I put it to you — isn't this strange?"

Rachel's smile broadened.

"You've found us out," Adam said. "But Father's not the only mushroom hunter in town. Plenty of professors from KSU out there too."

"What Dan does is commonplace in Europe. So much so that most police stations have mycologists available to help with identification. Here, not so common. Tell your Father I'd love to join him in a hunt sometime. My repertoire is modest, but I know what I know."

"Ok," said Adam. "Could you tell us a little more?"

She was holding their attention. "When you get to Latin, you'll discover, as did Caesar, that Gaul is divided into three parts. Once you learn that, you will start to realize that almost everything divides into three, from triangles to tricolors, tricycles to tridactyls, hat-tricks in hockey to trifectas in horseracing. Even your Christian God. And so, naturally, Dr. Freud divided our minds into three forces that, in combination, cause us to behave as we do. They are the _id_, named for the instinctual force that's hard to control, the _ego_, for the force that interacts with the world around us, and the _super-ego_, for the moral force that seeks to control the ego and channel it into good patterns of behavior."

Somewhere along this path, she lost them. "Enough Sigmund Freud for today. You said you were twelve. Approaching puberty. Aaron told me you were curious about that 'birds and the bees' stuff, as he put it. I bet he was boasting. Getting the attention of younger kids by shocking them with anatomy. He's done that before. I admit to being responsible for giving him a lot of information to soak up and, then, ring out for others. Much more than most kids his age get from their parents. Aaron, it's plainly your fault for picking a Freudian for a parent. Adam and Benno, I admit that Aaron and I are in cahoots. It's part of my training and mission to shine light in dark places, on matters often neglected or misunderstood, even by parents. The subject of sex is one on which our man Sigmund had much to say. Come back next week, same time, and we'll try out another pie."

Next week, they returned, following Aaron like cattle trailing after a Judas goat in the stockyard. Rachel was behind in pie preparation. Pie dough, a pair of clever pitting devices and all the other ingredients were lined up in the work space, all that is except the cherries, which still hung on the tree in bunches of two and three.

"My boys, see, here are baskets and there's the ladder. I know you've come from the farm, but it's only a matter of ten minutes work. We'll have enough for two pies."

While they picked, Dr. Rachel talked, seizing the moment to speak of birds and bees. Much later as grown-ups, the boys realized that Rachel was something of a zealot for Freudian ideas and the need to spread them around. Her influence on them was profound. She must have felt driven by her mentor to save Adam and Benno from a lifetime of repression caused by social and individual inhibitions. If, as she had been taught, the primary motivating factor in human behavior is the sex drive, and neuroses develop from rejecting, hiding or ignoring it, her mission, as the only carrier of this flame of truth to Manhattan, must be to educate the city's youth.

She used Aaron as the lure. Adam and Benno would be the first beneficiaries of her crusade. If Rachel's mission was filled with risk, as indeed it was, given her lack of status in the community and the taboos she was engaging for the benefit of children without their parent's consent, one would not know it from her mien, despite Isaiah's frequent predictions of peril for them both. "Imagine, Rachel, what you're proposing," Isaiah said. "Coming into a strange town with new-fangled ideas that you feel duty-bound to impose on the neighborhood, welcome or not. Don't do it, please."

Her zeal plowed through the thicket of worries planted by her husband as easily as a bear on a blackberry bender can trample a cabbage patch. She had twisted duty to the profession into the need to enlighten the neighborhood, starting with the Murdocks. Much in town, including, in particular, the town's acceptance of the Bernsteins, turned on the outcome of what she admitted to Isaiah was, perhaps, somewhat risky.

In perfunctory fashion, knowing the answer, she inquired as to the extent of their knowledge. She began to explain the uses to which the male and female bodies could be put in pursuit of progeny and pleasure. Or pleasure alone, a concept she claimed was normal, precisely because whatever could be done in pursuit of pleasure had long ago been done, and being done by humans, was for that reason alone sufficient to legitimate it.

By the time the baskets were filled, the boys' minds were swirling. Hearing for the first time of so many strange activities, done alone or with others of the same or opposite sex, might not be too shocking in the abstract, but a boy's mind cannot receive such knowledge without trying to imagine how it might apply to those in his circle of family and friends. Concretely. And in such imagining dwelt pure terror. With urgency akin to a much too long deferred bathroom stop, the boys had to escape. Rachel read desperation in their wide-eyed expressions. She backed off, realizing that the strange things she was saying should be delivered in small doses and, perhaps, repeated over time to seep into their minds, like water pooling on dry garden loam.

Benno said, "The pies are going to take too long. We must go now."

"You're right. I'll save one for next week, if you like. They'll stay fresh. I'm sure you have questions. Talk with Aaron if you like. And don't take any wooden nickels." Like squirrels surprised by a dog, the twins had vanished.

The cherries ripened over two weeks. Pie making lasted three. Rachel had the boys to herself for three sessions. Their embarrassment began to fade in the second session. By the third, Adam was open to asking questions, but not without blush or hesitation. Benno just listened, taking it all in without a word. Perhaps because, at twelve, the boys were too young immediately to translate theory into practice, or because of Rachel's didactic and dryly matter-of-fact method of delivery, the sessions seemed oddly clinical, detached from the emotive core of the stories Rachel was telling, all of which rested on the same foundation of sexual need, drive and desire.

There was one exception. It started when Adam asked Rachel if she had ever seen horses mate.

"Why no, Adam, that's a sight I've missed. Why do you ask?"

"We have. Often. We were wondering if humans and horses ... you know what I mean." Adam's ears burned, their redness spreading to his cheeks.

"Tell me about what you've seen," Rachel said in the soft, confident tone of one expecting a truthful answer.

"Father raises quarter-horses. Best in the country. His stud's named Cactus, for his color, not his appeal. Lots of mares come to our ranch. Father takes us out to watch."

"Father calls it 'God's transcendent treat,' or things like that," Benno said. "He takes us even though we've seen Cactus do it many times. We disappoint him."

True to her profession, Rachel's face had that questioning look, a mask blending serious perplexity with welcoming openness and a sly hint of that earthy wisdom that knows — come what may — the human condition is absurd.

Adam explained. "It doesn't seem like a 'treat' to us. It's violent. The mare's skittish. We're sure she's going to run away, but she doesn't. Do you think she likes it?"

"I suspect it's your Father's way of teaching you the facts of life. Passion and arousal are not too far from violence," she said, knowing as the words passed her lips that it was the wrong thing to say. The boys flinched.

"Horses mate when mares are in heat," Rachel explained. "They do so out of necessity, a Darwinian drive without which horses wouldn't survive. I'm sure your Father finds it a beautiful sight to see, and not just because of the stud fee he collects. Sounds like he finds there something divine. Humans are different. Yes, they make love to create a family. But they do it for pleasure too, taking care to avoid pregnancy. It's as natural for pleasure as for growing a family, and because pursuit of pleasure is entirely normal among well-balanced humans, it occurs often."

"One of our classmates said his mother told him she did it only because it was her duty as a wife," Adam said. "He claimed women don't enjoy it. When we heard that, it didn't sound right, given all you've said. We decided to ask Father."

Rachel could see the boys were confused. She guessed their minds were fraught with anxieties. Rachel's matter-of-fact teaching style got translated in the boys' far-ranging imaginations into scenes too bizarre to admit, even to oneself. Again and again, in the privacy of their bedroom, the boys tried to discuss what they'd heard, only to clam up. No other subject had had this effect on them. They were embarrassed.

"You decided," said Benno.

"Well, I went ahead, alone. Benno was right. He refused to say a word. Reminding us of the trips to see Cactus, he angrily asked us what more we needed to know."

"It was not really a question," Benno added.

"The rest are details," Adam said, quoting his Father's finishing touch.

"What your friend's mother claimed is nonsense. Society's to blame. Women were designed to enjoy sex every bit as much as men. And, long ago, in a state of nature, they did. Think of Adam and Eve getting plenty physical, joyfully and without shame, in the Garden of Eden. It was others in the community, more than the serpent's temptation, that ruined things. Today, women should be fighting these ideas. In a year or two you will be told girls are either 'good,' meaning they don't get physical with boys until they marry and then only out of duty, or 'bad,' meaning they kiss and do all sorts of other physical stuff with boys from puberty on. Don't believe it. As I said, nonsense."

———◆———

The Kaw swung around the town as if to cradle it. In late June, the cottonwoods, great giants lining the river's high sheer banks and leaning over its waters to form a canopy, shed feathered seed, white as paint, that descended through waves of Summer heat to brighten the dusty surroundings. Adam and Benno attended Manhattan High School. They walked the mile and a half twice a day, weather notwithstanding. With reverence for living remnants of ancient times instilled in them by their Father, they would occasionally, as Spring appeared in its bulging buds, pay homage to a massive white oak on the route, reputed to be over 200 years old. Its lower limbs, over a yard in diameter, spread at a right angle to the trunk to such a length that the town arborist had ordered supports against the levered effects of gravity.

Kansas adopted Prohibition in 1880. In an interesting way, it accounted for those living in Kansas at the twins' birth, being, for the most part, descendants of those who came in the 70's, 80's and 90's, originally from New England, pausing a generation or so in the middle states north of Ohio. Unlike Wisconsin, Minnesota, Iowa, the Dakotas and Nebraska, Kansas had almost none of the settlers from Germany and Northern Europe. By the time those Teutons and Scandinavians were spreading across the Middle West, Kansas had criminalized drinking. Given a choice, those immigrants avoided the puritanical enclave. To them, snaps and other spirits were like "mother's milk."

Although he used it in moderation, Dan Murdock considered alcohol the Devil's own brew, invented to tempt mankind into destructive ways. At the same time, he despised Prohibition because it meddled in man's lifelong struggle with the Devil. While rejecting paternalism by Government, Dan felt duty-bound to teach his sons the perils of alcohol. "And not just because it's bootleg. As long as you're around me, you'll not be touching a drop, whatever its source!" Thus, he would exclaim whenever a sermonizing mood came over him, as typically it did when, in the company of his sons, he came upon a Manhattanite under the influence. To drink in excess was to exhibit a serious character flaw, a lack of will, a weakness, an immorality beyond excuse. As Dan taught, so did his boys learn. Dan saw no inconsistency between his general view of alcohol and his love of single malt scotch, in which he daily indulged to a limit of one drink, or the pleasure he took in good wine with food. Indeed, Dan used Adam's challenge to the apparent clash of preaching and practice as a platform to parade the tight control he had learned to exert over his strong taste for scotch and his intolerance for those unwilling to control theirs.

In regard to alcohol, Adam and Benno absorbed their Father's attitude too well, becoming not just intolerant but allowing their contempt to show, parading an attitude at once superior and silly in front of others, much to the consternation of classmates, teachers and neighborhood friends. By chance, in their senior year in high school, they had an opportunity to advance the proposition, in state-wide debate, that "RESOLVED, the High Cost of Bootlegging ruins more lives than the Open Saloon and Five Cent Beer."

Their argument was rooted in Dan's notion that freedom to drink strengthens one's resolve to resist, whereas Prohibition insidiously erodes one's will. Under Dan's influence, the boys even claimed that all laws for social betterment were designed by Governments acting as disciples of the Devil to weaken and, ultimately destroy, the moral compass of mankind.

They swept the competition. Their opponents had made two mistakes. First, they had interpreted "high cost" narrowly to mean out-of-pocket expense to consumers. Second, they wandered from the main theme by trying to prove that bootlegging, in fact, didn't cost the consumer more than he would pay in open saloon. Upon hearing this argument, Adam adjusted his rebuttal by pointing out that his argument depended not a whit on the cost of alcohol to consumers. Cheap or dear, that cost was trivial. What mattered was the cost of paternalism. Adam argued that cost must be measured in ruined lives as countless as the feathered seeds of Manhattan's cottonwoods. Of course, Dan was delighted. Their victory, he imagined, would serve to prolong the ideological grip he held over them.

As if she were there, in the room, sharing responsibility, Dan often debated with Juanita all manner of questions about how to raise the twins. Perhaps because he knew animal husbandry from birth on, perhaps because he supported even the flimsiest opinions with far more self-assurance, or perhaps, because her arguments, in reality, flowed not from her but from his prejudiced imagination of what she might have thought, whatever the reason, Dan's judgments ruled the day.

Starting the day Juanita died, Dan developed a fear that, without a mother's presence, he would bend over backwards to compensate, and end up spoiling them, a sure way, he knew, to ruin their lives. As worry grew, so too did the harshness of his parental technique.

Clear on what not to do, Dan pondered with more difficulty the ways and means of developing his boys' characters. Although he would deny it if challenged, he wanted them to mimic his own. Repeatedly, he had tried to obtain Juanita's consent to name their first child, assumed to be a boy, "Dan Junior." By bestowing his name on the infant, he was convinced he could imprint his values there too. Despite repeated beratings, she refused, an uncommon act of disobedience rooted in having experienced what this act of selfishness had done to her Father, whose crippled personality clearly came from deep channeling from her Grandfather, beginning with the label "Junior."

At the right time in a child's development, Dan believed, there would be nothing better than a paper route to teach him how to get out of bed well before sunrise and carry through a tedious, repetitive task, day after day. He would also have them wash the family car every Sunday, as regular a duty as Manhattan's most devoted Christian might feel about attending church. In his effort to shape their minds, Dan was unconscious of a tendency to create a single mold.

Dan was also determined to control their bodies. He had studied Greek in college, where the professor's approach had been total immersion in the ways of Attica. His claim was that a student must be thoroughly dunked in Aegean waters to make the great language of that country come alive. Dan chose Sparta over Athens. So deeply did Dan admire the Spartan way that, from childhood, he had his boys go five two minute rounds with one another wearing not a stitch other than boxing gloves.

This Spartan outcropping was known only to a few of Dan Murdock's Humboldt Street neighbors, who tended to avert their minds by treating the story as malicious gossip not to be believed. Since the boys were instructed never to discuss what went on in their "temple," as Dan liked to call it, this odd behavior had been kept under wraps.

———◆———

The boys had a radio in their bedroom and listened to music while doing their homework. Having entered upon Dr. Bernstein's world, they began to appreciate in new ways the lyrics of hit tunes that came over the airwaves. It started with George Gershwin's *Do It Again*, which made the top five in 1922. The song seemed to be talking of kissing, but, now Adam and Benno could imagine other meanings.

I may say "no, no, no, no, no,"
But do it again.
Oh, no one is near.
I may cry "Oh, oh, oh, oh, oh,"
But no one will hear.
My mom will scold me, 'cause she told me that it's naughty, but then
Oh, do it again! Please do it again!

Each time they heard this tune, which came over the airwaves daily, they would re-enact the same scene:

"Look," Adam would say, "kisses aren't naughty." Laughter would erupt, as the boys gave each other knowing winks. "I bet a lot of saps in school don't get it, don't ya think?"

Benno nodded while trying to imagine the contradiction of saying no but meaning yes. It perplexed him. And so, too, did the boy's problem of distinguishing that case from one where the girl says "no" and means it.

He would leave it for another day.

The Gershwin tune was popular. One could count on hearing it over a frappe of coffee ice cream and chocolate sauce in the College Inn Café on Poyntz Avenue, Manhattan's main drag. When they had time on their hands and two bits in their pockets, the twins would go there hoping to get a booth and ogle the KSU students, who came in like packed sardines between classes. At the first note of *Do It Again*, they would crack up.

Four years later, when the Gershwin brothers launched *Oh Kay* on Broadway, the boys were quick to pick up on *Do, Do, Do,* a song that Gertrude Lawrence could be heard singing over the radio. At sixteen, with more sophistication and even a few tiny skirmishes with the opposite sex, they could savor the lyrics through more developed imaginations.

"Let's try again, Sigh again, Fly again to heaven" left little doubt in Adam's mind where Ira Gershwin was headed.

"Benno, this guy's got a fixation. First he wants to 'do it again' and then he's on his knees begging 'Oh, do, do, do what you've done, done, done before, baby!' All these song writers think about is sex."

"It sells. Or perhaps there's something in New York City water," said Benno. "Maybe, someday I'll try it."

Was it her nature never to hold back on a question that needed to be answered, or her Freudian education? Rachel Bernstein could never tease apart those two strands enough to know what drove her to a directness that seemed strange and unsettling to the citizens of Manhattan. Only weeks after hearing of the Spartan routine to which Adam and Benno were subjected, she saw Dan Murdock on the sidewalk beside his house and hailed him with a pleasant enough wave of her hand. She was not one for prolonged formalities. "A minute of your time, Dan. Greetings. I'm interested in the athletics you encourage your boys to play. Spartan wrestling. Have I got it right?" Rachel's English was correct but she delivered it with the heavy accent of an East European Jew, making her brash entry into a Kansas cattleman's privacy all the more jarring.

"Neighborly curiosity or something more professional?" Dan asked, trying hard to overlay his surprise and rising anger with matter-of-fact coolness.

"The Humboldt resident I heard the story from didn't take it seriously. Having met your sons, I do. Not that they told me. Not a thing. And, lest I be misunderstood, I am neither shocked nor disturbed. Nor do I object. What you do in your 'temple,' as I believe you call that large home of yours, is your business, not mine. Your boys are approaching puberty. People talk. Boys can be barbarically cruel to other boys who seem different. You've met my son, Aaron. He knows the cruelty of peers from a playground in Vienna. No broken bones, but plenty of psychic scars. Bones heal but those scars linger. I like your boys too much to see them hurt."

Rachel caught Dan's eyes, which appeared to be changing color as varying shades of red and purple crossed Dan's face.

"Not wrestling. Boxing. A noble sport in Sparta. Teaches self-defense. In Manhattan too. From the sound of it, something they will need. Good day, Dr. Bernstein." Whirling around, he strode back to his house, opened the imposing front door and quickly disappeared in the shadow of an unlighted vestibule. Less than a minute later, Dan reappeared. Rachel was walking swiftly back to her house when she heard his voice: "Dr. Bernstein." Turning around, she saw him running to catch up to her.

"My departure was rude. Forgive me. Your directness caught me up. Manhattanites beat around the bush. We banter our way along. Never hasty to get to the point. A peacock's dance. Infuriating at times. So, the boys box naked, except for gloves. Any harm in that, Doctor?"

"Let's be on a first name basis." She pursed her lips, wetting them with her tongue. Involuntarily, her face assumed that professional mien. "And what harm might you imagine, Dan?"

"You mentioned puberty." His voice dropping to a whisper, "You don't think this exercise could lead to them to prefer boys to girls?"

"Would you object?"

"Look, there's not one fairy, I mean, homosexual, in this town. I won't allow my sons to be the first."

"Many of us have a speck or two of 'queer' that we either don't know about or keep secret. There was plenty of homosexuality in Sparta. Do you admire that aspect of its society?"

"I can't believe we're having this conversation in public, on Humboldt Street. Strange as a two dollar bill. You think I cherry-picked Spartan life. You're right, although it hadn't occurred to me till now. Interesting how we can select what we like and discard the rest, as if it wasn't there."

"Yes, as if it wasn't even there. Dig around below the surface of rational analysis and you often find a substratum of bestial emotion, belief and suspicion."

"Rachel, I don't know what to make of you. But — I think I've told you before — I appreciate the friendship you've shown my boys. Cherry pies and all that. But, here, I've held you up, so please, be off."

"Why, Dan, that's a kind thing to say. I appreciate it. Raising twin boys as a single parent is nobody's cup of tea. And you're a stockman.

From what I see, you take the responsibility very seriously. Isaiah being busy making cement, dawn to dusk, gives me more time than my practice needs. I would be glad to help out where I could be useful. You know, school pick-ups, hikes, even mushrooming, where I had excellent training as a youngster in Austria."

Dan stared at Rachel for what seemed to her almost a minute, their eyes locked and unblinking. Suddenly, she realized that for the first time, he was seeing her as a mother and a woman. "I may take you up on that," he said, waving goodbye as he turned back towards his house.

———◆———

On the first day of class in the Fall of 1922, the Murdock boys arrived in their 7th grade classroom to find, written on the blackboard, the following: SPARTANS ARE HERE. Mr. Darby, the home room teacher, who had let his hair grow very long over the Summer, appeared nonplussed. Stammering, he asked who had put it there. The class, numbering 13 boys and 8 girls, remained silent.

"What does it mean?" he demanded.

Adam looked at Benno, who was staring down at his pencil. He glanced around the room. With the exception of Bill Spiker and George Brandley, all heads bent down towards their desks. Bill and George were looking intently at Benno. They seemed to be expecting something. Adam saw them exchange glances. And then he saw them turn their gaze to him, as if to force out the answer to Mr. Darby's question. He stared back, slinging a silent challenge either to speak up or abandon the game. Lowering their eyes, they disengaged.

On the way home, the boys debated what to do. They hadn't exercised in the Spartan way since mid-Summer, when their Father suggested they had outgrown the practice. It would be best, they thought, to ignore the incident, even though Adam boasted he knew who was behind the message.

"I stared them down," Adam said. "We've heard the last of this."

Benno replied. "I'm not sure."

Last year Bill Spiker and George Brandley had tied for the most demerits of anyone in 6th grade, a whopping 125. Since each demerit took an hour's work to erase, the trouble-makers spent a lot of their free time at janitorial chores. Adam and Benno wanted to know how Bill and George had found out. They decided not to tell Father.

The next day, the class saw another blackboard message: SPARTANS BOX NAKED. Each letter was upper case. Beside himself with anger, Mr. Darby again demanded answers, only to be greeted by more silence punctuated, this time, by muffled laughter. The Murdock boys sent Bill and George a message requesting a meeting at the northeast corner of the middle school football field right after classes ended.

Bill and George arrived first. With them was another classmate, Floyd Teas, a jokester who also was one of the largest boys in 7th grade, and a good athlete as well.

Adam opened the conversation. "What's the point?" he asked.

"We want to see you box," Bill replied. "Take off your clothes and give us a show, and we won't write again."

"Yea," said George, "You must be a snappy piece of work."

"Listen, you're balled up. We aren't Spartans. We don't box naked. I won't take off my clothes, but I will give you a show." Raising his fists, Adam advanced to within inches of Bill's face.

"What's eating you?" Bill said, backing off.

"You want me to box. Here's the show. "

Bill tried to protect his face, only to find Adam's fists sinking deep into his stomach. Lowering his fists to protect his body, Bill found himself pummeled in the head, on the chin and nose, which started to bleed, drops covering his cheeks and dripping down his white shirt. With surprising swiftness, the fight was over.

Benno had never enjoyed the Spartan play as much as Adam did. It was not a matter of being less skilled. Though somewhat lighter than Adam, Benno was quicker and gifted with exceptional coordination of eye and hand that more than compensated for his size and even his reluctance to cause physical pain to others. At home, he held his own with the far more aggressive Adam. Now, with Adam triumphant, Benno thought the awkward blackboard game was finished.

"Come on, Adam. Time to go home."

In fact, it was not. George had been supporting Bill, helping to stop the nosebleed and at the same time talking to him in urgent whispers. Floyd joined the tight group, which had all the hallmarks of a team seeking to recover its spirits after a lousy first half. The trio burst out of their huddle to turn on Adam, hitting him high, low and in-between. He had no chance to respond. He dropped first to his knees and then to the ground, where, for protection, he assumed a fetal position, allowing blows to land on his thighs, arms and the hands that covered his face and head. No member of the counter-attacking trio was willing to be the first to stop.

Although there was no response to Adam's first two cries for help, they were not in vain. Echoing in Benno's ears, they joined with his third cry to overcome Benno's instinct for preserving the peace, even at risk of personal ridicule or humiliation. Here, the peace had been ruptured and not he but his brother was suffering. He pulled Bill away first. Spinning him around, Benno caught his nose with a left hook. It hadn't much force, just enough to trigger more bleeding. Then he pulled George off his brother's fetal form. George faced Benno, then charged at him with fists pumping like a steam engine. Although George put plenty of energy behind his attack, he came up short on technique, despite having a longer reach than Benno. By clever footwork and timely twisting and ducking, Benno offered his body to George only at sharp angles, causing the boy's fists to glance off face and arms without serious impact. Benno seemed to be inviting attack, encouraging George to keep swinging wildly, not throwing punches himself. George didn't realize, until the deed was done, that he had been played to exhaustion. Picking the moment, Benno became the aggressor. Using left and right jabs, he bruised his knuckles against George's lean face, inflicting a cut at the cheekbone. Then, when George tried to parry a left jab, Benno saw an opening to the chin and followed through with a jarring uppercut. George's head snapped back and his teeth collided with an alarming clack. Benno watched George retreat, only to be replaced by a larger boy, who glared at him.

"OK, powder puff, let's see what you've got."

Floyd Teas was good at the popular sports. But he was also skilled at boxing, having learned the sport at the Summer camp he had attended for many years. After a minute of sparring, Benno knew he was in trouble. He wondered how long he could last. He wouldn't quit. Wouldn't because he couldn't. Father had seen to that. Dan called giving up an act of self-treason.

Floyd and Benno danced around, jabbing like probing doctors. As jabs turned to punches, knuckles began to bleed, grunts and groans grew louder, breathing quickened. Adam, bloody and bruised, got to his feet. He saw Bill, stretched out on the grass, head lifted to stop the bleeding, George, walking slowly backwards off in the distance, a watchful retreat, and Benno, close by, engaged with a more powerful opponent in what Father reverently called "the noble art of self-defense." He could see that Benno had been cut. Blood oozed from his eyebrow. Soft tissue around the eye was swelling, likely soon to impair vision.

"Break it up," Adam yelled, his voice weak from dirt in the throat. "Break it up now," he shouted, moving between them to put his body behind the command, absorbing a hit or two before the fisticuffs ceased. Whether due to Adam's intervention or the tacit agreement of combatants, the fight was over.

It had been a rough day for Dan. Despite training and retraining, a young cowpuncher had chased one of his Herefords too hard. Instead of backing off to allow the beast to calm down, the youth kept pursuing it with lasso at the ready. The cow was agile and wily, the quarter-horse, a yearling, too young to anticipate, and the rider too inexperienced, despite Dan's cautions, to grasp the risks. A good horse can think ahead and move on a cow as it starts in a new direction. Doing so slows the cow down, preventing it from reaching a speed dangerous to its heart. It was one of those unusually hot days that can arrive, like a Summer tornado, unannounced in September. Pushing too hard for too long, the cowpoke had to pull hard on the reins to avoid having his horse stumble over the cow, which suddenly collapsed in a dusty heap on a bed of bluestem grass. Dismounting, he rushed to the cow just as she uttered the ugly rattle of death.

This news alone was a blow for Dan, since he could count his herd asleep, and often did. Each Hereford was dear to him, its loss a cause for deep grieving. But, when, after explaining what had happened, the cowhand put all the blame on God, Dan flew into a rage.

"Listen here and listen close. We don't accept Acts of God on this ranch. Our God offers no excuse for messing up. We put all our faith in tenacity, perseverance and grit — just plain, old fashioned grit. Enough application and no matter what the odds, cowhands working here at Wyandot can be like the hero in a fairy tale and save the day. Like the weather, God's just an obstacle to overcome. Think hard about where you went wrong today. And come tell me about it tomorrow."

The boys dragged themselves through the front door. Adam's face was cut and bruised. Benno's right eye was closed. Splotches of dried blood clung to his eyebrow and streaked down both cheeks. Seeing them coming, Dan rushed from his study. Quickly sizing up the situation, he corralled the boys in his study. They knew what to expect, for this "behind the woodshed" moment had occurred many times before. They had even given it a name: the Manhattan Inquisition.

Dan knew spanking. Had experienced it on the receiving end many times growing up. His Father wasn't doctrinaire about the use of corporal punishment. He and his wife began child-rearing as agnostics, open through trial and error to whatever worked. They tried teaching, scolding, shaming, isolation and removal of privilege. They came close to withholding love, but whenever that idea arose, instinct intervened. Dan's parents concluded rather early in the game that to correct, deter or shape behavior, physical pain worked. In addition to being effective, it ended swiftly, an exclamation point, with parent and child able immediately to move on. It became their method of choice. Although not the way Dan remembered it, his Father aimed for the least amount of pain that would still work. He hoped the child's imagination would magnify the prospect beyond the reality. And, in Dan's case, it did. Too well.

No memory is perfect. One's mind bends the facts. Whether knowingly or not, to more or less extent, one disassembles them, shrinking some, expanding others, cutting, pasting, rearranging. Dan remembered his Father's spankings as exceedingly painful. Believing he had turned out well, Dan attributed too much to his Father's use of the rod. His approach to discipline lacked the subtlety of his Father. He never questioned the use of physical pain. He used it first, last and always. The possibility of unintended side effects never entered his mind. His medium of expression was the leather strap he kept in the bathroom for stropping his razor. Unfortunately for the boys, his faulty memory gave excuse to apply the strap with excessive force. After a beating, the boys could not sit for at least a day and, if they slept at all, it would be on their stomachs.

In addition to finding in his own success a warrant for physical punishment, Dan believed that, up to a certain age, his children were as one with his animals, to be motivated and trained in similar fashion. As for the age at which they would enter the human realm, Dan chose 12. While it was a nakedly arbitrary choice, he knew it was right. On their sixth birthday he informed the twins that in six years to the day, the strap would cease to be used for anything other than honing a razor's edge.

Dan's beatings had unanticipated consequences for the boys, but for better or worse, not ones that Dan ever caught a glimmer of over his remaining years. With lights out, through hours of pillow talk, each twin came to understand, through a bit of self-knowledge but much more from the insights of the other, the scars left by their Father's way of handling what he took to be unacceptable behavior. For Adam, an impatience and irritability with others, an intolerance and lack of kindness. Lucky he was to know the enemy, against which he would struggle throughout his years. For Benno, the beatings taught avoidance of conflict, building on his natural tendency toward shyness and reluctance to express certainty about anything.

Dan's study was cozy. A large oak desk occupied one corner of the room. In the opposite corner was a three-sided cabinet with open shelves. On the opposite side was a large casement window extending down to meet a window seat. On the pine-paneled walls were photographs of Dan with his prize-winning breeds. So covered were the walls that one didn't easily notice the absence of photographs of Juanita or the twins.

The boys sat on the window seat, Dan behind his desk.

"How do you account for this?" Dan had filled his pipe and was lighting it, drawing in air and exhaling smoke with the distinctive anise odor of Half & Half, Burley and Bright's famous brand and his favorite. The boys caught the whiff as the smoke blended with the smell of sweat-drenched clothing.

Adam told the story, omitting nothing. As it unfolded, Dan's body language spoke of far-ranging emotions, from anger to humiliation, from peak of pride to face of failure.

"You quit. Benno, you quit a fight," Dan said, his voice blending disappointment with resignation.

Adam jumped up. "No, he didn't. Listen Father, please. I told you what happened," his voice cracking, eyes wet with tears. "I broke it up. Got between them. They had no choice. I stopped the fight!" he shouted, arms crossing.

"Well, you had no cause. All these years I've taught you, never quit a fight, so long as it's fair. Act like a man and you'll become one. Cower like a dog and you won't. Winning or losing, it's all the same so long as you give it your best shot. But you've heard all this before. You've disappointed me, that's the nub of it."

They trooped out, heads bowed. At twelve, they knew shame. And injustice. Since two or three, they had lived for their Father's recognition and approval. From the start, he was a hard man to please and, perversely, with each passing year they saw the hurdle get higher.

Dan would invariably fling a final comment at the boys when they were just beyond the door. Today was no exception.

"One other thing, Adam. Stop fighting Benno's battles for him. First you intervene in the fight with Floyd. Then with me. You think you're helping him. As sure as heat can kill a steer, you're not. Quit it. And close the door as you leave."

———◆———

Dan was attracted to the Ku Klux Klan. He liked its defense of that great mass of Americans who claim ancestry to old pioneer stock. Dan brought his twins along, explaining why this group, whose presence in Manhattan was growing, appealed to him. He told them the Klan stood tall in support of people like the Murdocks, who were part of that blend of various peoples of the so-called Nordic race. "With all its faults," Dan asserted, "we Nordics have given the world almost the whole of modern civilization. Our country, heaven help us, has admitted to its shores aliens who became Americans for profit only. What politicians in search of votes call the 'melting pot' has been a ghastly failure. One of the alien races now threatening our pioneer stock are the Jews, who despite having coined that evocative phrase seem determined not to melt."

Adam and Benno tried to take it in. Thinking of Rachel Bernstein and her family, they were confused. After some moments' silence, Adam spoke.

"But Father, ..."

"Don't stammer, Adam. Say what you have to say, and mean it."

"Yes, I mean, I thought you liked the Bernsteins. You always spoke highly of the Doctor's brains."

"And encouraged us to make friends with Aaron," Benno added.

"And to visit over cherry pie. We thought you admired them as much as we do," Adam said, almost defiantly.

"So that's it. Look, I don't include the Bernsteins in those aliens. Not at all. They live on our street. They are our friends. A totally different kettle of fish. Don't confuse one with the other."

For Adam and Benno, at 14, the armor-plate encasing Father was starting to show a chink here and there.

The Klan's growing power was being felt in Kansas, which fast became one of its main strongholds. Dan enjoyed a strong and well exercised friendship with William Allen White, Editor and owner of *The Emporia Gazette* in Emporia. It would last while they lived, despite political and philosophical differences that at times challenged their friendship. An early test came with the Klan's presence in Kansas. In 1921, Bill had copied Dan on a letter he sent to Herbert Bayard Swope, editor of the *New York World* and leader of a crusade against the Klan. It was like a hard slap across the face of one caught unawares.

"An organizer of the Ku Klux Klan was in Emporia the other day, and the men whom he invited to join his band at ten dollars per join turned him down. The Emporians told him that they had no time for him. The proposition seems to be:
Anti foreigners; Anti Catholics; Anti Negroes.

There are, of course, bad foreigners and good ones, good Catholics and bad ones, and all kinds of Negroes. To make a case against a birthplace, a religion, or a race is wickedly un-American and cowardly.

It is to the everlasting credit of Emporia that the organizer found no suckers with $10 each to squander here. Whatever Emporia may be otherwise, it believes in law and order, and absolute freedom under the constitution for every man, no matter what birth or creed or race, to speak and meet and talk and act as a free law-abiding citizen. The picayunish cowardice of a man who would substitute Klan rule and mob law for what our American Fathers have died to establish and maintain should prove what a cheap screw outfit the Klan is."

As he had always done, Dan had responded immediately and at length.

Dear Bill,

About your letter to the *NY World*. Breathtaking. That is, from surprise and shock, it took breath away, leaving me feeling abandoned and forlorn. Why do I embrace the Klan? Indeed, how could I when faced with your contempt for that 'cheap screw outfit'? Every cause has good and bad sides. One can't be an activist, getting things done, without taking views offensive to some. Look, I concentrate on the affirmative things. I ignore the rest and cut them some slack to come round by day's end.

The aliens are tearing down the American standard of living, especially in the lower walks. I'm sure I've heard you make the same point. More important is the moral breakdown, going on now for two decades. The sacredness of our Sabbath, of our homes, of chastity, and finally even of our right to teach our own children in our own schools fundamental facts and truths was torn away from us. Those who maintained the old standards did so only in the face of constant ridicule.

The Klan stands up for old-stock Americans like you and me. They are removing the disguise that makes the steady flood of alien ideas spreading over the country appear as American. They are alerting the country to the dangers of the alien's attraction to low living and fast breeding, his ability to so far under-live the American as to force him out of all competitive labor.

The Klan says to us old-stock Americans, "Take back your country before it's too late." I hear the call. I applaud it. And I intend to heed it, as I'm sure, in your heart, you want to do too.

Enough of this. Spring is coming on a run. Tulips blaze in the garden and violets are blooming. This afternoon, I reckon, I'll take the boys for a drive to the pastures far up among the hills to see how the cows are making it. They are due to calve next month. The sows have mostly farrowed and likewise the ewes have lambed. A dull life, the farmer's? Hell, no. There's something doing every moment.

Affectionately,
Dan Murdock

Dan had only one sibling, a sister, Bridget. A decade older and widowed, she was among the few in town who openly admitted to being a member of the local Klan chapter. Bridget taught piano. She was a whiz at reading, but could play by ear as well, particularly the popular show tunes of the day. Dan's family and friends could be counted on to gather around his Steinway when Bridget was seated at the keyboard, singing favorites while their voices lasted.

There were only two Manhattan women who had joined the chapter, the Klan being chiefly a man's thing. Bridget wore her opinions on her sleeves, the better, she thought, to bring others along. It was an unreasoned loathing for Jews that brought her to the Klan and its gospel of superiority and hate. It was the Klan that deepened the mental ruts in which she would remain stuck for a lifetime. How this prejudice got started no one knew. A seed planted early, in childhood? If so, it grew in a sealed environment, cut off from the natural influences of others that bend, shape and reshape most people's minds through time.

Dan had somehow escaped Bridget's poisonous opinions. Perhaps because he was much younger, perhaps because he was a voracious reader, perhaps because he was instinctively open to test ideas, perhaps because he was forced by life's challenges to face a wide range of opinions and think hard about them, to weigh the evidence, to stretch his mind and follow in paths made uncomfortable by childhood teaching.

Not that Bridget's mind wasn't nimble. It easily could embrace two ideas so thoroughly at odds with one another that the boys would puzzle over it for years to come. She had mastered Brahms and Mozart well enough to teach her students. But she especially loved the popular music of the day written mainly for the stage. As Cole Porter might have put it, "nothing thrilled her half as much as" playing Broadway show tunes for the piano bench. And, of course, given her good taste, the music she chose invariably were songs composed by Jews: Irving Berlin, Jerome Kern, George and Ira Gershwin, Harold Arlen, Richard Rodgers, Lorenz Hart and Oscar Hammerstein. As composers, they were far and away the best, and as such adored by Bridget. Had she considered their origins, she would have believed that, as Jews, they must be of inferior immigrant stock, beneath her contempt.

In the Summer of 1924, while Bill White and his wife, Sallie, were visiting the Murdocks, Bridget came to dinner. Discussion turned to the Klan. Argument ensued, growing vigorous. Opinions veered close to the personal, becoming accusatory. What could easily have been kept civil were just Bill and Dan engaged, turned nasty through the presence of

Bridget, who was still active in the Klan and prepared, in defending it, to make explicit its worst motives.

The boys were ignored. Bill, Dan and Bridget rehearsed in the raw views they had often expressed, but never in the presence of young teenagers. Adam and Benno sat in silence. Their earlier confusion over Dan's attitude turned to shock. They each recognized in Bridget a more extreme form of the dissonance noted in their Father's opinions. Somehow, they had missed the fact of Bridget's Klan membership and her vile and hateful prejudices, so incompatible with the love songs she favored on piano and the happiness she evoked among those singing around her. They wondered what would happen if the Bernsteins were invited to join the singing. Even if unspoken, wouldn't they feel the animus? The boys had believed they loved Bridget. Now they saw a different Bridget, one they couldn't even understand, much less love.

During the Whites' visit, the Progressive Party nominated Senator Robert M. La Follette by acclamation and the platform upon which he wished to stand unanimously and without argument. Naturally enough, over dinner, the subject came up.

"He's a traitor to our party, Bill. The party that birthed and nourished him in Wisconsin," said Dan. "Now, don't mind me, I'm going to the sideboy to carve this beast."

The sound of steel against steel began.

"I always admire your sharpening technique, Dan. And your timing. Using it to punctuate one of those declarations you're fond of making — you know, the ones you intend to be unanswerable. A neat trick, turning your back on the enemy."

Dan winked at Adam and Benno, hoping they were following enough to share the humor.

Bridget exclaimed: "Your enemy has two voices, and one of them is here beside you."

Ignoring her, Bill declared: "If your Hereford beef tastes anything like as good as this gravy smells, we're in for a treat."

"Yes, indeedy," Sallie said. Look, Bill, beside the gravy, a dish of horseradish and sour cream. Very British."

"Have I softened you up? For what you say is downright uncharitable, Dan. La Follette just wants to use the Federal government in new ways. To alleviate suffering. The platform addresses the farm problem, and surely you won't argue that we don't have a problem, all across the mid-west? The Agriculture Secretary just reported that since 1920 in the principal wheat growing states — and that includes us — almost 600,000 farmers, or 26% of all farmers in these states, have lost their farms and been virtually bankrupted. All the while, the great industrial corporations are near to drowning in profit. La Follette is after what your pointy-headed academics here at state call 'distributive justice.' He's got the scent and will run it down, like a bird dog."

"I fear you're right." Dan turned to face the table, knife in hand. "But, hey, who says the Government's job is to alleviate all suffering? You and I grew up believing in some basic 'rules of the road.' First, the law of supply and demand is as certain as the law of gravity. Second, wealth is evidence of virtue; poverty, evidence of sin or, worse, weakness. Third, the acquisitive faculty is the only human talent in the busy world having survival value. And fourth, the only thing worse than being poor is to be one of those — like La Follette — who champions the poor, for they pander to poverty to profit by it. Sometimes, when I hear you talk, Bill, I feel a twinge in my belly, a fear that you might have abandoned these guideposts."

Wide-eyed, the boys exchanged confirming looks. Never before had they heard their Father describe his philosophy so clearly. Like so many facets of Dan's outlook, they saw inconsistency between his strident theories on poverty and his day-to-day behavior in Manhattan. They knew he gave generously to the town's private agencies serving the down-trodden and afflicted, regardless of cause. Indeed, they knew, because they had attended gatherings to honor him for his generosity.

Bill looked down at the round shape of his stomach. Putting his hands around it, he said "My belly's bigger now, and softer. Bigger belly, bigger appetite. So, when food like this is on hand, I eat more. That's all. Washington shouldn't step across the line. Protection and defense, yes. Coddling and mothering, no. But should the strong and predatory range unscathed? I say no. The bully and cheat should be yanked back into the arena of common decency and Christian morality. Mind you, Dan, not because of the victims they would despoil. No, just because it's naturally indecent for them to thrive. And because, eventually, it will wreck society."

Dan liked a bit of what his friend was saying. Looking appreciatively at Bill, he saw that his friend's attention had shifted to Adam, who had raised his hand, arm outstretched. Here was something new. Perhaps, thought Dan, at fourteen the boys were ready to engage.

"Who will yank them back?" Adam said.

"Good question, son. Solutions should begin at the smallest level of Government. From village to town, from city to state. But no further. So the community most affected by the bully and cheat should be the first line of defense. As for social welfare generally, I believe that each state with its own taxes should set up its own program of social welfare. Washington should stick to things that only Washington can do."

"So it's the job of Kansas?" Adam asked.

"Yes. First and ultimate. If we can't afford out of our own economic surplus to take care of our own poor, our crippled and disabled, our own problem of unemployment, then we are in a bad way."

Adam seemed satisfied. Bill was about to turn to a different subject when, catching the perplexed expression on Benno's face, he paused.

"I see you have something to say, Benno."

"Yes, I'm confused. You say Kansas bears ultimate responsibility. But suppose Kansas lacks the means. What then? We are one nation, after all. Where does the Federal Government come in? In school we learned that, with Hamilton's leadership, the Government assumed the war debts of the states, an essential element of becoming a country. Also, you are for every state defining social justice and treating it in its own way. Seems to me hunger and illness are the same across the country. Shouldn't they be treated the same wherever found?"

Bill was about to respond when Dan cut him off. "The nation, Benno, provides for national defense, treaties with other nations, foreign policy, that sort of thing. A body with sharply limited powers. You'll find it in the Constitution. The states have all powers not expressly granted to the Feds. I share Bill's philosophy. Apples shouldn't fall far from the tree. You get my drift. No more questions.

"We'll take coffee in the library. Boys, time for homework and bed. I'll be up to tuck you in."

———◆———

Upon reaching their fourteenth birthdays, the boys stopped visits to Rachel Bernstein's kitchen. It was not a decision consciously taken. Just a practice dropped by the wayside. Like dance partners drifting away from one another when the music stopped. Not that the dance hadn't been rewarding. The time had come for other things, and they all seemed to know it.

Of course, living on the same street, the boys saw Rachel from time to time. But never with time enough to talk beyond simple greetings. Then, one day in the Fall of 1926, Adam bumped into Rachel outside her house.

"Two years it's been since you stepped foot in my kitchen. I've missed those visits. How about coming over for breakfast next Sunday? No pie, but maybe some buttermilk pancakes, if that appeals. At eight?"

"It's a date. And I speak for Benno too."

Adam and Benno were precisely on time.

"You're sixteen now, if I have my dates right. Tell me, honestly, have you regretted anything you've learned from me? Have you been hurt by anything? Or helped?"

Adam was quick to answer. "Not a thing, Doctor. Our minds are filled with it; we parade around the Garden of Eden like old pros, aware we know things others do not."

"And you, Benno?"

"Knowing what I learned from you has hog-tied me with girls."

"How's that?" Rachel asked off-handedly, shifting to lean into the question.

Benno put both hands to his mouth, covering his lips. Out of habit, he tried to think while keeping a hawk-eye on Adam, who typically at times like this would answer for his brother.

Adam's big mouth had just opened when Benno found his voice. "You've showed me the path of romance, where it leads. It makes me afraid even to take the first step."

"Interesting. Very interesting. And unexpected. As good Christians, I'm sure you know your Bible. Benno's reaction is akin to Adam and Eve's shame after eating from the tree of knowledge. They clothed themselves. You wrap yourself in the fear of losing self-control. Perfectly normal." At this, Benno's heavy frown dropped away.

Adam's eyes danced. With laughter, he said "So, Adam and Eve started it all? Must be human."

"Tell me this. In school, have either of you had a teacher make a physical advance on you that felt like something sexual or, maybe preliminary to becoming sexual?"

"What makes you ask that?" Adam said, looking at Benno, who had dropped his eyes to the floor and was shifting hands from one pocket to another.

"Aaron came home the other day with stories. Because he's a careful reporter, they alarmed me. I touch on a delicate subject, but only out of concern for your welfare. In fact, I went to your dad with Aaron's tale, because I wanted to enlist him in advance. We talked over tea the other day. He approved of my taking this matter up with you."

"Ok. The answer's no," said Adam, looking at Rachel to catch her reaction. "But I know classmates who have," he added, turning to look again at Benno.

"What did Aaron tell you?"

Ignoring Adam's question, Rachel studied Benno.

"And you, Benno?"

"The Latin teacher does things," Benno said almost too softly to be understood.

"What sorts of things?"

Benno blushed, ear to ear. He felt trapped on a slippery incline, with no chance to get off. Shame clouded his mind.

"Go ahead, Benno. If she's going to help us, she needs to know."

"He calls us up to his desk, to come around to his side, and to read, or listen while he reads, or comments on written work. With me, he often puts his hand under my shirt and rubs my back. Sometimes, he pulls against my belt, trying to rub lower down."

"And what do you do when this happens?"

"Nothing. It makes me afraid, and ashamed lest classmates see what's happening. I just try to get through it as fast as possible and return to my seat."

"Does he do this to others?"

"I'm not the only one," said Benno.

Adam said, "He tried it with me and the first, and only time, I squirmed away, pulling his arm down. I looked at him hard, like, I guess, anger and fear combined, 'cause that's how I felt. It never happened again. As for others, there seems to be a conspiracy of silence. Benno hasn't told others and others haven't told him. Benno is fearful, and if there are others, and I'm sure there are, they are probably fearful, and ashamed too. We've heard from someone in French class that the teacher does the same sort of thing to him. He's an odd duck, taking the whole thing as normal; says he likes being rubbed — calls it 'French Massage' — Thinks it may help his grades. Even looks forward to that class."

"Do you think physical contact with the Latin or French teacher has gone beyond back massage? Or could? Benno?"

"I try not to think about it. To imagine it happening. To me or others. And, yet, sometimes I do. I visualize it and hate myself for these imaginings. They're disgusting."

"Bravo, Benno," Adam cried, aware, as only he could be, of his brother's brave spirit.

Rachel tried to restrain herself from giving Benno a hug. Failing, she grabbed him with both hands on his shoulders, pulling him to her in a tight embrace. Benno never had been inclined to embraces. At first, instinctively, he wriggled. But, then, appreciating this expression of empathy, Benno relaxed in her arms, welcoming the approval Rachel was demonstrably expressing.

"Now, as I understand it, you both have recently been confirmed into the faith — the Episcopalian faith — and that entitles you to take communion and partake of all that the church offers. First, my congratulations. You're helping to meet the need for more, and younger, parishioners. And, who knows? Perhaps this new armament will protect you from the roving hands and fertile minds of your French and Latin teachers."

"We don't feel comfortable with the Minister," Benno said in a whisper. "He plays nice, but I suspect he's a parental spy. He's always talking forgiveness, but I'm sure if we confess, he'll just pass it along. I don't see him spreading much charity around."

"He's not spreading much joy either," said Adam. "You should know, Rachel, that you're the only one in town we can open up with. If this is what psychoanalysis does, it should be a religion; your man, Freud, should be the Pope; and you, why not Archbishop?"

"Boys, boys enough of this. But, you may be onto something. Freudian doctrine could become a religion. It's heady stuff; students can easily get carried away with its powers, a kind of secular infallibility can take over."

"Sounds dangerous for patients," Benno whispered.

3

———◆———

To THE AMAZEMENT OF HER parents, Mariah finished Sweet Briar single and with academic honors. Her independence from parental wishes was complete. And she had accomplished this trick while preserving their support, financial and otherwise. Chalk it up to knowing oneself better than others do, even one's parents, and being right along most of the pathway to becoming a grown-up. With argument falling far short of full disclosure, Mariah easily gained parental support for graduate work at Newton Theological Seminary, beginning in the Fall of 1931.

One wintry day during her first year at Newton, Mariah went to The Harry Elkins Widener Memorial Library to study. Public transportation from Newton to Cambridge was fast. She came to Harvard's main library for a change of scene and for the chance to meet people outside her field. Especially those in pants. Before graduating from Sweet Briar, she had applied to Harvard Divinity School, only to be informed it was limited to men. As an alternative, the letter from Harvard suggested Yale, which had just started admitting women a couple of years earlier. She wanted the Boston area, however, and found Newton, where women had been welcomed since 1922.

Snow was falling as she marched through the Yard to Widener. Stamping her feet and brushing her coat to shake off the snow, she paused in front of the large bulletin board in Widener's vestibule, home to all manner of notices and offering of services, including thesis preparation and other typing services, dog-sitting, tutoring — you name it and there you would find it. A strange offering caught her eye:

SUMMER JOB OPPORTUNITY

**Do you believe the main trouble with this country today is
the unequal distribution of wealth?
If you answer YES, and want to do something about it,
Write to The Reverend Gerald L. K. Smith**

**P.O. Box 2228
New Orleans, Louisiana
And enclose your resume. He may have a job for you this Summer!**

Mariah's heart leapt. She had no plans for the Summer and was out of sorts with herself for not having even tried to develop any. Suddenly, she was staring at an opportunity resting on the chief focus of her life, the national dilemma that undergirded her decision to enter Newton. It was her youthful disgust over the concentration of so much southern wealth in the hands of so few — chief among whom were her parents, her parents' friends and the parents of her classmates at both St. Catherine's and Sweet Briar; indeed, virtually all the parents of both student bodies. Like loosestrife, her passion over this issue grew through her college years and, with the help of Willa Cather, was channeled into a youthful ambition to change things, fired by a belief that change could come through mastery of the human spirit. Graduate study in politics failed her notion of first principles. As form follows function, so she believed, politics follows the human spirit. Harness that and public policy will follow. Mariah's embrace of religion, any religion, was hesitant at best, as was her belief in God. Of course, such matters were better left unsaid at home. To the Admissions Office at Newton, she was forthcoming to a degree, successfully arguing that her shortcomings in religious faith should be of no concern. "If I had it all worked out, why would I need to enroll?"

First, among the boys of Richmond society, and later, among the young men who, like milling drones around a queen bee, clustered on the Sweet Briar campus at the first hint of Spring, Mariah had established a distinct reputation. Even at a distance, she looked intriguing. Always tall for her age, and willowy, she kept her blond hair long and in disarray, as if she'd just rolled out of bed, a possibility belied by the excessive make-up carefully applied to her face.

At a young age, she found a way to keep her would-be wooers off-balance. As this power grew, her approach to the opposite sex became increasingly self-conscious. In a kind of rapid-fire serial monogamy, one by one, she would draw them in with flirtatious talk and opportunistic use of hands and limbs to make physical contact. And, then, when she had them in raptures of anticipation over what lay ahead — and naturally enough, being males, they all thought along precisely the same lines and used precisely the same words when comparing notes — "making out," "feeling up," "petting," "scoring" and "going down" — she would find ways to chill the atmosphere, crushing these expectations. Those who hadn't fallen within her web thought her a vamp, whore or worse. Those on whom she practiced the dark art of manipulation were too proud and embarrassed to speak of the experience. As for Mariah, it was never clear, even to her, in these early years, whether she was afraid of losing control or too enthralled with her skill at domination to allow her own passion room for expression. Her behavior was oddly unemotional, more an exercise in power than an expression of caring. This continued to be the case even after she began, early in her college years, to add a full range of sexual practices to enhance her art.

Given her success in manipulating the desires of her suitors, it was a small step to suppose she could master the human spirit as well. If, as Marx had claimed, "religion was the opiate of the people," she would learn how to use it well. There was nothing more or less complicated behind her presence as a student at Newton. Now, suddenly, as if guided by the divine providence she questioned, she had found an appeal designed precisely for her.

Could this ad come from Senator Huey Long's office, she wondered? Although she hadn't heard of Reverend Smith, she knew of the "Kingfish," and had actually read his screed on wealth redistribution in *The Louisiana Progress,* the weekly newspaper he launched during his 1930 Senate campaign. It had found interest on the Newton campus, making the rounds among faculty and students.

She applied for the Summer post and was invited to New Orleans for an interview. Arriving as directed at the Hotel Roosevelt precisely at 10:30 AM, she asked the concierge for the Reverend Smith. He sent her to Room 1212. The door was ajar. Knocking, she heard a voice bark, "Come on in." On entering, she saw the senator striding towards her in lavender silk pajamas. She thought his handshake rambunctious. They seated themselves on opposite sides of a glass-topped coffee table.

"So, you're the one from Boston," he exclaimed, mockingly accenting the first syllable. "Talk to me. Why should I want to hire you?"

She saw her resume in his hand.

"Don't assume I looked at this thing," he said, waving it in the air, then tossing it on the rug. "Get on with it. I'm yours to sell."

Quickly, Mariah gave the senator a thumbnail sketch of her life, ending with her ambition to change the distribution of wealth in the country by changing the human spirit.

"It can be done. The Sally's been working on it for years. Bit by bit, spirits change. I'm inspired by your efforts."

"Jesus! Jesus Christ! Seen the eagle and heard the owl. Thought I knew it all. My young lady, have you considered how long it will take to re-distribute the wealth of this nation by changing spirits, one by one? Perhaps you and I have the same goal. But, you're cockeyed if you think concentration of wealth can be eliminated that way. Spiritual appeals my arse. Wild horses won't change the wealth-mongers. No, the only way is through a tiny little law that I'm going to write. A law that limits incomes and property ownership."

He paused, and Mariah pursed her lips, wanting to respond but not knowing just what to say. She was pretty sure she'd blown it. With small confidence, she said "Don't we first need to change the human spirit in order to get that little law?"

The senator jumped to his feet and called into the next room: "George! Get me a razor and a shaving-brush."

"Yes," he said, sitting down, "it's all in Plato. I hadn't read that idol before I started writing and speaking about wealth, and when I did, I found I had said almost exactly the same things. I felt as if I'd written *The Republic* myself. Isn't that funny?"

Thinking about his wish for a shave, Mariah examined the senator's face. She couldn't see much in the way of whiskers, but the vertical dimple on his chin stood out like the Grand Canyon. So deep that she imagined him forced to turn the razor to plumb its depths in safety. The following Winter, she happened to see *Madame Butterfly*, a new non-musical adaptation of Puccini's opera, starring the estimable Sylvia Sidney as Cho-Cho San and a new sensation, Cary Grant, looking extraordinarily handsome in his naval uniform as Lt. B.F. Pinkerton. She'd never seen Grant before. From the moment he appeared on screen, she thought of Huey Long. Of course, there was no possible resemblance, except, as she saw in a minute or two, for the same deeply etched dimple on his chin.

"And now, I'll tell you how the idea of writing this law came to me. Way back in 1914, when I was a law student, I wrote a letter to the Congressman from Louisiana — I can't find that letter now, to save my life — pointing out that the country couldn't continue more than fifteen years longer as it was going. And what happened? Exactly fifteen years later, the crash came! Concentration of wealth brought us down in '29. And it remains the greatest menace we have today!"

George appeared, holding out the requested implements. Without explanation or apology, the senator took them and disappeared from the room, George trotting behind. A few minutes later, he reappeared, face full of lather, to continue what Mariah realized was more lecture than interview, as he grazed his face with the razor and shook it into a towel.

"As I was saying, unless we provide for redistribution of wealth, the country's doomed. Now, my law would not be too radical at the start.

It would allow every man enough to be comfortable on, anyway. And, don't you worry about changing the human spirit. I know other ways to put a new law on the books."

The ablution was finished. Turning over the towel, he rubbed his face, then resumed. "After all, why should anyone go hungry when there is enough in the country for everyone to eat? Why should they go ragged, when there's enough to wear? You see, I am not in favor of abolishing private property. Only of limiting it. Don't think me naïve. It's either this or Communism." Pursing his lips and framing his tongue, he uttered a loud "raspberry." Mariah worried that his pajamas had come untied and were about to fall to the floor. The senator sat down and curled one leg under the other on the chair. Until the vulgarity, he had projected the pose of an earnest boy, talking with a magnetic gentleness that could herd cats.

Mariah was alternately terrified, shocked and amused. Most of all, she was smitten. She nodded through the entire tirade, a moon-faced smile confirming the high score he was racking up. He could actually pull it off, she kept thinking.

The senator seemed to have forgotten Mariah's purpose in being there. After an awkward silence, during which she imagined she was not forgotten but rejected, he leaned over to pick up her resume, pretended to examine it, and posed the question, "When did we ever, in a coon's age, hire a naïve seminary student bent on changing the human spirit, Sally style? George, come in here and escort Miss … Miss Massie to the elevator. Thank you very much, Miss Massie, for visiting us."

Crestfallen despite having tried to prepare herself, Mariah rose and accepted the senator's hand. George appeared and led her out the door. They stood together awkwardly, awaiting the elevator. Just as it reached the 12th floor, the senator opened the door to his hotel room and barked, "George, find out how soon that fetching Seminarian can start?"

———————

Spring came to Cambridge, bringing out breezy blouses and short skirts. Mariah delighted in cotton calicos of dappled pastel, a rainbow of colors displayed both day and night. She was scheduled to go to Huey Long's office in New Orleans right after the end of classes, the second week of June, 1932. He was often in the news that Spring, most astoundingly when he launched a one-man mutiny on the Senate floor the afternoon of April 29. Mariah read the *N. Y. Times* account with excitement and growing admiration for the man she would soon be working for. Without warning, the senator from Louisiana stunned his party and the country by attacking the leadership of Senator Robinson of Arkansas. He thereupon resigned from all committee assignments that Robinson had given him. No one could recall anything like this happening before. The revolt came after Senator Robinson repudiated a resolution offered by Long that would have directed the Finance Committee to work into its tax bill a rule preventing anyone from receiving yearly income of more than $1 million or inheritance of more than $5 million. Mariah reveled in the story, recognizing Long's resolution as the 'tiny little' law he had mentioned to her.

———◆———

Mariah arrived in the senator's suite on a hot June day. She was taken to his office. An overhead fan, operating at full speed, made a dreadful noise. Lifting his feet from the cluttered desk, the senator rose, put down the large bamboo fan he had been waving, tucked in his pink shirt and greeted her with a long embrace that left the side of her face dripping wet and smelling of perfume.

"Here to work. Well, work you will. We have an office for you. No fan, but a breeze. Guaranteed. Your first job's to investigate Joe Robinson's voting record laid against his law firm's major clients. I smell smoke; find me fire. Not an itty-bitty fire but a blaze, big enough to burn his house down. Do that and I'll take you with me to Chicago."

"Did you accuse him of conflict?" Mariah was subdued, disappointed not to be working on some angle for the wealth project.

"I'll give you the story." He snatched a paper off the desk. "I stood up in chamber and read from Martindale's — you know, the legal directory — the names of his firm's major clients. They include the largest power companies, banks and railroads in the Southeast. Of course, I was quickly admonished by one of Robinson's cronies for questioning the integrity of a colleague. We knew that would happen." Grasping a paper from his desk, the senator started reading with affect, as if auditioning for a part:

"I want now to disclaim that I have the slightest motive of saying, or that in my heart I believe, that such a man could to the slightest degree be influenced in any vote which he casts in this body by the fact that this association might mean hundreds of thousands and millions of dollars to him in the way of lucrative fees."

The senator beamed, sweating profusely, bathed in self-love.

"Do we know whether he takes money out of his firm?"

"We know very little other than what lurks in human nature — or the 'human spirit,' as you would say. There's not a soul who doesn't have to beg alms of another through this or that contrivance. Take that as a given, and get going. I may need your rap sheet for the Convention."

Mariah didn't see the senator for a week. A week of frustration. She was getting nowhere in the search for a fire to singe the Senate's Democratic leader. Then, early one morning, Huey passed by her office shouting, "Mariah, follow me. I need you."

The senator always appeared to have had three too many cups of coffee. Still, she'd never seen him so excited. Later in the Summer, she came to recognize this ultra-hyper condition as simply a state of intoxication caused by some new scheme he'd hatched. Plots to further his causes could inebriate him as thoroughly as a pint of fine Kentucky moonshine.

"Ever hear of Hattie Caraway?"

Mariah shook her head.

"Good. I want this to come fresh. Hattie's the other senator from Arkansas. Got there when her husband, Thaddeus, died last November. The Governor appointed her to fill that seat. Then Democratic leaders supported her in the special election required to be held in January. With only eight months 'til the regular Democratic primary, Joe Robinson and his boys considered the election of this hapless widow to be as harmless as granting an old ladybug space on your desk.

"So, she went to the Capitol, pursued by patronizing comment from wise guys in the press: 'Demure little woman. Belongs on a porch, in a rocking chair, mending socks.' But that dowdy dame's got more guts than a slaughterhouse. In May, despite there being six men lined up in the race for the Democratic nomination, Hattie announced she would seek a full term. The Arkansas pols thought she'd gone mad. She had no money, no identity except as widow of Thaddeus. In fact, she didn't even have a home, because the bank had just foreclosed for non-payment on the mortgage. I can see you want to know why I am telling you this?"

"Right. But, one thing I know. Somehow, there's going to be a way to scorch the senior senator from Arkansas."

"Smart girl. Hattie and I sit in the back row of the chamber. When I tell her she's a goner, a dead duck, she starts in to bawling. Next day, she looks worse. I see a brave little woman in distress. Well — and you know this — mine is a chivalric soul. I told her I would ride to the rescue. Mariah, get ready for the campaign swing of your life. We go to Arkansas after the Convention. Right after we get Roosevelt nominated. For Hattie. Those big shots won't know what hit 'em." The senator glowed like a bolt of lightning.

"A Presidential year and you have time for chivalry? Am I missing something?"

At that, the senator looked daggers. Then, with a wave of the hand he said, "Buy yourself a Packard. And get back to work on the rap sheet."

Later on, a seasoned staffer explained to Mariah that Hattie had a voting record almost identical to Long's; in particular, she had supported his effort to cap personal fortunes and had voted frequently against the senior senator from her state. If Long could pull off a victory for Hattie — an even more improbable outcome than Hoover's re-election — it would put the torch to Robinson's reputation.

"You missed the size of the scissors Huey's going to use to cut Robinson down to size," the staffer said, bubbling over with glee.

At times like this, the man's audacity stretched her capacity to invent.

———————

Joining the task force preparing Long's invasion of Arkansas, to be launched August 1, Mariah plunged into the madness with delight. The Kingfish welcomed creativity from all hands. It was her idea to define the campaign through a cartoon showing the bloated figure of "Uncle Trusty," personifying the power behind the great money interests. She could draw well enough. She displayed Uncle Trusty in a jacket covered with dollar signs, sitting at a desk, pudgy fingers holding a pen. The broadside explained he was signing an order "to his hired politicians to get busy day and night to see that Senator Caraway is not returned to the Senate."

In mid-July, advance workers blanketed Arkansas with the cartoon, together with Long's speaking schedule for the first week of August and the endorsement of Hattie by the American Federation of Labor.

On schedule, Long crossed the border August 1 with a fleet of sound trucks, literature vans and a loyal band of workers, thundering Old Testament quotations in his opening plea for Hattie Caraway — his theme, redistribution of wealth; his canon, the law of Moses. Mariah was part of the well-oiled advance party, consisting of two carloads of staffers, who arrived at each scheduled speaking site several hours ahead of Huey and Hattie. They drove Ford trucks with sound equipment mounted above to announce the time for speeches to begin. Repairing to the courthouse lawn or town square, they set up microphones. They used speaker's platforms or bandstands, if available; otherwise, they put table and chairs on the roof of the sound truck. For the final hour, they played loud country music. 1,000 gathered in Newport, 4,000 in Russellville, 5,000 in Hot Springs, 20,000 in Pine Bluffs, and in Little Rock, 30,000, the largest political gathering in Arkansas' history.

For Mariah, the week was a continuous, exhausting high. Looking back, it was hard to see through the fog, but the feelings — of intense immersion, concentrated focus, spirit and absolute commitment to the cause they all believed in — could never be forgotten. They slept hardly at all, using cheap hotels, if handy, or the back seat of a car. Racing over ill-paved bumpy roads from appearance to appearance, often at frantic speed, there was no time to stop for meals. Gas attendants were asked for something — anything — to eat, and often, while Mariah held the pump, would disappear into the station, quickly to return with peanut butter and jelly sandwiches. Knowing whose entourage it was, typically, they would refuse payment.

Mariah never tired of listening to the Kingfish, as he whipped audiences into a frenzy with denunciations of Wall Street bankers and their cronies in Washington. He used the wealth redistribution theme to attack Uncle Trusty's crew of powerful politicians, "who had conspired to remove this brave little woman from the Senate. I proposed it. Mrs. Caraway voted for it. So did I. But they killed it deader'n a doornail."

Mariah could quote the whole speech. She loved his guile. In support of a righteous cause, she believed, it served the higher reaches of morality. She saw a Seminary paper in this, if she could get back to Newton with time to write it.

"It's nip and tuck with us, up there in the Senate. If Wall Street and their trust gang succeed in defeating enough senators who have stood with the people — like this little woman senator from Arkansas has — they'll have the whip hand on you. You'll never be able to get anyone from this state to stand by you again."

Mariah was back in New Orleans on August 9, election day. Despite the stir Long's barnstorming created, political leaders in Arkansas continued smugly to predict that Caraway would place dead last. The results told a very different story, as reported in the *New York Times* on August 10 and 11. She had won by a landslide, garnering almost as many votes as her six male opponents combined. Arkansas was a one-party state. The primary victory meant she could keep her seat in the Senate.

In a press conference, Hattie gave the senator from Louisiana a large share of credit. "To him I would deny no meed of praise or thanks."

Two days after the primary, Huey took Mariah to breakfast in a fancy New Orleans hotel. He was honoring a gesture offered in the heat of battle, when, just before a rally in Arkansas, right in his face, Mariah fainted for a minute or two, more from dehydration than hunger, although she suffered from both. She fell forward and Huey caught her. Photographers seized the moment, which made it into the *Arkansas Gazette* the next morning above a caption announcing "Kingfish Caught a Keeper!"

They had scrambled eggs with lamb kidneys, country sausage, soda biscuits and grits ground on the premises, if the waiter was to be believed. Mariah declared it the best breakfast she'd ever had.

"From one who grew up in Richmond, that says a whole heap," Huey replied.

On the way out, the Kingfish spied John Nance Garner having breakfast.

"Look who's here, Mariah. That's Garner, Speaker of the House and Roosevelt's candidate for VP. Come on, I'll introduce you."

They walked over to his table. Long was beaming when the Congressman looked up. "Hello, Jack" Huey bellowed, forgetting he had just promised to introduce Mariah. "Thought you might wish to touch my garment. To bring you luck."

"Judging by what you did for Hattie, I think I ought to," Garner replied, tapping Huey's blue lapel three times.

Huey roared, turned on his heels and was almost out of sight before Mariah could gather her wits enough to trot along, trailing this divinity.

No sooner had they settled back in the senator's office, than Huey was handed a telegraph from Mrs. Theodore G. Bilbo, twice first lady of Mississippi, who had Congressional aspirations she knew could be fulfilled if — but only if — the Kingfish brought his sound trucks and oratory to her state. Huey handed it to Mariah, demanding advice on how he should respond.

Mariah knew she wasn't qualified to advise. Yet, here was this senator, red hot from having achieved the equivalent of a "Hail Mary" pass, asking for her judgment. Suddenly, on the cusp of taking him seriously, she realized it was a game. He played at advice-seeking. Never would he accept it unless it matched his own. And why should he, given the immense success he had achieved from following his own well-honed instincts. I'll play, she thought.

"This should be your reply: 'I have no intention of going into Mississippi.' And here's why, senator: Being knight errant to one lady politician is enough for this political season. More and I'll start to get a reputation."

Surprise broke out on Huey's face. "Why, that's good. Very good. And precisely what I'll do. Mariah, are you sure you have to return to Boston? I can use you right here. No. I need you. Heaven can wait. Ditto the seminary."

4

BEFORE HE LEARNED HER NAME, Adam felt he knew her. Often, on his way to lunch, he would see her bounding through the Yard. On first sighting, all one noticed was the hair, a great tangle, strands going this way and that, each fighting for a place in the sun. To a Kansas boy, her hair had the complexity of hay, the luster of straw, the shameless vibrancy of a long abandoned garden grown wild with weeds. It seemed to glow from within. As she came closer, there were other things. She had a tall, athletic figure with the telltale curves of her gender, a sharply chiseled face, intense hazel-green eyes set closer than usual, and flawless pale white skin kept out of the sun. Her mouth was large, broader across than the distance between her eyes, a feature that highlighted them both. In contrast to the riot of hair, her face was carefully, and to Adam, excessively made up with eye kohl, rouge and a heavy layer of bright red lipstick. Her clothes were like costume jewelry, worn simply as foils to direct one's attention to what they embellished. It took him time to discover how little they mattered to her. It took even longer to discover that, like her make-up, the hair was a product of design.

At the urging of Father, Adam had applied to and been accepted at the law schools of Columbia and Harvard. He picked Harvard.

Dan believed in legal training, even for running a farm, which he expected Adam to undertake in time. Dan likened law school to a bramble bush, not an original idea, for it had long been the analogy of choice for professors, who took it from an old rhyme Dan learned as a child and brought up in making the case with Adam.

> There was a man in our town
> And he was wondrous wise:
> He jumped into a bramble bush
> And scratched out both his eyes —
> And when he saw that he was blind,
> With all his might and main
> He jumped into another one
> And scratched them in again.

"I get it, Father." Then, laughing as he spoke, Adam said: "But the time and expense of losing one's sight and then regaining it seems a touch irrational, if one has both wisdom and sight before jumping in. But I'll do it. For my own reasons. And, before I do, we should be straight on one point. I don't intend to take over Wyandot."

"Well, we'll see about that." Dan grew red of face. Catching himself, he quickly added: "But let's not cross that bridge till you graduate."

———◆———

Adam began his studies in September, 1932. It was his custom, after the last morning class, to cut through the Yard, past Holworthy, to get to Massachusetts Avenue a bit East of Harvard Square and thence to Hazen's, his favorite lunch spot, where he would try for a corner table. He liked to banter with Hazel, a waitress fresh as salt air, who, it was said, at least once a day was forced to declare herself no relation to the proprietor.

"So, Adam, what'll it be today? Show some imagination."

"Hazel, I do. I do. I'll have today's special soup and sandwich. Since it's different every day, don't ya see, I'm showing imagination? And, what's more, courage, to allow your kitchen friends to decide for me. But, here's an idea. Instead of water, bring me a glass of buttermilk."

"Now you've gone too far. Stop teasing. I've never served buttermilk — to anyone. You're bughouse."

"Look, Hazel. It's right there on the menu. You just haven't waited on someone with enough imagination."

It was on that day, the day Hazel served buttermilk for the first time, that Mariah Massie entered what had become a crowded café with no tables free. Adam watched her, on the threshold, as she carefully checked out the partially occupied tables, then moved decisively in Adam's direction, made eye contact and said, in the inimitable accent of a Virginian to the plantation born, "Sir, would you mind company?"

"Of course not. Have a seat. I'm Adam. Adam Murdock." She kept him in a gaze that demanded more. "From Kansas. Manhattan, Kansas, home of KSU." Her expression shifted slightly as if to ask "What now?"

"Law school. First year." Hazel arrived, interrupting.

"What'll it be young lady? You can have what your friend here is having, what he's always having, or you can get creative."

"Thank you. I'll have a BLT on white toast, that soup and a coke with ice. Separate checks, please."

"I'm at Newton Theological Seminary. Second year. From Richmond, Virginia, as you might guess. Undergrad at Sweet Briar. What's KSU?"

———◆———

That Winter, Mariah and Adam began dating. Of course, if "dating" meant having lunch together at Hazen's, haphazardly, without formal arrangement, by each reckoning the odds of finding the other there around noon, then they had been dating for a couple of months. But, now, Adam was ringing Mariah up, when a phone was available, or dropping by her dormitory when not, to suggest a dinner, concert, play or whatnot. Neither one imagined having fallen in love, but they found much to discuss: Mariah with her growing passion for wealth redistribution, Adam with his growing awareness of how little wealth there was left in the country to be shared. Mariah was probing in asking about Adam's years in Manhattan. Unlike his brother, Adam was an easy valve to open. And so, too, was Mariah.

She was born in Virginia in 1908. She had grown up, as she put it with a touch of discomfort, "in Richmond society." Her Father had inherited over a thousand acres of prime tobacco fields and carried on a highly profitable family business that had been passed down from Massie to Massie for generations. Her mother claimed to be distantly related to Robert E. Lee. Her parents had never accepted Lincoln's interference with the rights of the people of that great Commonwealth. Their belief in social mobility had limits. Those born on second base could aspire to make the move to third or even home plate. For those just wanting a chance to get to first base, all bets were off.

Mariah lived in a large Georgian-revival house in the west end of town with ruddy bricks bearing the patina of age. A grand mix of tall azaleas and andromeda hugged the facade on either side of an impos-ing oak door, planted to trumpet the arrival of Spring in early March. Neatly groomed boxwood the height of a man lined either side of the gray pea gravel driveway for a distance of 40 yards. Beyond that, a riot of naturalized forget-me-nots blanketed the grass. And, because the ground sloped down from the long driveway's entrance to the house, it was often wet from underground seepage, which invited jack-in-the pulpits and hostas of immense size to spread out under the canopy of stately tulip poplars and oaks nicely spaced and well pruned to remove all branches below their crowns, a trompe l'oeil making the trees appear taller, thicker and altogether grander. The back of the house faced a sweeping greensward lined on either side with redbud and dogwood, extending down to the bank of the James River.

"Grand" was the family theme, and nothing was spared to achieve it with a grace designed to appear effortless.

In the Massie living room, three round tables of India mahogany with fluted edges were covered with family photos, each neatly framed in silver and precisely arranged by size. They were touched only by a daily dusting from live-in servants. The room had the look of a Potemkin village, and in truth, it was used only when the extended family gathered for christenings, marriages and funerals.

In the furnished front hall, just inside the imposing front door, were a table and two chairs. An up-to-date Bell telephone rested on the table. Beside it was a note pad with a silver sleeve for holding pencils and current copies of the membership books for the Garden Club, the Commonwealth Club and the Junior League, each a clearinghouse for status.

The Massies fitted into Richmond society as perfectly as the exquisitely crafted dovetail joints came together in the family's finest Hepplewhite highboy. With little thought and without the slightest objection, Mariah obliged her parents in their wish to have her presented at the Richmond German, accompanied by her Father in the long line of best-of-class debutantes invited to enter society through that elite venue. Like those ahead and behind her, she did the Figure, a graceful bow to the reviewing panel of Richmond's social lions of the day, and then turned back to her Father to waltz around the ballroom. Before this salute to one's coming of age, Mariah had studied piano with an ancient Hungarian whose command of English made oral instruction a challenge. She had taken dancing lessons with white-gloved boys pimply of face and far shorter than she. She had taken riding lessons at the Deep Run Hunt Club. And she had been given a vibrant bay gelding on which to practice her skills. Only much later did it occur to Mariah that little in these early years of growing up was left to chance, that each step of the way ineluctably followed the undisturbed pattern established long ago by earlier generations of Richmond society.

The nonchalance of Mariah's circle of friends mimicked that of the adults. It was a studied casualness, as if caring intensely was bad form. The Italian word: *sprezzatura*. While implying an acceptance of different ways of doing things and an openness to change, in fact, the circle in which Mariah and her parents moved was protected from disturbance by hardened custom.

So predictable were the patterns of her youth that one could imagine her a tiny fish in an exclusive school, synchronously swimming this way and that in response to the immutable signals of Richmond society.

She had a good mind. Until her senior year at St. Catherine's School, she used it for devising plots to ensnare boys from nearby St. Christopher's. With the backing of her parents, she rejected the invitation of Mr. Floyd, the teacher who knew her best and who happened to be the director of Upper School, to apply to college. Parroting her Father with such precision as to capture not only his words, but the strident tempo of his delivery, she explained that her mother hadn't gone to college, that woman's place was by husband's side, that the skills called for to serve this mission weren't taught in college and could only be perfected through practice and gritty common sense, something beyond the reach of what college could aspire to teach.

Left unsaid, because it was plain enough for others to see, was Mariah's evolving beauty. Her skin was soft, white and unblemished, her hair sandy, long, thick, yet fine, without a curl. Her tall figure was just what one of Classical bent might favor and her face was a lovely work in process. And, yet, she was unsatisfied, continuing to use make-up and tuberose perfume to excess.

Mr. Floyd did not push back against the parroting of her parents' expectations for her. But neither did he ignore her outburst. How could he, given his seldom-used role as what passed for a college adviser in this all-girls private high school. Mariah's opinions, if accurate, would eviscerate his mission. Beyond that, he saw in Mariah not just the physical endowments her Father liked to emphasize but something far more difficult to discern, the potential for intellectual growth. He saw it as an investment opportunity, risky but offering him the chance for a big return.

Already that Fall, at his suggestion, she had read and enjoyed Ulysses S. Grant's autobiography. Given the author and its subject matter, this voluntary undertaking was incomprehensible to her parents and not a little offensive. Mariah was pleased by their discomfort, and made it worse by mentioning that the book dealt almost exclusively with Grant's military triumphs over the Confederate Army.

When a student responded in this way, it was Mr. Floyd's custom to spend an hour or more over tea discussing what the student had read, hoping for vicarious reward through the student's enthusiasm. Mariah had been quick to grasp Grant's extraordinary ability in the field to issue precise, unambiguous orders to his officers. "They couldn't be misunderstood," she kept saying. "How did he do it?" And, then, she asked why he stopped his story with Appomattox, seeming to ignore his two terms as President. Mr. Floyd was pretty sure there was material here that, with luck, might be lifted out of the Richmond mold and set free.

And, so, a day or two later, he went to the library and dug out Willa Cather's high school oration, delivered in 1890. He also took out the most autobiographical of her novels, *The Song of the Lark*, written in 1915. Handing them to Mariah, he suggested that she might find them of interest.

"What are they about?" she asked, throwing him a suspicious smile.

"They're about migrations, physical and mental. Willa Cather graduated from Red Cloud High School in Nebraska, close by the Kansas border at the northern-most reaches of the High Plains. She was the only girl in a class of three. Her oration celebrates the pursuit of truth through experimentation, especially by novices. It marks the move away from superstition with Francis Bacon's *Novum Organum*, which you will recall studying. Towards the scientific method."

"And the novel?"

"Oh, the story of a Colorado girl who leaves a small town to go to a big city to become an opera singer. It's one of my favorites."

"Okey-dokey," she said, taking the books and turning to go.

"One other thing, Mariah," Mr. Floyd said. "Before we get together to discuss Willa Cather, dig out from the library a description of the original cover of Bacon's book. It's there for sure. I'd like you to explain it to me, in the context of Willa Cather's writings. For extra credit, of course."

"Mr. Floyd. You mustn't tell my classmates. They'd say I was sucking around. And my parents too." She swung her tall frame around again and was gone.

Right after Christmas, during vacation, Mariah sent word to Mr. Floyd that she was ready. On a dull cold afternoon, just before the New Year, they huddled together in the only café in town that boasted a large fireplace. Couches were drawn around in a semi-circle and on one of them Mariah and Mr. Floyd sat before a crackling fire, taking tea. They discussed the oration and novel in turn. Finally, oozing with youthful determination, she turned to face him.

"At first, I didn't think you had expected me to discover some big message in these writings. Even after finishing them, I wasn't sure. But, then, I found the cover to *Novum Organum*, and your project became clear."

"Tell me about it," he said, his face inscrutable.

"The cover shows a galleon passing between the famous pillars of Hercules, that stand on either side of the Strait of Gibraltar. The start of an exploration. The ship's passing from what's known into the Atlantic. Below this scene is some Latin, taken from the Book of Daniel. Its message: 'Many will travel and knowledge will be increased.' So, for the Mediterranean, substitute Richmond, for the Atlantic, college and for the galleon, me. It's of a piece with the message in *Song of the Lark*. As Isaiah said: 'Awake and Sing, all ye who dwell in the dust.' Do I pass?" She reached for his hand and squeezed it hard.

Mr. Floyd was surprised. And delighted. He said, "With colors flying, like the galleon."

"And so," she declared, "it came to pass that she went to college, that is she would go to college, if there were a college that would have her." Now she was laughing in his face, thrilled to see he had emerged from his customary mask of dull attentiveness to show delight in his triumph. She hid anxiety over the possibility, which she reckoned more likely than not, that her conversion came too late to get into college. At least the one she wanted to attend, Sweet Briar, a venerable women's institution situated in a rural setting of great beauty about 100 miles or so due west of Richmond.

"Leave that to me," he said, all chipper and cheerful. "I'll be in touch with some folks in admissions. No need to worry, yet. You have enough to do in convincing your parents. They hold the purse strings. My guess is it won't be easy."

"Funny how things turn out. Looking back, I'm not sure I ever fully accepted my parents' views on college. I told them I did, and my friends too, but did I tell myself and believe it? I'm not sure. And, I never accounted for the challenge you set nor the fun I would have in meeting it."

———◆———

Adam found Mariah's intellectual equipment remarkable. So much so that he couldn't connect this side of her to the other, that being what Dr. Bernstein had, with such thoroughness, prepared him to understand and enjoy. Despite her own intellectual accomplishments, the good doctor had left unstated the idea that womankind possessed brains capable of intellectual pursuits or political passions and (Adam imagined Rachel would add) should be encouraged to use them. Of course, she never denied the possibility, but her focus was always away from the intellectual and towards the wonder of female sexuality. She was, perhaps inadvertently, encouraging Adam and Benno to think and imagine nothing else. And Dan was not one to notice a woman's capacity for pursuits beyond the home. Indeed, he had often expressed to the twins his astonishment at Rachel's intellect, hinting darkly that it was strange, even occult. "Perhaps it should be pickled for display in a museum," he told them, laughing with pleasure at his cleverness. "Don't get me wrong, boys. I like her. A good neighbor. And good to you."

In the classrooms of both law and theology, the great struggle of principle between those who insisted on treating the destitute through private charity — the dole, as it was known — and those who believed it was the Federal Government's role to provide a safety net was being taught, not with the wisdom that comes from decades of studying the past, but experientially, day by day, as conditions around the country created an immediate and ever-changing laboratory. Adam's instincts favored Government intervention; Mariah's fixation on the human spirit led her to embrace what she called the responsibility of individual men and women to their neighbors. A hard intellectual divide of this magnitude could not easily be bridged, except perhaps through the softer realms of the flesh, which for a time lay outside Adam's experience.

Over dinner in February, 1933, Adam and Mariah launched into ferocious debate. He had studied the band of Arkansas farmers, 500 strong, who, desperate with hunger following another Summer's drought, in January 1931, invaded the little town of England, bearing shotguns and supported by clamorous wives, all with the intention of encouraging storekeepers to provide food. "Let me tell you their story," Adam said. "It illustrates the principle that divides us."

"More than one principle divides us, Adam. But, if you insist."

"They had first given the Red Cross a chance to feed them, but it lacked the means. Without actual violence, but an overhanging threat, the storekeepers doled out food. Hoover's Secretary of Agriculture, calling the drought the worst in history, sought relief money to feed farm animals. Congress sought to enlarge the bill to cover humans as well. The President denounced Congress, asserting that 'prosperity cannot be restored by raids on the public treasury.' The House saw food for people as a dole. The Senate insisted on putting farmers and their families on an equal footing with their mules. Finally, a so-called 'compromise' was reached, increasing appropriation for feed and seed but still no food. Now, surely, as a seminary student, you can see what a crime this is!"

Adam found it next to impossible to put Mariah on the defensive. Looking at her now, a cocky shit-eating smile beaming back at him, he knew he had failed.

"You think, because I'm at seminary, my head and heart are soft. Bad bet. As I see it, the problem is one of crossing a line, of letting go on a slippery slope," Mariah replied. "Once the Federal Government comes to the aid of families in distress, there will be no turning back. And worse, no stopping an expansion of the idea of 'distress.' Self-sufficiency, every tub on its own bottom, that's the American way, the Christian way. The question is whether the American people will maintain the spirit of charity and mutual self-help that Christ taught his followers. To deny us the chance to prove ourselves is to sap our will."

"Wasn't it Hoover, in an earlier life, who presided over feeding the victims of famine abroad? No one called that a dole. Look," he said, voice rising in frustration, "you can't rehabilitate a farm with a dead farmer."

Soft at the start, her voice became a whisper. Adam leaned forward.

"If the Federal Government feeds that farmer, his body may survive but his spirit will die. The spiritual life of the nation is at stake."

"Mariah, you won't appreciate the strength of the insult I am about to deliver," Adam said, all earnest. Opening her mouth wide, she inhaled, eyes bullfrog round and bulging, projecting the phony face of fear. "Oh, it's a pisscutter, all right."

"Let me compose myself," she implored with a friendly smirk.

Adam felt the wind drop from his sails. Momentum carried him forward. "At this moment, you remind me of Father, but let's save the 'why' for a separate evening."

Mariah nodded, feigning relief.

Their plates were removed, dessert offered and declined, coffee served.

His sails filling again, Adam turned to the debater's final refuge.

"Allow me one question. How can you square your love of Huey Long's idea for wealth redistribution with your abhorrence of the dole? It doesn't add up."

"I've been waiting for that curve ball. Bush league stuff, Adam. Consistency, as you must have picked up in Langdell, is the hobgoblin of petty minds, especially those training for the law. But, as a matter of fact, there's no inconsistency here. Wealth redistribution is ok because it's simply the result, the side-effect, of capping wealth at some reasonable level. The excess has to go somewhere, so why not to all the people in equal shares. This is very different from having Government bailout those who have fallen. They must be encouraged, and that will be the certain effect of redistribution, not discouraged by inducing dependence on the dole."

"Ok, I hear you. If a policy of soaking the rich results in giving their wealth to the poor, that's fine and dandy. But a policy designed to help the destitute, whether brought low by their own failing, a failed national policy or an Act of God, that's a corrupting misuse of Government power."

"Yes, yes. That's it exactly, like hiring a drunk to tend bar."

They were glaring across the table. Adam questioned being in the same room with this woman. Because he thought her reasoning faulty and the conclusions it led to odious, he wondered how he could be attracted to her. But only for a moment. Mariah leaned forward, taking Adam's hands in hers, and squeezed twice. "Next time, let's first try something we can both agree on, leaving the debates till afterwards."

———◆———

Adam and Mariah were together much of the Winter and Spring of 1933. Their left brains were constantly locked in combat, like two wrestlers condemned to engage with one another on sight and fated to continue without verdict. Their right brains followed mellow pathways of sensual exploration and enlarging discovery. Adam thought the gap between these braidings too wide to bridge. It discouraged him, because he knew he would be the only one caring to try. Mariah, though aware of the missing bridge, was unconcerned. For her, the relationship was ripening just the way she had planned. For she was a planner. Adam, it seemed, was intended to be a keeper.

Adam had difficulty taking the measure of this woman. His awareness of her began in what, digging deep into his feelings, he called fascination. Dr. Bernstein had taught the twins to be skeptical of "love," a word she claimed could be used for the most amazing variety of relationships, even the trickery that enables one to transform narcissistic self-regard into love for another. If asked, Adam would admit to being downright scared of "love," and even more afraid of "falling in love." He dwelled not a bit on the glories of these conditions but on the tragic consequences that so often follow in literature, as Shakespeare and many others taught. As their intimacies grew, Adam would admit to romance, a feeling of passion, even sexual infatuation, but never to "love," which, following Dr. Bernstein's lead, he defined as a condition of submission to one's emotions so powerful as to be, like a drought-driven wild fire, all consuming. He would not go there.

At the prosaic level, there was the simple matter of expressing passion without creating life. No Puritan ever feared the Devil as much as Adam feared fathering a child out of wedlock. This concern became palpable as the natural path of their growing intimacies opened up the possibility. It was here, as elsewhere in their expanding universe of pleasures, that Mariah led. She could count days, and did so with care. When, at times of exposure, they were pleasuring one another instead of fighting, she would tell him to use her belly. Her command of the mechanics captured him, dissipating fear.

Although Adam could remember even the details of Dr. Bernstein's kitchen talk, it was all in the realm of theory and dream-life, for he had experienced little through his college years. Whether from practice, mother wit, or other sources, Mariah seemed to know his body as well as hers, and was prepared, with exuberant patience, to lead Adam step by step, from one night to the next, much as Beatrice led Dante through Paradise to God. So profound was the journey at times that Adam's agnosticism could have been erased by any claimant to God's existence clever enough to offer as proof the sort of feelings Mariah could generate in him. He could see how Catholic hierarchy could view priestly intercourse as the undoing of discipline.

Adam thought her irrepressibly playful. When they sat side by side in a restaurant, one of her hands, the one closest to him, would disappear, its goal to make him cry "uncle" or something more embarrassing. Or, when seated opposite one another, she would challenge him to remove a shoe and sock and pleasure her with his toe. When going out, she never wore panties.

When their pleasures began to fade from repetition, she would pour old wine into new bottles by inventing games. She was matador to Adam's bull. She introduced him to Hieronymus Bosch's astonishing masterpiece, *The Garden of Earthly Delights*, a painting she had studied in the Prado. It was her favorite. She had a good facsimile that they pored over together. At her direction, they would take turns trying to word-paint what Bosch might have been thinking as he painted images so arresting and fantastic. It was a game, of course, the goal of which, as both of them knew, could never be fully realized, given Bosch's world of the unthinkable. The game's other purpose, however, never failed. In Mariah's hands, an unstoppable force.

Her period never interfered. She would ask Adam to invent other ways of satisfying her, speaking softly to him about what felt good, what better, what best. Afterwards, she would use her mouth to bring him to the same point of no return, capturing what he had to offer, then allowing it gently to flow out of her mouth and down his still engorged sex.

From the outset, Adam wondered how Mariah had learned all these things. One night, he asked her.

"What a question. Thought you'd never ask. After all, since I know I seem far more experienced than you, you had to be curious. Not from my parents, that's for sure. From them I heard a lot of bad ideas. No, I'll tell you. But are you jealous? Don't think I've done with others the things I'm doing with you. Through school and college, I played around, had many beaus, grew impatient pretty easily, always looking over the guy's shoulder for the next one. That's God's truth. Intercourse? Hardly ever."

"Did you keep count?"

"Yes, as a matter of fact, and you could get them onto one hand."

"Guess that makes you a quick study. Handful not enough for much trial and error."

"There were books. More important, there was vicarious experience. My girlfriends and I shared everything. Big multiplier. But I got off to a bad start. On the living room couch, without much of an idea, and with a guy who was even more clueless than I. Kept on most of our clothes. He had no understanding that my motor would take a lot more time than his to warm up. He came in seconds. Right after that, my mother announces herself by turning on the lights. It was a one-two punch that humiliated me in more ways than two. My mother thought we were just kissing. But in her mind that was a no-no for someone my age in the dark on a couch in her home."

"Didn't she see him pulling up his pants?"

"In the excitement of her gotcha, she must have missed exactly what had been going on. Or was in denial. Or pretending. Who knows."

———————◆———————

When Franklin D. Roosevelt was Governor of New York, in a special message to the Legislature, he argued successfully for a temporary relief program for the unemployed. Adam had come across the message in a course and, believing Mariah approved of FDR, wanted to tell her about it.

In truth, Mariah's approval of FDR was thinly felt. There was none of the enthusiasm she lavished on the Kingfish, who, she believed, had been responsible for getting FDR the nomination, and, given Hoover's hopelessness, the White House. Her acceptance of FDR probably derived from a need to be different from her parents, who hated the man. Nothing more positive than that.

Adam had in hand an excerpt from the address when they gathered in Hazen's over their customary order of tuna salad sandwiches on rye with lettuce, mayo and a slice of Swiss cheese, a couple of dill pickle quarters, chips and cold buttermilk.

"When FDR was Governor of New York, he got the legislature to fund a relief office for seven months, at $20 million. His argument was simple:

"Modern society owes the definite obligation to prevent the starvation or dire want of any of its fellow men and women who try to maintain themselves but cannot. To these unfortunate citizens aid must be extended by Government — not as a matter of charity but as a matter of social duty."

Mariah was unimpressed. "If I can get a check from the Government, why would I look for work? I know, perhaps because work will pay more. But at the margins, many recipients of the 'dole,' and that's its true moniker, will not search for work as hard as they would without the check."

"Just what I was expecting. Now, would it change your view to learn that Roosevelt nixed the use of money. Jobs were to be found for these people, and jobs wanting, food, fuel, clothes and shelter. Not money."

"Oh, get off it. That's a verbal trick. Excellent political strategy but only those too stupid or lazy to think could fall for it. How different is it from receiving a check to spend on those things?"

"You're tough, Mariah. But listen. Where was the Governor going to come up with the $20 million? He proposed to get it by increasing the already graduated state income tax by 50%. This was a perfect way to implement your policy of wealth redistribution. So, I ask you, what's wrong with that story?"

Mariah set her jaw. "Interesting, but I don't buy your attempt at equivalence to the kind of serious redistribution Huey's talking about. I'm sure you know the AFL has repeatedly rejected unemployment insurance — a fancy name for the dole, even though, you can bet your last coconut, they would favor redistribution. In my book the dole is comparable to slavery, in the sense that those employing slaves guaranteed shelter, food and work. The reciprocal of the dole is the power of Government to compel a man to take a job, whether he wants one or not. It subverts freedom."

"That's creative of you, Mariah. I admit it, especially since you're studying the realms of God and I'm studying the realms of law and public policy. But let me ask you this: Hoover gave "the dole" to the railroads and other lords of industry, to the international bankers, to the building and loan associations, even to foreign countries in distress. To these interests he gave billions, but to starving Americans — men, women and children — not a red cent. Is that your position? For if it is, you're a hothouse flower, out of touch with reality. And the reach of Newton."

Mariah flinched, color pulsing across her face, before regaining the control she demanded of herself.

They had finished their sandwiches and most of the buttermilk, signs of which clung to their upper lips. Hazel arrived to pick up the plates and ask about dessert or coffee. From her expression, Adam saw that she might be taking their disagreement too seriously, like an alarmed grandparent watching her grandsons roughhouse.

"Don't worry about this verbal jousting, Hazel; it's as regular as heartbeats. We have friendlier ways to engage. Two coffees, no dessert."

"He's right, Hazel. I only punish him in public places."

"I'll deal with this after the coffee comes. It's a base argument, Adam, not worthy of a man from the heartland."

"Leave Kansas out of it," Adam said, looking stern at her remarkable face, which was beginning to lose its glow. She had a tough-fibered brain, a nearly insult-proof armor and a peacock-like vanity that was almost always on display, come what may. Adam knew there would be more.

"It's absurd to claim that temporary protection of our means of production is a dole. Finance was stuck. By freeing it, loans would flow, industry would start up again, and through jobs and wages, prosperity would spread across the land. Helping the finance sector has a great multiplier effect on the economy. Corporations aren't like human beings. This sort of help won't erode the corporate will to work, to employ, to strive in competition, to reach for a moonful of profit. Your comparison's bogus — bogus and insulting."

Adam's face turned the color of Mariah's lipstick. He could handle most forms of abuse but not contempt. He stammered before regaining enough balance to express his anger.

"You're overbearing and overwrought. You defend the rights of the rich and powerful, heedless of your passion for wealth equality. You can't have it both ways. You play the Good Samaritan until a destitute crosses your path. Then you turn heel and run."

It was a rage he'd seldom felt before. He sought to wound, and that scared him. Then, almost immediately, the heat in his head, like forged iron plunged into cold water, disappeared. Hiss, steam, bubbles, silence. He felt remorse.

"Hey, let's pay and get out of here. I forgot I'm supposed to be well-bred."

This time, Mariah didn't flinch. Taking his hand, she intoned softly: "You're right; let's go." Had Adam, searching for cash to pay the check, looked into her face instead of Hazel's, he might have detected the bare outline of a satisfied smile.

———◆———

"I came across an old story about what the center of your cosmos did to Senator Robinson last Spring. The writer called Huey a 'comic opera star.'" They were lying side by side in Adam's bed, half asleep after allowing pleasure to overtake them.

"Are you kidding? What a giant of grit and integrity. Imagine attacking the hand that tried to feed him, then tossing the proffered food back into the Senate leader's face. What a glorious moment. Oh, to have been there. At least, I was in Arkansas last Summer, when the senator humiliated Robinson again by getting Hattie Caraway re-elected, against all the odds."

"I think he had planned the whole thing. That bright pink handkerchief the *Times* said he pulled out, waving it around, mopping his face. It was all an act. By a juvenile demagogue. In Manhattan we'd call the likes of Long a spoiled brat. Robinson blocked his proposal to tax away amounts people earn over one million or inherit over five million. Called it confiscation of private property, a doctrine he said, and I agree, violates party principles. I know it sounds better to say 'redistribution of wealth.' Tweedle dee, tweedle dum."

Mariah said, "You're the lawyer. So let me ask you: Is Huey's proposal unconstitutional?"

"I get Con-Law next year," Adam said, sitting up with arms extended to almost reach his toes. "But it sounds bad. Unlawful taking of private property. Due process, yes, but compensation, no. If Robinson asked me, I'd take the case."

Mariah sat up, her knee rubbing against his, her arms extended to reach her toes. "Congress has the power to tax. We both know that. We applaud the graduated income and estate taxes, which take more away from those who have more to give. No one questions constitutionality there. Huey's idea is just to take more from the rich than these taxes do. What's wrong with that?" Mariah sounded chipper.

Adam was again surprised at her grasp of subjects he was supposed to be mastering. Did she spend all her time studying political science and law? Was she some sort of polymath? Perhaps Newton didn't teach the spiritual realms any more than Yale taught the law. But damn, she was smart.

"That's good, Mariah. Very good, as far as it goes. But, look, we both know, too, that no power is unlimited…."

Mariah cut him off. "Tell that to the Pope, my friend."

"I forgot where you study. Should have said 'no earthly power.' But since you interrupted, allow me a small detour. I'm sure you know the Lord Acton quote: 'Power tends to corrupt, and absolute power corrupts absolutely.' Do you know who he had in mind?"

"No, but I could guess. Go on, I see you're eager to tell me." She smiled, her mouth widening, capacious, distracting.

He nodded, returning the smile. "Pope Pius IX. Acton tried to block the Church from adopting papal infallibility. Around 1870. I think he viewed Kings the same way. 'Great men are almost always bad men,' he said. Which reminds me of Huey Long.

"Congress can tax, yes it can, but only for the general welfare. If taxes are levied to build railroads across the country, it obviously serves the general welfare. But taxing the rich to give directly to the poor, that's an entirely different salad. How does it serve the general welfare to make some worse off in order to make others better off? Long's idea is too raw, too blatant, too simple a money grab to pass muster. But ask me in a couple of years; I'll have better reasons to shoot him down."

Mariah threw up her hands. "You're swell. Fine and dandy. But wild horses won't change you. Where's the passion? I don't need a dry lecture over an iced tea when all the ice is gone. You and I want the same things. In giving those in need a helping hand. In Isaiah: 'Awake and Sing, Ye who dwell in the dust.' And, yes, I believe in that prophet from Louisiana, a Moses for whom the Democratic Party has been waiting, the one to lead us into the promised land. Juicy passion for something, for anything, is better than all the squeezed out, desiccated, barren argument that marches under the heading of rational thought. It's not the stuff taught at Harvard that's the problem, it's the stiff and sterile way it's taught. That's not the real world, my friend. There's more passion in one class at Newton than in all of them at your tabernacle. I will ask the good senator from Louisiana to defend the constitutionality of his proposal. But your bed's lost its charm. I've had enough. From the looks of it, so have you. Tell me just one thing, where did you learn that stuff about Lord Acton?"

He bested her in argument yet felt defeated. Mariah could overcome even the enemy who had just laid her out flat. And she never hesitated to do so. What a dangerous woman to allow into your head. To Adam she was a contradiction: spontaneous and calculating at the same time.

"Father is an Acton admirer. Knows his story inside and out. Loved his sayings and adopted them as his own. All that Father loves, all his enthusiasms, he tries to infect us with."

"In some areas, I'd say he succeeded."

"Not politics."

———◆———

Winter turned toward Spring. Newton's grip on Mariah, never firm, began to slacken even more with the lengthening of days. If the promise of a weekday was glorious, she would skip class to visit the Arnold Arboretum, arguing to anyone who cared that she could not serve the human spirit of others until she had first nourished her own.

For Adam, Harvard's grip on his life tightened as the time for taking all-important final exams approached. They were the only measuring rod used in the academic year. On the outcome of these trials alone turned one's class ranking and the doors of opportunity.

"For goodness sakes, Adam, disenthrall yourself. A few hours away from Langdell won't matter."

At first, Adam thought Mariah just uninformed. Patiently, he explained the competitive aspect, how everything turned not on demonstrating some objective level of competence, as in the state bar exam, but on coming out ahead of the others.

To no avail. She persisted, even to the point of belittling him.

He tried a touch of sharp-edged humor.

"Hey, Mariah, you remind me of Carmen, singing the *Seguidilla* to Don Jose."

"You know I can't hit a note."

"That's my point. Unlike the Spaniard, I won't yield."

Distilling her machinations into unvarnished selfishness, his resolve grew, and with it his anger.

"I don't get it Mariah. You say you love me. You claim to want me to succeed at law. And yet you keep trying to shame me into playing your game rather than my own. When you know my success depends on putting in study time. Why?"

"All work and no play makes Adam a dullard. Take a break. A ramble in the arboretum will do you good."

"That's baloney and you know it. You're trying to control my life. It's what makes you happy. At bottom, you're a puppeteer."

Adam expected anger from her, realizing he had shot an obnoxious claim at her. She just absorbed it, showing no emotion, except a smile as she took his hands in hers before bidding him off to Langdell.

———◆———

Mariah seemed more under the senator's spell than ever. Adam claimed she was the besotted follower of a dangerous fascist in disguise, an uncanny sorcerer with power to bewitch.

She would admit only to being a sober-minded disciple of a man she claimed to be the most principled and powerful defender of the poor and needy, a modern-day Good Samaritan.

On Brattle Street, early one balmy afternoon in May, as they walked toward Langdell, where Mariah was expected to leave him, Adam exploded.

"He's a danger to the Democrats, Mariah. I'm surprised that you don't see that."

"He may win like a demagogue, but he delivers like a statesman. Don't go shaking your head, Adam. It's a fact. As Governor, he led the state's sad, enslaved people out of bondage. Deposed feudal lords: the kings of cotton, lumber, rice, oil, sugar. Imposed severance taxes, using the collections to cut gas, electric and telephone rates, give free school-books to children, open night schools to teach adults to read and write, pave the roads and provide free school buses. It's history, Adam, accomplished without a smidgeon of witchcraft. And he returned Hattie to the Senate. And now, it's time we went to see the Rhodo Show at the Arnold."

"I grant you he did a lot for Louisiana. But along the way, he created a dictatorship Stalin might envy. He controls all appointments. He commands a secret police force. My professors say he dictates the rulings of the state's Supreme Court. Oh, and by the way, did you let his hands get freewheeling around you?"

Mariah looked daggers, her face starting to glow red. Seconds passed. Then, speaking at half-speed, she said: "Not on your tintype, wise-guy. And don't ever suggest that again."

Adam was embarrassed, knowing he had gone too far. Mariah was furious. Her code of behavior with men was clear and firm. It was a source of pride that she had never allowed herself in the physical realm to submit to anything she didn't consciously want to happen. Adam should understand that by now, she thought.

In silence, they walked along. Gradually, a smile crept back to her face. Vivacious again, she said: "Now, look: you're talking nonsense. There can be no dictatorship here. And, for argument's sake, if Huey Long were a dictator, he could only be called the most benevolent one who ever lived. Consider this: By abolishing poll taxes, he enabled 300,000 to vote for the first time in their lives. By removing small homes and farms from the tax rolls, he freed 95% of Negroes from taxes. Hardly the sort of stuff a Roman Emperor would do. And, don't forget that your man Roosevelt wouldn't have gotten the nomination if my man Long hadn't threatened the Mississippi and Arkansas leaders after the fourth ballot failed. Or won if he hadn't sent his sound trucks to the Dakotas, Nebraska and Kansas to campaign. After what he did in Arkansas last Summer, Farley and the rest of the FDR crowd took note. They're thick as thieves now. Selfish, that's what you are, refusing to join me at Arnold."

Adam's frustration festered as her trick of using the pot to call the kettle black registered. As the intellectual bait switched to sensual wiles. And, then, as he turned over her two-sided assault in a mind distracted by study and striving to be reasonable, his anger subsided, changing to puzzlement.

"Look, my problem with the senator is simple: for him, the ends justify the means, however cruel. If you don't see that, you're naïve. Since I know you're not naïve, you must agree with this monster. That won't fly at Newton Theological Seminary, you know. And they'll find out."

Mariah took his hand. They continued walking.

"The stately ship of Christianity is filled to the gunwales with examples of ends justifying means. Autos-da-fé, racks and other hideous tortures, wars, all in the name of spreading the gospel of love. From the beginning, organized religions have gotten good people to do bad things. They even boast about it. I'm not defending the past. But, I believe in trade-offs, a balancing of one thing against another. No absolutes."

"No dice," he fairly shouted, his brain trying to deny the reality of her body close to his, using her hand as a signaling device by gently squeezing his. In dealing with Mariah at moments like this, how much better, Adam thought, to have finished law school.

"I'm calling time out. Enjoy the Arboretum, if that's where you're headed. I'm off to Langdell. Unlike religion, where everything is relative and one can make things up on the run, the law's got principles that don't come naturally. Like beer, one must work at acquiring the taste."

"Ok, ok. I will. And I won't let Huey come between us."

5

———◆———

From Emporia

Dear Dan,

Just back from covering Pat Harrison's hearings. Quite a show. I recall you asked for my report. Here it is.

FDR's overwhelming victory seemed to confirm that everyone in the country except, perhaps, Hoover, recognized the desperate straits the country had gotten itself into. It was almost as well known that FDR was a closed book. No one, even his closest confidants, knew what he was going to do.

During that murky void, in responding to the question "What is your philosophy?" the President-elect had replied "Philosophy? Philosophy? I am a Christian and a Democrat. That's all."

The shrewdest observers, and the ones who knew him best, thought Walt Whitman's famous lines about himself might apply: "Do I contradict myself? Very well then I contradict myself. (I am large, I contain multitudes.)"

Senator Harrison, as you know a very conservative Democrat, imagined that by giving the country's brightest businessmen a platform to offer their economic wisdom to a country in need, he could head off radical ideas and insinuate into the President-elect's head a package of business solutions to all that ailed the nation. It seemed a commendable idea — one Harrison, as chair of the Finance Committee, could actually carry out.

Dan, you just won't believe the results of Harrison's effort. It would be hard to imagine a better case for radicalism than what was the sum and substance of the businessmen's offerings. It was a parade of vapidity and empty slogans with an occasional honest admission of ignorance thrown in.

John W. Davis said he had nothing to offer, in fact or theory. General Atterbury of the Pennsylvania Railroad had no solution except to "hit the bottom."

Bernard Baruch, never one to duck, thought he had the solution. Insisting that the country's credit was almost used up and that Government could no longer borrow, he advanced this single unoriginal idea: "Balance budgets, stop spending money we haven't got. Sacrifice for frugality and revenue. Cut Government spending — cut it as rations are cut in a siege. Tax — tax everybody for everything."

Thinking, no doubt, not just that unemployment stood at 25%, but of the meaning of that statistic in terms of human pain and suffering, senators shook their heads, astonished.

Jackson Reynolds of the First National Bank of New York was asked if he had a solution. "I have not," he replied, "and I do not believe anybody else has."

Myron C. Taylor of United States Steel said "I have no remedy in mind." He supported the Baruch idea for retrenchment and budget balancing.

David F. Houston, who you will remember as President Wilson's Secretary of Agriculture and also of the Treasury, is now President of Mutual Life. His offering: "Avoid any unnecessary appropriations."

Edward D. Duffield of the Prudential? "The thing of primary importance is the balancing of the Federal Budget."

It was a parade of intellectual bankrupts. I imagined a new chapter to the Bankruptcy Code just to house them. Here was Paul Block of Block papers offering more Baruch medicine: "First in importance is the balancing of our Budget."

Nicholas Murray Butler, President of Columbia University, echoed his business chums: "Government economy and balanced budgets."

Bill Clayton of Clayton and Anderson: "Balance the Budget through a drastic reduction in the cost of Government."

Now, Dan, I don't want you to think there were none among the witnesses who were aware of things. John L. Lewis of the United Mine Workers spoke passionately, and as usual with him, just at the edge of uncontrolled anger, in favor of national planning. Then he scorched the room with this: "The balancing of the Budget will not in itself place a teaspoonful of milk in a hungry baby's stomach or remove the rags from its mother's back."

It was Lewis who limned most profoundly the plight of our people and the total disconnect between the single-minded corporate solution of Government retrenchment and any feasible prospect for that solution actually to help.

I can hear you, Dan, demanding to know my solution. Of course, I don't have one either, except to say that, now, in the fourth Winter of our depression, we have given free enterprise, rugged individualism, prayer and other non-Governmental approaches enough time to work, or at least to show some sign of working. You might recall I visited that commander-in-chief of all non-Governmental solutions the night before the election, as he was preparing his final broadcast. Hoover's eyes were red-rimmed and lusterless. As he spoke, his voice comes tired — how infinitely tired — and his words how hollow and how sad in disillusion. The atmosphere was funereal.

Hoover's way has run its course. The slack we cut him to try anything but a Governmental solution — is gone. I don't know what approach, or combination of approaches, will work to get this country back on its feet, but I do know we must use Government to find a way. What is Government for if not to solve societal problems that are beyond the means of private actors, even large, well-organized actors, to handle?

Take care of yourself. I agree we can't expect the Government to do that for you. And, when Spring calving permits, let me know where I'm off base.

By the way, I'm searching for an excuse to visit you later this Summer.

Bill

Sometime after Adam began his studies at Harvard, Dan copied Bill's letter and sent it to Adam, something he had never done before. And with it, an unprecedented request. "I'd like to know what you think of this."

Before Christmas, Adam replied.

Dear Father,

That parade of brain-dead captains of finance and industry was astounding. It dramatizes the importance to Democracy of the hearing process on Capitol Hill. Without Harrison's hearing, the public might have assumed, as Harrison did, that our business leaders had the answers. Far worse, FDR might have been seduced by their supporters, in the press and elsewhere, to appoint these types to Cabinet positions. Imagine the damage we could suffer were the President to bring into high office the very scoundrels who contributed to the country's demise.

And what a brilliant example that would be of unintended consequences!

I was delighted to learn that in January, FDR had assured a Hearst emissary that his would be a "radical" cabinet. He promised there would be no one in it who knows the way to 23 Wall Street, no one linked in any way with the power trust or with the international bankers. He shows every sign of intending to do exactly what he promised Hearst, this despite immense pressure from the John W. Davises of this world.

Early signs suggest that FDR is, above all else, a pragmatist. A bold one at that. The professors here who seem mostly in the know claim he's preparing to use the forces of Government to try anything that makes a modicum of sense and has a plausible reason in support. I like that. I understand you don't. But the public is applauding FDR's promise to experiment.

Except for the fact that he's the country's President, not a corporate leader, and that it's the Government he's deploying, not a company like GE, I'm certain you would be applauding too. If he were a horse breeder, for example, trying a new mix of breeds that had never been mated before, I bet you'd be first to applaud. Well, FDR's been given power only over the Government, so that's all he's got to work with. Should be enough.

Give Cactus' forehead a loving scratch or two. Say a fond hello to the Bernsteins when you see them. And love to you. I'll be home in June.

Adam

Bill White's report had stirred up anew Dan's anger over the election, left for half a year and more to simmer down, a quiescent volcano. Adam's response was not what he was looking for. It enraged him, imagining the cause to be that law school's influence and the enabler himself. What was he thinking in promising to cover three-years' tuition as well as travel and living expenses? He knew, of course he knew. But seeking for his son the reputation that came with the degree, he took the risk, hoping steady inoculation over formative years would protect Adam from Harvard's attempts at intellectual taint that he knew would come. He thrust the letter in a drawer where he kept press clippings, correspondence and the like that made him too angry to address right away. Since FDR's election, the pile had grown.

The name "Pecora" began to ring in student ears. A darling of the professors, Ferdinand Pecora was the new counsel to the Senate Banking and Currency Committee, appointed after the election to lead the investigation of banks and banking practices. Adam and his classmates, almost to a man, swiftly became fans. Finding Pecora must surely have been Committee Chairman Duncan U. Fletcher's crowning achievement. Early on Pecora demonstrated an extraordinary combination of brilliance, indefatigability and single-minded focus in the relentless pursuit of financial wrong-doing. Through the Spring and Summer of 1933, the hearings he masterfully conducted became the daily talk of faculty and students at the Law School, as well as grist for the mill of newspapers throughout the land, providing a daily feed of revelations proving Wall Street's greed and mendacity.

To Adam, Pecora could do no wrong. He was little David, taking on the great House of Morgan, the Goliath bestriding that all-powerful street and its center at number 23; he was an Athenian hoplite facing the immense forces of the Persian Empire from a mountain pass above the plain of Marathon.

To Dan, he was Don Quixote, mistaking windmills for giants, flocks of sheep for armies, a demagogic inquisitor parading as righteous tribune of the people in the exercise of excessive power granted him by a Government rank with the foul breath of communistic Russia.

On June 1, 1933, the son of the great J.P. Morgan, founder of the firm bearing his name, was seated in the Senate Caucus Room waiting to testify. A flock of partners formed a tight circle around him, with lawyers in the next ring and assistants in the third. Suddenly, breaking through these defenses, a press agent for Ringling Brothers, Barnum & Bailey Circus popped a midget named Lya Graf into Morgan's lap, announcing as he did so that "the smallest lady in the world wants to meet the richest man in the world."

Adam couldn't resist writing his Father about the incident, which, due to the connivance of a Scripps-Howard reporter, was generously spread across the front pages of the world's leading newspapers. He was unaware of putting match to the fuse of explosive material collected in his Father's desk.

Here, Father, is the final humiliation for a world-class scoundrel. After all, hadn't Pecora nailed him on having paid no income tax in '30, '31 or '32; indeed, except for "peanuts," the same applied to the whole lot of those Morgan bankers? Hadn't this extraordinarily talented Sicilian, he with the great pompadour of gray-black hair, shown the fidgety and flushed Mr. Morgan to have bribed a bunch of friends by selling them stock in Alleghany Corporation at prices far below market?

By the way, I haven't heard from you about my new Sicilian hero. I like to imagine you following him in the press, including the Emporia Gazette, and slowly becoming convinced.

Father, even the *New York Times*, not by any stretch an anti-Wall Street publication, condemned Morgan's system of endearment among men in high places as a "gross impropriety" and ruminated on why the most powerful banking house in the world should stoop to practice "the small arts of petty traders." Pecora made vivid through witnesses the gilded past that led directly to the nation's downfall and its present plight. The mind-boggling bonuses, the taxes avoided, the rigged stock market pools, the bonds knowingly palmed off to uninformed investors — not only did he document it all, he brought it all to life in ways that even the most trusting investor could grasp.

And that's not all. The evidence he adduced was a springboard to demonstrate, beyond doubt, the shallow canard that Wall Street can best be managed by allowing its leaders to engage in self-regulation as a matter of enlightened self-interest. He proved the necessity of saddling private sector finance with the bridle and crop of strong Government regulation.

Among enterprises of great importance to the nation's welfare, neither the management of financial risk nor the modulation of human greed can, willy-nilly, be turned over to those whose careers are defined by profit.

Pecora makes me proud of our Government. I hope that you are coming to feel the same way. If not, I bet, with the new-honed skills you're buying me at the law school, I can persuade you.

I'll be seeing you at home in little more than a week. Looking forward.

Love,

Adam

He wondered whether he should mail it. Why was he writing? Anger? Embarrassment? He knew letters offered a safe, tempered avenue for expression that, face to face, would likely be explosive. But wasn't he baiting his Father, as the one footing the bill. Did he really expect anything could change a cowboy philosophy entrenched through decades of practice? In the end, deciding his motives were essentially unknowable, he sealed the envelope and mailed it.

Dan took less than a day to reply.

Adam,

Your letter leaves me profoundly depressed. You're not yourself. And I know the reason why. It is the insidious influence of those around you — those, to be precise, who make up the faculty at that law school. FDR came from there and so too many of his closest advisers. Your mind has been seized by these people — who are really our country's enemies — and ripped, branch and root, from your family. And, calumny upon calumny, I am paying them to do it.

Now, as for the midget caper, no fair-minded comment could call this a "humiliation." With every right to be furious, Mr. Morgan was reliably reported to have shown only surprise and to have reacted with good-humored courtesy. Under trying circumstances, he displayed a dignified, grown-up humanity toward the little lady. Indeed, I'd love to replay that scene with Lya Graf being deposited on Pecora's lap. As to who would display more human decency and kindness, my bet would be on the WASP over the WOP.

As for the tax issue, there wasn't the slightest suggestion of illegality. His taxable income was erased by real stock market losses incurred in the Crash, losses the law permitted him to set off against taxable income down the road. You or I would do the same. Duty bound in fact.

And, now, I come to the preferred list of prominent swells the great House set out to befriend. What a silly canard this disclosure turns out to be. All the *New York Times* could accuse them of was stooping to "practice the small arts of petty traders." Absurd! It's the petty traders who learn these commonplace business practices from the giants. Business is built on mutual back-scratching, just as farming, ranching and such self-described "lofty" professions as medicine and the law are. Those on Morgan's preferred list were Wall Street's best. Real achievers deserving of Morgan's generosity. (Just as I was deserving of the help my Kansas neighbors provided in saving my farm.) There's nothing to criticize in doing it, but plenty if it is not done well. Pecora adduced evidence showing that, in doling out preferences, the House of Morgan was a class act.

As for your hero, Pecora is showing himself to be an ambitious, crusading demagogue, as single-minded and abusive as Inspector Javert. He symbolizes the corrupting effect that too much Government power in the hands of one person can have. That's the main lesson, an unintended consequence obviously, of his work. What greatly concerns me, as you might have guessed, is the prospect of the Pecora example being repeated by FDR on a much larger canvas.

Our President sees himself as an alchemist, designing Governmental solutions to solve all manner of private sector problems that, if left alone, would take care of themselves, which is simply another way of trusting in the divine. Without regard to the harm he is bound to cause, he proposes to experiment, but unlike a doctor studying the human body by exploring a cadaver, where no harm can result, your hero will practice on a living society, with great harm looming as the most likely consequence of this odd form of paternalism. Before the Government deigns to interfere with private ordering by free men, it must surmount a very high hurdle of confidence that the interference will achieve far more good for society than harm. For me, this hurdle will prove too high in all but the rarest case.

I'll tell you what your FDR is: an irresponsible dilettante given to feckless experiment. (Don't publish, I want to slap this label on him in a speech — and make it stick.)

So there you have it my son.

With love,

Father

—————•—————

Adam and Mariah continued to engage with one another in what to Adam seemed like two water-tight compartments. They were either debating or making love. There seemed no place where the pedestrian aspects of two lives intertwined could exist. Their intellectual disputes were endless. They found little to consider common ground, despite the fact that their friends thought them both to be "liberals."

Long's filibuster against Senator Glass' financial reforms divided them. The only uniting event was FDR's election, although even that swiftly soured over differences in weighing the contributions of the good senator from Louisiana.

In the other compartment, they played sybaritic games: their minds a stage for imaginary art, gateway to arousal. Having started at a distinct disadvantage, Adam swiftly advanced to approach Mariah's ingenuity in devising new pathways to pleasure. Initially, he had worried about pregnancy, but the meticulous care Mariah gave to the calendar caused those concerns to ebb.

It was a beautiful June evening. For law students, the night before the Summer break began. Mariah would head south to Richmond the next day. Adam was going first to New York to see what he could do to help Benno, and from there to Wyandot, where he resolved to try again, even harder, to love his Father. By plan they separated after dinner, with Mariah going to a bar in Cambridge Square, where she sat down in a booth far to the back of the large dining area and ordered a scotch and soda. Twenty minutes later Adam arrived. He sat at the bar and ordered draft beer. Soon a waiter came to Adam, handing him a note. Opening it, he read "Bring your beer and come sit by me."

"Where did you get this?" Adam asked the waiter, who responded by turning to face the booth where Mariah was seated. Swiftly, Adam crossed the room to sit beside her. They looked at each other, saying nothing. Mariah put her hand on Adam's back, pulled up his shirt and began a playful massage of his back. Her other hand got busy too, undoing his belt, unbuttoning his pants and opening the zipper. She found him ready.

These moves left Mariah feeling randy.

"Hurry up, Adam," she insisted as they walked through light rain the few blocks to his room at the top of a large house on Bryant Street.

Mariah started to disrobe in the common vestibule, handing Adam one piece of clothing after another until, by the time they had passed through the door to his room, she had nothing left but bra, panties and stockings. Rolling into bed, they dispensed with foreplay. Mariah reminded Adam that it was her fertile time. "Be careful. And slow," she said.

Adam kept his passion under control. When finally she came, it ignited his passion, putting him within seconds of coming, irreversibly so, a place he had been many times before and successfully handled. But this time something seemed to be holding him in place. Trying to withdraw accelerated the natural bodily function. This had never happened before. He paused, confused. Seconds ticked away and with them his margin of safety.

He was upset. Too much so to speak of what had just happened. He recognized the feeling that swept over him. Like getting hit from behind without warning, as often happens on the football field, or suddenly falling through pond ice you thought safe. Mariah seemed oblivious. Didn't she realize, he wondered.

"You look like you forgot an exam. What's wrong, my love?"

How could she not know, he thought. "Mariah, my timing. Didn't you feel it?"

"Are you kidding? It was fantastic. Honey, it won't be a problem. If something develops, we have plenty of time to handle it. I'm not one bit worried and neither should you be."

Adam looked closely at Mariah's face for signs of stress. He found none. Her broad smile was more innocent and captivating than ever. She was radiating that sure sense of being in charge. Her calm was eerie; his reaction, fear.

"I wonder if we should pray?" he asked.

"You're cockeyed! When was the last time you prayed?"

"Ok, you're the divinity student. It was just a test. And you're right about me. Someone quipped that God's the sort of guy who, when you have to go to him, he has to take you in. I don't buy it. Can't stand the rainy day sort of prayer, the kind of guy who makes nice with God only when in distress." Adam knew he wasn't making sense. Anxiety ran very deep.

"You're feeling better. Everything's going to be peaches and cream. Now to sleep. Sweet dreams of home."

Mariah's reactions, Adam realized, were still completely unpredictable, despite their many months together. That must be part of why I'm so attracted to her, he thought, before slumber overtook him.

Two hours later, he awoke from an ugly dream. He was standing in a court room, before a judge whose face he couldn't make out because a brilliant beam of sunlight splashed across it, making it glow like a foil without definition. Behind the judge, Adam's name was being added to a list mounted there on the wall. Turning, he saw behind him a woman in the first row. She was speaking to him. "I tried so hard." He thought she was someone he knew. Nearby he saw Benno, who, without showing recognition, bowed his head upon catching sight of Adam's gaze.

The judge spoke in familiar voice. "Adam Murdock, you have blotted your copy book and disgraced your family. I find you unfit for the Bar and sentence you to a lifetime of manual labor to care for this woman and your offspring." On waking, he realized the judge's voice was one he had grown up with.

His mind raced from one plausible outcome of what he had done to another.

Filled with foreboding, Adam left Cambridge for an overnight stay with Benno. The next day he boarded the *American*, Pennsylvania Railroad's crack train to St. Louis, and there connected with MoPac's *Sunflower* to Kansas City and thence made his way to Manhattan. It was a long trip, one he hoped would offer him time to sort things out.

———◆———

Dan met his son at the station in the old Ford. It was Adam's first visit home. They had exchanged numerous letters, but the issues that divided them were seldom mentioned and never resolved. Some nights, when nothing else lay heavy on his mind, Adam would awaken about two in the morning and then, for a couple of hours, rehearse and rehearse again what had caused a widening crevasse between Father and son. It had been Adam's intention to air their fissure during his visit, but now, haunted not only by his dream, but the waking fear of conception, the irreversibility of it, and the vast uncertainties that would ensue from a birth, he debated whether to add this subject to the list.

It probably began with their birth, when Juanita died in labor. In Dan's mind, the twins were somehow responsible. An absurd thought, and one Dan never mentioned to a soul. But, for precisely that reason, the idea persisted without challenge, hidden in the dark recesses of his mind. As the years passed, Dan set impossibly ambitious expectations for the twins, making it certain they would always be found wanting. Making matters worse, Dan was short on praise, long on critique. He never failed to measure and report the shortfall. This process tended to squeeze out the joyful juices of growing up.

The wounded relationship between Father and sons began to be recognized and discussed by the twins in high school. Perhaps it was the absence of a mother over those years. Juanita knew how to soften her husband's personality, whose hard edges were known to inflict pain on those unfortunate enough to be stuck in his presence when the steely side was on display. His sons had no easy escape. The mold he held out for them hardened shortly after their birth. He was determined to cram them into it and force them to conform. That or be rejected. Juanita wouldn't have allowed him to be his own worst self. She would have kept the lariat pin in place, preventing him from running loose. Much in the boys' lives, and Dan's as well, would have been different had her formidable heart not stopped at childbirth. All of this was clear to their neighbor, Rachel Bernstein, who, as self-appointed surrogate mother and more, would in time have opportunity to explain it to the boys.

Late in his senior year, Benno concluded that he was an artist. Not suddenly, like a revelation, but in waves of conviction that swept over him month to month. That he had talent, particularly in the medium of sculpture, was obvious from the school's repeated selection of his works for display.

Dan followed his successes in sculpture with curious interest, even pride, that a son of his could, like his adored Athenians, display skills in more than one field. He approved of what he called amateurs of the fine arts. He knew and admired men of consequence who sought relaxation in painting, woodwork or gardening. When Benno presented his Father with a wood carving of Cactus, Dan's esteemed stallion, his smile grew wide as a Kansas sky, and with it pride in Benno's accomplishment.

But when, upon graduation, Benno jumped the mold to decline college in favor of art, the Father's pride puddled into anger. Not your open-faced kind, that blows in hard and then is gone, but a midnight-dark anger that blends self-hurt with self-pity and survives by feeding on those human weaknesses long past the point of remembering their source.

Dan knew best, and being the kind of man he was, would impose his will on his offspring. Benno was cast out. Adam, who was to attend Kansas State in the Fall, tried repeatedly to intervene. To no avail. The most Adam could get Dan to promise was that, when Benno came back a confessed sinner, seeking redemption, Dan would "kill the fatted calf" for him, as in Luke's parable of the Prodigal Son.

"Of course I will," Dan assured Adam.

That was 1928, over two years ago. The calf was still in the pasture. Benno studied the visual arts, concentrating on sculpture, which he enjoyed, whether working in wood, stone or a bar of soap. For two years he worked in Manhattan, apprenticed to an art school, where he did maintenance work in exchange for lessons and the chance to create the restless art he could feel inside, seeking release like the famous marble prisoners sculpted by Michelangelo long ago.

Benno spent time with Adam in those years, but never with his Father, who, the town gossips reported, felt humiliated by Benno's role in the life of this small, transparent Kansas town. Like a wound that's left open to heal, their separation hardened. The possibility of reconciliation, at the outset considered by all a likely event, faded into the distance until, by the time Benno set forth on a voyage of hope and adventure to New York City in the Fall of 1930, it had vanished. Just before Benno left, Dan sent him a brief note: "I'd expected time would heal the wound you caused me but, now, upon your departure for the Big City, I know I am just not ready. I understand you chose to be an artist at risk of losing my affection, approval and support, and looking down the road I hope for your sake this decision will prove to be a good one. I hope someday you will be able to return and I to forgive."

He ended this note with "Dan Murdock."

———————

"Adam, welcome home. Dan extended his hand in the oddly formal way he had always greeted his boys. You look thin. Thin and pale. Too much library time, I reckon. We'll fatten you up, that's for sure. Roast pig tonight. Supremely succulent pig, just the way it used to be. My boy, in the old days, when we served pork, I had to pry the serving plate away from you, remember?"

"Bill White stopped off earlier this afternoon. He'll be with us overnight. Always on the move, that fellow. You'll enjoy catching up. And so will I. In our correspondence, we fight like alley cats. Over drinks and a meal, we behave, calmed by the civilizing force of the grape. By the way, how'd you do on the exams?"

Adam was having trouble taking it all in. The perfumes of Kansas in full Summer bloom had enveloped him as he stepped down from the train, small suitcase in hand. Memories rattled around in his head, bumping into each other, jarring his effort to sort them out. His Father's love of alliteration hadn't faded with age, nor his special way with words. Even at the cost of warping the meaning he intended his words to convey, Dan would favor like sounds and send them tripping from his tongue to dramatic effect. The infatuation continued. Adam smiled, thinking, if it was Dan's pork, it couldn't be otherwise.

"Oh, who knows? Results come in the mail at the end of July."

"I mean how'd you think you did? I could always tell."

"Ok, I guess."

Adam wondered if his Father cared about how much he learned or whether, like the blue ribbons he added to his bedecked wall each year for the prize herd he took to the Chicago stockyards, he just wanted to dine out on a blue ribbon garnered by his son in the classrooms of Harvard.

He was nine. It was mid-June. Kansas had been hit by a withering heat wave, with temperatures soaring to 105 degrees and staying there for a week. His Father's herd of hogs, three hundred or so, including that Spring's newborn, was housed in a closed-in shelter that allowed for little natural ventilation and lacked electricity that might have served to drive some fans. By the third day of this heat wave, the swine were beginning to curl up and die. Dan knew he had to move them to a space where air could circulate and electricity was available. He was able to borrow from the Fair Grounds, in exchange for the promise of pork, a circus tent and some large, freestanding fans. Pitching the tent as close as he could get to the hog shelter and still have electricity, Dan prepared his men to move the animals. The distance to be covered was the length of two football fields.

Dan had insisted that the twins be on hand that day to watch. It would be a lesson, he had told them — animal husbandry. They had learned not to play hooky from moments like that. Moving a herd of swine is never easy, and here, given the distance to be covered and the intense heat in the ground that had built up over several days, the task entailed large risks, even though they would undertake the move late in the day, just after sunset. Moving swine is like moving cattle, only more so. They spook easily. Stampedes can occur. Disasters can result.

Many farmhands were enlisted to shape the drive, moving the swine at a walk, speaking gently to them, guiding them toward the big tent across pasture land baked hard by the sun. As sunset turned to dusk and the sky darkened, it was easy for even experienced farmhands, concentrating as they were on the herd, to miss the black clouds coming fast out of the east or the giant thunderheads rising, like the Devil's own towers, far up into the sky. As the herd reached the midpoint in their journey of salvation, bolts of lightning flashed across the sky, zigzagging this way and that before touching down. These were followed by violent claps of thunder loud enough to frighten Jupiter. A cooling rain followed, but too late to break the hell-for-leather stampede triggered by these sights and sounds.

The farmhands never had a chance. The swine bolted, charging in random directions, trampling each other, grunting and squealing at frequencies seldom heard. The twins would never forget the wild and frightening chorus of sounds. Dust rose in clouds, counterpoint to the patter of raindrops. The men could barely see.

It was over in minutes, just before the downpour arrived to tamp down the dust and calm the heads and hearts of those few animals who had survived the rampage. Dead and dying swine lay everywhere. A brutal, ugly sight.

Dan accepted the destruction of his herd as an Act of God. He blamed no one, even though, with hindsight, it would have been safer to schedule the move at dawn, when the likelihood of thunderstorms was remote. Dan saw God's hand spread across all aspects of farming, as constant as stars in a night sky. Seeing his Father now, listening to him, Adam knew he hadn't changed. Just like Robert Frost's farmer Brown in *Brown's Descent*, Dan "bowed with grace to natural law and went round it on his feet, after the manner of our stock."

Recalling this incident, Adam saw how his Father's philosophy, which through Adam's childhood seemed only to affect a tight circle of family and farmhands, now infused his politics, leading to much wider impacts.

When it came to putting food on his table, Dan had the pick of wives from among his farmhands. He knew them for their strengths and weaknesses and would mix and match to deploy skill where it could make a difference. Sheila Chestnut, wife of Dan's general manager, was in the kitchen tonight, a signal that the pork would be served with the farm's applesauce and prunes, root vegetables and sweet potatoes.

Looking at his Father closely, Adam was shocked. He shouldn't have been. All Fathers age and tire. And most lose their hair. Dan was no different. In fact, he was better preserved than most of his peers, although Adam couldn't be expected to know that.

Dan smelled of horse, leather and manure. So, too, did his Ford. In this regard, nothing had changed. His face showed a three-day growth of white whiskers that stood out against deeply tanned skin below the shade line just below the eyes that his wide brimmed hat accounted for. When Dan took off his hat to climb into the pickup, Adam saw that his

Father's hair had thinned and receded, and that the little remaining had whitened.

Bill White arrived at 6 PM. Drinks were offered to Bill and Dan — single malt, neat for Bill, with ice for Dan. Adam was left to rustle up a bottle of beer from the kitchen. The family's odd specialty, uncooked carrots sliced across the grain and dabbed with peanut butter, was served. Adam had almost forgotten. Cheddar and crackers rounded out the fare. Even though it had been more than a year, the three men behaved as if they had last seen one another the day before. In no time, like Jersey cream in a milking can, politics surfaced, attracting attention, and with it public policy.

"What a Summer we had last year," said Bill, "what with the cry for a dictator to lead us out of our economic wilderness and the over-firm hand of Hoover in expelling the Bonus Army. Plenty to keep an old journalist like me out of trouble."

"I wondered how long it would take us to open up on these," Dan said. "Last year's rumblings about the need for a Mussolini had merit. Still do."

Adam had read a summary of the propaganda for dictatorship in the September issue of *Current History*, suggested to him by a left-leaning professor. It was authored by Frederic Ogg, editor of the *American Political Science Review*. He provided background to a screed published a year ago in June by 86 prominent citizens, including Edsel Ford, the President of the American Federation of Labor and retired rich men and active financiers and industrialists. It was an open plea for dictatorship. They begged the President to bring back the Council of National Defense. He swiftly rejected the idea, confirming in the minds of those most agitated the belief that Hoover wasn't the man to lead in time of martial law.

"How much of this do you know about, Dan?" Bill asked, his voice dropping almost to the whisper of one afraid of being overheard.

"I know a lot, as it turns out. The Elders, that group of 86, asked me to join them. This was just after they published their statement, so it was too late for me to become a signatory. But I pitched in, offering any help they might need. And they are going to need a lot of help."

Dan paused, taking in the open mouths. "You look shocked. And Adam, you too. Here's my point. Democracy in times of stress cannot be counted on. Constitutional edicts must not be allowed to interfere with a general when he's fighting a battle. The Constitution shouldn't interfere with remedies essential to get us out of this appalling depression. The Elders got the need right. But the country's stuck with the wrong man for the job."

"Who in this amazing land of ours is wise enough to know what those 'essential remedies' might be?" asked Bill, his voice much louder now. "Might there be one such genius? Might there be more than one? And, if so, suppose their remedies differed? How to proceed? Might we let some group decide? By majority vote perhaps? Who should be excluded from that vote? Those less educated? Those who rent rather than own? Those with darker skin? In the end, don't you see, my harebrained friend, in pursuit of common decency you are driven away from Fascism to embrace Democracy."

Adam listened, his mind stirred up by the exchange of views, especially his Father's complicity with the dictatorial set. Adam knew his Father wasn't a simple farmer who could easily be manipulated by eastern elites. Dan knew what he was doing. For Adam, it was like a hard punch in the gut. Wasn't he at Harvard, studying the law of the land, learning respect for legal institutions, mastering the most sacred document of all, the US Constitution? Could his own Father countenance throwing that document overboard in favor of rule by a few self-proclaimed wise men?

"Come now, Adam," Bill said, looking intently into Adam's reclusive eyes. "Tell us what you think."

Adam took a deep breath and a gulp of beer. "I think Americans, at least those who should know better, are losing their nerve. It's not useful or wise to take the measure of any system when all is hunky-dory. Democracy should be tested when it comes under stress. As now. But one doesn't walk away from it before it's failed, on the chance that it might, or more likely with these self-designated Elders," on the chance that democratically achieved solutions are not to their liking. Since the founding, we've weathered two big wars, springing back from each, growing more successful, and able to reject stupidity and injustice in high places through the ballot box. Perhaps I'm too young and inexperienced to lose my nerve."

"You have a fetching naiveté appropriate to your age," said Dan, a broad smile covering his face, the kind of smile that says, "Sonny boy, I've been around a lot longer than you." "But it's overlaid with the mindless exuberance of the theory class you are hanging out with in Cambridge. If I were given to prayer, I would pray not for your soul, but for your mind, before it's too late."

Smelling danger, Bill broke in. "Dan reports you've got a girl tucked away somewhere in Cambridge, Adam. Congratulations. What's her name?"

"Nothing serious, Bill. Just a second, I'm going to get another beer."

On returning, Adam saw that Bill had not moved on, as he hoped. "We argue a lot. She prevents me from swallowing whole hog Harvard's whoop-de-do. Mariah Massie. From Richmond. She attends Newton Seminary. Worked for Huey Long last Summer."

"You never mentioned that," Dan said.

"Did she like it?" Bill asked.

"He bewitched her," Adam replied, as he stood and took a step towards the dining room. "Huey's one of the things we fight over. I think dinner's ready."

Dan kept two hired girls to handle shopping and serving, to help out in the kitchen and do the cleaning and general upkeep of the house. He borrowed a farmhand to mow the lawn, a task that was passed around, just as the position of chef rotated among farmhand wives.

The table was well set with shining silver and Quimper pottery from Brittany. There were finger bowls of lead, with bas reliefs facing up through the water, each a different type of fish. They rested on crocheted doilies in white linen. At each place were tall glasses of water with ice cubes, a recent addition to patrician tables around town.

As cold butternut soup was served, Dan asked his son what, exactly, he and Mariah disagreed about in regard to the Kingfish.

"She loves his plan for wealth redistribution. Sees it as a religious cause. Wants to start with her parents' wealth, which drove her to seminary in search of a way to understand and deal with it. Doesn't see what a demagogue he is."

"Interesting. Very. Let's come back to Mariah after I get Bill's thoughts on Hoover's handling of the Bonus Army."

———◆———

After the Great War, the Government issued to its ex-soldiers certificates of value redeemable in 1945. In 1932, with unemployment rampant, the ex-soldiers began lobbying for immediate redemption, at least in part. They failed, but not entirely. Congress authorized holders to borrow up to 50% of the face value of the certificates. The aim was to put money in the men's pockets, thereby stimulating the economy. Hoover vetoed the bill. Congress overrode, and the bill became law. Within a few months, some two million five hundred thousand certificates had been pledged for loans, totaling one and a quarter billion dollars. The promised stimulation of business failed to appear. Most of the money went to pay old grocery bills, back rent and overdue debt installments.

To pay off the rest of the certificates would cost the Government about two and a quarter billion dollars more. In the Spring of 1932, 1,000 ex-soldiers appeared in Washington bearing a petition signed, they claimed, by over two million Americans. It demanded immediate payment of the bonus. By June, 2,500 men had arrived, camping in tents at Anacostia Park. Placards captured the mood: "Give us a bonus or give us a job."

They argued for the money because they needed it. So did millions of non-veterans who were out of work. They said the country owed them the money, both legally and morally. True, but a promise to pay in 1945 did not, by itself, support the claim for payment in 1932. Initial press reports claimed that the Bonus Army had become a mob, giving cover to Communists who stirred up disorder and discontent and turned to violence, leaving the President no choice but to call out the Army. That he did in July. Federal troops drove the Bonus Army out of Washington.

Later, contrary reports circulated. The Attorney General's report in September, being noticeably unbalanced, fed the doubters.

It claimed the Bonus Army refused to leave its headquarters in some abandoned and half-demolished Treasury buildings on Pennsylvania Avenue and Third when the Treasury pressed for possession, arguing the property was "urgently needed to carry on its program of public improvements." This expulsion triggered the violence that led to the president's call for Federal troops. General Pelham Glassford, Chief of Police for the District, was said in the AG's report to have requested Federal assistance because things were beyond the ability of his forces to control. Glassford directly contradicted this claim. Conspiracy theorists developed the idea that the Government had arranged for the use of Federal troops before the triggering event and had worked at provoking an otherwise law-abiding Army of Bonus Marchers until they fought back, thereby justifying the prearranged troop call.

For the first time in American history, Federal troops were summoned by the President to attack American citizens in the nation's Capitol. Not just citizens, but veterans of a World War. For the first time since the Civil War, Federal troops made war against American citizens who were not striking and not interfering with the processes of industry. Some saw in this incident something new and ominous, akin to Fascism.

General Douglas MacArthur was in command of the Federal troops, accompanied by his aide, Dwight D. Eisenhower. Marching on this bedraggled and unarmed Bonus Army were four troops of cavalry with sabres drawn, followed by six tanks with machine guns hooded and a column of infantry with fixed bayonets, steel helmets and, at their belts, gas masks and blue tear-gas bombs.

After his successful rout of the Bonus Army, MacArthur claimed that the "mob" was animated by "the essence of revolution" and, if allowed to remain in Washington much longer, would have seized control of the Government.

President Hoover said: "A challenge to the authority of the United States Government has been met. Order and tranquility are the first requisites in the great task of economic reconstruction."

———◆———

"I'm sure we're all familiar with the facts," said Bill. "At first I supported the President. As more information dribbled in, I began to doubt my first instinct. At some point after the AG's report had been shredded, I swung 180 degrees. In fact, I believe a great injustice was done to the Bonus Army." Referring to Hoover's explanation of why he called out the troops, Bill said, "You both will recall it was precisely to restore 'order and tranquility' that Mussolini marched on Rome."

"My man Bill, gone soft again. Surely you can distinguish between Mussolini's march and MacArthur's. These Bonus men were scum, and as such, lucky to escape the District with their lives."

"Father, I can't let you have that last word. You call them scum; I call them honorable veterans; I don't know what Bill calls them. But none of that counts. What's important is that, under a Government of laws, these men have constitutional rights. Rights that must be protected, even if, as you claim, they were 'scum.' In this country, even the most undeserving mortal must be protected in the exercise of his rights, and not just because he is entitled to that protection, but because he is the vicarious champion of each and every one of us. To the extent we fail to protect his rights, we erode our own. Enough of this kind of selective enforcement and our rights are gone."

"Bravo, Adam," said Bill.

"One other thing, Father. These "scum," as you call them, fought with you in the War. For all we know, some out there being attacked by their own Government may have been your friends. Damning them with so little knowledge is unbecoming, Father. It could turn my stomach."

Dan felt outnumbered. And angry at Adam, for the eloquence and logic of his views, at himself, for being talked into covering Adam's legal education at what was turning out to be a spawning ground for pinkos. As a man of honor, he couldn't break his promise of support. On top of all this, he also felt betrayed by his lifelong friend. He knew enough to back off but couldn't resist plunging further down the road.

"So, my sometime, when it suits him, friend, oh, so gentle Bill, tell me how your new champion, our President, he of Groton and Harvard stock, of pretense to farming and silviculture along the Hudson River, he with the bleeding heart, he who rumors say was known to girls on the Harvard campus as "feather duster," for his shallow and priggish qualities — tell me how he would have handled the shanty town on the Anacostia Flats?"

"That's one I can answer. You may have heard the Army is reforming in the District. We may find out how FDR would handle them. But had he been in office last year, I am confident of what he would have done: crushed them with kindness. And Eleanor would have joined in the conspiracy."

"Ha!" Dan uttered with withering scorn.

"I read skepticism in your face. How, you ask, would this be done? By treating them as they are: American veterans. By feeding them well. Providing countless pots of hot coffee and iced tea. Medical service. Inviting their leaders to the White House for consultation. Quiet encouragement to disband with free rail transportation to their homes. And, when he saw resolve beginning to melt from all this kindness, he would call upon Eleanor, his ultimate weapon of opportunity, to visit the camp and provide the coup de grace, an invitation to join her in singing that haunting tune they knew so well, 'There's a Long, Long Trail.'"

Dan sat speechless, wishing he had never asked the question. Then, recovering, his eyes narrowed. "And how much bonus money would your hero offer them?"

"Ah," replied Bill. "That's the beauty of his approach. Not a red cent."

Shifting to reach for the pepper, Adam knocked over his beer bottle. It was almost all gone. Dan said, "Come now Adam, you don't have to knock your drink over to justify reaching for another."

"Father, that joke's old and threadbare." Adam went into the kitchen, fetched a couple of dishrags and a fresh bottle of beer and was back in his seat before the conversation had resumed.

After the main course, the chef appeared with a large salad bowl and proceeded to toss it with olive oil and vinegar at the table. The girls then took servings on matching pottery to each diner's place.

"Look, Bill," Dan said, appearing to have cast off his defeat. "What happens in the District isn't my reality. In the Capitol, mirrors enlarge clever fallacies and pass them back and forth until they appear to be true. Here in Manhattan, reality is the scarlet tanager I saw this morning sitting on the top branch of a deep purple lilac bush, singing his heart out to the first rays of sunlight, which turned him burning red against the still dark sky. He was of a piece with the force that moves the stars. The force of nature, which man tinkers with at great risk. My scarlet friend seeks no hand-out. He will not cease singing in exchange for millet. He bows to no central authority, as we farmers are being asked to do. He is free within nature's constraints and yoked in joy to the destiny nature has in store for him. Oh, to be a bird!"

"If by that story you meant to say grace, it was apt and well put," said Bill. "An indigo bunting frequents our house in Emporia, returning from God knows where every June. In watching him, set against the pine he favors and white clouds above, I feel both humble — in the face of this magnificent force of nature — and grateful for his presence, for his power to bend my thoughts in his direction. Is he aware? I'd like to know."

"Amen," intoned Adam.

Dan considered the disturbing possibility that he was losing Bill as a fellow Republican.

"You've got me worried. More so than ever, although I confess to having started to worry about you many years ago, when you fell in love with Teddy Roosevelt and his Bull Moose heros. Long ago, when we first met, you and I were anchored by the same chain. We believed in Nature's laws and mankind's utter inability to control them. We accepted Nature's rules for supply and demand. And we believed in independent manhood. That's what the Republican Party stood for. And still does. It says to the weak man: 'Be strong or go under.' And to the strong: 'Only be fair and keep within the law.' And we believed in fighting, going to war if needs be, for what's right.

"Then you got mesmerized by Teddy and, along with him, tried to inaugurate 'Social and Industrial Justice' by man-made laws, instead of leaving the job to God Almighty. You were well-intentioned. But your efforts to interfere with natural laws have led directly to our present unhappy economic and political condition."

Adam couldn't help admire his Father's absurd argument about cause. As if Hoover had used any of the powers of Government to promote justice.

"As I recall it, Dan, you took something of a shine to Teddy too."

"He had an attractive way of presenting his ideas, making it all seem righteous and fine. No misplaced pity in his creed. Respect for the strenuous life, salvation by hard work. Up to that point, hard not to be attracted. But the idea that industrial and social reforms could be accomplished by legislation was false, at least if they tried to override natural law. For evidence, look what's happening now: attempts by our Savior to regulate hours and wages; to shunt onto the shoulders of the Federal Government every decent and natural obligation of the individual to society; the unjointing of our whole national economy until farm and industrial prices become utterly unrelated to each other."

Dan paused. His face wore the serene expression of conviction, a diamond-hard certainty that could not be dulled by lesser elements.

"Bill, you've changed a lot. You've moved toward socialism, toward an un-American doctrine of state paternalism. Under that theory, the man without means becomes the nation's ward, to be protected against the oppression of wealth, to be lifted up. And you've renounced war. I must know how you justify change so extreme?"

To Adam, the clamor of plates being gathered and carried into the kitchen became a roar as silence fell across the dining table. He could see that Bill was summoning his wits to respond.

"Yes, as an editor, I've evolved over nearly 50 years. Had to, in the face of changing facts. But consider this: There's a certain wisdom of the ages that is changeless. I am satisfied that there is some kind of a law of spiritual gravity which governs human happiness, that is as authentic and rigid as the law of physical gravity. For instance, I don't think a mean man can be happy, nor a stingy man, nor a revengeful man. But the social environment changes with the generations. That makes it impossible to say what is intelligent selfishness, as of, say, Cromwell's time and as of today. Once a man could be intelligently selfish and own slaves. He could be intelligently selfish and have serfs on his land. He could be intelligently selfish if he was a smuggler two hundred years ago in Massachusetts. But he couldn't do any of those things now and be intelligently selfish. And, yet, a lot of fellows in their labor relations feel that they are intelligently selfish when they look after No. 1. Today, we've got to consider No. 2 a lot more or bust — bust spiritually, bust financially, bust morally.

"I wish I could get this into your old thick head, which is above all a heart I love."

Adam began to imagine he was observing the kind of debate that produced the Federalist Papers. Their braiding of intellectual disagreement with human love was unmistakable, a far cry from the water-tight compartments in which his relationship with Mariah was conducted.

"Life's too cruel to endure on one's own?" Dan asked. "Well, fairly cruel but mighty lovely all the same. I reckon it's a hell of a back aching business to bear a baby, but it's just one of those good old processes of Nature and, unless women had the will to face it, we wouldn't be. It's a rebellion against the laws of Nature that's going to destroy us. Oh, Bill,

I do wish you'd take arms to quell that rebellion instead of abetting it. The only way we can save ourselves is by undoing the wrongs we have done. And now are threatening to do, in defiance of Nature's decrees. For instance, Teddy tried, and now FDR is going to try even harder, to use the state as an instrument for enhancing our well-being and for establishing 'social justice.' But the law of cost and compensation forbids the one and the laws of biology forbid the other. Have done with it. I'm prepared to end my days gallantly in a forlorn fight for Truth. Come now, Bill; won't you join me?"

"No, Dan, not that Truth. On the other hand, I see no reason to take the advice of Job's comforters and curse God and die —-yet! I am willing to send up a flare again and see where she lights. That things are bad, no one can doubt. That it could be worse, I'll bet a horse. That it may be worse, I'm willing to admit. But the end is not nigh. Democracy is a work-in-process. Always been; always will be. There's still a fighting chance."

"But, look at what your Democracy put in the White House!"

"Dan, my goodness. Your ideas remind me of a conversation I once heard between a waitress and a customer. Said he, 'Those canned peas are no good.' And she answered, 'Well, you wouldn't like them if they were good.' And he replied, 'How'd you know that?'

"I'm afraid you wouldn't like Democracy even if it worked. It never has worked. Neither has Christianity or any other faith. We've got about 15% residual Christianity in our Democracy and that's about as much decency as we could put into life with the human breed as it is. Though I think we are gradually improving the strain."

In silence, Adam wondered at this last point. Bill could conceal more dynamite in a handful of sentences than anyone he had ever listened to. His thoughts turned to Adolf Hitler. He knew of this man's rise to power through democratic processes at the head of the National Socialist Party in Germany, his being named Chancellor on a Nazi platform that allowed him to abolish Democracy in favor of dictatorship. He had read of Hitler's appeal to all that was insanely egotistical in the German national soul, all that was meanest and cruelest in the German mass man. Had he then known the full story of Nazism as it would play out on the world stage through 1945, silence would have been way out of line.

Dessert arrived. Stewed prunes drowned in fresh lemon juice and seasoned with a cinnamon stick and a touch of ground nutmeg. Their intellectual capital depleted, conversation turned to memories, old times, movies, old and new, and songs.

Dan leaned forward across the table in the direction of Bill, as if to verify something on the left side of Bill's face he had noticed. He wore a knowing, not unkindly, smile that in the eyes of some would be considered mischievous.

"What, exactly, are you up to, my saddle-reared friend, staring at me that way?" Bill said.

"It's just that patch of hair on your cheek, near the ear, that the razor missed. It stands out on a face I've enjoyed the sight of for a score of years and more, a face always tended with fastidious care."

Bill felt the left side of his face, quickly locating the uncut clump.

Adam was shocked at his Father's indiscretion. Where could he be headed with this rudeness?

"Bill, I wouldn't bring such personal hygienic matters to the dinner table, but for one thing. I identify with your problem. In fact, I can explain it. Like the cluster of hair I often miss, your clump is a sign of age. And here's why. At some point along our lifelines, and not so long ago at that, I decided, and my bet is you did too, that I could save time and energy by shaving in the shower instead of before, in front of a mirror. Both of us, being right-handed, hold the razor in our right hands, meaning we have to reach with arthritic joints to shave the left side of our faces. Without a mirror, we often miss the crouching clump near the ear. Case solved."

Bill burst into laughter, an acknowledgement of Dan's insight. Adam and Dan joined in the merriment.

"What you're telling me is 'It takes one to know one.'" Bill said. "A regular sleuth-hound you are."

Talk turned to Al Jolson, which led to Dan's wobbly rendition of his hit song, *Toot Toot Tootsie, Goodbye*. Bill reported Jolson was starring in a Depression-era comedy called *Hallelujah I'm a Bum*, designed to make beaten-down spirits soar. Trooping off to bed, the three men resolved to see this movie and compare notes.

———◆———

Even before boarding the train from Boston, Adam felt Rachel's pull. He would visit her, of course, but not to talk about his foremost worry. Too embarrassing. He imagined her humiliating him without intending to be mean. Freudian analysis just worked that way. Innocent venom. Sometimes, venom for the innocent.

He had let her know he was in town. Her response to his knock on the door was almost instantaneous. The door flung wide, there she stood, taking stock of him. And like the well-trained patient, he waited, suffering a scrutiny that seemed to penetrate, getting inside his head before he'd even crossed the threshold.

"Come in, Adam, and tell me how things are with you. It's been at least a year. But wait. First, I want a big hug."

Stepping across the threshold, Adam did as directed. Rachel held him in embrace, her head nestled in the hollow between shoulder and arm. "You feel fit, more like an athlete than a scholar."

"Can we have a coffee and sit at your kitchen table, like the old days?"

"My thought precisely. Come along. We have much catching up to do."

Her hair seemed dappled with more touches of gray but her face seemed unchanged. And her voice too. Musical, feminine, inviting, disarming. And, in the end, probing and intrusive. Skilled at mental seduction, able to coax one to disrobe one's mind in plain sight and feel comfortable doing so. These things he had known and experienced before. He came prepared. He would not succumb.

After preliminaries (how was law school, living away from home, the food, etc.), Rachel began gently to poke and pry.

"Adam, I can see at a distance you are vexed, and not only about women, although I think that's part of it. Talk to me. It's never done you in."

Adam spoke of his Father's treatment of Benno, for Rachel a case study of depraved fatherly disappointment in a son whose aspirations and interests deviated from plan. "Nothing's changed. He continues to be intolerant, unthinkingly so. Although much is left unspoken, it seems the more desperate Benno grows at being unable to earn a living as an artist, the more rigid Father becomes, as if determined never to accept his son's differences until they drive him into the poorhouse or worse. As if he's waiting for Benno to submit, to crawl back home admitting not just defeat but that he was wrong and Father was right. That's a high price for anyone to pay. For Benno, impossible."

"Have you discussed Benno with your Father on this visit?"

"He knew I had just come to Manhattan after visiting Benno but has yet to ask after him. Or mention his name. It's bizarre. As if Benno doesn't exist. Somehow, this pattern must be broken. A reconciliation arranged."

"The solution, if there is one, rests with your Father," Rachel said "And I do mean 'if,' for there may not be one. What will it take?"

"Rachel, I haven't a clue," Adam replied. "Given his hatred of Government's interference with private individual choice, I might have expected him to rejoice in Benno's independence and determination to make his own way in the world. But, since it's not Father's chosen way for Benno, he can only feel the bitterness of betrayal. I've come to realize that, once he forms an opinion, and that he does swiftly, Father won't change. To do so must be a risk to his manhood. Pathetic, but there it is."

"He says no to Government intrusion but yes to his own." Rachel had an insight. "Make him understand this inconsistency, and perhaps he will come around."

"That's a possibility. Father prides himself on honesty. I'll work on it."

"More coffee? "Rachel asked, holding the pot over Adam's empty cup.

Adam nodded, Rachel poured and then went to the larder for some thin ginger cookies, a favorite of hers that, in the excitement of their greeting, she had forgotten to offer.

"And now," Rachel said, a syrupy lilt to her voice, all expectant.

"Now what?" Adam replied, knowing exactly what she meant but pretending he didn't, in an effort to dodge the bullet.

"Tell me about the women in your life. Particularly the stuff you resolved not to tell me," she said with that warm-hearted, all knowing laugh that had for years been her passkey.

Adam knew of slippery slopes. One of his favorite poets, Robert Frost, had nailed this metaphor in *Brown's Descent,* depicting a Vermont farmer who got caught on icy crust atop his lofty farm while setting forth one late afternoon to do his chores.

Anticipation is the best defense, he thought. I will speak in measured ways. Unlike Farmer Brown, I can stop whenever I wish to.

And so, Adam spoke of Mariah Massie, recounting how they met and much more about their relationship, as Rachel's questions led him down a footpath that was narrow at first but soon widened into the broad avenue of disclosure Rachel intended.

"From your account of her Summer with Huey Long, it sounds like she had him eating out of her hand."

"Well put. I hadn't looked at it that way, but perhaps you're right, perhaps she was manipulating the master manipulator, himself. But what are you driving at?"

"My husband liked to tell new hires he made in Vienna about how the world of executives is divided into three types: Those who make things happen; those who watch things happen; and those who don't know what's happening. Of course, he would urge them to be among those who make good things happen in the company.

"I think your Mariah's the first type. Likes to control things."

"And what about me? What type am I?" He put the question hard on her comment about Mariah and immediately regretted doing so. He knew he had exposed an insecurity. One he hadn't recognized in himself until this moment. A sense of foolishness overcame him. His battle for cover was almost lost. Now, disrobed and in disarray, he realized he had revealed himself in regard to Mariah, as both insecure and foolish. Rachel hadn't broken a sweat.

"If you need to ask me that question, I would suggest you likely fall into the second grouping."

Although he would deny the comparison, like Farmer Brown, Adam found his resistance swept away by the subtle force of Rachel's questions. He couldn't stop himself.

"I know what you're thinking. If she can manipulate the senator from Louisiana, she can manipulate me. But you're wrong. We love one another. There's nothing about power in our relationship. Shouldn't I be the first to know? I don't feel manipulated." He spoke in an unnecessarily loud voice, as if determined to convince not just Rachel, who was seated close enough to hear the softest whisper.

"If that were true, our profession would be out of a job. Tell me, what do you like about the relationship?" Rachel's honeyed tones and even, quiet pace of questioning never changed, a foil to Adam's volatility, a snare to pry open his mind.

"The intellectual sparring. Whether its politics, role of Government, treatment of poverty. She's a tough partner, but I like it. There are sparks. She drives me to insights, to make connections I hadn't discovered on my own. And there's the sex. It's good. Very good. In certain ways, it was you who prepared me for this. We play games. We know how to please one another. I think even you'd be impressed with the scope of our play. But I'll tell you what I don't like. It's the divide. There are these two parts to what we share. They don't meet anywhere in the middle. Sometimes I fear something's missing, but I don't know what it is."

"What about kindness? Is that a word you might use to describe Mariah?"

Adam had never thought in these terms before. The first thing to enter his mind was a lost image of Mariah petting a dog. He couldn't bring it into focus. That's because it wasn't there. Never had been.

Mariah didn't change direction to pat dogs. He realized he'd never discussed pets with Mariah, didn't know if she grew up in a dog-loving family. And then he realized kindness to animals was not exactly the subject of Rachel's question.

"To be honest, I don't know. Determined, yes. Smart, yes. Focused on what she wants, you bet. With a plan, for sure. That's why I agree with your thought that she will make things happen. But kindness. That takes empathy, right? She doesn't suffer fools gladly. Even me. Especially me, when I'm being foolish, something that happens more than I like. I'm not sure. I'm not even sure I've got it. As the years pass, I find my Father increasingly hard to accept. If one can't think kind thoughts about one's Father, who can one be kind to?"

"Ah, but Adam, you know the old saw about familiarity and contempt. Don't be so harsh on yourself. So, if Mariah's a planner, a mover and shaker, as we've agreed, where might she be planning to take you?"

Like an unwelcome draft from an old window, Adam felt an icy chill run up and down his spine. "We've never spoken of marriage. Except, in my case, to rule it out at least until I finish law school and have a job. Right now, I think she's devoted to Huey Long, to furthering his plan to redistribute the nation's wealth."

"So, Adam, you believe she has eyes only for Huey Long. No plans for you; not even a sketch? This, despite womenfolk being far better at keeping two or three balls in the air."

Under any circumstance, marriage was a frightening prospect for Adam. Having not grown up within a marriage, he had no intimacy with it, no experienced appreciation for it, no opportunity to develop trust in its bonds. Compounding his anxiety was fear of pregnancy and the duties that would ensue, as certain as one breath following another. He had always assumed Mariah had no urge to marry. But, now, Rachel was planting seeds of doubt in a field already furrowed with fear.

"If she were a schemer, I'd know it. We play; we argue. We avoid commitment. That's it. That's what's missing between the two parts. And that's why I don't believe she's got some plan for me. And, by the way, I'm not sure what's missing will ever be supplied, by either of us. Look, I'm afraid of it and I think she is too."

"You're clear on the point. Good. Now, tell me this, my young friend. What might you do if those games you play with Mariah lead to pregnancy, accidental or not?"

Again the chill. Adam had wanted to cut the conversation off. Unlike Farmer Brown, he had resolved to dig in and stop the descent. But now it was too late. Rachel's skill had gotten Adam to a point too far, a speed too fast, to stop. Rachel's intuition had led her, in disarming fashion, to pose the one question that would open a door behind which suppressed fears crouched.

Later, traveling back to Cambridge, Adam realized with a stab of pain that he had twice gone beyond the point of return, once with Mariah and again with Rachel, whose technique he began to question. Surely, he thought, Freudian doctrine wouldn't expect the psychiatrist to create the very anxiety she then set out to treat. Could Rachel have been ignorant of the scary possibilities she was planting in his head? Not a chance. What about kindness? Was she trying to break us apart? Could she have a need to control as well as understand? Could she even have a mean streak? He couldn't make it all add up.

———————◆———————

Adam had a Summer job awaiting him in Cambridge. He would work for Professor Samuel Williston, author of the five-volume treatise, *The Law of Contracts*, and, for the past year, reporter to the first *Restatement of Contracts* undertaken by the American Law Institute. Adam's task was to help the Professor with the meticulous and time-consuming job of preparing the draft Restatement for submission to the project's advisers and ultimately to the Institute's membership. As the Professor explained it, a restatement was something less than a code but more than a treatise. Its success would be measured by its authority not to command but to persuade.

During his work for the Professor, Adam was distracted by his Father's apparent disregard for the drastic problems affecting the Farm Belt. Of course, Dan Murdock had some advantages over the pure dirt farmer. In fact, farming was a minor sideline of the Wyandot Farm. Its main business was beef cattle, Herefords that he fattened on the marvelous diet of tall blue-stem grass growing on 2,400 acres of abundant pastureland in the Flint Hills above Manhattan. And his stud operation for breeding quarter-horses was a separate source of income, helping to put bread on the table. Beyond this healthy diversification of earning streams, he had come from upper-middle-class surroundings, which gave him a leg up in getting started through inherited capital that only those with more would consider modest.

Adam knew next to nothing about his Father's balance sheet or income statement. It was a subject they never discussed. Dan succeeded in projecting very comfortable levels of wealth. As, for example, when, on principle, he denied Benno any financial support. Implicit in that disgraceful episode was the existence of sufficient wealth to carry Benno. Just as he was bearing Adam's cost of a law degree. He showed a deliberately insouciant attitude about money, a subject his demeanor suggested as being so insignificant as to be unworthy of even a minute of grown-up discourse.

Dan wasn't ignorant of the deplorable state in which farmers in and around Manhattan were struggling. Adam had heard Bill talk with Dan on the subject during his recent visit home. All the world knew that surplus crops had driven market prices well below the point where profits begin, down to levels under the cost of production. Bill described one county in Iowa that was burning corn to heat the courthouse, because it was cheaper than coal. And a county elevator in South Dakota paying minus three cents a bushel for corn. Their land is their life, Adam recalled Bill saying, to which his Father replied, "Yes, you take a man's horses and his plow away and the result? You deny him food and convict his family to starvation. It's just that simple."

They spoke of Milo Reno, leader of the Farmer's Holiday Association, of his determination to organize mass refusals to deliver farm products at less than production costs.

And, yet, that conversation never crossed the threshold of Dan's personal experience or sympathies. Like the invisible repelling force of two magnets, north to north. Untouchable, even without words to declare it so. Adam feared his Father was indifferent to the farmer's plight. It was incomprehensible except as the warped outcome of his philosophy.

———•———

The Le Mars incident caught the attention of the whole nation. In this Iowa town, there was a judge by the name of Bradley. He was gruff and arrogant. Ran a "no-nonsense, you do this, you do that, it's my court" sort of forum. Worst of all, he was inclined to do the bidding of the banks and insurance companies appearing before him to demand farm foreclosures. Increasingly desperate, the Iowa farmers, with nearly one-third of that state's farm values in hock, began to defend their property rights against these financial entities, using force if necessary. By their lights, resistance was not an expression of revolt but of patriotism. Thus, in Primghar, Iowa, foreclosure riots ended only after a deputy sheriff sank to his knees before an angry crowd of farmers and kissed the American flag.

At Le Mars, five hundred men gathered in Judge Bradley's courthouse to watch the farm of John A. Johnson go on auction. Knowing Bradley's tendency to permit foreclosure sales at less than full mortgage value and then issue deficiency judgments against the farmers, the lender's agent offered less than face value. A riot ensued, with the mob mauling the agent, then dragging Bradley down the court house steps and showing him a noose.

Throughout Iowa, farmers were organizing to save their brethren's farms through ten cent sales. When a farm went up for sale at foreclosure, neighbors would bid ten cents for a horse, twenty-five cents for a plow and so on, threatening the lender, who theoretically could make a credit bid up to the face amount of the mortgage, or anyone who might be thinking of offering a realistic cash bid. After the sale, the neighbors would return the farm, every bit of it, to the owner.

———◆———

When Adam was visiting in early Summer, one morning over breakfast, he put a question to Bill and his Father. "Are the farmers entitled?"

Bill replied, "Look Adam, poverty creates desperation, and desperation creates violence. We have police not just to enforce the law but to prevent private citizens from taking the law into their own hands. I have great sympathy for the farmers. As I've written, we need a mortgage moratorium against foreclosures."

"Hog wash, Bill. I can't let you get away with that sympathy stuff. Progressive beliefs, that's all. Beliefs that block your God-given common sense. Beliefs that Teddy Roosevelt infected you with. The Bull Moose bug. If Roosevelt and his wrecking crew, led by Henry Wallace, had kept Government out of it, I would have no sympathy for farmers who lose their farms in a fair fight against soil and weather, nature's rules of supply and demand, and the mighty mortgage holders. But if, as FDR insists, and you agree, alas alack, the Federal Government presumes to control the economy, and asserting responsibility, gets in the thick of it, then, of course, it starts fixing farm prices. But its responsibilities now extend far beyond that. Right down to the welfare and relief of farmers when prices fail to support their livelihood. And so, when the Federal Government, in its hellish, misguided pursuit, fails in these responsibilities, it must follow that the farmers are entitled to disregard the law in seizing what they have been promised."

"Why, Dan, with an edit here and there, I couldn't have explained it better. If we are not getting to agreement, at least our understanding of each other is improving."

"But Bill, I won't have the Federal Government assume those responsibilities. So, I don't share your sympathy for those farmers taking the law into their own hands. Banks have rights too, you will admit."

Adam recalled this conversation as, with surprise, he read a letter from his Father posted in August, 1933.

Dear Adam,

    I write to share with you the most difficult time I've been having over the past two years, culminating in a financial crisis that occurred soon after you returned to law school and was only resolved a couple of days ago. As you know, I've never spoken to you or Benno about my financial affairs. In my Father's house, a curtain was drawn on that subject. Until now, I have followed suit. What changed is the near-financial death experience I just passed through, and the realization that, without some understanding of my affairs, you and Benno could easily develop errors in how you view my situation; indeed, in how you view me.

    Until the Great Crash, I always had a large enough cushion of liquid assets — stocks and bonds — to survive with comfort, even against the natural vicissitudes of farming. Much of my wealth was lost in that deluge. What I could salvage I divided between the Manhattan State Bank and bonds of the most well-financed and highly regarded business corporations. Then, two years ago, the bank failed. I lost all the savings I had placed there. Before that happened, I took out a mortgage on the farm, with a view to replacing the large barn, which, as you know, was on its last legs, and building some much needed stables and accessory structures. I also was going to pick up a few hundred more acres of Blue-stem. Interest rates were low, payment terms favorable and revenues more than sufficient to meet debt service with a large margin of safety.

    As you know, there followed Summers of drought that, atop the on-going depression, put my revenue streams through a wringer. I was unable to keep current on debt service. Smelling opportunity, the lender, a rinky-dink insurance company I once mistakenly admired, refused to reset terms. In August, they commenced foreclosure. I was in a state of shock.

You know my corn-fed philosophy: A farmer's success or failure from year to year is, and must always be, determined very largely by the whims of nature. However, even under conditions now prevailing, a good farm intelligently operated should, with hard work, produce the necessary comforts of life. As one with much intelligence, good education and sound philosophy, I have always had a keen appreciation of the fact that spiritual returns from cultivating the soil and husbanding animals are far more important than the material product of a farmer's business. And, so, I believed I could be permanently contented, hopeful and happy on the soil. And was until now. But my philosophy has been shaken to its roots by these successive hammer blows of bad fortune.

I grew desperate as the day of foreclosure sale grew near. I called friends for help, tried to find another financing entity that might take out the scoundrel holding my mortgage, renewed pleadings, all to no avail. I felt under sentence of death, as you can appreciate, knowing how much of my life is in Wyandot.

And then, at the scene of sale, a miracle arrived. A large number of farmers from Manhattan, but not just Manhattan, from other nearby towns too, gathered at the auction site. They were angry and fearful, seeing my plight today as theirs tomorrow. The bidding commenced, and the insurance representative, new to these parts, blundered. His bid was far below my mortgage's face value. But, more important, it was clearly below any realistic market value for the farm. As in Iowa, the farmers let forth a cry, surging forward to seize the agent and drive him away, and sure enough, he ran, fearing for his life. I stood in amazement as, returning, they followed the ten-cent bid gambit to complete the sale and then, with quiet ceremony, returned all title to me.

So, I hear you asking me what I make of this extraordinary experience. Humankind, like the animals it husbands, if left to its own devices, is capable of great acts of compassion and generosity. Humans will support one another, if given a chance. I call this a miracle. I don't mean that in the sense of God's intercession. It's the doings of humankind at its best, pure and simple. I was a deserving farmer in need and my fellow farmers, knowing my condition, responded.

The chance of this sort of thing happening to one whose life has been meritorious — and of course that element is the key — that chance is removed when Government interferes, as it now threatens under Roosevelt to do with so-called Farm Relief. Trying to do something for the farmer through legislation is a fool's errand. Its main achievement will be to sap the instinct of humankind to look after itself, one for all and all for one, fearless and independent. The kindness of friends. Of course, but better yet, the kindness of strangers.

Were the farmers entitled to liquidate the mortgage in this fashion? Of course they were. Didn't the agent try to steal my farm with his low-ball bid? He set the moral code and we followed it. Turns out to be a rather grand example of private ordering, free of Government interference.

With mortgage debt discharged, even my reduced revenues suffice to survive more or less comfortably. I am refreshed; I look to Spring planting with rekindled joy and high hopes that the days of drought are over.

You may share this letter, or at least its tidings, with your brother.

As ever,
Father

Adam's memory of his Father's opinions of the Iowa farmers was too vivid to permit him to cut the old man much slack. Dan's monstrously strained reasoning could only be the product of one tone-deaf to how he might sound to others. Adam found the letter infuriating. He was mortified. Too much so to discuss it with Mariah, at least right away. Of course, he would send it to Benno. Father embraces the tale of the Good Samaritan when he's the one in need. Would he become the Good Samaritan if the tables were turned? Adam feared he knew the answer, and that was one source of his anger.

6

———————

SOON AFTER HIS RETURN FROM Manhattan, Adam found a note under his door. From Mariah, it contained many ideas, none touching the intellect. They came together for dinner near Harvard Square. They sat side by side. It took just minutes after ordering for Mariah's hands to get freewheeling below Adam's belt. He sensed her hunger, a yearning that surprised him, considering that it had been only two weeks since they last played in the same bed. In her face he saw not a care in the world, nothing but passion.

Adam was as solemn as she was playful. "Have you missed your period?" he asked, unable to amble up to the subject now consuming him, as it had in Manhattan, as it did throughout his visit with Rachel.

She deflected the question. "If that ever happens, Adam, you'll be the first to know. Look my love, my overly nervous love, there's nothing to worry about."

———◆———

Mariah left for another Summer with the senator. She returned to Cambridge in mid-August, earlier than planned. And, true to her word, because she then knew she was pregnant, she told Adam without a trace of remorse, fear or concern. To the contrary, she used a lilting voice, gilded with gladness. As each of them knew, the die was cast. What were they going to do about it, that was the question Adam desperately wanted to resolve within a period that would permit pursuit of all options. He finally got Mariah's agreement to sort the thing out over a meal later that month.

"Let's start with this," Mariah said. Rubbing her stomach, she continued, "We love each other, have from the start, and this — this is the product of our love."

"You're right. But neither of us signed on to becoming parents, or the marriage contract that often follows. We have some options that need to be discussed."

"I know you'd do the right thing if we decided to have the baby. There are options, I agree. Let's speak of them."

"Well, there's Zurich or Geneva."

"You're speaking of having me abort in a Swiss hospital. To end the quickening life within me. Ok, and the other option is to carry to term and offer the babe for adoption. Anything else?"

Adam could feel the cords of Mariah's determination tightening around him. Rachel's warnings rang in his ears. His fear of commitment was palpable. Her drive to achieve the result she wanted was crystal clear. Need he ask who wins, when one who fears an outcome is pitted against one who seeks it?

"This fetus is yours and mine. Its quickening is solely our doing. But, beyond that, in all this world, it's unique. We could try and try again for another, and another, but never could we recreate the unique human being flourishing in my tummy. That's my problem with abortions."

Mariah looked deeply philosophical, even a touch detached, as if it weren't her fetus they were discussing.

"Ok, I get it. But, if we identify with this fetus, wouldn't it be hard to put the baby up for adoption? And, how could it be done quietly, without notice, compared, say, to a trip to Switzerland?"

"I'm trying not to think of the social aspects of this, even though I know, given Richmond society, they will demand attention, once we figure out what we want to do. Here's the rub, Adam: Surely you know the last thing I want is to have you marry me out of a sense of duty, some absurd sense of what an honorable man is expected to do under these circumstances. To be driven under pressure, No! That I would puncture at the first sign. But, since we know we love one another, a duty-driven marriage is not on the table, don't you agree?"

"I see the options running away, like rats abandoning a sinking ship. All options, save one. Am I right?"

"Now hold on." There was a fierceness to Mariah's expression and voice. "Which one of us is that 'sinking ship?" You're cockeyed if you think that simile fits the case. The promise of life should be glorious, cause for celebration. We — you and I — have accomplished something real, something many would consider divine. And here you're speaking of 'rats.'"

Watching Mariah, Adam imagined her a Scythian warrior, dismounting in midst of battle to dispose of her enemy with short axe.

"Ok, tasteless joke. But if you rule out abortion, adoption and single parenting, the only way is marriage, which must not happen, you argue, if it's the result of pressure. I'm a law student, supposed to be good at analysis, so I'm driven to ask how there could not be pressure for the only acceptable course of action, 'the right thing' as you called it. For me, it's a Hobson's choice."

"I never said I wouldn't raise the baby as a single parent. It's just that, knowing you, knowing our feelings for each other, knowing this fetus belongs not to one but both of us in equal, indivisible measure, I couldn't imagine you allowing me to escape with the baby that way."

Adam could see he was licked. He didn't fully grasp the ways and means of her success, nor did he particularly care to figure it out. What astounded him, however, was the completeness of what she called "our Richmond plan." She seemed to have worked out every detail. Absurdly, he imagined her taking it down from a shelf where it had been stored for a long time. Perhaps under the label "Marriage Plans, If Pregnant." He would be the Father in the fullest sense of that role as dictated by Richmond society. They would marry. She and her parents would join as one in confronting and repulsing the wagging tongues of that town's upper crust. The wedding would be scheduled for the following June.

"What about pregnancy and birth of our child before marriage, a big square peg in a small round hole, if there ever were one," Adam said.

"I've thought that one through. It's not a problem," Mariah asserted. "There would be no effort to hide my condition; indeed, we will glory in it by seizing the initiative, proclaiming it the result of our decision to marry and the twin desires of wanting our marriage and the start of a family to occur before we left the sheltering life of academia. Awkward but necessary, as all would understand. We will show Richmond that ours is a determined love, one that brooks no conventional thinking or societal mores that might stand in the way of marital duty and bliss. And consider this: by wedding time our babe will be old enough to offer laughing eyes to the curious."

In Mariah's hands Adam would be molded to fit a palatable story, one Richmond could digest, bestowing on him a husband's zealous sense of duty to provide for wife and child and on Mariah those fine sacrificial motives and heroics that southern aristocracy adores. He would be packaged and sold by Richmond's leading divinity student, whose natural marketing skills could persuade a devout Muslim to embrace the Holy Ghost.

———◆———

Mariah planned to take Adam with her to Richmond in late August. She saw the trip as a joyful one to work together on the announcement and the wedding to follow in June. Just before they were due to leave, Adam came down with a high fever, perhaps from too many late evenings of work for Professor Williston, perhaps from a Summer flu that had invaded Cambridge. Rather than wait, Mariah boarded the train alone.

From Richmond, she phoned him. "How could you go and get yourself sick just when we're needed at home. If you weren't running such a fever, I'd suspect you of deliberately trying to escape this 'ordeal.' Good Lord-a-mercy, Adam, you've shown little interest or talent for planning. I know you hate it all; I sometimes imagine you'd prefer just to stop off at the local Justice of the Peace and get it over with in a jiffy. But that's not our way. Not the Richmond way, with child or not."

"Look, honey, I'll be up for travel in a day or two. I'll join you as soon as I can." Adam was croaking like a tired out-of-luck raven. Of course, she was right. He despised even the thought of wedding preparations.

Dan was kept in the dark. Again and again, Adam postponed the letter that would let his Father in on the secret. Mariah kept pestering him to write. To no avail. Rachel had nailed Mariah's character in identifying the overriding need to be in charge. Under the banner of 'marriage preparation,' she was trying to dictate how Adam should engage not just with her family, but with his. Resentment grew with each demand she made. He felt anger inside and at first couldn't explain it. Her pestering, he realized, could so easily have been handled with humor. (Hey, Mariah, don't you think your mother's enough of a project? Here's the deal: when you've got her all wrapped up and tied with ribbons, I'll give you Father to handle.) He knew how, but he wouldn't do it.

It finally dawned on him why he hadn't written his Father. The cardinal character trait his Father had insisted upon for his sons was Athenian-like self-control, precisely what he believed he had lost in getting Mariah pregnant. He had failed at something as simple as *coitus interruptus*, as his Father would surely label it. The humiliation required to explain this to Father was too painful for Adam to accept. Indeed, it was too painful even to explain to Mariah, who might have desisted had she understood.

Now, with only a few months to go before the invitation would be mailed, Adam decided to wait until then to contact his Father. Benno knew but was in no position to help with the planning, although he did agree to serve as best man. Whatever would be done on behalf of the Murdocks would be done by the groom alone.

Adam knew Mariah was competitive. What he hadn't anticipated, however, was just how similar her mother was to her, how all-consuming would be their fight for dominance in planning the event. Adam's best image was a motorcycle with empty sidecar, the women all arms and legs fighting to control the seat, handlebars and throttle. Mariah and her mother occupied a two-person elevator, a ski lift for two, an exclusive dance card, a tea for two, a double bed, whatever accommodates two and no more. Even if he could have squeezed in, they would have sucked up all the oxygen, leaving him gasping for breath. In the game they were playing, he had no position on the field, not even a uniform to wear on the sidelines.

It got worse. Though an essential participant in the day's events, he soon realized he was just a prop. If the world would revolve around him, as Mariah promised him it would, it would do so because he was stage center, an immobile, functionless, manikin placed there for all to see, a check-the-box sort of necessity whose appearance alone would suffice, whose efforts to go beyond would be considered rude, even uncouth.

Mariah called every day. Her mind was crammed full of details about the ways and means to the altar according to Richmond rules. Like a bucket loader filled to the brim, she dumped it all on him, for what purpose, he couldn't imagine.

"We need final lists from you now. You know, the bridal dinner list and the one for the wedding. How soon can you get them to us? A wire will do, or, if there aren't too many, maybe we could do it on the phone. Saw a final version of the invitation. Terrific. We are booked at the Commonwealth Club for the bridal dinner Friday night. Remember, it's just family, godparents, members of wedding party and one or two special out-of-town guests. I meet the chef today to review menus. Have I told you about their Oyster Special, it's a broiled oyster appetizer like nothing you've ever tasted, Darling, it's fabulous, and imagine, if you were here, you could sample it this afternoon. But you're not and Mother says no need for you to travel down, given your cold. How's it coming, by the way? I mean going, Ha- Ha. Darling, I can't describe what an exciting madhouse we have here."

"Breathless," Adam said to himself and then, into the phone, croaked that black bird's call from deep in his chest.

"Did you say something, Darling? I missed it. Hurry up and get well. Caterer just arrived. I'll call later."

This wedding project had turned Mariah into someone Adam could hardy recognize, at least on the phone. She embodied a contradiction in the story line. Rejecting Richmond society and her family's place in it, she had journeyed to Newton to break the bonds. And, yet, now, with marriage and motherhood looming, she seemed to be wrapping herself in the coils of Richmond's most traditional society. Adam saw this divide, but couldn't comprehend.

The urgency to button everything up had more to do with getting a wedding invitation out before word of pregnancy leaked around town than with Mariah's need to return for Fall semester. Adam rewound the story as he had done over and over again since late Summer, each time hoping for new insight. How did I get myself into this? Wasn't I terrified over precisely this outcome? Why am I marrying her? Love? Yes, but not in every way. I'm seeing things I dislike. Like her incessant drive to have it her way. Patience, acceptance, tolerance, and kindness aren't in her vocabulary. Would I marry her if she weren't with child? But why do I repeat this story? If the "right thing to do" is marriage, then I am compelled to go ahead with it. But why? Is it my genes, my sense of what Father would expect of me? I don't believe I could not go through with it. It all turns on what's the "right thing to do." The rabbit in the hat. But who decides what's right? Mariah declared it so, even before I had thought it through for myself. What about Rachel? She claimed marriage was just a societal device for enabling one who's responsible for creating a new life to discharge the nurturing responsibility that follows. Not the only device. One could pay for someone else to raise the child. Or place the child in an orphanage or arrange for an adoption. I alone am Father to the child. That's why, if Mariah happened to be pregnant by someone else, marriage would not be the only "right thing to do." But suppose I had been exquisitely careful but, breaking our bond, Mariah had been careless and it was her carelessness that caused the pregnancy. What then? Not so black-and-white. But, I can hear my torts professor intoning, one who engages in an activity rife with life-creating potential should be held to have assumed the risk of precisely that outcome, regardless of which partner was more directly accountable. I'm onto something. Playing with a pistol is inherently dangerous and, if an accident occurs, the actor's not relieved of responsibility just because he didn't load the weapon. Free will doesn't mean one can do whatever one wants. As life is lived, as choices are made, as certain roads are taken while others are not, free will becomes more and more circumscribed until one day the only choice is simply whether to live another day or not. It's like living the Darwinian chart of ancestors backwards.

I'm boxed in by fortune, whether brought about by my own actions or those of Mariah. It's my life, the only one I have to live, and I've stumbled into my worst nightmare. But, who's to say that Mariah will turn out to be any worse a wife and mother than another woman I might have found in the exercise of free will. Better to call it the apparent exercise of free will, for even without the driving tailwind of pregnancy, there would no doubt be other constraining factors, recognized or not. Isn't this possibility the joker in the card deck? I don't know. How little I know about anything I do when I do it, especially anything fraught with life-bending potential.

We change and others change around us, sometimes driven by our change, sometimes not, sometimes by exogenous events, sometimes not. And all at all times unknown and unknowable. And, yet, how certain we can be, of causes and effects, of motivations and beliefs, of outcomes. How absurd we are. What a grand and glorious joke God plays on us. Or, if God is missing, what, in the exercise of free will, an equally grand and glorious joke we play on ourselves.

It took all of Mariah's stay in Richmond for Adam to recover, at least physically. Mariah's frequent, unscheduled calls to report on doings at the Massie household, if not linked by objective evidence to the slowness of his recovery became the procuring cause in Adam's feverish head. Her calls exuded a certain focused gaiety, focused, that is, solely on the self, and without a hint of self-consciousness. To Adam, each call seemed like the beginning of a new game in a tennis match that Mariah was playing to the applause of an unseen crowd. He came to dread her calls.

Over these nights, Adam had more than one dream about the wedding. The theme was always the same. Having been drilled in the customs of Richmond society and the process and protocol expected of those who would seek its grace in matrimony, Mariah and her mother would stand over Adam, testing his mastery of the details.

"At the bridal dinner, dancing?"

"No," Adam responded, "but plenty of dancing at the wedding reception. Toasts, poems and songs perhaps, verbal cleverness, with Benno as the emcee."

"Where are the wedding presents?"

"In your house, a room near the garden, where the reception tent will be pitched. A dedicated room you call the Wedding Present Room, with rented tables covered in white damask tablecloths and displaying presents, each with the giver's visiting card."

"Bravo, Adam," Mrs. Massie fairly shouted in his ear. "Now, tell us about the bride's dress."

It was always the same. Two correct answers followed by paralysis and failure. He couldn't remember a thing about Mariah's dress.

"Remind me," he said, all sheepish and ashamed.

"Adam, it's coming from Montaldo's of course, with the Brussels lace veil worn by my grandmother and re-designed by Montaldo's top hat person. How could you forget that?" hissed Mariah, making a loud, repulsive sound like that of the off-key Good Humor truck that would often rescue Adam from these turbulent slumbers.

In time for the start of classes, Mariah returned to Newton triumphant. After weeks of skirmishing with her mother by letter and telephone, her trip to Richmond gave opportunity for close-in combat, a duel where brainpower was the chosen weapon and endurance the winning game. Surrender occurred three days after Mariah's arrival, the tipping point coming when her mother gave up on the menu for the bridal dinner. From that moment forward, decisions came easily and with confidence. To an acute observer, it might have appeared that this seminary student had spent time in leadership training at Harvard's famed business school.

For Adam, something was changing in their relationship. Something connected to the pregnancy but extending beyond. Mariah wanted to resume lovemaking; indeed, immediately upon her reunion with Adam, she seemed positively bewitched by the idea of sharing Adam's member with the fetus growing within. The thought was repellent to Adam, and so too even the idea of intercourse with a woman in the family way.

Adam struggled to understand his feelings toward Mariah, to tease apart the old feelings of love from the newer ones that had come to mind with the planning process for marriage and then advanced as that work progressed. He had the sense that Mariah had completed much more than wedding plans. She had her man, check. She was with child, check. The meals, music and minister, the sundry suppliers, servers, cooks and attendants, all were booked, check. The invitation drafted and mailing list complete, check. Marriage was like the "closing" of a financial trans-action. When all was in readiness it was time to move on to the next big thing, which in Mariah's case was finding a way, despite the change in circumstance, to help Huey Long.

For Adam, marriage was a foreign land, seen "through a glass, darkly," as Paul put it to the Corinthians. He would soon follow his con-science into that *terra incognita*, come "face-to-face" with it but only as the beginning of what he still hoped, with faith in the future, would grow into a mature love for his wife. But, sadly, he now felt left behind by Mariah, for whom love was more noun than verb.

In the 18th week Mariah noticed some weight loss. It gladdened her heart, for she had become a cautious eater, hoping through diet control to lessen the difficulty of childbirth. The pleasure was short-lived. Within days, she began to experience contractions. Their frequency increased to, perhaps, one every 15 to 20 minutes. In the beginning there was pain. Then much more pain. Followed by bleeding. Despite her thoroughness in most things personal, she had made no inquiry regarding miscarriage Of course, she didn't need medical advice to fear what was happening.

By the time she saw a doctor, the pregnancy was over. Adam was clueless. With surprise, he noticed that Mariah had dropped the demand for sex. He concluded she had, at last, and in good spirits, accepted his point of view, an uncommon event but one, he hoped, might be a promising augury of things to come.

Without sex, Adam had no occasion to feel or even see the growing curve of Mariah's tummy, the pressure evident on her belly button or the rewarding enlargement of her breasts. Lacking these sightings, he had failed to notice the more recent changes that were occurring. The day for mailing the wedding invitations was at hand, and still he was in the dark. By coincidence, that morning he had visited his internist for the regular tri-annual checkup. The internist's office was shared with other doctors, including Mariah's obstetrician. On his way out, Adam passed the desk of the new receptionist, an inexperienced woman bent on ingratiating herself with patients. She offered condolence. He had never seen the woman and couldn't imagine what she was whimpering about. "The good news, Mr. Murdock, is the D&C went beautifully; you'll have many more times at bat, as one might say, Ha, ha."

Adam was on the verge of giving the receptionist a piece of his mind for jabbering so incoherently when her meaning hit him — a thunderbolt from a cloudless sky. To make sure, he lifted a medical dictionary from his doctor's bookshelf to look up D&C.

Adam's mind raced during his walk to Mariah's apartment. Feelings of despair and relief were flying around, bumping into each other, creating a new feeling of guilt. *The heartbeats of our infant stopped. Our* babe lost. Marriage postponed. Everything on the table again. Why did this happen? Why didn't she tell me? Wasn't she devastated? Forget why. How could she have hidden such a thing? Was she ashamed? Am I just clueless or was she masterfully clever at concealment? Or what? And how about the wedding invitations? Were they to go out without my knowledge of what, quite literally, was a life-changing event? If so, what sort of trust was this?

He found her on the phone to her mother, issuing last-minute instructions about the invitation list. Not given to rage, a part of him stood apart, astonished by the emotions bubbling up from inside.

"I must talk with you, Mariah."

Mariah waved him away.

"Now, please." His face burned with frustration.

Again, she waved him off.

He yanked the wire free from its baseboard connection. Mariah saw it dangling from the phone's cradle. The receiver she still held to her ear was dead.

"You've had a miscarriage."

"That new receptionist. She must have said something. Right?" Her tone prideful.

Adam stared at her. "Why didn't you tell me?"

"Oh, Adam," she said, sweet but not cloying. "To spare you pain, of course. And, you'll understand, it's a private matter for me and my doctor. I'd have let you know soon enough. And we can try again. My doctor says there's nothing to prevent a successful one next time. "

Adam couldn't read his wife-to-be. Many possibilities. Was she tormented by the miscarriage, to the point of not thinking clearly? Covering a sense of shame with bravado? Perhaps, for much the same reason he felt blocked from telling his Father of the forthcoming marriage, Mariah couldn't tell him about her changed condition. Could she really think it a matter so private, so trivial to their relationship, that informing him could await full recovery. Or was she afraid that he might abandon her on the threshold of marriage. He understood that possibility. If marriage was "the right thing to do" upon her becoming pregnant, wasn't it no longer the "right thing to do" when pregnancy ceased to exist?

He needed time to plumb her mind. But not that alone. He must plunge deeply into his own head, and his heart too, to search out where values reside, where scales are found for weighing virtues that compete, self-definitions that contradict, the defining essences of the life one aspires to live. The stream of life flows on, leaving behind the indelible record of one's behavior at each point along the way, without the slightest chance of second thoughts, course corrections or makeovers. He had to get this one right. What appeared simple to her was complicated for him. Exhaustingly so.

"Mariah, we need some time to think, and to talk this over. Until we do, the invitations should not go out." Adam saw Mariah flinch like a fighter absorbing a blow and then, turning defiant, strike back.

"The wedding's set. No reason to change the mailing schedule, unless you want to undo all that we've worked so long and hard to accomplish. You could think on this for a week and still your conscience wouldn't allow you to alter our plans. Given my family and all those others in Richmond who have acted on our decision, that's impossible. I miscarry and you abort. Unthinkable." Mariah held him in a wild and wide-eyed stare.

It was Adam's turn to flinch. He was slow to respond, breaking away to examine the floor while collecting his thoughts. When finally he spoke, it was slow and deliberate.

"Our marriage, to deserve the name, must be entered freely on both sides. This is a big deal. We need time to reflect. You control the levers for mailing. How you use them will, willy-nilly, affect us. Please, Mariah, weigh very carefully the choice of a delayed single mailing against the possible need for a second one. On this point, it might be wise to consult your mother."

Following the miscarriage, Mariah's mother regained the upper hand in their lifelong duel. The invitations were dumped in the waste basket. And, at her urging, Mariah accepted Adam's proposal to put their relationship on hold, or, as he put it, "in a lock-box at Cambridge Trust" for the remainder of the academic year and through the Summer.

"Think of it as a time out, what football teams do under stress," Adam said. "Let's test ourselves with freedom from commitment for a few months. Convene in the Fall and compare notes. See where it leads."

In fact, she and Adam had not really come to grips with the fallout from his decision. Whatever "time out" meant to Adam, for Mariah it didn't mean they would not marry or that they would no longer engage the two sides of their lives together, whether in combat or under the covers.

Mariah was not one to pout or sit despondently licking her wounds. Many girls can't even get pregnant, she thought. I got there on the first try. If the fetus had been ok, it wouldn't have aborted. We were blessed. There will be many more chances to come.

Let go the past; seize the present, plan the future — her coat of arms.

She accepted the senator's request that she rejoin his merry band for the remaining weeks of Summer, and longer if she could arrange it. In place of the awkwardness of being a mother at the altar, Mariah now only needed to explain why a long-planned marriage had been called off. In Richmond, the word offered was simply a newfound freedom for the lovebirds to finish their studies before getting hitched. It went forth without fanfare, as if this result had always been there — as if those detailed wedding plans had been just an enjoyable exercise, a rehearsal for a show that insiders knew all along might not open on the original schedule.

To those surrounding her in the senator's office that Summer, recovery from this jolt seemed swift and complete. She seemed to shoo the whole thing off like a horse swats flies.

For Adam, the relationship was all topsy-turvy, something he knew would take time to sort out, to tease apart the jumble of emotions crowding his mind. Father always insisted one remount immediately after being thrown from a horse. And he always did. Now, the thought occupying his mind was whether he should follow Father's advice with respect to this particular horse, or putting pride aside, just move on.

Mariah's assignment that Summer was to help Huey Long with *Every Man a King*, the autobiography he had been working on intermittently for over a year. Mariah knew how to use the English language. She had a reporter's instinct for getting the full story. And she had the drive to take on and complete a project like this, one Huey had found easy to put aside. Helping the senator with his book project, she discovered, called upon a different skill, one she had often practiced growing up. Remarkably for one attending a theological seminary, she found it easy to subjugate other values to the supremacy of ends justifying means. This was an idea essential to the book. She had to leave behind not just her refined literary skills and zeal for the whole story but, ultimately, outside the deeply personal realm, her belief in telling the truth.

As she explained to Adam in a letter posted in mid-July, "With warts and all, I accept him as our vehicle for redistribution of the wealth. That's his goal. It's mine too, and was, even before I met him. It was the cause that, naively perhaps, brought me to Newton. Now it summons my best thinking to present the Huey Long story in its most favorable light. This book will not lie. Not outright. But neither will it try for Athenian balance. To spread zeal for wealth redistribution, we must rally around the heroic farmer who is trying to plant that seed across the land. And do so at whatever cost. I'm pretty excited about *Every Man a King*. It's going to work."

Being lodged cheek by jowl with the senator over the Summer of 1933 meant for Mariah early access to the flow of his increasingly incendiary attacks on the New Deal juggernaut that FDR was deploying on Capitol Hill in the first hundred days. She wasted no time in adopting the senator's colors.

When her boss denounced FDR's keystone program, the National Industrial Recovery Act, not for its public-works expenditures, which he supported, but for the system of wage and price codes, Mariah laid out her boss' critique in a letter to Adam, ignoring the pain her support for the Kingfish would cause. She knew Adam found it difficult to keep the emotional part of his relationship with her separate from, and unaffected by, their political differences. And, yet, confident she could get away with embracing both senator and student without loss, she blew caution away.

Huey's attack on the NIRA wasn't crazy. He predicted that FDR's codes would be written by the leaders of the industries sought to be regulated, becoming a Government-sponsored excuse for price-fixing and cartelization, with the result that large interests would drive small ones out of business. Mariah claimed to Adam that time would prove him right. As things turned out, it did.

She reported to Adam when Long took aim at many of FDR's appointees, who by his lights had been summoned to high office despite having been prominent pigs feasting at the trough of a financial system that brought the country to its knees. He called Lewis Douglas, the conservative director of the budget, a "tool of the financial interests." He claimed that Hugh Johnson, the first director of the National Recovery Administration, was "linked in a corrupt alliance with spokesmen for the major banks." And most damning of all, he denounced William H. Woodin, the President's choice for Secretary of the Treasury, as being "mired with the mud of Wall Street and the House of Morgan."

Here, of course, he had the benefit of learning, through Pecora's dramatic inquiry, that Woodin had been among the preferred clients of the House of Morgan and, despite great wealth accumulated as President of American Car and Foundry Company, had accepted its *douceur.* "Doesn't the President know," the senator had blurted out to Mariah as he fumed over appointments, "that servitude to the House of Morgan, even with padding for the golden chains, will still be servitude? Freedom's one of those things that's absolute or nothing."

Mariah recalled Adam's delight over FDR's promise, before taking office, that his would be a "radical" cabinet, that there would be no one in it who knew the way to 23 Wall Street, no one linked in any way with the power trust or with the international bankers. At the time, she, too, had taken great comfort in this pledge and even participated in writing Adam's long, post-election letter to his Father claiming, with apparent justification, that FDR was going to be different.

The temptation to call out Adam as hopelessly naïve in believing FDR's claim was too delicious to avoid, even though she knew he would take it badly. With Mariah, winning was everything. It seems she had never learned that sometimes it's better to hide rather than flaunt one's brilliance.

Her letter to Adam recounting all these things began with an under-scored quote from a speech the senator had delivered in the Senate, where it had resonated deep in the marrow of that body:

> Despite campaign promises solemnly given, despite daily remind-ers of the squalid ethics, abuse of trust and other outrages to common decency inflicted upon the people of this country by men who had been our financial leaders, our President has wel-comed the money-changers back to the temple.

"How could this be happening?" she challenged Adam to explain, before ending the letter with another quote:

> No, I will not participate in the Democratic victory tonight. I do not care for my share in a victory that means that the poor and downtrodden, the blind, the helpless, the orphaned, the bleed-ing, the wounded, the hungry and the distressed, will be the victims.

"I know you think my man, Huey, is a charlatan, but in charging FDR with hypocrisy, he's nailed your man, dead to rights."

Adam reacted to Mariah's screed with resignation born of expe-rience. Of course, she was right. Adam had no explanation for FDR's behavior. News of his pick of Woodin came like a rabbit punch. And then, his Father piled on with a letter of his own, crowing about FDR's choice for Treasury, calling it a miracle bestowed on the right-minded of the country, a moment when the President honored his Grotonian roots to assure continuity of experience and skill in Government.

Adam was surprised to find, enclosed with Dan's letter, one to Dan from Bill White, written before any of FDR's appointments were made. It lamented the tone of business leaders who caused the nation's downfall and expressed the hope that FDR would do better in picking his cabinet. Dan told Adam that he was absolutely certain that Woodin would get three cheers of approval from his friend. Adam sat down to give the always sensible words of Bill White a careful read.

Dear Dan:

I hope you won't think me too proud in defining myself, in small ways, as a practitioner of what I firmly believe is the best American trait, that being "intelligent discontent." We have much to be discontented over, but what has increasingly been attracting my notice are the findings of the Pecora hearings.

Some wise wag once said a great city should be judged not by its numbers but by its great men. I like that idea, and tragically, it turns out, apply it to that great 'city' of finance, Wall Street. Where's the tragedy I hear you ask. It's plumb in our faces if we weren't such dumb bunnies as to ignore the Pecora record.

The Wall Street gang keeps trying to sell the country on the idea of one or two "bad apples" in an otherwise commendable barrel full of leading men, outstanding characters befitting their self-assumed role as masters of the universe. With almost plodding deliberation, Pecora keeps throwing this nonsense back in their faces. He's right. The rot runs riot up and down that famous street. Here's just one of any number of stories that make the point.

We know Samuel Insull, Chicago-based builder of a utilities empire, was brought down last year, after trying desperately to save his crumbling estate through new loans and other astounding shenanigans. After resigning his eighty-five directorships, sixty-five chairmanships and eleven presidencies, he departed for Europe. Here's what *The New York Times,* that famous molder of elite opinion, had to say as he left our shores:

"Mr. Insull fell, not because his ideals were wrong, but because of his persistent optimism…. He stands withal as one of the foremost and greatest builders of American industrial empires."

Within months, a Cook County grand jury had indicted Insull for embezzlement. The slender threads holding in place the gross fiction of his life, as depicted by the *Times,* broke. By coded telegrams, his lawyers advised him to seek refuge beyond extradition in Greece.

And, now, dear friend, I come to the point. Insull couldn't grasp the cause and effect of the shambles he'd made of his life. "Why am I not more popular in the United States?" he asked. "What have I done that every banker and business magnate has not done in the course of business?"

In those words, Insull didn't merely convict himself, he convicted an entire class of American leaders. Therein lies the problem we face, the problem I hope our new President will confront in every way he can. For the true significance of Samuel Insull's career lies in the fact that his sins were commonplace rather than exceptional.

Weather's turning nippy. Hope all's well in town and up in the Flint Hills. How I long to be with you for a gallop on one of your cow ponies. I can feel the wind and see the sun flashing in the blue stem as we thunder through. Be good.

Bill

P.S. Please share this with that law student son of yours.

Adam had trouble imagining how his Father could conceivably conclude from Bill White's letter that Bill would find Woodin's background compatible with what the country needed, rather than just a continuation of the abominable practice of putting in positions of immense power those who got us deep in trouble. Evidence of his Father's blindness to reality continued to mount. Adam likened him to an old cannon loose on the deck in a storm. Thank God, he thought, it would never be the ship of state. Alas, none of this helped Adam address Mariah's challenge to his beloved President's choice for Treasury. Apparently, to "contain multitudes" in the political sphere means to indulge all manner of conflicting interests.

The Summer proved difficult for the Kingfish, and the turbulence he kept stirring up was felt by all his troops. Most damaging was an incident at a party held at a country club in Sands Beach, Long Island. Mariah had gone with the senator on a brief Summer visit to New York. She couldn't avoid noticing a change in his mien since working with him in Arkansas the Summer before. His lifestyle had become more loose, flamboyant and bizarrely risky to himself and those around him. Or so she believed, keeping that thought to herself.

At the party he quickly consumed alcohol in amounts even excessive by his standards. He worked the tables with tipsy exuberance, flirted with the women and backslapped the men. Mariah saw him suddenly turn away from the dining room, look imploringly at her and then wheel around in the direction she pointed to make a dash for the bathroom. Among his staff he was known to be chronically late in acknowledging the demands of his plumbing. When he returned, he had a bleeding and badly swollen eye. Mariah fetched a handkerchief from her purse and moved to dab the flow of blood. The senator brushed her away, declaring, "It's nothing. Get our things and round up the troops, we're leaving."

They exited without a word, returning to New York City. As to how his face got messed up, Huey had nothing to say. The press was all over the mystery like hornets whose nest had been kicked like a soccer ball. The most reliable reports claimed that the Kingfish, finding all urinals occupied, had tried to relieve himself between the legs of a big man in front of him, whose trousers were soaked in the experiment.

With swiftness, Huey developed an alternative account, getting it out through his powerful publicity machine. At first his story of being attacked by dark forces in the men's room was too vague as to persons and motives to be believed, even by those inclined toward the senator. With no anchor of truth to constrain her, Mariah imagined a more specific story.

"Why not tie the attack to J.P. Morgan," she offered. "They're the central seat of concentrated wealth in the country and, as such, the most threatened by your redistribution program." The senator jumped to his feet, shouting "You've got it, Mariah. Once more into the breach you go." He smothered her with hugs. In no time the senator's public relations team was hard at work circulating the story that "hit men hired by the House of Morgan had tried to eliminate the nation's most powerful threat to financial oligarchy."

As the incident grew in notoriety, the senator considered addressing it in his autobiography, then nearing completion. He consulted Mariah and others. She was at a loss. If included, it would have to come somewhere at the end of the story. Not exactly a high point to finish with, she thought.

"I'd just ignore it. Your last chapter sets out the Long Plan for redistributing the wealth, ending with references to those — like Jefferson, Jackson, Webster, Teddy Roosevelt and Bryan — in whose footsteps you follow with the banner of *Every Man a King*. From this 'Valhalla', as you call it, how could you descend into the gutter to speak like a journalist about Sands Beach?"

"Listen here Mariah. It's my story, not yours. You've grown too attached. Pride of authorship and such. It'll end where and how I say."

Mariah backed off, but not down. Remarkably, Huey compromised. It would come at the end, but not as a final chapter. To Mariah's dismay, it would take the form of an open letter from the senator to Al Capone, addressed to him at the Penitentiary in Atlanta. It would appear under the heading *Incidental Publicity*, with a subtitle of *J.P. Morgan & Company Points Way for Capone's Release.* In it, Huey would claim that *Collier's Weekly,* owned by Morgan, was taking contributions to give to the unknown criminals who assaulted the senator. The letter would urge Capone to claim the money.

For the first time since starting her odyssey with the Kingfish, Mariah was embarrassed. This was too much. She tried to rescue the book and its author from appearing absurd. No dice. Mariah saw in this ridiculous coda to an otherwise worthy autobiography a sad truth about the man not otherwise found in the book. He could play the clown with absolutely no awareness of how hurtful his childish behavior would be to his noble aims. Beyond embarrassment was sorrow. He had crushed her high hopes for change against the rocks of self-deceit.

Mariah finished her work on *Every Man a King* in early September. After what seemed a quick final review by the senator, she put the manuscript safely in the hands of the publisher, the National Book Company of New Orleans, a property of the senator and some associates, with the release date set for October, just three weeks from submission. An initial printing of 50,000 copies was planned. Three hundred review copies were sent out. Circulars were mailed to bookstores and rental libraries all over the country.

When the review copies were in hand, Mariah sent one, autographed by the senator, to Adam. Holding his nose while admiring Mariah's skill in capturing the special dialect of her boss and writing what his legal training and experience told him was a brief of gargantuan exaggerations, omissions and refractions of fact, he read the book. It was a paean of piety and praise for this selfless soul who bent every effort to aid, succor and protect the common people of America. It was bound in a resplendent gold jacket bearing five pictures of the senator. It was priced at one dollar. After selling 20,000 copies, Huey ordered the remainder given away.

The reviews came out shortly after Mariah had returned to Newton. She read them with relief. No comment on the coda. With a chuckle, she imagined that the reviewers might never have gotten that far. In their sneering critiques, the reviewers had missed the whole purpose of the exercise. She was proudest of the comment in *The New York Times Book Review* stating: "There is hardly a law of English usage or a rule of English grammar that its author does not break somewhere."

With uncommon zeal, Mariah wanted Adam's reaction to the book. She had already imagined his appreciation for the voice her writing had achieved. They had gotten together over coffee in a shop on Brattle Street.

"Adam, that was high praise from atop the priesthood," she said, beside herself with pleasure. "And the truth of that claim would change not a whit if the gray lady's reviewer had been informed enough to insert the adverb 'knowingly' in front of the verb 'break.' I hope you admired my touch."

Adam's mind was filled with the dangers to the country he saw in her mentor. *Every Man a King* would heighten those dangers. And here, facing him with chirping pride of authorship, was a woman he had almost married, a woman who expected that marriage to occur, a woman seemingly oblivious of the pain her conduct with Huey caused him. He took recourse in a false smile of approval and silence.

———◆———

A stunning change came over the senator as the Winter months of 1934 turned to Spring and early Summer. He gave up drinking. He gave up nightclubs. And through rigorous dieting, he gave up more than 30 pounds. It was obvious to Mariah that Sands Point had been a galvanizing event for the Kingfish, a rare moment of shame, when ridicule and laughter over his bizarre behavior brought near panic, then firm resolution. His ambition had never wavered, but the ways and means for carrying it forward had been foolish. He had failed. He would change. And, that Summer, as Mariah saw up close, day to day, he did.

Increasingly, he was using the radio to reach millions of Americans across the country. He enlisted Mariah to help with his addresses. She was particularly involved with preparation for a speech titled *"Every Man a King,"* to be delivered over the National Broadcasting System. It would advance the senator's new political organization: the *Share Our Wealth Society,* open to all and consisting of a nationwide system of local clubs. It would describe the basic problem with the country, a problem simple to describe and simple to fix. It was Mariah's delight to put the senator's thoughts into words. What Adam thought to be her good luck in playing this role, having come to Newton precisely to advance her cause for redistribution and then being allowed to yoke her cause to his, was, to Mariah, her grand destiny. Here's how she crafted the crux of the matter:

> The nation's wealth is abundant but limited. Each citizen has a basic right to a decent share of that wealth. But the Government has allowed a few rich men to own so large a proportion of that wealth that there is not enough left for all the others. To fix this problem, all one needs to do is redistribute the wealth, which divided equally comes to about $15,000 per family. We won't guarantee equality. But we will guarantee a minimum family wealth of $5,000, enough for a home, an automobile, a radio, and the ordinary conveniences, and the opportunity to educate their children. And, thereafter, we will guarantee to that family a fair share of the income of this land so there will be no such thing as merely the select having those things, and so there will be no such thing as a family living in poverty and distress.

Mariah exchanged letters with Adam after the speech had been given, sending him a copy. He read it with care and a fair-mindedness that surprised him. "I'm aware," he wrote back, "that many critics have denounced Huey's *Share Our Wealth* movement as nothing more than cynical, backwoods demagoguery that panders to the ignorance and prejudice of our populace. It's easy to say those things, and I feel somewhat the same way. However, I see what he's about as addressing a fundamental issue that the country faces today. Excessive concentration of wealth is our central dilemma. It accounts for the insufficient distribution of purchasing power among the people, a principal cause of our depression. His solution may be totally impractical — on this point I just read somewhere that he admitted the need 'to call in some great minds to help me' — but he's on to something basic and appealing to the people. The White House should take it seriously."

Mariah stayed with the senator until September, when she returned to Newton to finish her last year, graduating in June 1935 around the same time Adam graduated from law school. She had seen him only occasionally, and only during daylight hours for coffee, since they put things on hold, although their correspondence had preserved one of the two big elements of what Mariah doggedly thought of as their continuing relationship.

Once their Fall semesters began, lunches at Hazen's replaced letter writing. Their intellectual affair waxed as the months passed. Mariah's initial edge in verbal combat began to erode as Adam continued to be exposed to the animating laws of the country and the caldron of new ideas stirred up on Capitol Hill. The other part of their relationship, put on ice by Adam following the miscarriage, remained there, despite Mariah's efforts, throughout the Fall, to melt the ice away.

In their first academic year together, each part of the relationship, though kept in a watertight compartment, had seemed to gather strength from the other. Now, it seemed, as their intellectual engagement deepened, it served for Adam as a barrier to carnal desire, or even emotional intimacy. And he took advantage of this barrier, hiding behind it, fearing, as he finally admitted to himself, that any physical contact with Mariah would put him on a slope too slippery to resist.

From reading *Of Human Bondage* in high school, Adam retained a haunting image of Mildred Rogers, the cold, tawdry waitress for whom Maugham's protagonist, Philip Carey, develops a sexual infatuation. At the time, Carey's behavior puzzled Adam. Now, in trying to understand his feelings, he drew rough parallels between himself and Philip Carey, between Mariah and Mildred. Absurdly rough, he knew, but the association was planted in his head. Seeing Bette Davis in the film version that Fall, with Leslie Howard as Philip, fertilized the thought.

For as long as he could contain the dormant passion for this woman, he would police their relationship, assuring that they were workmates, not playmates.

Early in January, they had gotten together to discuss FDR's State of the Union address, presented on the 4th to overwhelming Democratic majorities in both houses — the surprising result of midterm elections. In particular, Adam wanted to defend FDR's call for a "single new and greatly enlarged" work program, a call he was sure Mariah would reject. He brought a transcript of the speech to the table at Hazen's. After they were seated, and Hazel had taken their order, so unvarying that she needn't have bothered, and wouldn't have but for the glasses of water, Adam handed Mariah the speech.

"Have a look at what he said. It's not long, took me five minutes or so, and you're a much faster reader than I." Adam smiled, a look of embarrassment crossing his face at this puny effort to cage her.

"How many times have you said that? Of course, you believe no one can read at my speed and comprehend. You believe I miss things that, plodding along, you catch. Your conceit, Adam. And risk."

Soup of the day was black bean. Too hot to touch. "I'll have this read before the soup cools," Mariah boasted, lowering her head to engage the President's prose, pencil in hand. The soup still steamed when she put down the last page.

"I've marked the two big messages in this thing. One of them, coming straight from the Kingfish, I like. Of course, it would be too much to expect the President to credit Huey for having gotten there first. Which, the record shows, he did. The other, well, you know where I stand on FDR's work program."

"Ok. Start with the good stuff."

"He's adopted the senator's passion for social justice. It's woven throughout, but particularly in these passages:

In spite of our efforts and in spite of our talk, we have not weeded out the over-privileged and we have not effectively lifted up the under-privileged. Both of these manifestations of injustice have retarded happiness.

"And this:

We have, however, a clear mandate from the people, that Americans must forswear that conception of the acquisition of wealth which, through excessive profits, creates undue private power over private affairs and, to our misfortune, over public affairs as well. We continue to recognize the greater ability of some to earn more than others. But we do assert that the ambition of the individual to obtain for him and his a proper security, a reasonable leisure, and a decent living throughout life, is an ambition to be preferred to the appetite for great wealth and great power.

"He's not as clear or strong as the Kingfish, but he sure seems to be pushing for Government interference with private affairs to 'weed out' the overprivileged. It's a stealthy way to advance Huey's *Share the Wealth Plan*."

"You may be right," Adam acknowledged. "I see the thread of social justice running through it all."

"But he overpromises. Over the top. As you know better than anyone, I'm not naturally a good woman but I have been scared to death so many times — personally and vicariously through the Kingfish — that I have learned, regretfully, sadly and often, that honesty is the best policy."

Again, for the thousandth time, Adam couldn't help admiring Mariah's tough-fibered brain and skill with words — a kind of verbal carpentry. He was less admiring of her self-deception. Did she really think she practiced honesty? Like most of us, he realized, she isn't what she thinks she is.

"I wish you were as sharp on the substance of policy as you are in debating it." Adam was smiling.

"Now, let's talk about putting men to work."

"Adam, yes, let's, but first I'm going to cross wires on you by posing this question: Why is it, since we've returned to Cambridge, you've gone so far out of your way to avoid what you once called my 'physical charms'? Remember calling them 'devastating and irresistible'? Remember telling me you could never get enough? Why won't you renew that physical connection? Looking in the mirror, I detect little change. But you've changed. What's going on in that studious, mid-western head of yours?"

Adam recoiled in surprise. Had he been so transparent?

"When we first met, I was terribly young. Rachel thought I was very slow at college. When I left for law school, she cautioned that I was 'full of sap and ripe for some girl.' She quoted a Kansas quip about the inexperienced male. 'A girl had only to spread her apron and shake the cottonwood tree and he would fall into it.' And she was right. But then, after our close encounter with marriage and a baby, I felt suddenly old. You spoke just now of being scared to death. Well, the events of last year scared me that way. I lost control. We both paid a big price. I resolved, above all else, to take control of my life and hold onto it. If to do so, like a priest, I had to avoid carnal pleasures, so be it. That's the story, as best I can read my feelings, which at times like this isn't all that well."

"I think you're selling yourself short. To mix a metaphor, you don't need such a short leash."

"Not with every woman. No. But you're different. Used to getting your way. Practiced in it and skilled. And insistent. You frightened me once. I won't risk being frightened again."

It was Mariah's turn to recoil. Knowing exactly what he meant, and agreeing with it, did not make acceptance of his resolve any easier. Mariah wasn't bruised easily. From childhood days, she had refused to exploit others by playing the hurt feelings game. She wouldn't start now, even though his candor landed some well-aimed blows. Blows to what? Not her pride in who she was. Not to her determination, which was only strengthened by his story. They were just like hits one takes in football, momentarily jarring, even painful, but just part of a game one plays to win.

"Thanks for that, Adam. I understand. I can be patient — as well as provocative and unpredictable. Now, about FDR's jobs program." She picked up the long dill pickle beside her tuna fish and cheddar cheese sandwich, looked hard at Adam, locking his eyes to hers, then moved the pickle in and out of her mouth a couple of times before biting it in half.

As if it were a shield, Adam held up the President's text.

"Yes, moving right along. Here's what he says:

The lessons of history, confirmed by the evidence immediately before me, show conclusively that continued dependence upon relief induces a spiritual and moral disintegration fundamentally destructive to the national fibre. To dole out relief in this way is to administer a narcotic, a subtle destroyer of the human spirit. It is inimical to the dictates of sound policy, it is in violation of the traditions of America. Work must be found for able-bodied but destitute workers.

"He's going to take three and a half million off relief and put them to work. A bold ambition, and worthy, won't you agree?"

"Adam, you know me. I'm not moved by platitudes. Everything he says about relief destroying self-respect, self-reliance, courage, determination, and so on, I embrace with enthusiasm. But, I can't buy the sharp distinction he makes between relief through cash to buy food and relief through a make-work job that pays for the same things. Two forms of narcotic. And he goes on to expect the Government, as a regular matter and not just for emergencies, to provide unemployment insurance. Why isn't that precisely the sort of relief he so eloquently condemns?"

"He's talking about real work, not shovel-leaning stuff. As for unemployment insurance, I assume he's talking about a short period. You know. Breathing space to find a job. Anyway, we both want Government to set policy that interferes with private ordering. Our difference is over what policies we like."

7

ONE MORNING, WHEN DAN WAS walking his coal black cocker spaniel along Humboldt Street, he passed the Bernstein house just as Rachel emerged. She hurried down to the sidewalk, lest he escape.

"Dan, I've wanted to talk with you about Wyandot."

Dan flinched, coloring across his face. Recovering, he said in a breezy way, "Good morning, Rachel. May I ask how'd you hear about that?"

"Yes, good morning. Why, I'm sure you know it's the talk of the town, for days now. I wondered how you and your sons were coping? I know you kept the farm. I mean the fallout. And I'd like to catch up on those boys too. Would you come for tea this afternoon?"

"Why, that's downright good of you to offer. But why not come to my house for tea.?" I have some freshly made cakes. We can give them a try. It'd be a shame to eat them alone. You know something? It's long past time since I invited you to see the inside of my house. Will four suit your schedule?"

"Perfectly, Dan. I'll be there."

Rachel liked to be punctual. Dan expected she would be and, on opening the front door, noticed she was carefully made-up and had changed into a cocktail dress cinched tight at the waist with a neckline that defined the point at which a sufficient cleavage began.

Dan's observant eye was equaled by Rachel's, who saw that Dan had shaved away the stubble evident in the morning and, judging by all the rest that showed, had scrubbed himself clean. He wore a checkered Harris Tweed sport coat with leather buttons and elbow pads, showing years of use. A blue bandana had been stuffed in the lapel pocket. He emitted the fresh smell of Old Spice. The house retained the musty odor of horse and tobacco.

They settled down in Dan's study, where the maid had arranged on a large silver tray the necessaries for tea and two well-iced cakes, one chocolate, the other carrot.

"That foreclosure experience must have been terrible. Tell me how you survived," Rachel said.

"It wasn't much fun. You're right. I wrote Adam. I count myself blessed. Not at the outset, but as things turned out."

"No question. What do you take away from it all, now that some time has passed?"

"No one's asked me that before. Let's see. You know, I couldn't have imagined what an invasion of privacy an event like that causes. My financial situation as well as Wyandot's laid bare. To the whole town. Even more painful, to Adam and Benno."

"Painful, how would you say?"

"You're making this difficult. Painful, that's all. What else is there to say?" Dan sounded a note of irritation. Then he paused, dropping his eyes, which had been held by Rachel's earnest look. "I know what you're looking for. You want me to say how humiliating it was for me to be discovered. To have pretended for so long to be so rich, a scion of the town, and then, in an instant, to be found out — a fraud." Dan dropped his arms, embracing his legs tightly and cried softly.

"Dan, I know in your head, buried somewhere, you imagine yourself a fraud. But it's not true. You have never strutted your wealth. Never tried to show off with money. Never lorded it over those having less. Your pride — not a bad thing by the way — got in the way of your self-perception, leading you to conclude something about yourself that just isn't so. But tell me, did you write your sons about the foreclosure?" Rachel leaned forward in that special way psychiatrists do when they've picked up a scent.

"I don't communicate with Benno. Adam will have passed along my news. He always does." Dan's voice changed with the mention of Benno. Stiff, staccato. He appeared sullen, a contrast to the momentary breakdown.

"That privacy point. I can understand. But there were public things about you in the paper I never knew. Wonderful things, like the years of support you've given to Manhattan Welfare, and the medal of exemplary service to the community that the Masons pinned on you at that dinner in your honor. It all gave a balance to your life — the very conservative side of it, I mean, that you're famous for around Manhattan. And has affected your sons."

"Yes, I suppose your right. A more positive way to think about it. Do you believe my sons see that balance?"

"Do you care?"

"That's funny. I'd say yes and no. I mean I want them to know the whole of me, but at the same time I don't because they might think I'm being inconsistent. What's most important to me is defending my conservative beliefs. But not only that. Bending other minds to embrace them."

"Why haven't you remarried, Dan. It's been two decades and more."

"I bet you could use more tea. And another slice. Here, let me pour."

"I know that's a very personal question, but I have been wanting to know." Rachel caught his eyes and held them. Her smile was natural, calming.

"Wanting! You think just wanting to know excuses you? If that were true there would be no secrets left in this town. It's a question never put to me before. But, ok. Here goes. I never remarried because I never missed being in that state. My life is full. In the beginning, I thought I should remarry quickly, for the twins. But as time passed, and being a single Father seemed to work, of course with a lot of help from nurses, farmhand wives and the like, I realized I could handle the twins, and with just me to influence their characters and values, I'd have an easier time controlling things."

"And female companionship? Don't you miss that at all?"

"You're something, Rachel. I'm surprised you stopped at 'companionship.' Is this a Jewish thing or just your training? I know I don't talk much, ask few personal questions and answer even less. A WASP trait, I suppose. But you're different from me, and from most of the good people in town." Rachel's face clouded.

"Oh, my, was that a booboo? Didn't mean to suggest, to — not a bit — that you weren't a good person. Look, yes, at first, a little. But, and you'd know this too, the less one has something like that around, the less one misses it. What's the expression, 'Out of sight, out of mind.' Like candy. And, now, about you. I never see you and your husband out together. How does your marriage work?"

"Good question. We lead very separate lives, united in caring for Aaron, but otherwise independent."

"With plenty of privacy, I bet. Don't ever get foreclosed on!"

Rachel's answer started something in Dan's mind that hadn't been there for many years. He stared at Rachel with eyes opened wide by a mind considering new possibilities. For the first time he saw Rachel as a woman instead of a Doctor. A woman with earthy appeal.

Even one not trained in Freudian methods would notice a change in the room. The air seemed charged, expectant. Rachel understood and made a decision.

"This has been fun, Dan. Next time, my house. And now I must go." Rachel rose and walked slowly out of Dan's study headed toward the front door. Dan followed. At the door, he put his arms around her waist, turning her to face him, pulling her close. He sought her lips.

"Dan, I think you've mistaken independence for easy ways with sex. A bad bet." She offered her cheek and he took it, letting his arms fall away.

"As you noticed, I'm out of practice," Dan said, a sheepish smile developing across his deeply lined face. Rachel looked at Dan intently.

"I like the lines in your face. They say a lot. They tell me your fore-closure experience was no accident. You earned what you got from the farmers, who could read those lines too. Next time, let's make it for drinks, and a toast to friendship."

8

FROM UNION STATION, ADAM WALKED briskly to the Walker-Johnson Building at 1734 New York Avenue, where the WPA had set up shop. It was a large structure, utterly lacking in character. It appeared bare, hardly used, perhaps even empty. Appearances lie. The WPA was a hurricane of activity, people, mostly young, hugely energetic, coming and going as if bent on the most important mission of a lifetime.

Adam couldn't reckon his chance of getting a job. On the one hand, competition was severe. On the other, here he was, invited by WPA recruiters in Cambridge to be interviewed by Harry Hopkins in Washington. He took the rickety elevator to Mr. Hopkins' office. In the anteroom a secretary greeted him, took his name, turned it over in her mind and said, in the brusque fashion that typified New Dealers, "Why! I just mailed a letter to you from Mr. Baker, thanking you for your interest in the WPA and advising that the position you sought had been filled."

Adam was dumbfounded. "A letter to me? Are you sure? Mr. Carmody, who was interviewing with Mr. Baker, invited me here today to meet Mr. Hopkins. There must be some mistake. May I speak with Mr. Carmody?"

"He's still in Boston. Mr. Baker's word is final. I'm sure they talked. Perhaps you misunderstood." Finality rang in her voice.

Adam was torn between raising a ruckus, as would nine out of ten lawyers, or accepting this woman's edict and keeping his powder dry to fight for a better outcome another day. He was still undecided when Mr. Hopkins burst out of his office through a cloud of cigarette smoke.

"What have we here?" he exclaimed, pointing a long skinny index finger in Adam's direction.

The secretary began to answer. Raising his voice just enough to be heard, Adam said, "I think that question was addressed to me."

He had the administrator's attention. "Go on. Go on then," he said.

Adam told his story. Mr. Hopkins' eyes darted this way and that until Adam had finished.

"We're just getting organized. Obviously, communication within our ranks could be improved. Follow me." He spun around and returned to his office, sitting in a swivel chair behind a desk swept clean but for two overflowing ashtrays. The room was clockless, the walls peeling. Behind the Administrator were large uncurtained windows allowing a fine view of the city.

"Close the door behind you. Coffee? Ok, ask Mildred. Tell her how you take it."

Adam put in the order, closed the door and sat in one of two chairs facing the Administrator's desk.

"Smoke?" He held out a package of Lucky Strikes, which Adam declined. Hopkins lighted up. Adam felt electricity in the room. Examining his host, Adam saw in a smart dark blue suit and pale blue shirt a restless, gangling man. His face was handsome, good-natured and sardonic, with intense brown eyes shining out curiously, or perhaps suspiciously, at the young law student.

"Got a cv for me to look at?"

"Certainly," Adam said, pulling the extra copy he had luckily thought, at the last minute, to bring with him, despite having furnished two copies to Messrs. Baker and Carmody in Langdell the day before. He did so not expecting to hand it out to interviewers but for his own use as an aid to memory of all the things he had said about himself in print.

"Not on the Law Review, I see. You must have dicked around."

"Actually, that's not true. I played in college. Entering law school, I assumed that I could be as good as I wanted to be, that it was just a matter of effort. I would be first. I resolved to work hard, as hard or harder than anyone else. And I did. First year results put me in the top 30%. Not bad, but far below what I expected, given the assumption. I found myself surrounded by a number of brilliant classmates who were quicker in analytical skills and more articulate and facile on their feet than I. By third year, I had concluded that intelligence came in many forms, that to be effective it had to be applied with motivation and good judgment. In that department I concluded that none of them was better than me. Oops. Better than I. My first year's anxieties ebbed in year two; now they're gone. I feel ok in my own skin."

"Not bad. Not bad at all, as rationalizations go. I went to Grinnell. Some of my happiest days. One of the best things about college is the sheer fun of it. What do you value in a fellow human being?"

"Tolerance, compassion, kindness. Not my strong suits growing up. Perhaps, that's why I value them. My twin brother, Benno, has them in spades."

Hopkins leaned forward over his desk as if trying to get within reach of Adam. "We admire things we don't have. Why work for the WPA?" He shook another Lucky Strike out of the pack, lighted it and took a slow deep draw, exhaling slowly in the direction of his coffee cup. Absurdly, Adam imagined the man taking smoke in his coffee instead of cream.

"Lots of reasons. I voted for FDR. I believe in the role of Government to put a safety net under its citizens. A job — any job — in this Administration became my goal." Adam paused, deliberating whether to take it to a deeper level.

Hopkins showed impatience. "You haven't answered my question," he said, directing his next puff of smoke in Adam's direction.

Ignoring the cloud, Adam said, "I wasn't finished. I come from a Republican family. Deeply Jeffersonian. My Father's a rancher and farmer in Manhattan, Kansas. He believes passionately in the individual's ability — and duty — to make his way in this world without the aid of Government. To him, poverty and want are human failings. If one's unemployed, that's a choice. One of Father's favorite quotations — I've heard it a hundred times — is Cassius' claim to Brutus:

Men at some time are masters of their fates:
The fault, dear Brutus, is not in our stars,
But in ourselves, that we are underlings.

"My brother lives in the other Manhattan. He's an artist, a sculptor. He's unemployed but not by choice. Before we had graduated from high school, my brother had rejected our Father's social views. I was slower in moving toward the same place. Three years of law school scrubbed my mind a lot, leading me to question Father's faith, again and again. Working for the WPA would give me a chance to carry forward my own views, to help the destitute, including, in some way or other, my brother, and to put an exclamation mark on the running arguments I have with Father."

Hopkins finished the last of his coffee and stuck the butt of his cigarette in the overflowing ashtray. His quizzical expression turned into a smile. In a voice barely more than a whisper, he said "How do you account for the difference between you and your Father?"

Adam hesitated. Then, on instinct, he plunged in.

"It started in grade school. Benno and I were different from the other boys. Father saw to that. He was enthralled with Ancient Greece and Rome."

"Of course he was."

As kids he would have us practice boxing. And memorize ancient passages from the Greeks, or Lincoln's great speeches. And recite them before guests. He required that on Sundays, we witness his superb quarter-horse earn the large stud fees paid for the stallion's services. In myriad ways, you see, we were different. And our classmates punished us for it. Longing for tolerance, we learned to value it — Benno more than I — to look for it in others, to befriend those who had it. Father has tolerance and those other things I told you I valued, but more for animals than humans, more for those who show strength in the face of adversity and are still defeated than for those who, by his lights, give up too soon. I credit Harvard Law with pushing me in the opposite direction."

Hopkins stood up and beckoned to the door. The interview was over. Ushered out to the waiting room, Adam paused. Hopkins moved swiftly to the door leading to the outer hallway, opened it and, just as Adam was moving past the threshold, said "When can you start?"

Turning around, Adam saw a broad grin on Hopkins' face. "As soon as you can use me," he replied.

"Ok, go back to Cambridge, get your things together and come as soon as you can. If you'd like, there are a couple of other new hires planning on getting an apartment together and they could probably use a third roommate to share the rent. I'll put you in touch. And hang onto your receipts. Travel's on us."

Adam dashed out and headed for Union Station. He felt dazed by the sudden turn of fortune. I'm going to work for Harry Hopkins, he said to himself, over and over. One of FDR's great men. Inspiring leader, imaginative genius, chain-smoking public servant in a smart suit.

———◆———

It was his first office job, the real thing at last, his first as a professional, the start, perhaps, of something grand, if only he could avoid "blotting his copybook," Dan Murdock's antique way of cautioning his boys not to screw up. Furtively, he caressed these thoughts, afraid they would bring bad luck were he to confront them head-on. Adam had been given plenty of advice when those who cared for him got wind of the job offer. Be the first to arrive and the last to leave, Father wrote. Just accept the fact you've always been good at whatever you do, enjoy the fact you have a job and try to relax now and then, advised Benno.

Mariah passed on her uncle's story of how he made himself invaluable as a young lawyer in Hunton & Williams, the principal Richmond law firm for Philip Morris and, therefore, the City's most powerful. The trick, she said, was to sneak into the senior partner's office after he had left for the day, take a critical document from his desk and, then, next day, when he couldn't find it and was growing desperate, pretend to have found it for him.

"Take it with a grain of salt," she cautioned.

"At least two grains. Did he make partner?" Adam asked, a smile widening across his face.

"That's funny. After a couple of years, he left to grow tobacco. I had never made the connection. Must have filched one too many documents."

Growing up, Adam had never failed at work. True enough. Whether garden clean-up and yard work over Spring holidays from school or working for one of Dan's farm teams over Summer months, he seemed naturally — or was it his Father's relentless lectures on what it means to be a man — to grasp each assignment well and instinctively overshoot, so that when the work was complete, it was obvious he had done a little bit more than expected of him. To Dan, his son's achievement was nothing more than sound genetic material well molded by a skillful parent. For Adam, there was always doubt. His Father's prominence and success, his apparent wealth, posed an issue for him. Fear lurked behind his growing sense of accomplishment, fear that the true measure of his success might have fallen far short of appearances were he not the son of Dan Murdock.

As Rachel put it to the boys one day: "Never forget your origins. From the start you young fellows have been privileged, and to some degree, immeasurable yet certain enough, these privileges add up to a head start. So don't be fooled. Don't act like the kid born on third who thought he'd hit a triple. Always look to test your mettle with those who have nothing to gain through flattery."

Adam's first assignment was to analyze the pros and cons of establishing New York City, uniquely as it turned out, as a separate WPA unit equivalent to a state unit — the 49th state, as some called it. He traveled to New York and Albany on this assignment, meeting with politicians to collect the arguments. On receiving his memorandum, Harry Hopkins could immediately discern two things about this young new arrival: one, he could think about an issue from multiple angles; and two, he could write with clarity. No, better than that: felicitous clarity.

Hopkins was starting to imagine writing a book about the WPA and its predecessor, the Federal Emergency Relief Administration. He knew he couldn't do it quickly even with help, and he also knew that help would be required to do it at all. He hated writing. His style, whether managing the development of policy within the agency or political support for policy in the White House or on Capitol Hill, was all sensory, and not just through the voice, but that combined with the language of face and body, the message from one hand to another, the warm embrace or the arm around shoulder or waist. The quick joke and even quicker wink. Above all else, the visual power of being trustworthy, a man of his word, the flip side of being direct, frank, sometimes brutally frank, a crude form of honesty that Hopkins came to naturally. He lacked the patience to practice persuasion through the written word. And it showed, particularly in delivering written speeches when he didn't have time to prepare enough to break away from the text. In the Capitol, the big thing separating doers from strivers was truthfulness and reliability. Saying what you planned to do and then doing it. Limiting promises to those one could keep. Few among the flood of FDR followers to Washington could achieve these things or even appreciate their shortcomings.

The book would have to detail the prelude to FERA; documenting the rise of unemployment from 1929 on and the Hoover response. Why not get someone started on this part? A second reading of Adam's memo sufficed to convince Hopkins his newest employee might be the man for the job.

Adam was summoned to the corner office, tucked away in the ancient Walker-Johnson building. He hadn't been there since his interview. It was just as he remembered it: small, about the size of a decent hotel room, dark and untidy, with an incoherent collection of hideous Government furniture but a redeeming view of the city. The doors were warped, paint peeled in protest, curving out from ceiling and wall, except where bare water pipes lining the walls blocked their progress. Upon entering, Adam picked up the odor of insecticide, used in desperate abandon to cope with the mounting cockroach population. Adam's first thought was to imagine the office a calculated attempt by its occupant to align himself and his agency with the afflicted he was trying to help. On reflection, he knew better. The man didn't care enough for office appearances to waste a minute on them. After all, Adam reflected, the office fit this wiry, tall leader, whose suit, from day to day, could make him look race-track flashy or bread-line disheveled, depending on how late a night he logged at the office. Hopkins had been variously described as a matchstick, a piece of shredded wheat, an Ichabod Crane. True, Adam thought, but hardly enough. A "fiery" matchstick or "animated" piece of shredded wheat, perhaps. Hopkins burned with an inner glow of intellectual energy that could be focused for as long as it took.

In rumpled blue shirt with sleeves rolled above his elbows and collar too large for his skinny neck, Hopkins was on the phone, his back to the door as Adam entered. Putting his hand over the receiver, he said, "I liked the NYC memo, Adam. It'll be the subject of an all hands meeting. Let you know when." Thinking that was all, Adam turned to leave.

Still on the phone, Hopkins swiveled around to recall Adam, who took a seat in front of a cluttered desk, where U.S. Printing Office documents wrestled with draft memos in various stages of review, some marked "urgent," others "HH eyes only" or "legal/confidential." Under last night's unempted coffee cups and ashtrays were typewritten riders cut to size with straight pins at the ready to be used to place the riders beside the text they modified. To Adam, the desk was a palpable presence, a throbbing extension of the man occupying the swivel chair behind it. He recalled the clean desk top of his first visit.

"If you want me to, Mr. President, of course I'll see him. The press goes crazy over us, falling all over themselves to uncover hostility, when it's just not there. Now, Mr. President, don't you fall for that ridiculous stuff."

Again cupping the receiver in his hand, he said: "How'd you like to write a book with me?"

"Why, Mr. Hopkins, Sir. I ...." Adam was too nonplussed to continue. Here was the czar of WPA, speaking to the President by phone and, at the same time, to him across the desk. And not only that. Inviting him, the agency's newest arrival, to become his co-author. Finally, as Hopkins finished his call with a "Yes, Mr. President, I'll be there," Adam came to.

"I'd love to, Mr. Hopkins. What's the subject?"

"Ok, ok. Let's get one thing straight. To you, I'm Harry. Nothing more; nothing less. Now, here's the idea: to account for all we've been doing. But it needs context. It will only be compelling if one understands what came before, the story of a Government unable to imagine its proper role, the nuts and bolts of what did, and did not happen pre-New Deal. That's the beginning. What I want you to write is the first draft. Getting the low-down on what happened won't be easy. You're going to have to gumshoe around, interviewing, poking, probing, ingratiating yourself if possible, making yourself obnoxious if necessary. You'll be putting Hooverites on the defensive. It's going to be politically sensitive stuff. It's got to be hard-hitting, like a brief, but accurate, believable, defensible before the court that counts."

He paused, as if inviting Adam to complete the thought. Trying to think like a politician, Adam had the letters "FDR" on the tip of his tongue when Harry continued with emphasis.

"The people's court. Get the picture?"

———◆———

The assignment took Adam to Capitol Hill, the National Archives and New York City, where there were many people to be interviewed and where he was able to spend a little time with Benno and Violet. In fact, duty and pleasure merged in Adam's visits. Although he hadn't planned it that way, what better people could he find to experience vicariously the horrors of hopelessness, of being destitute and unemployed despite being young, with something of value to offer and plenty of energy to offer it, which both Benno and Violet had tried to do, time and again.

Adam was torn up over Benno's situation. Wanting to help financially, he had been rebuffed by Benno, who, as a matter of pride and with few exceptions, refused to accept, even indirectly, money from his Father. And during his years at law school, that would have been the source of the help offered by Adam. Now, with a WPA salary, perhaps Benno would be more open to help. Especially, since Violet had come into his life.

Since they were solid witnesses, Adam considered taking Benno and Violet to meals on his expense account. But there was an appearance problem. He recalled a pep talk Harry had given his troops just after Adam came on board. Reminding them of the public trust that Government employees undertook, Hopkins urged them to apply the sort of litmus test he had been taught during college days. "Boys, test everything by the standard of whether you could live with it if a story appeared in next day's newspaper. For me, at Grinnell, this was just a theoretical exercise. But for us, at the WPA, things come up every day. The press is relentless. And because we have limited funds measured against unlimited needs, for every staunch friend out there, we've got hundreds of potential enemies. In all you do, bend over forward and be alert."

———◆———

"So, who are you here to interview?" Benno asked his brother, as they sat in Chinatown at one of the many dim sum palaces offering brunch one Sunday at noon.

"Where's Violet?" Adam said, a slightly sinister smile appearing on his face. "I hope you're not still pretending to be living apart, for God's sake. Not to me, your brother."

Benno shrugged, a look of helplessness in his eyes.

"We're not together in the way you think. We live apart, each in our own hovel, claiming to be an apartment. We are not the couple you imagine. So lay off."

Just then Violet arrived, slipping into a chair close to Benno. "I'm so happy to see you, Adam. Just looking at your smiling face tells me WPA work's agreeable. What an accomplishment to land a job there. We are clients, you might say, and we can't easily get their attention."

"Or hold it," Benno added.

A waiter appeared, holding a large tray of oval plates containing steamed pork dumplings and chives.

"Yes to those," exclaimed Adam, "We'll take three plates, won't we? And, please, we use chop sticks. Could you bring us some white vinegar and hot sauce?"

"Last time Benno told me about your work, Adam, you were searching for unemployment numbers. Any luck?"

"I've got numbers. More important, I've got a meeting today with the guy who created them. Robert Nathan, an economist who served on Hoover's Committee on Economic Security. His estimates are the best around. By March 1929, well before the Crash, close to 3 million and by December, more; a year later, almost 7 million, or 14% of our total workforce. The peak came in March 1933, with somewhere between 13 and 18 million, or close to 30%. No one knew the numbers then."

"No, but people like us felt them," Violet said.

"Last trip you were going to see Colonel Woods," Benno said. The oil and vinegar had arrived, along with the chop sticks, which they wielded with some success against the slippery dumplings.

"The Colonel saw me. He minced no words. Perhaps he had no choice, given that I had access to the records of his committee. But he seemed like a straight-shooter. I trusted him."

"I don't think I ever heard what his position was, exactly?" said Benno.

"No wonder. He was appointed in October 1930 under the title 'Director General of Unemployment.' He laughed about it. Admitted it was a big boner."

"Sure captures Hoover's regard for the condition," Violet said.

"Some P.R. guy quickly got in the act, and they ended up with 'President's Committee for Employment.' Of course, as Woods put it, his committee was just a clearing house for gathering information from the states and sharing it to spread 'best practice.' All Hoover did rested on the assumption that voluntary contributions to community chests would do the trick.

"In fact, with the help of sampling by the Metropolitan Life Insurance Company, Colonel Woods became very well informed. What they discovered was a country in spiraling distress. When Hoover's State of the Union speech was set for December 2, 1930, the Colonel decided to present the President with the truth, knowing it would likely be unwelcome. He offered detailed drafting suggestions for the speech. Figuring I had nothing to lose, I asked him for a copy. And to my surprise he said sure. I now understand why. Knowing of Hopkins' book, he was keen to set the record straight."

"You mean to enable you to set the record straight, without his being disloyal," Benno suggested.

"Maybe. But getting hold of this material made my day."

Adam had just lifted a rice noodle shrimp dumpling, dripping with hot oil and vinegar, to his mouth. Distracted by the story, he got careless. The chop sticks slipped, releasing the nearly translucent, pearly white dumpling, which tumbled down his front like a toboggan hugging a path, leaving orange colored blotches of oil the length of his new silk tie.

Violet saw it coming and was quick with a wet napkin.

"What a pisser. I should know better than to pretend I can use these things as well as my brother. Water's no use against oil, I'm afraid. Damn. Another expensive tie I can't afford wasted."

"Is silk part of the WPA dress code?" Benno said, chuckling.

"No," Adam said. "The truth, if you really must know, is simply that my boss loves silk ties and he's become my all-round mentor. Pathetic, I admit."

"You were about to tell us what the Colonel advised Hoover," said Benno.

"Right. It was eloquent and moving. Yes, I mean it, moving in its design to get the President to ask Congress for a two billion dollar public construction program. Remarkable because Woods was a staunch

Republican. A leading capitalist. He put the number of unemployed in the millions. He compared the ravages of unemployment to those of war and disease.

"What's chilling is the fact that Hoover didn't just ignore the Colonel's plea. Denying the Colonel's findings of fact, he lied to the American people, boasting that 'the fundamental strength of the nation's economic life is unimpaired.' He put the blame for our weak recovery on unwarranted fears created by forces beyond our shores. And he cut in half the Colonel's highly reliable unemployment numbers. This sorry episode is going to be Exhibit A for the book."

"Tragic, really, when one considers it needn't have been that way," said Benno.

"Tragic? Yes, at the least," Violet cried. "But for me what makes all this beyond tragedy is Hoover's elevation of principle over facts collected by his own people. I was in Dalhart the Winter of '30. A dreadful time of dusters and drought. All of us on the high plains were suffering. Living on locusts and hoppers covered in a fine coating of what had once been our topsoil. We heard that both houses of Congress passed resolutions calling for aid. Then we read about Arthur Hyde, Hoover's well named Secretary of Agriculture. He refused, testifying that food for farmers would set a dangerous precedent, putting the country on a slippery slope to the dole. If we start feeding drought-stricken farmers, he said, the next thing you know we might be feeding the unemployed in our cities.

"And here's the irony: he had approved loans to us for seed and fertilizer, fuel for tractors, even food for livestock. Oh, how we despised Hoover and stooges like Hyde."

"You speak of irony," Adam said. "Consider this. In the '20s, our Government appropriated millions to relieve human suffering in Europe. Hoover was then Secretary of Commerce. His passion for this relief carried the day, earning for him the title 'great humanitarian.' When $10 million was appropriated by the House for relief of German women and children but then spurned by the Senate, Hoover appealed to the Foreign Affairs Committee. He claimed German children would be stunted from undernourishment unless the Senate acted.

"And it gets worse. On January 27, 1931, Myron Taylor, chairman of the Finance Committee of US Steel, delivered a radio address under the auspices of the Woods Committee. In truth, he was a shill for Hoover. "When I asked the Colonel about Taylor's remarks, he blushed with embarrassment, admitting he had been asked by the White House to give Taylor the platform and had no idea what message he would convey. Here, if I can find it in my notebook, I want to read you a short piece of what Taylor said:

> While the number of unemployed is considerable, the number in real distress is relatively few, because the masses have been provident and are caring for themselves and each other.
>
> One solution, and a basic one, in the adjustment of the conditions which affect the individual, is his own attitude and conduct toward life and the sincerity with which he undertakes to work. The individual with a will to work must fit himself into the new scheme of things. The slacker must give way to the man of action. The drone must not obstruct the way, or, like his prototype the bee, he will be expelled from the hive.

On hearing these words, Violet turned to Benno, who was wincing, then rolling his shoulders forward as if cudgeled from behind.

"Adam, I know you don't mean it, but these stories bury me in pain. Look, like me, the great majority of unemployed had nothing left to save. Like me, those with the 'will to work' find it impossible to 'fit themselves into the new scheme of things,' because, no matter how strong that will, there is no work to be found. I am a 'man of action,' but I am compelled by strange forces beyond my ken to become a 'slacker.' The hives I frequent have no more honey. Like me, the industrious and thrifty are being expelled just as ruthlessly as the drones."

"Bravo," Violet said softly. She could see he was fighting back tears, releasing some of her own.

Awkward seconds passed, as embarrassed, those around the table awaited the composure that was bound to come.

Finally, Benno said, "Adam, has it occurred to you that Father has been right there with Hoover from the beginning?"

"I'm planning a trip to see Father, just as soon as I get this project finished. I plan to beard him in his den, put my politics on the table and demand that he do the same. Sparks may fly."

"We'll be able to hear you from here," said Benno, laughing softly. "Someday, Violet, you've got to meet Father...."

"Who ain't in heaven," Adam added, joining the necessary silliness. "I'm sure Violet's not wild to meet Father. But, listen. There's a new movie playing. Astaire and Rogers again. We can make the 3 o'clock if we get that waitress' attention. My treat."

Adam paid the bill, adding 20% for the downtrodden waitress. They raced off to Broadway and the RKO Radio Pictures presentation of *Roberta*. Having seen this team in *The Gay Divorcee*, Adam had some notion of what to expect. He recalled them vividly as they sang and danced to Cole Porter's *Night and Day*. Entering the theater clueless, Benno and Violet emerged spellbound.

Jerome Kern wrote the music and Otto Harbach the lyrics. Although the film had an entirely predictable plot, the music and dancing were transcendent. The highlight was Ginger singing *I'll be Hard to Handle* with a heavy Russian accent, followed by an Astaire and Rogers dance routine to the same music. Violet was in rapture. "My God," she exclaimed, "the ease, the elegance they project in each other's arms, it's too much to believe and yet I saw it: perfection of movement and expression. And they make it appear unrehearsed and spontaneous."

The trio floated out into the evening. Violet grabbed Benno, putting an arm around his waist, leading him to dance on the sidewalk while crooning "They asked me how I knew, my true love was true? I of course replied, something here inside cannot be denied." Adam began to imitate the master in his solo to the song *I Won't Dance*, moving furiously across the sidewalk and into the street, where traffic was heavy, horns blowing like an ornery brass section.

"Adam," Benno exclaimed, "you're jigging around like a cricket on a hot grill. Get out of the street before you get hit by a fat Packard."

———◆———

"How's my ghost writer doing?"

Harry had summoned Adam to get a briefing on his interview with Walter Gifford, whom Hoover had appointed in August of 1931 to head up a follow-on committee to that of Colonel Woods. Its title: "The President's Organization on Unemployment Relief." Its stated mission: "to mobilize the national, state and local agencies of every kind which will have charge of the activities arising out of unemployment in various parts of the nation this Winter."

Gifford was head of AT&T and President of the Charity Organization Society of New York. A big man around town. To get an appointment, Hopkins had to intervene, using back channels to big business. Fearing for his reputation, Gifford refused several appeals. "No surprise," Hopkins acknowledged to his most promising back channel operative, "but I won't accept this. We must have an interview. Put it to him this way: Look, Walter: you served one President and Hopkins is serving another. You had the same job to do in coping with unemployment as he does. Don't you see, it's your duty as a patriot and national leader to help him carry your fight forward."

Sitting in Harry's office listening to this argument as it flowed from the city's foremost wizard of influence, Adam was again, and for the hundredth time, dazzled. And amused, too, when he saw Harry's wink and tight-fisted punch at the imaginary forces of darkness as he uttered the word "fight."

How many times had Adam reminded himself of the sheer fun he was having as part of Harry's lean army. Or how lucky he had been to stumble into this job.

He couldn't count all the reasons he loved what he was doing. Near the top, of course, was just being an avid Hopkins watcher. The more contact with the great man one had, the more seasoned a connoisseur one became. And the more one stood in awe. Adam quickly realized that here was a game that united the staff, top to bottom. All worshipped the man, built fantasies around all that he did, turned weaknesses into strengths and abandoned critical thinking for fervor resting on unwavering faith. A secular religion no less, and, if not organized, still highly addictive. Or, in Marine Corps language, " Esprit de corps."

Whatever truth there might be in the aphorism that 'familiarity breeds contempt,' it was turned on its head in regard to Harry Hopkins. Consider the speed and energy of the man, a trait even a tyro picked up immediately. He was like a quarterhorse that never rested, a hockey forward on a one-line team going full tilt until the whistle blew. Incessant and often impertinent impatience fueled the man's pace. At formal meetings, whether chaired by him or others, he could reliably be seen checking off each agenda item with the flourish of his pencil, invariably well ahead of the moment when that item was, in fact, completed. No one could miss the man's one-handed clap, the silent exhortation to think faster, act faster, finish faster and move on to what's next.

Harry was eager for a report.

"Tell all, my boy. Tell it so I can imagine being there with you." Harry ordered a couple of coffees, then leaned back in his swivel chair, put his feet up on the desk and closed his eyes.

"You're such a swell dresser, Harry, I thought perhaps you should know there's a hole in your right shoe."

"Of course there is, Adam. I put it there. But the left, it's ok. The story."

"His office was immense, with vistas of Manhattan on all sides from what felt like an eagle's aerie. A squad of secretaries guarded his nest, but they all seemed to know about me and competed in offering kind attention as I was passed slowly through successive anterooms from one to another. They suggested I might linger over the art. Prints of the City and the Harbor filled the walls, including two surprising lithographs by Currier & Ives. For me, unforgettable. They depicted the decorous start and disorderly finish of a 'Great Oyster-Eating Match between The

Dark Town Cormorant and The Blackville Buster'. Each contestant had a 'second' to open his oysters. The subtext for the Finish, voiced by the timer and judge was 'Yous is a tie: De one dat gags fust, am a gone coon.'"

"How did they make you feel?" Harry asked, face a blank.

"Honestly, the more I looked the more uncomfortable I became. I understand how funny they would have appeared to the white clientele that Currier & Ives catered to just after the Civil War. But, today, over six decades later, to hang such racially loaded scenes in the public space of our country's largest telephone company — a public utility open to all and serving a vital national interest — seems a tasteless act. And given AT&T's prestige, a bad act for society."

"You hit the nail on the head."

"He gave me plenty of his time. And most important, he had set aside for me to examine the committee's correspondence file, which turned out to be a gold mine of information. He was less defensive than I expected. I think he had rationalized his work as being the only correct response to unemployment conditions prevailing before FDR took over. Thereafter, with conditions having changed dramatically, he could understand the need for a different approach. Using Nathan's figures, he pointed out that there were 'only' (his words) eight million unemployed when his committee was established, compared to about 15 million when FDR was sworn in."

"Did he appreciate the cause?"

"I asked. He refused to consider the possibility that earlier intervention at the Federal level could have helped."

Adam fought against personalizing the subject matter of his work for Harry. But feelings for the plight of Benno and Violet intruded. In his head there was no such thing as an impersonal work force.

"Here's the big picture I draw from the interview. Hoover feared national responsibility more than he feared national unemployment. Gifford was his lackey, chairing a committee whose real mission was to inspire local relief committees to assume financial responsibility for the unemployed and thereby to counteract the persistent campaign for Federal aid. Gifford as much as admitted that his assignment was to help the President justify his refusal to assist the states and municipalities whose coffers were bare, whose resources to aid the destitute were exhausted. As to why Hoover was so steadfast, the correspondence was eye-opening. For example, I saw letters from the DuPonts and other business leaders begging Gifford to use his influence to block Congress from raising income taxes.

"Before we go on, I need to confess something. I recall your caution to the troops about conflicts of interest and the hovering press, always looking for some tidbit to use in embarrassing us. I've tried to be objective in fact-gathering and reporting. But I am eternally conscious of my brother Benno's condition and that of his girlfriend Violet in New York. They came from different circumstances, but landed in the same impoverished state. You need to know that I share their pain, so much so that I fear it could warp my work in ways I can't easily spot. I hope this isn't cause for dropping me."

"I get it. Don't worry, your position's safe. You've handled this just right. Knowing the background, I can be on the lookout for bias, but I'm confident there won't be any. Now, back to Gifford. Of all local relief funding, do you have any idea of how much comes from private funds and how much from tax receipts? I bet it's disproportionate."

Adam had seen numbers on this question, contained in an article by Gifford Pinchot, the wise and sensibly compassionate Governor of Pennsylvania.

"You're right. Russell Sage Foundation studied eighty-one cities. It found that private funds supplied only 28% of relief with tax receipts the rest."

"So, here's the point," Harry said. "Local relief means higher property taxes, a kind of enforced charity. Higher property taxes means reduced consuming power, furthering our economic maladjustment, sinking us further into the hole. At the Federal level, dollars can be printed, Treasury bonds can be sold, all without reducing the consumer's ability to spend. OK, what's next?"

Adam hadn't carried his thinking this far. Appearing to be half asleep, Harry surprised him with this quick insight.

Despite much of their populace being on the verge of starvation, many Governors responded to the President's urgent request for support in opposing what was considered a "dole," if provided by the Federal government.

"Here's a quote from one Governor's letter to the White House: 'I think I am speaking for a great majority of the people of the State of Vermont when I say to you that the people of Vermont are for a Government supported by the people rather than a people supported by the Government.'

"I put this question to Gifford: Whenever one requests Federal aid, the cry from Hooverites is 'dole, dole, dole,' as if it were a loathsome, contagious disease. Why should it be that aid given by a nation is a 'dole,' when precisely the same form of aid given by a state or city is not a 'dole'? His answer? An embarrassing and extended silence, followed by the same argument he advanced in December 1931 before the La Follette-Costigan Committee:

> The net result might well be that the unemployed who are in need would be worse instead of better off.

"With disarming honesty, Gifford answered La Follette's question of why, if assistance at the Federal level was contrary to public policy, his national organization had been created.

> It was created principally to stimulate the local organizations and keep them busy on the problem."

"Great stuff. Give me another coffin nail or two and then get back to your desk." Harry had removed his feet from the desk and was sitting up straight in his chair, leaning forward with the feline grin of a cat who had just broken a robin's wing. "Insisting on that interview was not so dumb, after all."

"So many nails, Harry. It's hard to pick the best. What you have in the pre-FDR years is compelling data to support it all — all that the WPA stands for. Publish and never again will this country allow its people to become destitute."

"Hey, cut pontificating. That's where I come in. Just gimme the nails."

"Ok. Here's Senate testimony by Clarence E. Pickett, Secretary of the American Friends Service Committee, in response to the claim by the Governor of West Virginia that Federal help for relief was opposed by its people. The AFSC had been requested to go into the bituminous mining communities in West Virginia and Kentucky to care for starving children.

> Pickett: 'Now we are studying each community, so that we prob-
> ably will have to include a good many more, because we are
> putting our feeding on the basis of the weight of the child,
> and also certain other factors which we discover by a case
> study of families. The first thing we do is to weigh all the
> children in the school, and automatically put on the list to
> be fed all who are 10 per cent underweight.'
>
> La Follette: 'In these surveys of the schools, what percentage of
> the school children did you find underweight?'
>
> Pickett: 'It ranges from 20 to 90 per cent. We found in one school
> of 100 children that 99 were underweight. That is the worst
> we have found. We have found a good many that were 85 to
> 90 per cent, and then ranging down as low as 20.'
>
> Costigan: 'Are the children retarded in their physical
> development?'
>
> Pickett: 'I do not think you would find many cases of seriously
> retarded physical development. We find drowsiness, leth-
> argy, and sleepiness.'
>
> Costigan: 'A mental retardation?'
>
> Pickett: 'A mental retardation, but not often physical retardation.'"

Harry leaned forward, downed his cup and cried softly, "Thus do we use institutions as fronts to mask the cruelties we inflict on our fellow human beings." Then, he leaned back, swiveled toward the window and croaked, "Ok, great material, but can't you give me one more nail for Gifford's personal coffin?"

"As a matter of fact, I can. Here's an exchange between our man from AT&T and Senator Costigan:

> Costigan: 'May I ask with respect to another question by Senator La Follette which you answered, what evidence of human need in America would be required to satisfy you that the Federal Government should make an appropriation?'
>
> Gifford: 'I think if a state Government were absolutely broke and could not raise any more money by taxes or otherwise, that would be pretty satisfactory, assuming now that the local communities and counties could not do the thing directly and state aid was asked and the state legislature met and they could not sell any bonds and the tax limits had been reached and they could not tax anybody. I think that would be pretty good evidence.'"

"Indeed! Adam my friend, we are pursuing the white whale and you are in the bow of the boat, pen raised — a harpoon. Now, off to your office and write."

9

—◆—

"You're swell, Violet. more, pour it on."

They were back in the Horn & Hardart where the braiding of their lives had begun. Violet was recounting last night's dream. Benno was admiring her passion, the poignancy of her words.

"Yea, that's when we and our neighbors, we all got jobs; we abandoned the stinking, rat-infested tenement houses we live in without plumbing, those shelters made of rusted-out car bodies and orange crate shacks; yea, traded them for clean apartments with heat, hot and cold running water, beds with clean sheets and nary a cockroach.

"Benno, where can we go to find these things? What can we do to make it happen? To recover our pride? You know, I'm embarrassed to have your brother see us this way. And I bet you are too."

"I'm embarrassed just to have you see me. But maybe a bit less so than before we met. The endurance of each when two share the same plight seems much greater. At times I feel empowered by you. At other times, thinking of the berating that Father would give me for not taking better care of you, like a man, to deserve the name, must with his "lady," I feel worse. There's nothing theoretical about our actual condition, and that's the point, no matter what we think of it.

"By the way, I learned something at the ERB office today. From that sweetheart case worker, Hillary. Might interest you. ERB has funded Actors' Equity to launch a Gilbert & Sullivan operetta this Summer. Auditions start next Monday for an opening in June. They're doing something called *Pirates of Penzance.* Ever heard of it? You might give it a try?"

"Nope. But time to put fear aside. That movie continues to give. It's been a tonic all right. I could touch the moon."

Being a natural worrier, Benno scrunched up his face until it began to resemble black clouds. Luckily, Violet didn't see them.

"The problem with feel-good movies like *Roberta,* where all turns out swell, and *Love Me Tonight,* where tailor gets princess, is they raise our hopes, allowing us to believe a dream can come true, just as it did on the screen. We're lifted up, and that's good, but when the fuel feeding the dream runs out, that's bad because the fall is all the more painful."

As he delivered this fatuous homily, Benno watched Violet's spirits sag like a popover fresh from the oven that no one remembered to puncture. How could he be so stupid?

"But you came to the right city. If wishes are ever going to be granted, it will happen first in New York."

They left the automat, heading back to their dreary tenements. As they walked side by side, Benno felt desire, which waxed from block to block in equal measure with fear. He knew desire. Had experienced it many times, often when alone. And, of course, he knew how to release himself from its grip. The fear was something new, brought on by Violet's presence. He lacked experience. But so what, he thought. Every man begins without it. His problem was being self-consciously aware that, despite Dr. Bernstein's efforts, he was woefully short on confidence. Remarkably, although they had been together for months, they had never braided physically. Although Violet's smile came naturally and was expressed without regard to sex, it wasn't intended to turn men on to her, and indeed, it hadn't. Quite unlike the effect Mariah's smile had on the male sex, a smile intended to interest and even excite. Mariah was practiced in this feminine art, and used it with gusto, despite having been cautioned at a young age to avoid smiling at men, because, if given encouragement, they would just end up wasting your time.

They were strolling down 3rd Avenue. The mood was just right, he could feel it. Violet's arm brushed against his. He should take her hand. She would welcome it. But suppose she didn't? Benno was ashamed, a disappointment to himself but also, he rued, to Rachel, who seemed to perch in a corner of his mind, her influence as palpable now as it had been in those Manhattan days. Fear swallowed desire. He felt forlorn. Violet had fallen a couple of steps behind. A scruffy looking street bum appeared out of an unlighted tenement doorway and grabbed her arm, trying to drag her into the darkness of the doorway. She cried out. Turning, Benno was able to grasp her hand and yank her away from the man's grip. "Let's go," Benno said, and they began running, hand in hand, a link that remained long after they had resumed their walk south to the lower east side, toward their separate rooms in the smelly, rat-infested and thoroughly squalid tenements they called home. It took a bum to break the ice, Benno thought. Now what?

Benno was too ashamed of the degrading space he lived in to consider inviting Violet up the five flights of squeaky, tilting steps to his cold water flat. But he thought of her more and more with the passing days of early Spring, especially when he was in the bathtub or urinating, moments that brought to mind the same wild fantasies he had enjoyed since puberty, although now there was a face in them he recognized. He didn't understand this process, although it should have been obvious. Where, he wondered, could they find clean space and privacy?

———◆———

Violet arrived at the theater early, just after the super. The auditions were to begin at 10 am. He let her in.

"Look, lady, there ain't nobody here yet. I know you're looking for an edge. I mean, aren't we all? But you're an hour too soon."

The super looked old enough to be Violet's Father. His face was weathered by time and gathering disappointments; his body was shaped like a boa that had swallowed a pig. Although Violet didn't detect it, to a

New Yorker, his voice would betray a childhood wasted at the corner of Flatbush and Avenue Q.

Violet shrugged. "I'm used to waiting. I'll just sit down in the orchestra if you don't mind. Never had a seat so close." She smiled; the super melted.

"Lady, if you follow me, I can get you a nice cup of coffee."

He led her into his office, squirreled away behind the stage and dressing rooms. It smelled like the well-used locker room of a high school football team with limited shower facilities, except in place of dried towels and Ben-Gay there were dried mops and buckets partially filled with murky water and half-spent bottles of ammonia. There was a desk, its top buried under papers, a couple of light bulbs and various ancient hand tools. At one corner stood the super's pride, an electric percolator, the cleanest, shiniest object in the room. Behind the desk was a deep sink, above which was a white porcelain cabinet with scratched doors heavily rusted from years of unvented humidity. The super filled the percolator with water from the tap above the sink, then with ground coffee from a stash in the cabinet. Returning this precious device to his desk, he plugged in the cord, announcing there would be freshly brewed coffee in ten minutes. Returning to the cabinet, he grabbed two mugs, rinsed them out and set them on the desk beside the percolator, which had started to burble.

"Listen," he said. "Don't you love that sound? Trust me, a gorgeous smell's right behind.

"So, what's it about these Gilberts and Sullivans? What did you say your name was? Call me Bernie. You know why you're here, don't you? I liked your smile. No, no, don't think I'm making a pass. Too old for that malarkey. Leave it to the directors. I figured you different. Come from somewhere else. Saw it in your eyes. I'd like to know."

"Black. I take it black," Violet said, worried about losing her place in line. "You're a curious one. No harm in that, I reckon. Yep. You nailed me right. Hail from Texas. Dalhart, Texas. My name's Violet Long."

"I know Texas, but never heard of Dalhart. Where's that?"

"A town of the High Plains. Ambitious, self-confident town, tucked away in the northwest corner of the panhandle. Hey, Bernie, perking's stopped. How about the coffee? I got to get back." Violet had grabbed the mug that said "STRONGER" and was holding it out in the direction of the pot.

"You're all ambition, that's for sure. Self-confidence too. Seen it in the successful ones. See it in you. Here, take your coffee and run. Break-a-leg, Violet."

She was still first to arrive, and first to audition. By the time she was up on stage, alone with piano, accompanist and spotlight, it dawned on her that going first might not be the advantage she had assumed; in fact, given fallible memories and the impact of fresh impressions, it might be a disadvantage. As she waited to take her position on stage, the line of contenders kept growing. It became obvious that her eagerness to arrive early could hurt, that a line to audition for the theater was entirely different from a line to buy tickets to the theater. She felt the silly hick. Had she consulted Benno, he would have cautioned her as, she now recalled with a ripple of fear down her back, he had cautioned his brother.

The Director and his staff sat in third row center, although Violet couldn't make them out through the lights.

"Can you sing us a song from *Pirates*?" came the Director's voice.

"No. I don't know any Gilbert and Sullivan. I only brought one piece of sheet music with me from Texas: *The Picture That is Turned Toward the Wall*." My daddy insisted I take it as a joke because it's about a girl who leaves home."

"Ok, save the life story bit. Give it to Al and let's get started."

Violet wasn't at her best. Perhaps she hadn't warmed up enough. Or perhaps the 'shot to her foot' from being first had sapped her confidence. And, of course, the song wasn't likely to thrill any audience, especially this one.

"Is that the best you can do? There's something — something unusual — about your voice that I like but — Ouch! I mean, come on, where's the punch, where's the acting?" The voice behind the lights was rough gravel, whipping across her face like Dalhart dust. "You came early, eager beaver from Texas, wearing that rain barrel of a calico dress. Sorry. Next."

Violet recoiled, her face a map of grief. Seconds passed as she stood absolutely still, the stop frame of a motion picture. It was over. The next candidate had appeared on stage. As Violet was gathering her things, one of the staff appeared at the side of the stage.

"Look, if there's something else you'd like to try, and if you stick around, we might have time to give you another shot. Interested?"

"For that chance, I've got nothing but time," Violet said. "I'll sit near the front so you won't forget me."

Her grief had suddenly vanished, pushed away by the same wellspring of hope that had lifted her out of Dalhart and brought her east. It was a long wait. But right after a short lunch break, the director called her name. Despite the numbers, the auditions had gone quickly and had failed to excite.

"Ok, Calico, what ya got?"

As she climbed to the stage, she thought of Bernie, who said he had seen something, something she now seized upon: an ambitious and self-confident woman — a Texan no less.

"Al, I bet you know *A Bird in a Gilded Cage*.

"You better believe it." He played a few bars of the introduction, and then whispered "No one gets to bat twice, kid. Don't waste our time."

Violet poured herself into the song. It was one of her favorites, and not just because she had won a singing contest with it in Dalhart. It had a compelling melody. It offered scope for acting. The words evoked easy to imagine images of the old man and the young beauty, who could not mate with age. She put wings on that song, making it soar, filling the theater with a limpid sound that came from an unlabored voice.

Total silence followed her last note. She bowed into the lights, which denied her the chance to read the expressions on the faces of the Director and staff.

"Thanks Calico. Take a seat, please. It will be quite some time before we're through. If you go out for a bite, don't stray too far or long. Bonnie Stapleton, you're next."

She found a seat in a row filled with hopefuls who had made it through the first cut. As she sat down, she caught sight of Bernie off to the side. He was waving to her and, then, when she looked his way, he signaled with both thumbs up. She threw him her best smile. He beamed. They shared a bond; both of them knew it.

It was past three when she and four others were summoned back to the stage.

The Director joined the singers at the piano. "How many of you know *Pirates*? Three raised their hands. "Ok. The song I want you to try is Mabel's first big one, *Poor Wandering One*. You all claim to be readers, so it shouldn't matter much whether you know the piece or not. Violet, here's the score. Why don't you go first."

Violet blanched. Not the same mistake twice in one day. As an argument formed in her head, she took a chance.

"I think a fairer approach would be to have the three who know the piece go first. This will at least give the rest of us a chance to hear it, and to look over the score. And, while I'm at it, why not reverse the order from this morning?"

The Director looked surprised at such boldness. "Good thinking, Calico. That's how we'll proceed. There are enough scores for all. Al, show 'em how it's going to sound. My assistant, Joanie, will cover the women and I'll struggle with Frederic. Now, let's get started."

Violet could see from a quick look at the score that this song was going to be a challenge. It was highly ornamented, requiring a soprano's full range. After hearing the first finalist, she compared it to what Mozart sought from his "Queen of the Night." Not that she had ever performed that role. But in Dalhart she had been loaned a score and had practiced with the piano enough to appreciate its vocal demands and technique.

The Director didn't bother with plot, and to Violet's surprise, the four singers who preceded her didn't show much appreciation for Mabel's situation. Violet's score was complete, making it possible for her to grasp the context. When Al began with *Poor Wandering One,* Violet objected, saying she'd like to start with Frederic's "Not one?"

"You can handle that, can't you Al?"

This gave her the chance to hurl herself into the role by rushing to the edge of the stage, throwing up her arms and singing the repeat "Yes, one!" She missed a note here and there, but her portrayal of the deviously clever Mabel proved a triumph.

The Director and his team moved off-stage, back to the third row orchestra, to confer. The five girls stood across the stage, spaced a yard or so apart, fearful and expectant. In less than a minute, the Director was back on his feet.

Emily, Sarah and Joan, we thank you for the day's effort. You each have something special, and a promising future. I'm sorry it didn't work out. Good luck. Jennifer, you will be an understudy for Mabel and perhaps other roles. Calico, congratulations. Rehearsals start next Monday. Keep the scores. First day, 8 AM. See the bursar in the back office before you leave. He has an advance against salary for you."

On her way out, Violet passed Bernie's door. She knocked. Opening the door, he stood there, the world's widest smile stretched full across his face. She hugged him, squeezing his girth as far around as her arms would reach.

She let go. Bernie said, "I hear you're going to be sticking around this joint for a while. That's good news, kid."

"Bernie, you don't know how important you were to bringing Mabel to me. Thanks for what you said, and the coffee."

———◆———

"Two in one flat. Think of that," Benno rhymed as they set out in search of something clean and affordable. By sharing an apartment, they could get home relief to pay half the rent for Benno. Violet's salary would carry the rest. In the Houston-Canal Street area, they found on the third floor of a five-floor, 25 foot brownstone facing east — a floor-through apartment with a small kitchen and eating nook, a bedroom barely wide enough for twin beds, a tiny bathroom and living room with two windows facing the rising sun. What clinched the deal were things they did not find: obnoxious kitchen or bathroom odors or telltale water stains on walls and ceiling, or droppings in kitchen drawers or closets or even a single cockroach, large or small, black or tan, known throughout the city to be an irrefutable leading indicator of trouble ahead.

Things seemed to be going their way. Benno landed home relief. Then Violet landed a lead. Now, they were able to drop their rotten, separate quarters for something dignified, civilized and civilizing. There was a hitch, however. Moving in together, looking ahead eagerly to clean sheets and firm mattresses, they weren't close to being even young lovers, much less engaged or married. Together, all they knew was a touch of hands. And, by a peculiar destiny, separately, neither one had carnal experience beyond that. It was the prospect of clean sheets that thrilled them. For Violet, fresh bedding was a distant memory covered over by layer upon layer of gritty black dust that made getting under sheets like trying to slide over coarse sandpaper. For Benno, the memory dated back to his days in Kansas.

"How should we think of ourselves," Benno asked, breaking an uncomfortable silence that had suddenly intruded upon their joy in being in the newly rented space for the first time. He sounded awkward.

"Necessity. It threw us together. Think of us as roommates," Violet said.

"I won't take advantage, I promise you that. There hasn't been much romance in our relationship," Benno said, his guileless smile turning dour as he realized even this was an exaggeration. Then, thinking of Rachel, and recalling her advice in times like this to say what you feel, regardless, he added, "Although I hope that will change. What worries me, honestly, is the possibility that our living together could block romance, and stop it from flowering. Do you know what I mean?"

"I admit, we've got things a bit backward. But, my goodness, Benno. Come off it. Why do you always see the bottle half empty? I think it is obvious each of us cares for the other. Is attracted to each other, in many ways. We are not being honest not to acknowledge these facts. That all we've done physically is hold hands changes these feelings not at all. And think about this. We are free to do what we want. We have no parents, guardians, social protectors or guilt-mongers to appease. The society we occupy has no pretense; no standards to drop: a Garden of Eden without the snake. This arrangement will be the purest exercise of two free wills. Don't bind up that freedom before we've even reached the starting line."

Benno looked chagrined. "You've pegged me. I know I should fight it. Too many disappointments growing up. Can't change that."

"For instance."

"Disappointed I wasn't as popular as Adam; or as easy and outgoing; or determined; or as good with girls. Disappointed that my Father rejected me. Disappointed in my lack of success as a sculptor; in not having a job, and, especially now, in not having experience with women. Want more?"

"Ok, but these have mostly to do with other people. You bear no responsibility. As for success or having a job, that's so much a matter of luck, of who you know, of economic conditions and a lot of other things that are all beyond your control. Success can strengthen self-esteem but it's not essential. You know you're good. I know it too. And what's more, I know that, in time, you'll be recognized. So, there."

Violet looked fearsome, like a bobcat shielding her cubs. She moved toward Benno until they almost touched. She took his hands in hers, pulling them swiftly behind her. Looking up at him, his face just inches away from hers, she bridged the gap with her lips, softly touching his, dusting them back and forth, then kissing him with forceful intent.

And then, as suddenly as it had begun, it was over. She pulled away, releasing his hands. At first, he overflowed with glorious feelings, especially the belief that he had just experienced the most yielding, exquisitely soft and sensual lips in the world. But, then, true to form, doubt crept in. What if he might never again encounter such a lovely human connection.

Of course, neither of them had experienced the first-time thrill of lying naked between clean sheets beside another human being. They had read novels. But even the best of them couldn't prepare one for that epiphany; just as poking around in someone else's garden couldn't anticipate the thrill one experiences when the green shoots of one's own bulbs, planted in Fall, first appear in Spring, exactly where one intended them to be.

Despite Benno's promise, it took only a few months of communal apartment life for them to reach for pleasures beyond that first kiss.

Benno suggested they plot the ways and means of surrendering their virginity. Violet refused, arguing that would eliminate surprise and passion. "That's crazy thinking, Benno. I'm going to pretend I never heard it. No, that you never said it."

Benno feared he wouldn't be able to control himself. Rachel had told the boys this problem was common. Many males couldn't. Whether because of that fear or just the way he was, Benno's concern was well founded, and it very nearly undid him. Indeed, with someone more demanding or less understanding and patient than Violet, Benno's future with women could have been irrevocably damaged.

Gradually, with Violet guiding the conversation, they put their feelings on the table. With shared sighs of relief, Benno admitted his fears and Violet her frustrations. Unfortunately, having never experienced the epiphany that Violet had been led, as all girls are, one way or another, to expect from intercourse, she was in the dark about precisely what she was missing. A thoroughly experienced woman might, depending on her attitude, either have had much less patience with Benno, giving up on him as a suitable playmate in bed, or been able to coach him on how to overcome his lack of control. Violet did neither. Together they tried to dissect the process. While doing so, Benno remembered a trick Rachel had suggested to address precisely this problem. It was a prescription for diverting the male mind by doing multiplications in one's head. Benno began with the number three. In his head he saw a blackboard and on it he wrote in white chalk 3x3 =9. 3x9=27. 3x27=81. 3x81=243. 3x243=729. 3x729=What? He couldn't do it. And like a ship that has veered off course for a while only to return to the designated way, his mind snapped back to where it had been at the start, resulting in the same early expression of his ardor. Like one unable to sleep who is told to just concentrate on his breathing, and discovers that it helps not at all, Benno grew frustrated with the experiment. He felt helpless.

Violet tried humor. "Your math's rusty. Do some trial runs till you've got more sequences. Whoever said making love was simple but not easy knew a thing or two."

"Violet, I don't know why you're not more upset by my short-comings. Perhaps you are and just conceal it well."

Violet looked hard at Benno. Then smiled. "Did you say 'short-comings?' That's good Benno, very good." Now she was laughing. "Here's how I see it. Any disappointment I feel is offset by pride in what surely must be my overpowering appeal. I bet you didn't need to multiply a thing with all those other girls."

"There were no other girls, and you know it."

Benno joined her in laughter, realizing as he did so that she was more capable at thinking things through and getting them right than anyone he'd ever known. "Mother Wit," that's what Manhattanites called it.

"You're amazing, Violet. With any other woman, by now I'd be reduced to child-like insecurity and paranoia." Perhaps even driven, he thought, recalling something Rachel had said, to take up with other men for fear of failure with women. Yes, he thought, Violet is something else: steadfast emotions, iron-clad rationality, and an ever-present sense of humor. All this, despite her own frustrations, which must be magnified in her mind by lack of experience. I must figure out how to tell her.

———◆———

Benno had never seen G&S. Nor did he know the tunes. At Violet's urging, he had read through the libretto. The word play delighted him: a marvel of sophisticated humor and casual poignancy about the human condition. There were lines he couldn't forget. Ruth's moving responses to young Frederic's charge that she was old, with gray hair: "It gradually got so," she replies. Mabel's scathing rebuttal to the Policemen's song about going off to do their duty. "But you don't go," she scoffs.

Sitting center Orchestra, Benno was prepared to savor every word. As for the music, it was a blank slate since he couldn't read notes, and Violet had not tried to practice her songs at home. With surprise and growing delight, he listened to the Overture. By the end, he was hooked. When the curtain dropped for the last time, sadness overtook him. He recognized it as precisely the same feeling he had long ago when the curtain came down on his first circus, the one that came to Manhattan when he was 10. As the lights dimmed following the finale, and the audience filed out of the great tent, Benno had wept. Now, it was happening again, although he did his best to wipe away tears he didn't want anyone to notice. He was in rapture over the show, every element of it, the topsy-turveydom of G&S, and, quite naturally, in particular rapture over the role of Mabel. So, too, was the rest of the audience, if one were to judge from the sound and duration of applause she attracted.

Backstage, in the Green Room, a crowd had emerged, seemingly out of nowhere. Like waves in a pounding surf, well-wishers blocked Benno's efforts to get close enough to Violet to have a quiet word. No sooner had he elbowed his way past one fan than another materialized in front of him. The hell with it. What he had to say could wait till they walked back to the apartment. This was her night. It wouldn't do for him to stand in the way of even a single enthusiastic admirer looking for a break in the crowd to get close. He backed away, limply waving a hand, knowing she wouldn't see it, imagining the room a hive and Violet its queen bee, tightly encircled by attendant worker bees, the worshipful ones, tongues out, slobbering praise.

10

———————

Harry gave adam's first draft of the Hoover period a close read. He wanted more on the way the Emergency Relief and Construction Act of 1932 became law.

"Look, Adam, wasn't it the only law ever enacted under the Hoover Administration that carried provisions for the Federal relief of unemployment? Wasn't it bitterly opposed by Hoover himself until, after being passed by Congress and vetoed, it was passed again and signed by the President? Pretty fraught stuff, I'd say."

"Yes, yes," said Adam. "In a speech later that year, Hoover actually claimed he had been 'compelled finally to accept it.' He called the $322 million ear-marked for the states an 'expenditure forced upon the Government by the Democratic leaders.'"

"And the Senate hearings that Summer, weren't they rich with disbelief by Hooverites about the state of the country?"

Adam nodded.

"So, let's try to develop material on this sad story. Go see the players, Governor Pinchot, for example, Ogden Mills, for another. That's it. See those two Republicans. An exercise in contrast. Agreed? Ok, get on it." Pointing towards the door, Harry dismissed Adam with a wave of his hand.

Adam stood up, turned to go and then sat down again, testing his boss' patience. "As you know I've looked through those hearings. Have my notes here. There's one item worth mentioning right now. Just to crown your instinct about how revealing they were, listen to what

Dr. John Ryan of Catholic University reported to the committee. In 1930, he had organized a group of prominent citizens to urge the President to get Congress to create a public works program — to appropriate $3 billion to put men to work. The WPA idea, exactly. The group met with Hoover and made their pitch. He replied: 'Gentlemen, you have come sixty days too late. The depression is over.'"

"Did I say rich! Even FDR's PR geniuses couldn't make this stuff up. Thank God it's in the hearing record. Have a go at it my friend. If you hit a road-block on getting interviews, let me know."

The Hopkins name proved irresistible for Mills and Pinchot. Interviews were arranged for New York City and Philadelphia. Adam researched the careers of these men and then reviewed their testimony.

The Mills profile was a paradigm for leadership within the Republican party: inherited wealth, undergraduate and law degrees from Harvard, legal and society lion of New York City, Army Officer serving in the Great War, Congressman from New York's 17th District. He was appointed by President Coolidge as Under Secretary of the Treasury under Andrew Mellon and by President Hoover as the 50th Secretary of the Treasury. Directorships included Lackawanna Steel Company and Atchison, Topeka and Santa Fe Railway.

Mills despised FDR and his New Deal and often wrote and spoke out against both.

Adam met the former Secretary of the Treasury in the elegant corner office he maintained on Wall Street. He burst through a private door to the reception area, large Cuban cigar half smoked in his left hand. His greeting was robust, his handshake firm, his eyes intense as they caught and held Adam's attention. He was dressed in a Navy blue double-breasted suit, white dress shirt with gold cufflinks in the shape of elephants, and a pale blue silk tie with a slender knot almost concealed by a long white collar. His finely etched face and neatly combed silver gray hair, now noticeably set farther back on his forehead than in years past, all showed signs of having led the good life with modest damage, not enough to promote a change in his ways.

Ushered into the Secretary's office, Adam was directed to a high-backed Windsor chair. Mills displayed an insouciance typical of the high society from which he came. It could mask feelings of uncertainty and reputational risk that naturally would arise from the prospect of an on-the-record meeting with a New Deal zealot serving the notorious Harry Hopkins, a power within FDR's circle of trusted aides whose influence with the press verged on the unnatural. In his watching brief for Mills, Adam saw Mariah. He realized that, in the rarified realms of society from which they came, it didn't matter whether one dwelled north or south of the Mason-Dixon line. The affect seemed genetic. But how could that be?

"Now, my young friend, how can I help?"

"I read your May 9 piece in the *Tribune* dealing with our concentration of wealth. I wonder if you might elaborate a bit."

"Well, as you know, I'm deeply concerned over the large number of those in this country with little or no property to their name. I see it as the biggest challenge to American civilization. We need a system where freedom combines with security through distribution of property among so large a number of families as to fix our society's character forever."

"I follow. But what would the character of such a system be?" Adam said.

"Not Communist, not Fascist, but Proprietary." With that, Mills leaned back in exquisite comfort and inhaled a final drag on his much diminished cigar. His look suggested an inventive accomplishment akin to Thomas Edison's light bulb.

"I see. With slight adjustments, I could fit your system into the creed of Huey Long. But I can't imagine you accept his share-the-wealth campaign."

"Indeed not, my friend." Adam caught a flicker of concern crossing his face, a tiny fluster that vanished as quickly as it had appeared. "Yes, the country's undue concentration of wealth is of concern to many on all sides of the aisle, but solutions differ greatly. Mine starts by inscribing those words — 'Neither Communist nor Fascist but Proprietary' — on our Republican banner. And, then, by inspired leadership, through attitudinal change over time, the Proprietary system will evolve."

"Let's go back to the Senate hearings you appeared at in June 1932. The subject, you recall, was the idea of granting relief to the states through an appropriation of some $300 million for public works. I'd like to try to understand your position on this bill."

"Gladly. Your question follows many others that have come my way since those hearings. I'm pretty well rehearsed. Of course, I was representing the Hoover administration in all I had to say. Happily, all of it jibed with my personal views. The country had lost belief in itself. We needed to restore confidence. And we needed to restore credit. Cheap money for a long time. The Government had to lend money in much larger amounts to private corporations for use in the development of industry. As I said to the senators at the time, when you attempt to bust this depression with a $300 million appropriation for public works, it's just like asking a 10-year-old boy to go and pick up the Washington Monument and bring it to this room."

"I see. You espoused the Hamiltonian theory that if the top of the financial structure is taken care of with credit and subsidy, prosperity will percolate down to the rest of the population."

"That's it, exactly." Mills had fetched another cigar from inside his suit coat and was in the process of lighting it. He looked triumphant, possibly because he was reliving his appearance before the senators.

"As I recall, Senator Wagner didn't buy your argument. He asserted that what the people needed was work for themselves, unlimited credit for large industry. If $300 million was too small a package for relief, why couldn't you have suggested $3 billion?"

"Because one must treat disease at the head first, letting the curative effects ripple down to the people, which they will, as surely night follows day. Starting with public works that smack of the dole is doomed to failure. We opposed it in every way we could. And if the Wagner-Rainey Act hadn't been passed a second time after the President vetoed it, nothing of the kind would have become law under Hoover."

"You've been clear. So, let me ask you a question. I'm sure you're familiar with The Brookings Institution Report on distribution of incomes in the country, published just last year. It found that in 1929, before the crash, family income of $2,000 was enough only to supply basic necessities. And that 16 million families, or 60% of all families in the country, had incomes less than that $2,000 threshold. Indeed, that 21% of those 16 million had incomes less than half that. So, my question is simply this: if the Hamiltonian theory is sound, why at a time of soaring prosperity did so vast a number of American families live below even the most minimal level?"

"That's a good question. But, I'll be honest with you, I never saw the Brookings Report. I'm inclined to suspect liberal bias. Also, it could be simply a timing issue. Hard to evaluate the study without knowing the authors, their methodology, standards for research, and all that. 60%. It's a huge number and hard to swallow. When I looked out to the people of this great country, I just didn't see anywhere near 60% suffering from malnutrition and whatnot. One swallow does not a Spring make. It would take more than one Brookings study to repudiate Hamilton, Hoover and Mills."

With that, rather abruptly Mills rose from his seat, extended his hand to Adam and guided him to the door leading back to the reception area.

"I trust you have all you came for. It's been my pleasure. I regret another appointment awaits. Give my good wishes to Mr. Hopkins, won't you."

———◆———

Governor Pinchot's office in Philadelphia was a modest affair, befitting a state under stress. A secretary showed Adam into the Governor's office, overlooking the City's central business district from the perch of a 12th floor office building. The Governor rose from behind a large cluttered desk and came forward to greet his guest, hand extended in enthusiastic welcome. Here was another patrician with stature and bearing comparable to that of Mills. Cut from the same cloth.

The Governor sported a robust and slightly wayward mustache of salt and pepper hues. Adam noticed a prominent nose, clear, kindly eyes, a high forehead reaching to a distinct hair line. Overall, the look was European more than American. Adam thought the lines on the Governor's face revealed an open and independent personality. And possibly a touch of the guileless.

Adam had done his homework. Exeter, then Yale, where Governor Pinchot was inducted into Skull and Bones, the super-secret society. While born into a patrician family and educated in the manner expected of one so privileged, from the earliest days of his political career, Gifford Pinchot was a Progressive first, Republican second. His compassion for those less well-off was equaled by a belief that Government must shoulder the duty to relieve family hardships. In this he fit the mold of Theodore Roosevelt, who was his patron. It was Pinchot's advocacy for Roosevelt, and against W.H. Taft and his wing of the party, that got him fired from his job as chief of the U.S. Forest Service when Taft became President in 1908.

Adam had obtained a copy of the Governor's book, *The Fight for Conservation*, written in 1910. He had copied into his notebook some passages he considered extraordinary and would later read to his boss:

> Because the special interests are in politics, we as a nation have lost confidence in Congress. ... The people of the United States believe that, as a whole, the Senate and the House no longer represent the voters by whom they were elected, but the special interests by whom they are controlled. They believe so because they have so often seen Congress reject what the people desire, and do instead what the interests demand.
>
> The loss of confidence in Congress is a matter for deep concern to every thinking American.
>
> Many of the old style leaders ... have grown old in the belief that money has the right to rule.

The people of the United States demand a new deal and a square deal.

"Governor, let me say at the start how much I have admired your leadership in creating, with Teddy Roosevelt and a handful of others, the conservation movement in this country. I'd love to speak with you about those accomplishments — your coining the term 'conservation ethic,' your founding of the National Conservation Association, your leadership as the first chief of the U.S. Forest Service — but I can't. In the limited time you've offered me, I'm here to talk about your role as Governor in supporting unemployment relief. As a Republican politician, you offer an interesting contrast to other Republicans, such as, for example, Ogden Mills."

The Governor didn't take the bait. "Ok. Where do you want to start?"

"How about President Hoover's aversion to the dole?"

"Just right. It was high principle with him. If the Federal Government gave food or clothing or even money to those starving, that principle would be violated. But not if a city or state Government did it.

"A delicate distinction. Made even more so by the fact that, for Hoover, there was no limit to the money which the Federal Government could advance to banks or industrial corporations. The Hoover principle attracted diverse support, some of it surprising. The AFL rejected unemployment insurance as un-American. That was in 1932. In the same year, Silas Strawn, President of the US Chamber, said 'it would be deplorable if this country ever voted a dole. When we do that, we've hit the toboggan as a nation.'"

"That was the year I wrote the President, asking for a special session of Congress to deal with unemployment and make appropriations for relief of the needy. David Reed, my own senator, rebuked me for this, claiming the problems of starvation were vastly exaggerated, that such hardships as existed were being nicely handled by city and state. To prove the point more generally, Hoover enlisted Hiram Bingham, senator from Connecticut, to telegraph all the governors, asking whether any of them had noticed starvation in their communities. Thirty-nine of the first forty to respond said they had never heard of it. I was the only one to admit that in Pennsylvania we knew starvation. We knew it was widespread and getting worse."

"I see. Starvation, like sales tax, must stop at the state line. Governor, Harry Hopkins told me that Lorena Hickok, the crack reporter he sent around the country to assess the condition of people as an ordinary citizen would see it, came first to see you."

"Yes, we had some 1,150,000 unemployed. And many others on short hours. Not more than 40% of our normal work force had full-time work. When, kicking and screaming, Hoover was forced to sign the Emergency Relief Act of 1932, I applied for $45 million, the maximum permitted a single state. I pointed out that even if we got $60 million out of the $300, spreading it around those in need, $60 million would give each jobless citizen only 13 cents worth of food per day and that for one year only. In its wisdom, the Government gave us $11.3 million. In fact, by the end of 1932, only $30 million, or 10%, of the sum authorized, had actually been allotted for relief."

"The Act cast RFC's largesse in the form of loans, I believe."

"Exactly. Repayable with interest in July of this year. Loans rather than grants. For Hoover, another key principle. You know, the President was either misled by his staff or blind to realities. He actually believed that in urban centers like Philly and New York, people left their jobs for the more profitable one of selling apples on street corners."

Adam was scribbling furiously. Looking up from his notes, he threw a fat pitch.

"Hoover claimed to be opposed to Federal relief out of a concern for the moral health of those in need. Do you buy that idea?"

"Let's be honest. The force behind opposition to Federal relief is fear of taxes. Fear of higher taxes on concentrated wealth. Local relief means making the poor man pay."

Adam didn't follow Pinchot's last point and asked him to explain.

"Most local relief comes from taxes. Russell Sage has reported private funds supply only 28%. Taxes at the local level come mainly from real estate, affecting almost all residents. So, increased taxes to meet local demands for relief reduces the buying power of residents by exactly the amount of the increase. It comes out of consumption. And that can only serve to further our economic maladjustment and to sink us deeper in the hole. In contrast, the feds, if they had the will, could run deficits, to be made up in good times."

Adam recalled Harry Hopkins making the same point. Now embarrassed, Adam saw that he had not understood his boss.

Adam blurted out inanely, "And that's precisely what FDR's doing. Well, I've taken too much of your time. Would you permit me another question of a more personal nature. Of course, you needn't answer. So, I've interviewed Ogden Mills and now you. Both of you come from families of immense wealth and were educated at Harvard and Yale, two of the top universities in the country. Both of you are Republicans. Both of you entered public service. And, yet, despite these similarities, the role of Government in serving the public, as each of you see it, couldn't possibly be further apart. I puzzle over why?"

"Interesting question. Very interesting. And in the end, of course, unanswerable. But, since I know you won't let me off the hook with that excuse, let me try out some ideas. And chime in, won't you? It can't be the schools. A particular professor? Possibly, but not in my case. Peer influences? Again, possibly. But I wager unlikely. Because we are shaped in these respects by the time we reach college and choose our friends, and our courses too."

"So, that leaves family, doesn't it?"

"Precisely. And its influences are shaped by the influences of one's parents' parents and so on back in history. If one traced my parents and those of Ogden Mills, and went even further back in our family histories, I bet you'd find an explanation for our different approaches. But how about your background? How did it happen that you went from law school to the WPA?"

"Instead of Wall Street?" Adam said with a comfortable laugh. "My case falls outside your reckoning. My Father trained my twin brother and me to be Republicans. Rigidly trained, we were to be libertarian style Republicans. Somewhere along the way, we started to question his philosophy. Bill White, who I know was a fellow Progressive with you and Harold Ickes in the twilight days of the Bull Moose crusade of 1920, is a life-long friend of my Father, a frequent visitor to our home in Manhattan, Kansas. When Father and Bill White talked, my brother and I listened. As we grew up, Bill turned our heads toward progressive thinking. So, too, did a Freudian psychiatrist who lived on our street. We were influenced by long talks with her over cold milk and warm cherry pie."

"What about your mother?"

"She died in childbirth. Father raised us with some help, now and then, from surrogates; the psychiatrist, for example. By the time I got to law school, I was prepped to adopt a large view of Government's role. And, I should add that the legal method of thinking about the role of law bends one's head towards that idea. I was taught that well shaped laws work, that laws can be designed to improve man's lot. That's why law schools graduate more liberals than conservatives."

"So, neither nurture nor nature rule the day. As I said, your question remains essentially unanswerable, even by ourselves. Any more questions?"

"When you became the first chief of the Forest Service, back in 1905, you are recorded as saying that job was 'worth more to me than all the treasures of all the pirates of history.' Why?"

"A domain of sixty million acres. Something to protect, for the earth belongs of right to all its people, and here was a chance to preserve a very small, but important, piece of it. As I've said many times, humans must never take more from the earth than they put back. This idea is simple, an American virtue, the very stuff of which Democracy is made. But look, I thought you came here to talk jobs."

They both rose; the office door was opened by the Governor's secretary, and the Governor bade Adam good-bye, extending very best wishes to Harry Hopkins. "I applaud what you're doing. With all my heart I do. Keep at it."

Adam turned to leave, hesitated, and turning again, said "One last question?'

The Governor nodded, glancing at his watch.

"In your seminal book on conservation, published in 1910 I believe, you said 'The people of the United States demand a new deal, a fair deal.' May I assume you named our President's program for fixing the Depression?"

The Governor's smile widened. "It's been my pleasure," he said, as the door to his office closed.

The interview confirmed Adam's initial reading of the man, particularly in regard to independence and integrity. Leaving the building, Adam thought of Cyrano de Bergerac and his *panache blanche*. And he thought of Father and Bill White, and how, over a dinner of perfectly roasted pork, they would debate the merits of these two public servants.

11

———•———

BENNO WAITED PATIENTLY FOR VIOLET to join him. He was seated on a bench outside the theater and away from the outflowing theater crowd. It had been a magnificent New York City day, ushered in by a steady wind from the Northwest, the kind that sweeps away all haze and humidity, scrubbing the air as if to prepare it for the feast of perfumes that mark the arrival of April's floral bounty. Benno felt the evening breeze on his face, across the nape of his neck and along his sleeveless arms, like water lapping at the side of a boat.

It was a tranquil moment. His mood was uncommonly mellow, more so than at any time since he arrived in the City. And why not? Violet was on the WPA payroll, singing her heart out as the indomitable Mabel. And he had made it to Home Relief and now was headed for a possible job opening in a sculpture shop. Suddenly there were prospects to hope for. He felt a stir of yearnings that, crushed to numbness, had lain dormant for years. Could that crystalline sky arching over him, bejeweled with countless sparkling stars, be a new symbol, as fresh as the Northwest wind? Perhaps a dome of protection against want, whether of food, shelter or the dignity of work?

When Violet appeared, Benno was close to sleep, sheltered by the protective armor of his imagination. It was late. They walked home through quiet streets, she brimming with the energy of conquest by stage, he sharing her exuberance vicariously while imagining good things for himself the next day. Her energy level continued through the trip home and into bed, where her desires pushed beyond Benno's experience. Resting before sleep overtook them, Violet let out a little cry.

"Oh, Benno," she said. "After a day like this, I thought I'd come home exhausted and go right off to sleep."

"Pure happiness. That's it, Violet. No stimulant's more powerful."

Benno left at 6:30 AM the next morning to walk the diagonal to the 85th Street transverse, cutting west to 5th, then north past the Metropolitan Museum of Art to enter the Park at 85th. He figured an hour, leaving 30 minutes in reserve before the scheduled start. He carried a backpack containing as many stone carvings as he could manage. En route he rummaged around his head, trying to rehearse lessons learned in Manhattan about the craft of stone carving, design and lettering. Knowing nothing of what the WPA sought, he wanted to be ready for anything. At first his mind moved like cold maple syrup. But by the time he had reached the Public Library at 42nd and 5th, remembrances were starting to flow. Upon reaching 85th Street, the master stone carvers who had taught him came into focus.

Benno found the sculpture shop easily enough. It was in a low-ceiling building on the south side of the 85th transverse, plumb in the middle of the park. But there was no hiring. Hillary had jumped the gun. The building was empty save for an old man Benno saw sitting on a bench. He had a considerable beard, pepper and salt, descending unkempt past high cheekbones sharply etched by taut cellophane-thin skin that, Benno knew, was the telltale sign of not getting enough food.

Benno took him for a stone carver and, indeed, there were the remains of one about him. With a gleam in his eye, the man told Benno he'd been trained on Hopton-Wood limestone by the masters of Derbyshire. It took Benno further questioning, at risk of appearing stupid and unskilled in stone work, to discover that Hopton-Wood was the material used in the great Cathedral of St. Paul's atop Ludgate Hill.

"Letter carvers all come from England, far as I know. Steven Horay's my name. I'm the caretaker of this space. What's your business, young man?"

Benno dropped his backpack, grown heavy with time and distance. On hearing Benno's purpose, Steven said, "Sorry to disappoint you. It's clear from that satchel you were all puckered up to make an impression. Wish I had a job to offer. Plenty of carving to be done. And rumors are there will be jobs. But nothing yet. And I've heard it before, many times. Plenty of confusion now, as ERB stops before WPA gets under way. Give me your name. I'll make a note of it. You're the first to apply for stone carving, at least the first without a proper accent. So, what entitles you to that title?"

Benno's face betrayed an heroic effort to overcome the shock of this news, which hit him like a fist to the jaw.

"That's a load of stone you lugged up here. Even in the dark, I can feel your disappointment."

Steven's comment was like a shot of adrenaline to Benno. Recovering, he unpeeled his pent-up love for the profession he had chosen in high school, layer by layer.

Horay heard him out, then asked, "Do you do lettering or just free form sculpture." Steven's question betrayed nothing. "Craftsman or artist, how do you see yourself?"

The question agitated Benno and his general disappointment caused him to cast off customary caution. "Mr. Horay, may I speak frankly? I hate that distinction. For me it doesn't exist. I sculpt objects of art, objects of my own devising, and I have samples in my pack should you be interested. But I also do lettering. In my first year's classes, I felt something like primeval awe in the presence of Roman Lettering on slate. History came alive for me at that moment. The idea of permanence, of creating a record for future generations, perhaps, even, for the sensitive ones, of inviting them to ponder the carver himself. Whenever I carve letters, these feelings return. They make me happy."

———◆———

Benno carried his disappointment back to the apartment, walking the distance in a steady Spring rain that soaked him through before the half-way point. He was chilled, but not by the rain, which was warm, but by the colder air through which it moved. Memories of home crowded his head. "Morels pop up after the first warm rain of Spring," Dan told the boys, as they prepared to hunt this treasure. "'Morchella deliciosa' — as McIlvaine's puts it." Dan knew where to look. Along Wildcat Creek where it runs into the Kaw, and beside Kerry Creek under the cotton-woods, usually in sandy soil. And especially in burnt pastureland. Benno recalled the smell and taste, after their bounty had been sautéed in butter, minced garlic, a dash of sherry and some grated nutmeg. These thoughts turned him maudlin, sadder even than before the rain.

By the time Violet returned, his body and clothes had dried out but, as she quickly detected, his spirits were still damp. She had a way of getting him to talk and knew, intuitively, when to call on this skill. She got him to run the day's movie backwards. When he'd finished, she took his hand in both of hers.

"Benno, you won't believe this, but Stephen, the guy who plays Frederic, is a mushroom hunter. Just last week he told me about mush-rooming around the City, even in Central Park. Said last year he'd found that mushroom you mentioned, way up north."

"Morels?" Benno looked skeptical.

"Remember, Benno, the City's full of surprises. Imagine a mush-room — what'd you call it — a morel — hiding in plain sight among millions of New Yorkers. Take me there, won't you? On a hunt. From what your Father used to say, the next few days should be perfect."

Excited by her idea, she tried kissing him. He turned away, this way and that. "Oh, you must. Let's see the bottle half full for a change," she said, still trying to land a kiss.

"Ok, Ok. I get the point. Until I become a sculptor, I'm a mycologist."

Three days later they walked to the north end of the Park. Benno carried a basket borrowed from the show and two pairs of scissors. Just beyond the northernmost transverse, Benno noticed the tops of tall syc-amores growing beside a creek flowing east to west. "That's the spot, if one exists," he announced. "Let's have a look."

Skilled, lucky or blessed, in less than five minutes they were staring down at a generous patch of fine morels, looking fresh as newborns, which in fact they were. Benno showed Violet how to cut the mushrooms at the base and then tap them to leave spores behind for next year. Busing back to the lower east side, they created quite the stir when the bandana covering the basket blew off. Looking down at the pockmarked brown and grey matter, riders were dumbfounded to hear what they were and where they came from (a place only described as Central Park). One, who moved away to the door as the bus slowed at his stop, couldn't restrain himself as he exited the bus:

"You gotta be nuts to eat those things. They look diseased. They're still moving."

Back in their neighborhood, they picked up some fresh bread and butter, a head of garlic and a bottle of cheap chianti. It was a day to remember. In the middle of the night, Violet awoke to the thought that they had left not a single morel for Stephen. Waking Benno, she tried to infect him with her shame.

"Good grief, Violet. You woke me for this? He had the same chance. Better, since he knew the spot. Go back to sleep." She did, but not until it occurred to her that, as there was more than one sycamore in the Park, there must be more than one patch of morels.

———————◆———————

It was not until Monday, August 26th that Benno was able, again, to seek work as a sculptor. By then the WPA had become established in New York City, occupying the same offices in the Port Authority Building that the work-relief center for the CWA had used. Harry Hopkins, after hearing from Mayor La Guardia that the relief administration needed 'drama,' had announced in June the appointment of General Hugh S. Johnson as Works Progress Administrator for New York City. Johnson was known for being the hard charging, outspoken and highly opinionated chief of the National Reconstruction Administration. But, in case that didn't create enough drama by way of anticipation, Hopkins informed the New York State Administrator that, in deference to the size and prominence of New York City, he was dividing the state's territory so that, for purposes of the WPA, the city would become the "forty-ninth state," with Johnson reporting not to Albany but directly to Hopkins in Washington.

Again tipped off by Hillary, more accurately this time, Benno arrived before dawn at the WPA's placement offices, which opened at Eighteenth Street and Second Avenue. The line was already long and growing. Similar lines were forming at the ERB home-relief offices around town. Five thousand applicants were assigned WPA jobs that day, among them Benno, who, without testing or even a cursory look at his work, was accepted for the sculpture shop on the 85th street transverse in Central Park.

General Johnson led the City's office under the banner "Put men to work," a compassionate creed of urgency that reverberated along the canyons of Manhattan, resulting in thousands being hurried into "shovel ready" jobs of one kind or another, whether or not they knew which end of the shovel to use.

Benno's excitement over winning the job was tempered by the realization that his ability as a sculptor had been irrelevant. Take what you get and be grateful, that's my philosophy, he said to himself. Yes, and every man for himself, that too had become his philosophy, one he attributed to living in the big city. The Good Samaritan story, while uplifting and precisely on point, was just a story. Looking out for the other guy, Benno knew, became increasingly unrealistic as one's own conditions declined. Once a certain level of depravity was reached, and each human being had his own point, it became a "dog eat dog" existence, with consideration of others becoming an unaffordable luxury.

Luckily for Benno, he had reached the intake officer on the first day. By Tuesday, 20,000 job seekers stormed home-relief offices, unmoved by the WPA's ability to process only 5,000 a day. In the ensuing bedlam, skills were often not well fitted to the jobs. If Benno had delayed, a plumber might have been assigned to carve the stones that Benno, by chance, was hired to fashion. With patience and persistence, the City's leaders hoped that everyone in need could secure work. By the end of September, the WPA had provided jobs to 170,000 New Yorkers. The numbers continued to climb, reaching 207,000 by General Johnson's retirement in 1936.

Steven Horay welcomed Benno back, recalling their discussion in the Spring. He seemed friendly and genuinely interested in Benno's training and experience. Benno imagined commissions pouring in from all over town, from across the state, commissions that would challenge his imagination, tax his creative energies, fulfill his dream of becoming a recognized artist and even coax back to life the childish optimism he had left behind in Kansas so long ago. As Horay assigned spaces to the men, Benno's hopes rose, despite the caution he had learned from so many disappointments. He had visions of marble busts, reliefs in schist, stone buildings in Romanesque style. His spirits soared throughout the day and, that evening, grew contagious as Violet caught the fresh breeze that had carried him home.

Benno arrived early the next day, ready for work, with his tools sharpened, head clear, hand steady. He imagined performing heroic service in the cause of "art that works," as Harry Hopkins, defending his commitment to enabling artists to earn bread as well as blue collar types, had playfully dubbed the WPA arts projects.

For his first assignment, Steven handed him a sketch of what he was to carve on the natural cleft surface of a 1 x 2 foot stone, two inches thick. "You said you're a stone carver, Benno, that you love carving letters. I have no slate to offer but this granite will test your mettle. Off with you now. Remember, this is not a race. Measure twice. Cut once."

Benno tried unsuccessfully to hide his disappointment. From heavenly imagings of statuary to rival those found in the Tivoli Gardens, he plunged earthward to the reality of carving "W P A" on a granite plaque, with "1935" beneath it. Roman Lettering, of course. Nothing more or less. His spirits sagged, then collapsed. Over the next few hours of work, though, diverted by the intense concentration that his slightly rusted trade demanded, he began to revive. Far beneath Benno's acquired instinct for caution was a native-born Kansas boy's simple belief that life's fortunes, like the weather, even out over time.

Here, he realized, was a plain test of skill. With what Benno believed was typical British restraint, so natural to an island race, Steven must want to see how well he could do on a plaque before assigning him one of the challenging commissions he had dreamed of. For now, he would be content to prove himself.

———————

Violet continued happily in the role of Mabel through the Fall and into 1936. It was still difficult to get her arms around the idea that she was being paid to have so much fun. In January a man came backstage before she could scurry out into a cloudless night of bitter cold. He introduced himself as Lehman Engel, a composer and conductor.

"You might have heard of me. We have the same employer," he said with a sly chuckle.

Violet drew a blank. Undeterred, the man pressed the search for recognition, behavior that, on recounting to Benno later that night, she couldn't explain.

"I can," Benno said. "Conductors wield a lot of power over others and with that comes egos of large size."

"Perhaps you saw Sean O'Casey's *Within the Gates*," Engel continued. "I did the incidental music for that. And for the more recent production of T.S. Eliot's *Murder in the Cathedral.*"

"I wish I could have seen those. There just isn't time for everything, is there, Mr. Engel. And what may I do for you before I run home through this awful cold?"

"I know it's late. I'll be brief. You have a fine voice. A soprano instrument with potential. I am organizing a small choral group to perform Madrigals and would like to have you audition. This G&S show won't last forever, and, as you know, the longer you play the more pressure there is for turnover. My group will be under the wing of Federal One. It will be paid to rehearse, will do so frequently, and will perform around town and on radio."

"Mr. Engel, I know …"

"Please, Violet, it's 'Lehman.'"

"…next to nothing about madrigals. Never sung one, at least any I knew was a madrigal. I don't think it would work, even if I got picked."

"Auditions will start in a couple of weeks. At the new WPA Theater of Music, 254 West 54th. If you change your mind, just swing by and, if there's still room for a soprano, I'll give you a chance. By the way, I understand you'd never heard of G&S before playing Mabel. In our field sometimes less is more. And, now, you should make a dash for home."

Violet found Benno in bed. Undressing quickly and still cold throughout, she slid under the covers beside him and rubbed her frigid nose against his warm cheek, a token of her overall condition. Benno was always many degrees warmer than Violet, a puzzling delight on Winter nights.

"'Madrigals,' that's what they're going to sing. What's that mean to you?"

"If that nose of yours is a sample of your body heat, or lack of it, you need some thawing out." He gently moved his hand to the small of her back, then pulled her to him, body to body, head to toe.

"Part singing of the sort done in England and Italy around the 16th and 17th centuries. Father loves that kind of music. We heard it often. Mostly love songs but other secular stuff, especially about nature. Which is why he loved them. Let's see, can I remember the composers? Well, Purcell, certainly. And Thomas Morley. Monteverdi. But don't ask me to sing anything. I'm only good for nose warming."

"Do you think I'd like this sort of thing? Strange, but since I was a kid I've only done solos. Engel was certainly engaging. Hugely energetic. And he made the chorus sound rather special. You know, exceptional in size (small) and talent (large)."

"Sounds like he tickled your ego. It could be fun. And very different from playing Mabel every night. If you're not careful, soon you'll be earning a living wage."

Benno was getting aroused. He wanted more than Violet's nose. But they still had not succeeded in bed. Violet loved Benno and he loved her. Both believed that, under these conditions, making love should be simple. But from experience, they now knew it was hard. What they believed should be happening between the sheets wasn't. The more they worked the problem the more it worried them and the more it worried them the more elusive a solution seemed to become.

Feeling Benno's condition, Violet said "Shall we give it a try?"

"Sure." But, then, predictably, anxiety crashed Benno's party to chase arousal away, leaving them irretrievably sad.

"It's ok, Benno. Not tonight. We're both tired. Roll over so I can spoon up to you. It always puts me to sleep."

———— • ————

In February, at the direction of Hallie Flanagan, leader of Federal One, the leads in *Pirates* were changed. Violet got two weeks' notice. She went immediately to the Federal Music Project's offices in the long abandoned Friars Club on 48th Street, hoping to find it still possible to audition for Lehman Engel's choral group.

She found Mr. Engel there, alone in the large ballroom auditorium. He had come early to work on program notes for what would be the Madrigal Singers' first public concert. The group, sixteen in all, had already been selected out of countless numbers of out-of-work singers, virtually all of them professionally trained and qualified through active vocalizing until the Depression took hold. Gorgeous voices, many of big solo-quality that were a challenge to blend, a veritable League of Nations, with Italians, Jews, Germans, Russians and Poles, among others.

"Violet, what a surprise. I gave up on you some time ago."

"As you predicted, I was just shoved off the Pirates ship. Came right over."

"Too late, love. But there's a waiting list. Things happen in this business. So I'll add you to the sopranos. I don't follow first in line. If an opening comes up, I invite those suitable for the part to audition. Since you're here, if you have some time, let's see what you sound like up close. Try some scales, shall we?"

He tested her up and down the register. And, then, he said: "Sing anything you wish, other than what G&S wrote for Mabel."

Violet responded with Cole Porter's *Don't Fence Me In,* a song that called up the happier moments of her Dalhart life.

Mr. Engel then handed her the score of Purcell's *In These Delightful Pleasant Groves.*

"I bet you've never sung this before."

"Right. Among so much else one hears in this city."

"Try to sight read as best you can. "

"Ok, but give me a few minutes, if you don't mind."

Violet was a good reader. She managed the piece, but barely, with no loss of dignity.

"A good first try. Nicely sung, Violet. I think I should point out, before you leave, that we rehearse for two and one half hours, five days a week. We expect to perform one or two times a week, so you can see this is a full time job. Does it still seem like your cup of tea?"

"Maybe."

———————

In March Violet got a letter postmarked Dalhart, Texas. It was from her mother. She described her husband as a broken man. Broken physically from a back frayed numb in service to a mind unwilling to yield even a square yard to the wrath of Nature. Broken mentally from seepage, the heart-breaking state of hopelessness that slowly found its way into even the most iron-clad minds of Dalhart men "Unstoppable," she said. "Just like the dusters that penetrated our doors and windows. And there's nothing, absolutely nothing, I can do about it. Nor can anyone else. The town is filled with broken men just like your daddy."

She spoke not a word of her own condition, leaving Violet to imagine the daily drudgery, suffering and pain that were her lot. Violet assumed the Dalhart women gathered together to help one another by sharing their common agonies. The thought lessened her vicarious ache. In fact, however, for the most part these women bore their troubles alone, feeling too mortified by the condition of their homes and family to reach out to others. Their pride was stubborn and harder than a hammer to dent.

She reported news of the town. Big news. A filmmaker named Pare Lorentz, apparently with backing from the U.S. Government, had picked Dalhart to center a documentary on how the Great Plains had been settled and then brought to ruination. He had filmed in Kansas, Colorado and Oklahoma too. But Dalhart's own Bam White, whom Violet knew growing up, had been picked by Lorentz to be a central figure in the film. This little man with the handlebar mustache would become the iconic plainsman. Bam was thrilled, Violet's mother wrote. All he had to do was look himself as he hitched his horse to a plow and pulled it through a field. The film was finished, her mother wrote, and would be shown in the White House very soon, with an opening thereafter in New York City. She didn't know where. Didn't even know what Lorentz was calling his film. But she hoped Violet could track it down.

"I think it's something you'll want to see," her mother ventured, "being as it's got a lot of Dalhart in it and Bam White too. Parts, I reckon, could be painful. But I hope you'll give it a chance and write me."

Her mother's letter brought Violet's parents vividly to mind. Her heart ached. She had been close to them growing up. Love flowed both ways. But in New York, where she had run to with their unqualified blessing, that homesick feeling swiftly waned. She missed them only when she was really down or when letters arrived. She had anticipated her daddy's downfall but kept that likelihood at arm's length with thoughts like "It's way down the road." Or "I'll have plenty of time." Even if Benno and Violet pooled their resources, they'd lack the means for Violet to travel to Dalhart. They could save nothing to give them room to meet the unexpected. On reading her mother's letter, Benno wanted to write his Father seeking help. He would shape the letter as an appeal for Violet only, to let her journey home one last time to see her ailing parents. Violet refused. Tears flowed as she found pen and paper to respond in the only way she could afford.

With little difficulty, Violet discovered plans for rolling out the Lorentz film. It was going to open in June at the Rialto Theater, playing alongside *It Happened One Night.* Lorentz's documentary, they learned, was titled *The Plow That Broke the Plains.* They understood why it was being paired with that screwball comedy.

From opening night, there were lines to see the films. Benno and Violet waited their turn. Violet's anxiety grew as they got closer to the box office. Benno caught the scent and vicariously shared it, aware that the film could carry Violet back two thousand miles to the town where she grew up, the town she watched go from boom to bust and thence to dust. Once dredged up and exposed, her memories could be cruelly painful. In fact, waiting in line brought on uncontrollable sobbing, almost causing Violet to abandon this nostalgic journey. Standing there, she saw Bam White, Pare Lorentz's iconic farmer, then her daddy, both wrinkled, wizened and very old. She watched them merge into one and die. But for her mother's request, Violet would have turned away.

Benno couldn't know of these imaginings, but he understood the source of her tears. He took her arm, looked into her eyes and whispered "Shall we skip it?" They had reached the booth. Violet stepped forward. "Tickets for two, please."

The narrator's voice was at once foreboding and steeped in vicarious suffering. The music, composed by Virgil Thomson, dovetailed perfectly with the subject matter. The film began with a map depicting the ten states that, in part and together, accounted for the Great Plains, an area of 625,000 square miles, 400 million acres, spreading up from the Texas

Panhandle to the Canadian border. As the narrator put it, speaking very slowly in a voice drenched in pathos, "It was a country of windswept grasslands, of high winds and sun, high winds and sun, without rivers, without streams, with little rain."

There followed pictures of the grasslands, oceans of tall blue-stem grass waving in the wind, a sight Violet whispered to Benno she'd never seen. "A cattleman's paradise," the narrator called it.

Violet's eyes welled up again.

"First came the cattle," the narrator intoned. "Up from the Rio Grande. Cattle rolled into the old buffalo range. Once again, the plow-man followed the herder. Make way for the plowman."

Suddenly, on screen, Violet saw her friend Bam White, looking gaunt and sad as the narrator spoke in a voice fraught with danger: "Settler, plow at your peril."

She imagined her daddy atop his tractor, plowing deep furrows, planting his crop of wheat. So happy he looked. Wheat prices had soared as war shrank supply while increasing demand, with President Wilson joining the battle. "Wheat to win the war" was the cry, lending patriotic fervor to an already overheated expectation of fabulous profits, the fitting reward for the exhaustingly hard work of growing wheat on the High Plains.

What followed were scenes of broken tractors and rusted plows, the detritus of a wheat bonanza gone bad. It was all too vivid for Violet, who now was crying freely as the film started to depict the dusters, blowing in from the north, children running for cover, fences buried in dirt, corn swept away in a torrent of wind-driven dust.

The Plow came first, then *It Happened One Night.* For Violet, the searing experience of revisiting her hometown could not be expelled by slapstick romance, even with the likes of Claudette Colbert, playing the pampered socialite, and Clark Gable, the roguish reporter.

"Perhaps a little too much stimulation for one evening," Benno suggested, as they left the theater. "I half expected to emerge into a duster, but instead I'm looking up at this brilliant canopy of bright stars on a moonless night in June. Ah, New York," Benno said. "Tell me how you feel."

"Shredded," Violet said. "My mind's torn apart, like a rag doll in the mouth of a puppy. I know I will be seeing *The Plow* in my dreams for a long time, and it won't be pleasant, believe me."

"One thing about *The Plow* amazes me," Benno said. "It's a devastating critique of Government policy gone bad. An environmental disaster of Olympian size. The unintended result of our interference with Nature."

"Excuse me, but aren't you sounding an awful lot like your old man? You know, the one who cast out his son."

"You're right, of course. It hadn't occurred to me. I was trying to explain why the film shocked me. Because this harsh critique was financed by the very same entity that caused the colossal damage in the first place. The Government seems to be telling us 'Look, we made a mistake,' and there's a lesson here for us to ponder. The whole thing's extraordinary. Behavior reflecting the best in Government. And that's something you won't hear Father say."

———◆———

"What's a brother for, if not this, Violet?"

Benno was trying to get Violet's consent to ask Adam to put his finger on the scales Lehman Engel would use in picking a new soprano. Better yet, one of Harry Hopkins' fingers. After several months of rehearsals, the Madrigal Singers lost one of its sopranos, who was taken ill with parathyroid imbalance. Lehman had called in those on his waiting list, and after auditions, was taking his time in deciding who would fill the slot.

"Do you think I want it if it comes — what did you call it — through 'pull?'"

"What I know is how much you want this job. I'm determined to help you get it. Assume, for a minute, that in the Maestro's opinion, you and the three other candidates are about equal. That he'd be happy with any of you. By the way, that's the sort of outcome that occurs all the time in art and business, in all kinds of jobs, public and private. You look askance. I know because, more than once, Father told me that's the way of the world. First hand, you and I are ignorant. But Father knows, believe me. So, wouldn't it be better all-around for Mr. Engel to pick on the basis of connections rather than the flip of a coin?"

"Here's something else. You've never asked for Adam's help with his boss before. Even when we were in much tougher shape. Why? I know you've talked with your brother about using his position to be helpful. You told me how sensitive he was to appearances, to conflicts and such things. So, why now?"

"Adam gives us what he can spare, which isn't much given his living costs and threadbare pay. When I was really down, before I met you, I thought of asking Adam, but the WPA wasn't running things then, and Adam had told me of his boss' already storied sensitivity to misuse of office for personal benefit. Even a whiff.

"I saw your case as different. You're not his sister. And you're a talent deserving of a place, on the merits. All I'd be asking for is help in tipping the balance where other factors are the same."

Violet folded. Benno got Adam on the phone in his DC office. Benno told the story. Patiently, Adam listened, hoping his instinct about the call wasn't true.

"That's a tight race you're describing. I sure hope she wins. I know it means a lot to have work. Especially to Violet. And not just the money part. Fingers crossed. Anything else?"

Benno realized he'd been a touch too subtle, too hopeful in expecting Adam to offer without being asked.

"Yes, one thing. Could you help, you know, yourself or Mr. Hopkins, I mean have a talk with Mr. Engel so that Violet gets picked. Assuming, naturally, as we are sure is the case, that he would be as happy with her as with the others. You know, given where you are, I just thought it would be wrong not to use the family connection to help out. Doing so hurts no one."

It was a request Adam knew would come, sooner or later. He had often considered the fact that, until now, Benno had never asked him to use influence. This despite many instances where he knew, as Benno did, that it could have helped. The difference in this case, he quickly saw, was that Benno was asking not for himself, a fact that had broken through his impressive self-restraint.

"Look, I know you want to help her. I'd like to help her too, but not this way. You say it won't hurt anyone. You're wrong. It will hurt the WPA. Not a day goes by that Harry doesn't go into the ring to fight against corruption in assigning jobs, efforts by pols — mostly Democrats, by the way — to get their buddies plum jobs in the states. It's an endless fight. And one that we must win or it'll be the end of the WPA. Now, don't you see how impossible it is for me to do what we spend so much time fighting to prevent others from doing?"

Benno took time to respond. "Didn't see that angle at first, Adam. You explained it well, as you always do. Don't worry, I won't try this stunt again."

———◆———

Benno accepted Adam's rejection. But he would not let the matter rest. Violet was too reticent, he thought, to sell herself as he could sell her. He went to the Federal Music Project's offices to find Lehman Engel. Asked to wait, he plotted an approach, carried forward on the wings of instinct alone. Being an artist, Benno wasn't given to tight analysis or the weighing of alternatives.

When Engel returned to his office, Benno was ready, jumping up from a chair to follow him into a sparse room, essentially nothing more than a small space between two doors.

"And you are?"

"Benno Murdock, Mr. Engel. Here as Violet's companion, but without her knowledge, and surely without her willingness had she known, to lay down some reasons for her getting the opening in your chorus."

"A touch irregular, don't you think?" Engel sat behind a small, clean desk. There was no place for Benno to sit, and Engel seemed not the slightest disturbed over the fact that Benno was left standing. "I will choose on the merits. The chorus is the first casualty of doing it any other way. May we consider this meeting concluded?"

Benno launched his attack. He told of first meeting Violet in a breadline, disguised as a man, of her recent life in Dalhart, of her weeping throughout Pare Lorentz's masterpiece, to which Engel had gone mostly to hear Virgil Thomson's music, but had departed the theater deeply moved by all that he saw in and around Dalhart. In what could have been a stroke of genius, he ended the argument by describing Adam and his position at WPA, Benno's effort to have him tip the scales through Harry Hopkins and his brother's refusal to consider the idea.

"You're an unusual young man, if I may say so. What's your profession?"

"The unemployed, until recently. I'm a sculptor, now on the City's payroll, hired to carve letters in stone." The bitterness in his voice was unmistakable.

"Good day, Mr. Murdock. I wish you luck. And Violet too. Rest assured. Times are changing as a new wind blows out of Washington."

Violet was out when Mr. Engel called, a week later. Picking up his call, Benno was the first to learn that the maestro had selected Violet. That night they celebrated at the neighborhood Automat. On the way home they bought a bottle of sauterne. "Why not," Benno had argued. "Didn't we just save a bundle by supping at Horn & Hardart."

In no time, Violet had fallen under the spell of Lehman Engel, whose passion for the music was contagious. He made rehearsals a quiet pleasure to anticipate, a robust joy to experience. Often she would arrive at the Friars Club early, finding Lehman there alone. He was pretty high on himself, a talkative young man prone to storytelling. Fortunately, he had plenty to talk about. On one occasion, Violet asked Lehman what he thought of the President.

"He's the best. That's not just my opinion; it's the truth. And to prove it, I'll tell you a story. Sit down, please.

"A while ago I got a telegram from the White House, actually signed by the President, asking me to participate in a conference on the Federal Projects. At first blush, I was amazed he knew of me. Then, reviewing my connection to Federal Theater and Music, I realized I had actually attracted some attention since 1934. That's when I did my first incidental music score for Sean O'Casey's *Within the Gates*."

"Oh, yes, you mentioned that before. Was it a Federal Theater production?"

"No, no. Actually it was Broadway, starring Lillian Gish and directed by Melvyn Douglas. O'Casey came over here and we became very, very good friends. He was such a funny Irishman, nearly blind, and he was full of admiration when he wrote Melvyn a long letter. It was my music he liked best. And I had done some other stuff. Ballets for Martha Graham, a choral piece for Madame Dessoff performed with her choirs in Town Hall. So, I was getting around even then.

"Well, Edward Goodman, who was a biggie at Federal Theater, contacted me and asked if I would write incidental music for *Murder in the Cathedral*. And, I said yes, although it was totally dishonest of me because, when I read the play, being young and snide, I was by then only 25, I just thought that anything about religion must be pure hogwash. I could go on but — didn't you ask me about FDR?"

"Yes, so let's hold *Murder* for another time. You had gotten this personally signed note."

"Well, I RSVP'd right away and showed up at the White House and was ushered into a small room and two minutes after I got there, perhaps even faster than that, President Roosevelt was wheeled in and I remember feeling a tremendous emotional shock because I had never seen him in a wheelchair; I had always thought he could walk. A black servant brought him and left him there, facing me. He greeted me, shook hands. It wasn't going to be a conference. I was the only person, because apparently he had asked various people opinions about someone to come and discuss the project and since I was doing so many different things, I think that was the reason.

"He had a long yellow pad, a legal pad it was, and a pencil. He was very pleasant, thanked me profusely for coming, and then asked me — I was so impressed — because he asked me what I considered to be the most pertinent questions. Such as did I think the projects were doing any good for the people who were on them. Did I feel that the general public was interested in what was being offered? Did I think that the general quality was high? Those kinds of things. They were all very pertinent and he took notes on my answers. He asked a lot of questions and the time seemed to go by in a second and the same black servant came back and said, 'Mr. President, I think it is time to go,' and he said, 'Oh, I am so sorry,' and shook hands with me and thanked me again profusely and he said, 'But don't go, because a friend of yours wants you to stay to have tea with her,' and of course it could only be one person and I said, 'Mr. President, as much as that would please me, I am sure that Mrs. Roosevelt is doing it to give me a reward for coming here, but I have already had my reward and I think she could use the hour much better if I decline.' And I shook hands and left."

Although it would not seem possible, in Violet's head, Lehman's stature grew right before her loving gaze. So, too, his ego, but no matter.

"That's a great story. And so honorable. You made the right call. I'm sure I would have accepted."

Other singers trooped in, breaking the spell. Lehman instructed the chorus to take their places. Rehearsal began.

"First, a word about this program. It's American Music. I selected the pieces to depict the growth of our country — or if you prefer — a musical picture of the life of our people. We begin with obscure 18th Century songs: *The Death of Brave General Wolfe, Old Colony Times* and *The American Hero* — or *Bunker Hill* — *A Sapphick Ode*. These songs represent the victory of secular music — the historical ballad — over the 'puritan' attitude that had long rendered instrumental music taboo and limited songs to the spiritual. You might find this hard to believe — I certainly do — but in America's early days, non-religious music was declared by law improper. Indeed, even after 1750, all public performances of secular music in Boston, referred to by the pious Bostonians as 'sacrilegious,' were prohibited as 'tending to discourage industry and frugality, and greatly increase impiety.'

"We will follow up with more familiar songs of the Civil War period, divided between Songs of Peace (*The Burman Lover, Lubly Fan, Will You Come Out Tonight* and *Lilly Dale*) and Songs of War (*The Battle Hymn of the Republic, Marching Through Georgia, Stand up for Uncle Sam, My Boys* and *Tramp, Tramp, Tramp*). I want you, and, of course, our audience to see this section as transitional, a living chronicle of the country's growing freedom.

"We will then perform Randall Thompson's *Peaceable Kingdom*, recently commissioned by the League of Composers. It calls for double chorus and treats the ancient text of Isaiah in the musical tongue of our day."

Violet had never heard of Thompson or his new work. Nor did she know of the inspiration for it, a painting called the *Peaceable Kingdom* by Edward Hicks, depicting William Penn making peace with the Indians and Daniel making peace with a group of lions.

"We will end the concert with a cluster of rollicking folksongs: *The Monkey's Wedding, Jenny Fair, Sourwood Mountain, Brother Green, Don't You Weep No More, Mary* and, finally, those barroom classics you all know: *Cocaine Lil* and *Frankie and Johnny*. Now, to work."

Lehman had them warm up with scales, using "hee-hee" and "hah-hah," a favorite silliness of his that got the job done with a touch of serious fun.

In many ways it was an extraordinary rehearsal, one Violet described to Benno in detail.

"We were in the middle of *Old Colony Times* when Orson Welles came through the door, an impish grin on his face, and took up a position among the basses. We all recognized him, of course, and were amazed. He looked much younger than I supposed.

"'Orson, you're late,' Lehman said, stopping us in mid-phrase. He then explained that Orson had invited himself to the rehearsal, having claimed to have nothing better to do that afternoon. Orson was taking Lehman out to dinner and then they were going to the Henry Street Settlement, where Orson was staging a children's opera that Lehman got Aaron Copland to write for Henry Street's Music School. 'Busy night,' he allowed, before keying the chorus to begin the *Old Colony* piece again.

"Lehman has the energy of fifty border collies," Violet said, sounding breathless.

"I'm beginning to understand," replied Benno. "Rachel told us that people like Engel, who are on fire at a young age, tend to burn themselves out by the time they hit middle age. She said we all have limited supplies of intellectual capital. Most of us never exhaust what we have, because we just don't maximize our potential, even over a lifetime. Others do, spreading it out. And then there are the fire-eaters like Engel — and Orson Welles would be cut from the same cloth — who use up their supply before middle age."

"I'd like to meet your Dr. Rachel someday. She seems to have had more influence over you than your Father does, or I could ever hope to. I don't buy her story. It's like claiming that our heart has only a certain number of beats before pooping out, beats we can use up slowly by avoiding exercise, or quickly by running and doing other heart-pumping exercise all the time. I believe this is nonsense, that we are dynamic, not static. That intellectual capital grows with use. Ditto the heart. Perhaps ditto the sensual pleasures, although there, as you know, I'm wanting in depth of experience."

"We're so different. Excessive Kansas caution sharing a room with Dalhartian over-confidence."

"Ok, but there *is* a right answer. How about putting this question to Dr. Rachel: Had Mozart exhausted his intellectual capital by the time he died — what age was it? Thirty-seven? Just posing the question makes the idea laughable."

———◆———

Violet's relationship with Lehman Engel deepened as weeks and months with the Madrigal Singers flowed on. At first, she saw his interest as gearing up for something. As his attentions grew, becoming unmistakably outsized in relation to those he directed to others, Violet pondered the obvious — flirtation preparatory to making a pass or what? Did he linger after rehearsals just to talk with her? She wasn't by any stretch the most musically talented or sophisticated among the singers. Nor was she a provocative dresser, as some of the others strained to be. Or the best looking, for, as with most choruses, the range was vast.

His attentions were cerebral. He wanted to hear more than Benno had given him about her background, where she came from, what kind of family, what pulled (or drove) her to New York City. She felt comfortable with his interest, flattered in fact. But nothing approaching a heat wave. Whatever his scent, she couldn't catch it. Were men his thing or was he so awkward with women that he couldn't show his sexual side? Violet never found out, although, from observation and experience, she became convinced that awkwardness wasn't blocking desire.

One night early in December, 1936, Lehman invited Violet to stay behind after rehearsal. He said he had a record, on the blue Decca label, that he wanted her to hear. This sort of thing had happened a number of times, always resulting in something new, something she had never imagined, something other than a pass. Typically, it was fun.

Producing the record, he put it on his player.

"Lehman, I'm wondering what's up. May I see the label?"

He handed it over. "Right you are," he said. "I was a bit hasty. It's a bluesy, jazzy thing performed by the Harlem Hamfats, who are out of Chicago actually. Recorded in early October. Kansas Joe McCoy wrote the song. Called it '*Weed Smoker's Dream*,' with subtitle '*Why Don't You Do*

Now.' When I heard it I immediately saw you, all slinky in sequins, singing beside a concert grand."

He returned the disc to the player where it began to revolve. The tune was infectious. There was a lead trumpet, with guitar, drums and piano adding a propulsive beat. Violet couldn't catch the words in the first verse, but by the second she had them all:

> May's a good looking frail,
> She live down by the jail on her back,
> Though she's got hot stuff for sale.
> Why don't you do now like the millionaires do?
> Put your stuff on the market and make a million too.

"I love that song," Violet cried, when the needle had done its job.

"Not exactly the sort of stuff we sing, though," she added.

"I knew you'd like it. Perhaps I can get the sheet music and you can have a go. I have to say that your voice, your whole manner, are made to deliver this song. That's why we're here."

Violet braced herself for the advance that would crown this little episode. It didn't happen. Violet never knew why, or for that matter, how she would have handled it, despite anticipation, which is something very different from preparation.

12

———◆———

ADAM LEARNED OF HIS FATHER'S connection to the American Liberty League quite by accident. Summoned to the corner office at the Walker-Johnson Building in late June, 1935, he took his customary seat facing Harry Hopkins, who, sitting particularly tall, dressed to the nines and looking particularly spare and thin that day, offered his very wide mouth full of teeth in beamish smile. He looked amiable enough as he studied Adam with those steely eyes, even kindly one might say, but there was something in the smile suggesting trouble ahead. Perhaps the smile of a cat ready to pounce and certain — absolutely certain — of its prey.

Silence reigned a few moments too long, making Adam nervous, which he tried to wipe away with a rash stab at humor.

"What elegance! Bound for the race track today?"

"I didn't invite you here to admire my dress. Appreciated, though. Adam, you hail from Manhattan if I recall?"

"Indeed. The one in Kansas."

"Yes, yes. Of course. And your Father still lives there? A cowman I believe."

Adam detected a struggle in this most impatient and crafty of bosses to appear patient and ingenuous.

"Yes, he feeds Herefords on blue-stem grass in the Flint Hills."

"Ever hear of The Farmers' Independence Council of America?"

"No. Should I?"

"Your Father's its President. It was organized here, at the Raleigh Hotel, on April 11. Although the Council denies it, the same industrialists who sponsored the American Liberty League also backed the Council, along with the meat packers, Swift, Wilson and Cudahy. I'm sure you've read about the League. Rex Tugwell called this crowd a strange grouping of rabid reactionaries, financiers, big businessmen and corporation lawyers. People like Alfred Sloan and William Knudsen of GM; at least a dozen strong from the Du Pont family; Al Smith and his patron, John Raskob; John W. Davis and Sewell Avery. Party be damned, they are Con-Serva-tive! They see the country on the verge of socialism, bankruptcy and tyranny — all three, all at once."

Adam dropped his jaw in surprise, arms akimbo, face reddening in embarrassment. Questions tumbled over each other in his mind, leaving him speechless.

"You must be wondering how I know these things. The President keeps me informed about the Liberty League, which has promised an unremitting fight against us, under the banner of blocking Government encroachments upon the rights of citizens. We were quick to discover the Council, bastard child of the League, and learned of your Father's engagement. I caught Murdock's first radio broadcast just a few days after the Council's birth. His address was carried on NBC from Chicago. He called it *The Farmer and the AAA Amendments*. At first, I missed the connection to our Murdock."

"Well?" Adam said, fear swelling across his chest.

"I can see, now, the source of your verve and punch in the written word. But the ideas? No family resemblance. Your dad excoriated us — Henry Wallace and Chester Davis in particular — for the AAA program. He said it violated every fundamental law of mankind, including the laws of nature and of life, the law of supply and demand and, quite simply, the law of evolution, this by insuring survival of those least fit to survive. Cockeyed. But, oh, boy, it was a hum-dinger alright. He seems to lack even a hint of your coy modesty."

Adam was beyond dismay, his face showing the anguish of having his boss open the door to a dark family closet of whose contents even he was unaware. And pair him with his Father. Angling away from the radio address, he said "What's the Council's purpose?"

"Claims to be a genuine farmers' organization originating in the Corn Belt. Claims to be both patriotic and non-partisan. Claims to have been founded by farmers to protect themselves from further loss of their individual rights. Claims to espouse principles of 'Americanism' in contrast to the 'destructive radicalism' of FDR's administration. Oh, and by the way, your dad made much of his status as a farmer. Never used the word 'rancher' or 'cowman' in the address. Stated, flat out: 'I am a Kansas farmer and have no other occupation.' And he claimed, more aggressively and repeatedly than would seem to have been necessary had his claim been true, that he was speaking for no one but himself. This but five days after the Council was formed and made him its first President."

Adam felt heavy in the chair, too shamed to respond, unable to excuse himself for not responding, unable to stand up and depart, a dead leaf twisting in the wind.

"I'm not holding back because I hope you can help with your dad. His fiery passion, in combination with his powerful ability with words, his uncompromising nature and his access to the national airways — it all could be toxic for us. If you're willing, and I know this is delicate, I hope you'd have a go at the old man. We've learned he's a man of integrity — as one source put it, 'a man who rode straight in the saddle' — a contradictory blend of violent adversary and gentle friend."

"I hope you don't think I was aware. This is news, shocking news, believe me."

"Of course. I never imagined you knew. Or was his spy. Ha! Relax on that account." "He's not doing it for money, if that's what you mean. Look, Harry, I'll do what I can. Boy, your news is distressing. He has taken his fundamentalist beliefs a step too far. As you might guess, Father and I have fought over this sort of thing for years. He's a wily foe. In battle he uses all the leverage of a parent. Of being Father. To be honest, I can't count the number of times I've left his study with ears flattened and tail between my legs. Don't expect too much."

With that, Adam found his legs, stood up and left the office, carrying with him the awful weight of knowing that Father had now spread his despicable beliefs over the airwaves, 'from sea to shining sea' as the patriotic song puts it.

Adam first wrote Benno, reporting what he'd learned from Harry and more through the PR team at WPA, who were willing to probe NBC. They learned that Dan Murdock's next radio broadcast was scheduled for July 7. Benno cautioned Adam to avoid an immediate clash. "Look, we haven't heard what he's been saying. Don't assume the worst. After all, isn't he still a bosom buddy of Bill White?"

Sadly, in fact, Adam had read Father's recent radio talk and knew how far his philosophy and gift for rhetoric had carried him into the public arena.

Adam wrote his Father, asking about the Council and his role in it, using tones of gray, and inviting him to send a copy of his forthcoming address in July.

Dan mistook Adam's neutral tones for bright colors of support; an outcome Adam had never considered possible. A final draft of the address was forwarded by return mail with a four word cover note: "Thanks for your support."

Adam was appalled by what he read. It wasn't Father's opinions that were so upsetting. He had heard most of these rants before, in one form or another. But he had also seen him bend and sometimes even bow, in response to Bill White's rational arguments, offered in the privacy of the Murdock home in Manhattan.

The radio address was, in tone, shrill, and in substance, extreme.

"My purpose is to arouse all patriotic Americans to a sense of the peril which now threatens our liberty.... Steps already taken dangerously commit this nation in the direction of socialization, state capitalism and the tyranny of the dictator."

It was dishonest.

"I am a Kansas farmer and have no other occupation."

Was it because there was no one around to push back? Adam wanted to believe that explanation, but darker ones loomed large and insistent in his mind. Perhaps he was being blackmailed into performing this function. He hated the idea and rejected it for the same reason Adam was sure Father wasn't doing it for money. The worst explanation, and yet the most plausible to Adam, was that Father had become a tool of the eastern industrialists, wooed by big-shot flattery to serve as the spearhead of a conservative attack on the New Deal's solution to the farm problem — or, even worse, a tool without knowing it.

Harry had claimed that the League was spending much more than the Republican Party itself in an effort to kill the New Deal. It had called AAA a "trend toward Fascist control of agriculture." In the talk, his Father had called it "a contemptible device," one "as clearly unconstitutional" as the NRA. Adam was, of course, familiar with the recent practice of the League to sponsor constitutional prejudgments regarding New Deal laws, written by eminent counsel and given wide circulation in hopes of discrediting the legislation in the mind of the public and perhaps even influencing the courts.

As for the substantive arguments contained in the radio address, Adam realized that, so closely did they match up with the League's current propaganda, they could have come directly from that source. But he knew Father's style and his insistence on writing his own speeches, no matter what the subject matter or audience. It was definitely a Dan Murdock product, but one that tracked the League's screeds too closely to be an accident.

And, so, to this effect Adam wrote his Father, appealing to his immense reputation and pride as a cowman and breeder of the quarter-horse; to stop lending his good name to the preposterous program of the League; to resign as President of this newly formed Council; and to cease parading as a "dirt farmer," when all his friends and colleagues knew full well he was nothing of the sort.

At Harry Hopkins' suggestion, Adam included a quote from FDR's June 1934 fireside chat, an effort to put down his Father's repeated and extravagant claims that, like a thief in the night, the New Deal was stealing the farmer's freedom.

"Answer this question out of the facts of your life," FDR told his audience. "Have you lost any of your rights or liberty or constitutional freedom of action and choice? Turn to the Constitution, read each provision of the Bill of Rights, and ask yourself whether you personally have suffered the impairment of a single jot of these great assurances?"

"Father, your address contains not one example of liberty lost or freedom denied," Adam wrote. "Give this project up. Give it up, now, I beg you. If not, it will ruin you." He had first written "our family" but changed it to "you." Better to concentrate on Father and avoid an opening to allow Father to attack him as selfish.

Adam tingled with nervousness as he folded the letter and stuffed it in the already addressed and stamped envelope, the backward ordering of this simple process itself a sign of his agitation. Never before had he so bluntly accused Father of duplicity. Dan Murdock lived in a world of his own design and important elements of it were divorced from the normal perceptions and understandings of those around him. As his sons knew from experience, having seen their opinions of their Father's views of the world evolve from admiring wonderment to contempt, dragged down by the weight of the truth and a sense that Father was downright weird. In recent years, he recognized in the public utterances of many conservative leaders Father's tendency to build fantasies and swiftly come to believe them. In consequence, Adam had mellowed toward Father a little, but never enough to join his brother in leaning towards acceptance rather than contempt.

Adam was edgy waiting for his Father's answer. Anxiety often awoke him around four in the morning, lingering for the hour or so it took for him to rehearse the most difficult moments of growing up with Father. There was nothing voluntary in this process, which, willy-nilly, kept reoccurring, like practicing a Bach Partita.

A response never came. Adam surmised his Father had chosen to bottle up what anger he felt, ignoring both charges and pleas. Through the Summer and Fall and into the new year, there ensued a flow of brief transmittal notes from his Father, containing only the radio addresses and speeches to be given, together with dates, times and places. It dawned on Adam that Father was using this public material to speak privately to his son. The assertions of being just an independent dirt farmer grew more insistent. The claims that New Deal policies took away individual economic freedoms through bribery and destroyed political liberty became more textured and fulsome.

Finally a real letter arrived. Dated January 10, 1936, it informed Adam that Father was going to New York City to give a speech to the National Republican Club on the 15th of March. A draft was enclosed. He urged his son to come to NYC to hear the speech and meet for dinner the night before. And he gloated over the Supreme Court's 6 to 3 decision in <u>U.S. v. Butler</u>, handed down just days before, declaring AAA an unconstitutional invasion of rights reserved to the states.

"Justice Roberts got it right, as I predicted. AAA has now shared the fate of NRA, both killed by the Court standing staunchly in defense of our liberty, upholding rights reserved to the people. Thank God for the Supreme Court and for its wisdom — well, at least the wisdom of two-thirds of the Court — Justices who recognized AAA for what it was: FDR's ugly conceit that he could build better than God. I'm sure you noticed that Brandeis and Cardozo, the two Jews on the bench, joined in Stone's dissent."

13

———————

Violet first heard of halle Flanagan's idea from Lehman Engel. It was February, 1936. Lehman had invited a few of his singers to dine with him after an afternoon concert at the Theater of Music on West 54th Street. They had performed, among other crown jewels in the Madrigal Singers all-Brahms necklace, both *Liebeslieder Walzer* and *Zigeunerlieder*. It was Engel's practice to treat his choir to dinner in small groups. Violet was not unaware of being tapped more often than fair rotation would warrant.

Lehman led the selected group to a small French bistro he favored. The droll maître d', barely five foot one with an unruly handlebar mustache, eyes that sparkled like headlights in the rain and the odor of chopped garlic, ushered the group to a well-used round table far to the rear of the room, near the kitchen, where darkness was only partially overcome by candlelight.

One of the singers had asked Lehman if he knew Elmer Rice. It was the kind of opening Lehman couldn't resist. As a couple of large carafes of house wine, a pinot noir and chardonnay, were put down with glasses, Lehman said, in that formal and often ambiguous way he favored, "My dear friend, 'knowing Elmer' is hardly adequate to describe our relationship." Arched eyes were flung across the table as singers adjusted themselves to be slowly, elaborately entertained. Filling his glass with the red, Lehman began to talk about Elmer, going straight into his brief tenure as New York Director of Hallie's Federal Theater Project.

"So, Elmer was a successful producer and playwright in New York. Like many others, he was unable to resist Hallie Flanagan's passionate plea to join Federal One. Hallie had returned from a European tour of theaters with an idea drawn from the Soviet. As we all know, they use propaganda to glorify the revolution. With Rice, she developed an entirely original form of drama that she called the Living Newspaper. Contrary to what you might think, the Newspaper Guild became a sponsor of the program. Hallie could sell you the Brooklyn Bridge."

A singer asked if propaganda isn't just selling lies to the gullible and uninformed. She said she'd heard the first show, something called *Ethiopia*, was blocked by the White House, scotching the whole idea.

"Hardly," Lehman said. "But, wait a minute. Propaganda can sell the truth too. And Hallie's idea was rooted in accurate, hard-hitting journalism. She's a small but determined fighter. *Ethiopia* didn't stop her. She used that case of censorship, jujitsu fashion, to deepen the promise Harry had given her. And it seemed to work. In fact, as its next effort to dramatize a news event, the Living Newspaper is doing the demise of AAA. It's being written right now. They're calling it *Triple-A Plowed Under*, a nifty title. I'm told it's an essay on agriculture and public policy."

Violet left the dinner table that evening determined to make a pitch for a role in *Triple-A*. After all, didn't she know a thing or two about what happened to the farmer on the high plains? Here was a drama she could relate to, all the way down to the marrow of her bones. There had to be a part for her.

The script for *Triple-A* was still being finalized when auditions began at the end of February. Violet discovered the performance would be given in the Biltmore, on 47th Street near Eighth Avenue, despite initial resistance from the commercial producers to allow the Theater Project to perform within the ten-block heart of Broadway.

There were twenty-five scenes in the play, beginning with the inflation of 1917 ("Farmer, save the nation!" "Plant more wheat!"), then the deflation of the 1920s ("The fact is, agriculture is no longer a lucrative investment. Now do you see that I must call in your paper?"), then the unemployment of the 1930s ("I can't use you anymore." "I can't eat."), followed by milk strikes, farm auctions, the paradox of plenty ("As our economic system now works, the greater the surplus of wheat on Nebraska farms, the larger the breadlines in New York City."), the enactment of AAA, the drought of 1934 ("The sun bakes the soil. Dust covers the land. All green things wither. Cattle die for lack of food and water."), the Supreme Court's decision ending AAA and the consequences that followed.

Violet appeared for auditions at the Biltmore. She got a script and quickly read it through, looking for a part she could throw herself into. She found it in a short, powerful scene centered on Mrs. Dorothy Sherwood, a young mother from Newburgh, New York, whose story was reported in the *Daily News* on August 21, 1935. Even better, she got the part, despite what might have appeared to be "double-dipping" into the WPA well, given her employment as a Madrigal Singer, or perhaps, she wondered, because of it, given the friendship between Lehman Engel and Arthur Arent, the director of *Triple-A* responsible for casting as well as supervising the editorial staff.

Excited by victory, Violet raced home through dark streets now blanketed with an inch and more of snow, the soft kind composed of small, light and perfectly formed crystals preserved by intense cold in dry and unblemished condition, the kind that hushes city noises and cushions one's step with a whispered crunch. Violet journeyed gaily east, directly into the white wind of a nor'easter.

Her energy level unabated, upon reaching the apartment, Violet tried to share it with Benno. No dice. Benno was in a funk over his work. He could feel the electricity Violet brought through the door, but only vicariously; it left no charge. For months he had felt his brain cells, especially those on the right side, atrophying. Today had been a landmark of sorts. He had finished his 50th identical stone plaque, the one bearing the letters "WPA" and the date "1935." His boss, Steve Horay, who being British, liked to be called Steven, hadn't even told him where they had gone.

"I hadn't anticipated the demand or thought you could keep up. It's quite wonderful. I see no end in sight."

Steven's words, offered as a kind of reward, were received in quiet horror by Benno. Finally, the stone carver spoke.

"Where do they go? Ever seen one installed?"

"No, but they're flying out of here as fast as you can complete them. They're used for bridges and retaining walls, you know, that sort of thing, all over the east. I happen to know ten went up river to Bear Mountain."

"For the bears? Better than for the birds, I suppose." Benno wasn't even trying to hide his disappointment.

He had walked home through the same snowstorm that Violet later would charge into with triumph. Benno's hike was sodden, but not by the exquisitely dry snow. He was soaked from the inside out, his spirits crushed by the ironic weight of success.

Violet had an idea for saving the evening.

"I'm going to make you happy, whether you want me to or not. Then who knows what you may feel up for."

Laughing despite himself, Benno went from resignation to revival, obliging Violet as she cleared his head of the day's regrets, making good things happen.

———◆———

Triple-A Plowed Under was to open March 14, by coincidence the night before Dan Murdock was scheduled to speak to the National Republican Club. At his Father's invitation, Adam was coming to the city to hear the speech and join Dan for dinner. When Adam learned of Violet's involvement with *Triple-A* and the opening date, he saw a chance, all at once, to bring his family together, to lobby his Father to quit the Council, to have him reconcile with Benno and even get a taste of what his tax dollars, via the WPA, were able to stage through the Theater Project, the most politically outspoken of Federal One's four undertakings. It was a bold dream. He had often imagined playing the role of reconciler, and made pathetic stabs at it from time to time, but never anything this ambitious.

He first lined up Benno, who said "yes" on condition that Dan was agreeable. Writing Father, Adam reported on the coincidence of dates, the opportunity to see the opening of a Living Newspaper play about the farmer, precisely the subject Dan would be addressing the next night, the chance to see Benno, who, Adam wrote "was looking forward to the family gathering," the chance to meet Violet, the wheat farmer's daughter from Dalhart who Dan had only heard rumors about, and even the chance, as Adam carefully put it, to "iron out differences between us," as if they were tiny wrinkles on a dress shirt. He wondered if he should have gone first to Dan. Perhaps, it wouldn't have mattered. More likely that, Adam concluded.

Dan wrote back, rejecting any possibility of seeing Benno. "He's wasting his life. It's bad enough to feed at the Government trough, but to carve plaques that celebrate the glory of the agency providing the handout is beyond my ken. It would spoil the evening to spend any part of it with him."

As for *Triple-A*, he said, "I'm glad to hear that not all of the WPA crowd are lazy shovel leaners. I'm open to art. Artists work hard for little return. Giving them a leg up is civilized. Book us seats in the orchestra. We'll have dinner afterwards. It'll have to be opening night, though, since I have to get home right after the speech and was planning to take the Kansas City Chief that afternoon." Dan either forgot or ignored Adam's idea of having Violet join them.

The situation was fraught with the danger of moving dysfunctional family relationships from bad to worse. Like trying to lighten the shade of blue on a water-color painting. A screwed up family dynamic can often mend when eyes are averted but worsen from too much attention, however well-meaning.

"This would all be funny, like a Charlie Chaplin scene, if it weren't downright dangerous," Adam said on a call with Benno. "Father won't see his son, but demands tickets to the opening of a show starring his son's girl, but without showing any sign of interest in meeting her. Naturally, the girl expects the son at the opening and the son wants to go. Inexplicable, that's what it is. But what do we do?"

"I like the stuff about artists. How did he suddenly make that up? No one would ever accuse Father of being consistent. The man's riddled with conflicting, turbulent emotions, that he spackles over like sheet-rock riddled with holes."

Conflicts addressed through letter writing have the advantage of time. A reader who's enraged by a missive has time to simmer down before responding, unlike a verbal bombshell tossed face-to-face. Benno was hurt by his Father's response to his openness, which carried precisely the risk now realized. In fact, it was worse than Benno knew because Adam, in writing his Father, had changed Benno's willingness to strong desire.

"Let's shave over it a couple of days, Adam. We have the time. I'll talk to Violet."

Benno's reasonableness caused Adam's frustration to bubble over.

"No. I can't abide Father's behavior another minute. The problem's not of Violet's making or hers to solve. I'm going to disinvite him and explain exactly why."

"That won't do. It's a shot to your own foot. Really. I don't need days to figure this out. You've gotten the old man this far — dinner with you and a WPA performance. I can see *Triple-A* the next night. Father will see her perform. Then who knows? He may even want to meet her. Your goal was to make the evening an exercise in mending and building. Obviously there's a better chance of that happening without me."

———◆———

Father and son had house seats, third row center. The play's twenty-five short scenes were presented, without staging, through pantomime, skits and radio broadcasts. They depicted the plight of the farmer, tracing its history and effect on the country.

Scene Twenty-One belonged to Violet.

VOICE OF LIVING
NEWSPAPER
(over the loudspeaker)

Newburgh, New York! August 20th, 1935. Mrs. Dorothy Sherwood.[*]

(Police desk on stage right. Light up on desk with POLICE LIEUTENANT behind it. Enter MRS. SHERWOOD stage left, with dead infant in her arms. She walks toward the desk. Light her with overhead spot, center)

MRS. SHERWOOD

He's dead. I drowned him.

LIEUTENANT

You what?

MRS. SHERWOOD

I just drowned my son. I couldn't feed him, and I couldn't bear to see him hungry. I let him wade in the creek until he got tired. Then I led him out into the middle, and held him there until he stopped moving.

LIEUTENANT

(calling out loudly)

John!

(POLICEMAN approaches)

Take the body. Book this woman for murder.

(POLICEMAN takes child from her)

(BLACKOUT on everything except MRS. SHERWOOD. She is picked out by the solitary overhead light. Offstage voice comes through the loudspeaker.)

---

[*] *Daily News*, August 21, 1935

VOICE

Why did you do it?

MRS. SHERWOOD

I couldn't feed him. I had only five cents.

VOICE

Your own child. Did you think you were doing the right thing?

MRS. SHERWOOD

I just thought it had to be done, that's all. It was the best thing to do.

VOICE

How could a mother kill her own child?

MRS. SHERWOOD

He was hungry, I tell you. Hungry, hungry, hungry, hungry, <u>hungry</u>!

(as her voice mounts it is blended with that of another which commences a progression of nine voices crying 'Guilty'! These come over the loudspeaker and are varied in color, but increasing in fervor until ……DIMOUT)

They waited at the stage door for Violet. The audience that night had been primed to applaud or boo as the various scenes were presented. But they couldn't do it, receiving in silence scenes too painful to react to with voice. There was Scene Sixteen, about the drought of 1934, when the radio always reported the weather to be "fair and warmer" as the soil turned to dust. Having recently seen the Lorentz film and thinking of her Father's travails, Violet teared up each time that scene was rehearsed. On opening night, it was the same, but with a multiple of the emotional impact as, already keyed up, she waited in the wings for her turn.

Violet emerged looking subdued, not what one would expect from an actress who had just given a powerful performance on opening night. "I know how bad I look," she blurted out to no one in particular. "I feel drained. It's this show. It gets to all of us." And then, softly, just as Adam moved forward to introduce his Father, she began to cry.

Adam had only met Violet a couple of times and never seen her on stage. He felt drawn as he watched her playing Mrs. Sherwood. She would be Exhibit A to any explanation he might offer of what the WPA was trying to do. Yes, he thought, this must explain his attraction.

Ignoring Dan, he reached out, taking her gently into his arms, her head resting on his shoulder, her body beginning to press against his. They stood there in a cold clear March night, Dan nearby watching the scene until he could wait no longer. By nature he was impatient with people so undisciplined as to lose control of their emotions, especially in public.

"Hey, you two. I'm standing here waiting to meet this High Plains actress. And there isn't even a line."

Dan moved smartly forward, right hand thrown out. The scene was taut, Benno on everyone's mind in different ways. Violet hated Dan before she met him. Yet, for Benno's sake as well as the whole family, she had resolved to find a way to be civil but also honest — or at least not dishonest, which she knew was not the same thing.

"I've wanted to meet you, Mr. Murdock," Violet said, taking his hand in hers. His grip closed tight. Through drying tears she caught his eyes and, with a not unfriendly expression, held them as tightly as he held her hand.

"I hope you enjoyed the opening," she said. There's a lot of material in the play that I know you can relate to."

Dan turned to his son.

"Let's go, Adam. We'll be late for our table. Come along Violet, you can't refuse a Murdock." Adam saw that he was oblivious of the charged atmosphere, despite being chiefly responsible for it.

Turning, Dan struck off briskly with the confident air of a dog trainer expecting his unleashed charges to follow close on his heels.

Dan had reserved a table at Keen's Chop House, a restaurant with roots stretching back to the 1880s. Famous for massive mutton chops and a large selection of single malt scotch, it was located on West 36th Street near 6th Avenue. Until 1905, it admitted men only, but in that year Lily Langtry, the actress and paramour to King Edward of England, went to court to open the place to women and, in fact, succeeded. A seductive portrait of her reclining in the nude hung over the bar, an identifying feature almost as well known as the blackened clay pipes that hung from the ceiling throughout the restaurant.

To Adam's relief, the cold air retrieved Violet's naturally affirmative affect. On arrival at Keen's, they were taken to a table a bit out of the main room. They were forced to wade through a sea of revelers feasting on loud conversation and a sumptuous spread of oysters, shrimp, mutton and wine.

Dan was revved up. "Adam, we've got a lot to talk about, starting with the *Butler* decision. But first, I want to get acquainted with this Texas gal. Violet, I confess, your acting moved me to tears. It was a brilliant piece of work, worthy of Greek tragedy, something I know about. And I gather Mrs. Sherwood did the things you said she did in that town. And so, my question to Adam is why the community of ... of, what was it called, oh, yes, Newburgh. Don't even know where it is. Anyway, why those people would allow Mrs. Sherwood's son to starve? I can promise you that in Manhattan, the community wouldn't have permitted such a terrible situation to last more than a minute. We have unemployment and, in its wake, poverty. Food's scarce. But we've all pitched in to help feed those who can't feed themselves. Adam, I can't recall whether I told you I'm the chairman of our local charity. We raise a lot of money to help the poor, as you can imagine. But we also collect in kind, food, appliances, pots, pans, plates, whatever's useful to those with nothing. And we don't need any WPA or other New Deal nonsense to help us."

"Newburgh's in New York, on the west side of the Hudson, above West Point," Adam said, his voice a touch testy. "I don't believe the people there are any less charitable, any less imbued with Samaritan goodness. You're right, charity begins at home, among neighbors, and radiates out into the community. But the suffering has grown far beyond the ability of most communities to handle. The breaking point was reached long ago, in fact before FDR was elected. At this point only the Federal Government has the resources to meet the people's needs."

Dan stuck out his arm to corral a passing waiter. "Drinks. We want drinks, my friend. Violet, what would you like? A single malt? Some wine, perhaps? Here's the wine list. Let Adam choose something special. These Washington types devote a lot of taxpayer-supported time to picking New Deal wines."

Violet had felt the tension since emerging from the theater. And she felt it grow like lettuce at their cozy table. She decided to jump into the ring, like a referee bent on being there when the combatants must be separated.

"What's a New Deal wine?" she asked.

"It's fabulously expensive wine made from the few grapes FDR lets the farmers grow. You see, Henry Wallace's gang, using taxpayer dollars, bribes the growers to feed their grapes to raccoons." Dan was delighted with himself. He laughed uproariously into the silent stares of Adam and Violet. Had they missed the joke just as Dan had missed their reaction to it?.

The waiter's patience wore thin "I'll have a double single malt. I know Keen's has a vast selection. You pick what you think a crusty old cattleman from Kansas would favor. Now, Adam, the wine, please, so this gentleman can get on with his business."

Dan had said the dinner was on him. Adam jumped at this rare chance to order an expensive Cote de Beaune, a red he knew by reputation only. Violet mused over the menu, worrying at the sky-high price tags and the awkwardness of having tagged along as a last-minute guest. But of whom?

"Now, Violet, tell me your story. You grew up in Texas, I know that much from the way you shape your words. Fill in the gaps, please."

Violet felt summoned back to the stage. Was he serious? He cared not at all for the man I care for a heap. How could he, in the face of having refused to dine with his outcast son, show this kind of interest in a stranger, not just any stranger, but one living with and loving that son? She had pledged civility, and that she would honor.

"I'm the daughter of a dirt farmer. From the town of Dalhart, in the panhandle of Texas. It was a town that believed in its farmers. Believed they were saving the world with their wheat, as Scene One put it."

"We have much in common. I know, direct and up close, many of the scenes your play depicts. The auction scene, for one, left me shaking from memories I had hoped to forget. For another, that line where the man says 'Something is depriving one-third of our population of the God-given right to earn their bread by the sweat of their labor.' When I heard that, I said 'A-men.' The 'something' is FDR and his New Deal. It's that simple."

"Father, weren't you moved by the one about the terrible drought of '34?"

"Of course, son. Of course I was."

Violet joined in. "Mr. Murdock, as a Dalhartian, I can say the Voice of Living Newspaper speaks truth. Yes, that was Dalhart: nothing but high winds and dust, stinging, blinding dust that you had to spit out like tobacco juice. I left Dalhart on account of the drought, that and the dusters it kicked up on the High Plains. Manhattan, I reckon, was too far east to be hit by them."

"Of course not. Manhattan was in drought country. But the Flint Hills had plenty of water to be tapped, and we managed somehow to pull through that Summer with little loss of cattle. Hogs are another story. Wallace's program to destroy well over 6 million hogs demonstrates the impossible pretensions of AAA. I happen to be a maker of pork as well as beef and mutton. The way that law affected my rights to raise hogs —it's what first angered me about AAA. I suddenly realized the loss of liberty that senseless law would cause."

"Could you explain that, Father?"

"Here's how. My plant's equipped for 70 Duroc Jersey and Poland-China sows. By the law's decree, I was to discard 18 of them. And, if the remainder were to produce an unauthorized number of hogs, the overplus must either be destroyed or made subject to confiscatory tax."

Drinks had arrived. Expectantly the waiter stood by, ready to take orders. Dan asked Violet to begin. She ordered shrimp cocktail and mutton. Adam and Dan echoed her order. The waiter departed.

"Why'd you say you left Dalhart, lovely girl?"

"Now wait a minute. Hold onto your answer, Violet. I have to respond here. Father, you're not being fair. As Secretary Wallace says in the show, AAA was designed to increase the purchasing power of farmers. How? Well, the best minds in the country decided it should be done by getting farmers, in exchange for benefit payments, to reduce acreage and curtail production, with funding coming not out of general tax revenues but from a special tax on the processors who turn farm produce into consumer goods."

"Best minds? The minds of red professors whose hands have never felt the soil. As for that wise-guy, Wallace, don't let me get started or we'll never finish dinner. I hear he rides up to farm doors in a big car with chauffeur and radio. A big shot. Looking to have his picture on a postage stamp. Violet's show depicted well — poignantly in fact — how screwed up things become when the Government starts meddling with the laws of nature. Violet, I'm going to enlist our greatest thinker and patriot, Thomas Jefferson, just for the fun of it. Don't think for a minute I need him to help me answer Adam's misguided opinions. But, do you know what he wrote in 1821. Listen up: 'When we are told from Washington when to plant and when to reap, we shall soon want bread.' He was right then, and what's happening now proves him right again."

Adam became angry. At Father for tone deaf single-mindedness and at himself for falling victim to Father's bile. He felt trapped on a slippery slope, carrying him away from the place where mending occurs. He wondered how Benno would be doing, if he were sitting at the table?

Well into the single malt, Dan kept the floor. He was now speaking only to Violet.

"That processing tax immediately drove up the price of food and clothing, making the Mrs. Sherwoods around this country even more desperate for food they couldn't afford, adding millions to the ranks of poverty-stricken families. Government interference always breeds harmful, unintended side effects. Consider this irony: of the quarter billion pounds of pork resulting from the hog slaughter, some was thrown away as waste. But hundreds of millions of pounds were processed into fertilizer. Fertilizer? How could that be in a program intended to limit agricultural production? And how was it that only a bare tenth of the meat was distributed to hungry families on relief?"

Violet was moved by Dan's outburst. And confused. Dan's point about side effects, she realized, could easily explain the dust bowl debacle. Wasn't it Government support for wheat production that turned this magnificent grasslands, that had sustained first the buffalo and then the cattle, into a giant dustbowl barely fit for jackrabbits? Better to keep quiet.

Adam could see Violet's fork drop in a hand limp from lack of direction. Had a battle for her mind developed? Might he be losing?

"Father, FDR was elected with a mandate to use the Government to help people in need. The people wanted him to try things, see what works and pursue it. If something didn't work, to stop it and try something else."

Dan ignored his son.

"From the beginning, Violet, I'm proud to say I've indicted this abominable AAA on many counts."

"Father, I suspect you of rehearsing for tomorrow."

"You might think that, but I'm more concerned about Violet's mind than of tomorrow's Republican audience. That's preaching to the choir. Violet's a challenge, here and now. Well, Violet, your show ends with the formation of the Farmer-Labor Party. Do you know about those heroes?"

"A bit. They explained the background to each story. I'm not expert enough to know if you think them real 'heros,' or are being sarcastic."

"It's the brain-storm of Floyd Olson, Governor of Minnesota. Native son of American radicalism. His Party demands Government ownership of key industries. Goes far beyond Roosevelt's form of socialism. Capitalism must be destroyed. Where I predicted AAA would lead is exactly where your show ends up. It's shocking. And to think my taxes are funding it."

"And both our salaries, Father." Adam had raised his voice. "You're an insult to real dirt farmers. As you well know but chose to ignore, the

National Farm Bureau, the Grange and the Farmer's Union, together with leading farmers throughout the midwest, developed the hog program you ridicule. They can't all be wrong."

Violet had jumped into the ring to break up a fight. Now, she sensed, as the fight began, they had tossed her out.

"And, you, my own son, are a disgrace to the Murdock clan. This reunion, as you called it, feels more like a divorce. Ties of blood demand respect for the views of one's parents, as they respected the views of theirs. Not respect alone. Acceptance. Energetic support. Such is the history of the Murdock tribe. But none of it have I experienced from you since you entered that Red-riddled institution on the Charles. This Living Newspaper plays fast and loose with facts. Its selection of news distorts truth. Taking me to such a paean for socialism leads away from family love and reconciliation. I'm out of single malt and beyond patience. Violet's a charming girl but ill-advised by city scoundrels. Reunion finished. Take her home."

Adam seethed. Was the hatred he felt aimed at his Father or the things he stood for? He couldn't tease the two possibilities apart, at least not at that moment. Fuming, he rose from the table. Peering at Violet, he saw dismay on her face, but something more, a look of shock, as if she had been vicariously slapped in the face, a stand-in for Benno.

"Come, Violet. Father's boozy and getting ugly. We'd best be off."

Adam helped Violet to her feet and swiftly steered her away from the table. She mumbled "Thank you for dinner, Mr. Murdock," but it was in a voice too soft and uncertain to be believed.

Retrieving their coats, they left Keen's with knots in their stomachs.

"Are you up for a walk?" Adam asked. "I've got to unwind."

It was Violet's turn to provide comfort. "Yes, yes. I felt your rage. I understand. Don't be embarrassed on my account." She gave him a little hug, then turned away and they set off for the east side of town. "Benno had filled me in. He even forewarned me that the evening might disintegrate over your Father's penchant for 'in your face, my way only' politics, and your impulse to respond in kind. Here you are, twins, and yet, so different. Benno, with far more justification for hating your Father, seems to accept his behavior, despite being revolted by his politics. He seems able to forgive. You, on the other hand, being the son who is respected for having done the things your Father expected his sons to do, are far more judgmental and unforgiving. The relationship's highly inflammable."

"As we saw tonight," said Adam, who, oddly, felt no resistance to Violet's insight. The knot in his tummy subsided, to be replaced by a slow surge in his groin that might have had some connection to the hug she gave him. Was he turning a mole hill into a mountain? He knew how pathetic this idea was.

"I can't speak for Benno. He's always been more open, more accepting of other people's follies and failings than I. I'm outspoken, like Father, I suppose, and Benno's understated, unassertive. It's always been this way. We're different, and perhaps that's an important reason why we love one another. But, as for why I rage at Father, it has to do with my legal training and my present job at WPA. Legal training instills a certain arrogance, a sure sense that the optimum social policy for the country can be found in cold analysis freed of hot passion and bias. That's the boast of law schools. I was taught and became a believer. Working for the WPA has cemented the idea. Father's belief in jungle law is hateful. Despicable. And the older I get the stronger these feelings become. Forgiveness is one of Benno's strengths. It's not my cup of tea."

"Are you saying your anger is simply the result of differing political views?" Violet asked.

"Exactly."

"I got the impression your Father makes you feel ashamed. That he embarrasses you. That your feelings were developed in a childhood bereft of a mother who might have softened and explained your Father's heavy, never-in-doubt, opinionated hand."

Adam recoiled. He stopped, staring at her with a quizzical expression.

"Now, that insight caught me off-guard. Father fervently believes in a collection of idiotic, faith-based, fundamentalist and ante-diluvian ideas. It's true, I'm ashamed of him. He's not what I think a Father ought to be, the one I wanted, the one I deserved. All this makes me very angry, although till now I've never told anyone, anyone other than Benno. And even there, we never gave these kinds of feelings a full dress exchange."

They resumed walking. Sensing how wrought Adam was over the confessions she had extracted, Violet took his hand.

Benno wasn't in the apartment when they arrived. No note told them where he might have gone. Violet was exhausted from the excitement of opening night and the tension that followed. She knew it was time to sleep. Yet the raw intimacy of her evening with Adam, and the sorrow she felt over his dismal relationship with his Father, made her reluctant to let him leave.

The rational side of Adam's brain told him it was time to go, time to allow Violet to climb into bed. The other side of his brain put forth the idea of holding this woman in his arms, testing her resistance. For it dawned on him during their walk, that somewhere along the way he had become attracted to her. She seemed to be everything that Mariah wasn't, and her appeal tempted him, despite her being his brother's 'girl.' Or, could it be because of it?

Violet stood in soft light facing Adam, just inside the apartment door.

"I'd invite you to stay a while, but I'd fall asleep in your face." She took his hand again.

"I must go."

Dropping her hand, he enclosed her with his arms. He held her close, then closer. He felt her pull back, stiffly resisting. He was about to release her when she turned soft in his arms. His lips found hers. She responded with an eagerness that surprised them both.

"What are we doing?" she said.

He offered her a final kiss, but, glimpsing the future, she pulled away, frightened." He released her.

"Sleep well."

He wheeled around and was gone.

14

"No doubt, somewhere around the water fountain you picked up the story of how I censured Hallie Flanagan's idea for the Living Newspaper." Harry Hopkins had invited Adam to join him one Summer afternoon at the racetrack, wrapping the invitation in a cryptic comment about "this time there's no need for writing." "Just bring a dollar or two. The racetrack lacks juice without skin in the game, to mix metaphors."

At the track, the boss took a deep and terminal drag on the stub of a Lucky Strike, reached for another one, discovered the pack empty, squeezed it tight and stuffed it in his pocket. He looked expectantly at Adam, his hand opening, his motions as instinctual and practiced as those of Phillies star Blondy Ryan, executing a double play. Adam produced the new pack, wondering if this was to be his only function that afternoon.

"I've heard a bit — not much detail — about the *Ethiopia* incident. I know it caused Mr. Rice to quit as New York's Theater Director."

"Elmer Rice, a stormy petrel if ever there was one. It's bad enough to be regarded as Apostle of the New Deal, hated by all its enemies, but to be hated as well by the likes of Elmer Rice for censuring my own children, that's too much. Let me set you straight."

Adam hadn't asked to be set straight. And knowing Hopkins never to banter with staff, Adam saw the story as prologue to an assignment. But what?

"The Living Newspaper was Hallie's brainchild. Her answer to how the tidal wave of out-of-work actors could be usefully deployed. She wouldn't try to use them all in plays, which take a lot of time to mount. She'd dramatize the news and do it without expensive scenery — just living actors, light, music, movement. A brilliant solution to the obvious problem that even unemployed artists had to eat."

Adam thought the boss excessively agitated and jumpy in telling this old story.

"In fact, it was the Living Newspaper idea that brought Elmer Rice around to accept the post. He threw himself into the first New York production, a Living Newspaper to be called *Ethiopia*. At first, it seemed a compelling idea. The subject was big news. And one of the first groups of actors sent to Rice from the relief office was a troupe of African Negroes who came here as an operatic company and got stranded. Although they couldn't speak English, Hallie and Elmer decided they could beat drums, sing and shout on a set of Haile Selassie's courtyard.

"At first, Steve Early and Louis Howe liked the idea of kicking Mussolini in the ass. Presumably, since they were close advisers to FDR, he knew and approved as well. Rice worked non-stop. The show was ready. A letter, believed by Hallie and Company to be pro forma, had gone to the White House requesting permission to use the transcript of a broadcast by FDR, which would be juxtaposed against speeches by Haile Selassie and Mussolini.

"My PR guy at the time, Jack Durham, was in Hallie's office when the call came from Steve Early, saying 'no soap, Hallie, you can't put on the play.' Jack said Hallie, who had worked on this so hard with Elmer, the first original production of Federal Theater, broke up, bawling without shame, tears cascading. A miserable moment, a dreadful event flying directly in the face of my promise. I had been naïve to think I could speak for the Government in making that promise. She had been naïve in believing me. Elmer too."

"What was the promise?"

"Time out for the race about to start." The story his boss was telling seemed too important to be slotting it in between races. But Harry was a genius at multi-tasking.

"That hers would be a free, adult, uncensored theater. Before taking the job, she demanded it. She was right to do so, as I said at the time. But on the first test, I couldn't deliver."

Adam was wide-eyed at these revelations. His mind, as it was trained to do, focused on details. "How did Jack handle it?"

"He put his arm around her and said 'Don't cry. Go on and do another.' It was just right. She could well have quit over that. But Hallie's made of steel, with an iron will."

"What was the White House problem?"

Before the words were out of Adam's mouth, Hopkins had popped out of his seat and dashed for the men's room. "Hang on. I'll be right back," he cried before disappearing in the like-minded crowd. Adam understood. "Success?" he inquired as his boss reappeared in less than ten minutes with a couple of draft beers in his hand. Lighting up, he began a rapid fire response.

"As you know, Ethiopia had been an independent country for two score years. Mussolini's invasion used biplanes and bombers to destroy whole villages with mustard gas and heavy bombs. The League of Nations protested. The invasion continued. FDR requested a ban on arms exports to Italy. Isolationists carried the day. Hallie and Elmer wanted to use these atrocities to define fascism. The script, which Hallie approved, called for a goosestepping Il Duce."

"Did you see it?"

"No. Honestly, had I reviewed it, I probably would have given her a green light. We weren't savvy about the extreme sensitivities of state's cookie pushers. We must not depict foreign dignitaries, they declared. And that was the end of it.

"Licking her wounds, Hallie continued the fight for censure-free theater. Elmer, au contraire, submitted his resignation, something he had done more than once before, only to have it refused. Alas, this time we had no choice but to accept. And, guess what he did then? Elmer was a New York playwright, very, very New York. He issued a press release declaring he had been fighting censorship for fifteen years and would not remain servant to a Government that plays partisan politics at the expense of freedom. Next day, he invited the press to a private showing of *Ethiopia*. Elmer's dramatic, and well covered, exit, with attendant press coverage, led the public to believe that plays with serious social messages would all be banned."

"It could help you fight censorship."

"You're right." Hopkins ground his unfinished cigarette in the bench and took a gulp of beer. "But with anyone other than Hallie in charge, the Theater Project's ambitions would have been chilled. Hallie's undeterred. Her latest project is getting Sinclair Lewis to adapt his best seller, *It Can't Happen Here,* for the stage. She's got a big head of steam to open the play in a bunch of cities on the same night — October 27. The press is all over this thing. Some to the effect that it proves Federal Theater communistic. Others that it's driven by New Deal politics, given the election in November. And some that it makes us subconsciously fascist. They play up the fact that the motion picture companies turned it down as too controversial. MGM had shelled out 200 grand for the rights. I'm sending you to Hallie to dope all this out. Read the script, talk to her. Let's try, this time, to stay ahead of state. We wouldn't want to anger any sympathizers of Hitler and Mussolini, or who knows what else."

Adam was about to ask his customary question, when Hopkins resumed.

"Immediately, of course. First train out tomorrow. You know the calendar as well as I."

***

Adam found Hallie at the Essex House, where Sinclair Lewis had an apartment. When he called to book a meeting, she suggested tea following his arrival by train. He met her in the cocktail lounge, a short woman with cheerful face, drawn at the edges and under the eyes with lack of sleep, a distinctive wide-brimmed black hat set back at an angle on her head, said by some to be her talismanic touch. She handed him the playscript.

"This is the latest edition. There will be many others; it's undergoing constant revision. But it will give you the picture. I bet you've heard from Harry that, post *Ethiopia,* there's been zero censorship. He's actually made that claim to me. But don't believe it. Indeed, why would you, considering your present assignment."

"I wasn't sent to censor. In fact, I'm here to help you avoid anything like that. Could you tell me of the others?" Adam asked, thinking it wise to try to get the whole picture, as she saw it.

"While Elmer was perfecting the *Ethiopia* script, our Chicago unit was finalizing a play called *Model Tenement,* by Meyer Levin. Rehearsals were underway when word came from Washington to stop the show. Apparently, the rent strike theme was viewed by some highly placed local hero, probably the Mayor, as too anti-landlord to be staged. A double whammy for Project One before it could grow flight feathers."

"Something similar happened in Boston, of all places, with the play *Valley Forge,* runner up for the Pulitzer. Despite its subject matter and heaps of praise from historians, church leaders and a state commander of the American Legion, the state administrator blocked its launch in Boston. Why? As so often the case, he took at face value wild charges by a small opposition and ducked what he imagined to be an inflammable situation. There will be others before we are through, but not, over my small body," *It Can't Happen Here.* Not after all we've invested. Not after all Mr. Lewis has done, he and Jack Moffitt and their agents, and, I might add, the harassed staff of this fine House. Fair warning, my young friend."

Adam had admired Hallie's fiery spirit from afar, but now, seeing it close up, he wanted to salute her. He especially appreciated how easily she could let you feel the force of her personality, worn so easily on the sleeve, not to mention the negotiating technique.

"If you're willing, please tell me how the idea for *Can't Happen* got started."

"When Harry asked me to take this job, he took my philosophy too. Knowingly. I told him, no matter how wild the idea, if it has theatrical validity, if it's experimental, I'm going to be interested and willing to explore it. And, so, when Francis Bosworth advanced the Lewis idea, I said 'work on it.' You see Francis had read the book and thought it might work for the stage. So he went up to Vermont, to Lewis' farm, and presented the idea. Lewis wasn't interested in doing just one production at $50 a week. Not enough money, and more important to Lewis, not nearly enough fame. Out of desperation Francis said, 'But, look, you don't understand. We want to do this in as many productions, and in as many languages, as we can, all opening on the same night.' Lewis jumped. Francis came back very excited. I thought it a perfect brainstorm. We figured on about twenty theaters in some sixteen or seventeen states. As things stand it will be twenty-one in seventeen. Now, here's a little secret. Our publicity department, through some mistake, announced not just the plan but an opening date. We had nothing, not a word written. I nearly fainted at the news. There was nothing we could do but try to make it happen, to coin a phrase."

"Amazing. October 27th, only eight weeks away. I see where your reputation for grit comes from. So, here's what I'd like to understand. Why did the motion picture companies and commercial theaters reject it?"

"Controversial, no doubt. It's a play against dictatorships. Germany, Italy and Russia have them. There are plenty of people here who come, or whose parents came, from those countries. People who admire those dictators. Why, there're people here who loved Huey Long, who revere his memory. In fact, it's for that reason that New Orleans officials denied us a production there. But only the film industry actually banned it. Just the other day Red explained things to the press rather well. He said that, in spite of commercial offers from theater companies, he preferred to give it to Federal Theater. And, in explaining why, he tossed us a bouquet. Told them he had two reasons: one, his tremendous enthusiasm for our work. The other, because he could depend on us to present a non-partisan point of view."

"Interesting. Especially the second point. So, with so little time till curtain, how's it going?"

Hallie summoned the waiter and asked for hot tea. "You must be hungry. What do you say to some nice watercress sandwiches. Bread's always fresh here, and crusts go to the Sally." Adam nodded.

"Something new every day. You know we brought Red down here to Essex House. Only possible way. His co-playwright, Jack Moffitt, is here too. I guess you know Red's married to Dorothy Thompson, the *Herald Tribune* correspondent. *It Can't Happen Here* was her story. She reported from Berlin. He fictionalized it. Moved it to America. Anyway, he's writing, editing, acting the parts, rewriting; it goes on every day, and once a day we take what he done and rush it back to our project, where it's translated into Yiddish, Spanish, German and French. And, then, some days, Dorothy comes into his apartment — she isn't living with him right now, another place in the City — and he reads her what he's done, asks her what she thinks — he's very close to her, very much in love, the ideal of an uxorious mate — and she says 'It stinks.' I've been there and heard her say it. She sweeps out of the room and he tears up the work. And when it happens, I have visions of the translations then in process — the French, the German, the Yiddish and the Spanish — all stopping, grinding to a halt, and we are working against this crazy deadline. That, my friend, is how it's going."

"I'd have dropped my tea cup just explaining that kind of pressure," said Adam. "Are any of the companies telling you it's impossible?"

"I must say I'm rather set on opening in twenty-one. But I have gotten a few calls saying 'Look, we have to postpone this. It's going to be a disaster if we open on October 27.' No doubt, I'll get more. My answer's the same. 'We're not postponing it. If you can't do it, we'll put somebody in there who can!' And, then, I pound my little fists on the table. So far, it's worked."

"Give me an idea of this play's importance?"

"I've thought about that. Talked with Dorothy, too. She was in Germany the Summer Hitler came to power. She met no German who thought what happened there could possibly happen there. Not one. The theme of *It Can't Happen Here* is that fascism gets hold of things because well-meaning people don't recognize it for what it is. If you are not entirely immune to that process, this play will make you think, think hard about what fascism could do to American Democracy. In a nutshell, that's its value."

Adam would read the playscript the next morning, on the train back to DC. He couldn't imagine it would change his mind. If he had anything to do about it, there would be no censorship of this play.

That night he slept on the floor of Benno's apartment. Violet joined them for a late dinner. Adam felt drawn to her, as before, and he sensed she knew and imagined she had similar feelings. But nothing was revealed that night or the next morning, when, as Adam was departing for the train, Violet gave him an extra warm kiss on the cheek that brushed across his lips and he, in turn, pulled her to him with extra force, holding her there, against his body, while his lips gently touched her ear. Neither act stood out enough to be noticed, but anyone studying the matter could not have thought politeness alone accounted for their behavior.

15

—◆—

THE WINTER WEEKS PASSED SLOWLY for Benno. The eight hours daily he
devoted to stone carving in Central Park seemed to grow longer, keeping pace with the lengthening light of day as the job became increasingly rote. Benno allowed himself to daydream. In a dark corner of the
room where he worked, there lay on its long side a large chunk of marble. Benno began to project onto that stone a lovely, fanciful story, one
that he spun out over days, rationing its chapters and refining them to
prolong the fantasy. Finally, he could carry the dream no further, the
marble having been turned into a wondrous sculpture, discovered by
critics, displayed at the Public Library, bid upon by leading museums of
the world and sold to the Met for a King Richard-size ransom, making
Benno a wealthy artist released from monotony to pursue his demon-
strable talent.

On a blustery April day, Benno left work at 3 PM to meet Violet in
Greenwich Village, at the New School for Social Research, where they
would search out two prominent works of mural art commissioned by
that institution at the start of the decade. One, by Thomas Hart Benton,
consisted of nine panels. He called it *America Today*. Begun in 1930, the
panels depicted the country's greatness, unaffected by the depression
that began to be felt after Benton had finished all but one of the panels.

The other was a revolutionary mural by Jose Clemente Orozco,
started and finished over roughly the same period. It depicted tyranny,
poverty and revolution around the world, cast in Communistic hues

befitting the political persuasion of the artist. Benno had long wanted to see these murals. He knew that, somehow, both artists were surviving the depression through commissions and the sale of their art, without help from Federal One. He would look for inspiration from what they had done for the New School. Who knows, Violet suggested, perhaps by snooping around he might even discover their secret. There had to be one.

At five cents a ride, the subway was always a bargain for longer travel around town. Traveling separately, they met at the recently completed New School building on 12th Street West of 5th Avenue. Bespeaking the functional style widely known as "international" with its wrap-around strip windows on the main façade, it was an elegant, streamlined structure, designed by the internationally recognized Austrian architect, Joseph Urban.

Finding the rooms housing the murals was easy. They had attracted over 20,000 visitors within the first ten weeks.

On reaching the fifth floor lounge and dining room where Orozco's murals were located, Benno and Violet saw an attendant whose function, it turned out, was both to deny any of the City's maniacs a chance to despoil the murals and to educate the curious as to the ways, means and meanings of this work of art.

Three of the murals were allegorical. The other two were political-historical and included perhaps the first wall paintings in the United States to represent Vladimir Lenin and Joseph Stalin.

Benno and Violet were astounded to learn that first Orozco, and then Benton, had offered to donate their murals to the New School as tributes to the institution's ideals. Orozco's ambition since arriving in the United States in 1927 was to carve out an important place for himself in the New York art world. His was a high profile public gambit to get command of a wall within a modern, international-style building devoted to liberal education and modernism. Benton's offer sprung from much the same ground. Having studied mural technique in France and Italy, and established through easel paintings a uniquely American style, as much so as Mark Twain or Walt Whitman, he hungered for a means to present his art as a mural painter.

Violet said, "Don't you see? They're making investments. These will be donations that give back, year after year. And when you start selling your stuff to the rich for their homes instead of giving it away for mountings on bridges and stone walls, you could take a few New School courses."

She hadn't meant it as a goad, but Benno, more sensitive than usual, thought her disappointed in him.

"And you, Violet, wouldn't you like to do the same?"

"Yea. Love to, when my ship comes in."

Leaving the New School, they walked west, headed at Violet's urging, for the Washington Retail Market, a block-square building on Washington Street between Fulton and Vesey, bounded on the west by West Street and the Hudson River. Owned by the city, the building leased stalls, whose tenants offered a cornucopia of delicacies from around the world. And, for the most part, at reasonable prices. The place was jammed, the noise level too high for them to hear each other. In silence, but with plenty of joyous eye contact, they sampled, smorgasbord style, caviar from Siberia, Gorgonzola cheese from Italy, sardines from Norway and juicy slices of barbecued bear and venison steak. They took a near-empty cross-town bus home. Benno was deep in thought the whole way.

"Penny for your thoughts," Violet said.

"Marble, that's what I see."

———◆———

Benno came early to work the next day. He had a plan. By the time Steven Horay arrived, he had taken measurements of the only real thing in his daydreams.

"Morning, Steven. I've been thinking about that old piece of marble in the corner. Doesn't seem to be any use for it. What would you say to my having a go — after regular working hours, of course."

"I see a glint, Benno. Something that's been missing this year. Got yourself a project, eh? Look, that piece of marble was here before we came. Probably put there by Olmstead or Vaux when they were planning statues for the park. I'd call it surplus. WPA didn't pay for it, has no use for it and probably doesn't own it. So consider it yours to fashion as you wish — but something beautiful."

Benno was like a cricket jigging on a hot grill.

After work that day, Benno built a wooden frame to hold the marble upright. His next step was to make a sketch. He didn't have an exact subject in mind. Only an idea — what Violet called the Orozco-Benton dream — that, at some point along the way, he would propose to New School managers a donation, to be housed with the murals, and they would agree.

Months before Benno broached the sculpting idea with his boss, Lehman Engel had given Violet a book he wanted her to read. In the course of discussing Homer's epic works one night over beer with a few of his singers, Lehman had pointed out that there was a much older work well worth reading. It was the *Epic of Gilgamesh,* what he claimed to be the first great masterpiece of world literature. It was, he said "a story linking East and West, antiquity and modernity, poetry and history. Echoes of it can be found in Homer, and the Bible, too."

Violet devoured *Gilgamesh,* and so too did Benno, who had heard his Father praise the story repeatedly growing up. Benno recalled his Father urging the twins to read what he called mankind's first novel, but, without fanfare, they avoided the assignment.

Violet and Benno read their favorite passages to each other. They tried to understand why the story was so compelling. Mainly, they decided, it was the dichotomy between the age of the story and its contemporary feeling, in the sense of being a searching meditation on the nature of humankind, the meaning of life, the possibility of immortality and what one should strive to be remembered for after death.

Benno's favorite lines addressed the humanizing of Enkidu, the wild man of nature whom Gilgamesh tames by directing a temple prostitute named Shamhat to free Enkidu of his Eden-like sexual innocence.

Shamhat unfastened the cloth of her loins,
she bared her sex and he took in her charms.
She did not recoil, she took in his scent:
she spread her clothing and he lay upon her.
She did for the man the work of a woman,
his passion caressed and embraced her.
For six days and seven nights
Enkidu was erect, as he coupled with Shamhat.

These lines never failed to arouse them. However, this was not the only reason Benno found the lines riveting. He couldn't shake the image of Enkidu standing there, exactly at the moment he experienced sexual attraction. What was his expression at this extraordinary moment? Did the feeling in his groin capture his brain at the same instant? Of course, he shared these thoughts with Violet, who responded with ideas of her own. She compared this event to Adam and Eve, where their discovery was the result of a serpent's temptation. For the *Gilgamesh* epic, sex is a humanizing force; in the Bible, it is occasion for humankind's eternal shame. "Take your pick," Benno said. "Unfortunately for mankind, only the Bible is lodged in hotel rooms."

When Benno returned to their apartment all fired up about the marble but uncertain as to what he would try to carve, Violet was quick with a suggestion.

"Look, Benno. For months after reading *Gilgamesh* you have fixated on that divine moment when Enkidu felt desire. Why not sculpt Enkidu at that moment. I can't imagine the scene, but I bet you'll be able to."

For months Benno worked on the statue, stealing time here, there, everywhere he could without endangering his reputation for hard work. Repeatedly, he would call to mind Michelangelo's description of a Carrara marble block as a prisoner waiting for the sculptor to release him. Enkidu was the prisoner whose escape he was fashioning, chip by chip, shaving by shaving. He would call it *The Education of Enkidu*. Finally, it was finished. Benno moved it into the corner from which it had come, now a cognitive human-like presence glistening where, as an unthinking piece of marble, it had rested for who knows how many decades. Benno had contacted the New School. They showed interest. In time, they came to the park to inspect. And liked what they saw. Terms were discussed. Then finalized. They signed a letter committing to accept Benno's donation of the sculpture and transport it to the New School, where it would rest in a corner of the Director's office. This plan was not precisely as Benno had dreamed things might develop but close enough to stimulate the heart. Benno felt airborne.

He was at work carving his 155th plaque when the new Administrator for the city's WPA effort, Colonel Brehon B. Somervell, formerly of the US Army of Engineers, came to the shop to look around. He was touring all WPA sites in the City to get what he called a "hands-on" feel.

He was introduced to Steven Horay by his chief of staff. In turn, Steve introduced him to the sculptors. Standing over Benno as hammer struck chisel, cutting away the final chink of stone to complete the letter "A" in the plaque, the Colonel said, "Nicely done. I bet this isn't your first one."

Benno nodded, struggling against the instinct to say more.

"And what have we here?" the Colonel exclaimed, pointing to the nearby marble. "It has a definite appeal. A savage transformed into an angel? The man's expression is unusual. Compelling in some strange way. Who knows? A remarkable piece of art. Is it spoken for? I might have the perfect corner space in my office. At the moment rather sparse, you know."

Benno jumped to his feet. "Oh, that's something I did off hours," he said. "It's going to the New School for Social Research."

"But that's a private school. How could they get a Federal One public work?" The Colonel looked puzzled. So did his chief of staff.

"You see, it's not a public work. I sculpted it from an old chunk of marble that had been abandoned in that corner over there, way before the WPA appeared on the scene. Steven gave it to me to spend time on it before and after regular working hours. I've been at it for more than six months."

"And how is the New School acquiring it?" asked the Colonel's chief of staff. "Is a payment involved?"

"No, I'm making a donation to them," said Benno. "We have a letter." As he spoke, it dawned on him for the first time that the project he had created for himself suffered from an appearance problem. At the New School's insistence, the letter provided for payment to Benno of $300 to cover cost of materials. The presumed cost. Benno had resisted this term of the deal, but the New School pushed the matter, telling him that cost of materials had been paid to both Orozco and Benton. He finally agreed, not mentioning the fact that the marble had been given to him. How could he have missed this problem until now? At some level he must have known. *The Education of Enkidu* was too grand and far too good to pass unnoticed.

"Mr. Horay, is this how it went?" asked the Colonel.

"Not exactly, sir. I said I wouldn't stop Benno, if he wished to work on something in addition to his stone carving. But, if he used the marble that was lying in the corner, it would be at his own risk since I had no authority to give it to him."

"I see. Thank you, Mr. Horay, for being clear. I believe our rules say that all movable works of art produced by Federal One, unless committed to some public location, belong to the Federal Government and may be placed only in public spaces. Of course, the artist is recognized. I believe the central office in Washington decides this question for works created in the city. In any case, we will look into the matter and give you our decision."

Benno stood stone still. His heart was pounding. Silence had always been his refuge, from early childhood days when Adam dominated every conversation. To silence he now turned, deciding not to call his boss a liar in front of the Colonel. He would fight for what he believed to be his, but in another way.

By the time he reached the apartment that night, Benno was a jumble of nerves. He laid out the story for Violet, whose empathy for the plight of others had been summoned so often on the plains of Dalhart that it was always there for the asking, hair-trigger ready.

Violet knew, up close, the energy and time Benno had put into this project. The hope he had invested in it. So much, in fact, that it had come between them, soaking up most of the free time they might otherwise have enjoyed together.

Of course, she sided with Benno. Hadn't the marble been abandoned by the City long before WPA came on the scene? Even if that agency could claim title, hadn't his boss given it to him, and only later, in order to ingratiate himself with the Colonel, lied about what he had done? Hadn't Benno, acting in reliance on what his boss said, crafted a work of art wholly on his own time? How could it not belong to him? She would help him write to the Colonel, laying out the facts. "Don't worry, Benno, your case is solid. No need now to speak to the New School."

"But the $300. It's a problem," Benno said, still depressed.

"I wish you had mentioned that little item at the time. Makes things messy. Obviously, you should have told the school you were given the marble. But we can explain. You won't take the money."

Suddenly, like a knife in his back, a ripple of fear engulfed him. "Adam. I forgot about Adam and his sensitivities to conflict, to appearances of conflict. What if this matter comes across his desk? It's not a risk I can take, Violet."

"Actually, I had thought about Adam, but decided not to worry you about it. Here's my point. If you refuse the money, there is nothing for you to worry about. All you are trying to do is give a superb piece of sculpture to a not-for-profit, tax-exempt school that is pre-eminent in the city where the abandoned marble was found. If you were misled into thinking the gift was possible, then you will give it, or whatever rights over it you as the artist enjoy, to your employer. In either case, your reward is to have this work of art enjoyed. The more it is enjoyed by the public, the happier you are. As to your contract with the New School, it may have been entered into by you with a misunderstanding, but clearly in good faith, which is all that matters. Don't worry about Adam."

———◆———

It would be hard to find Adam's job on an organization chart. He told outsiders that he was chief dabbler for the agency, doing a little of this, a little of that. In fact, he did things too well ever to be thought a dabbler. Among senior management he had proved himself so reliable across so many different tasks that he was considered the "indispensable man" to several, each of whom believed he worked mainly for him. Only Harry Hopkins knew the full scope of Adam's absurdly full book. And for good reason. As top dog, Hopkins was in position to pre-empt Adam's time and, to do so, he needed to know what other things were keeping him up late.

One hot Summer day, Harry forwarded to Adam, for analysis and recommendation, a lengthy letter from Colonel Somervell, enclosing other letters and memoranda and requesting an opinion on the application of the WPA's ownership policy for public works of art to an unusual set of facts. Although Hopkins knew in a general way that Adam's twin brother was employed by the agency, he didn't make the connection when hurriedly looking over the file.

Adam saw at once that the sculptor in the center of this controversy was his brother. On reading the file, Adam realized that it would not be easy to resolve the matter under the written policy. That policy, in effect since March of 1934, granted the Federal Government title to "all works of art <u>produced by the project</u>." Is a work of art produced by a WPA artist on his own time, without pay, without direction from his boss but with the boss' permission, a work of art <u>produced by the project</u>? Would the answer be different if the chunk of marble was deemed to belong to the WPA and Steven Horay either didn't give it to the sculptor, or if he tried to, title didn't pass because he was acting outside the scope of his authority? Adam learned from the file that the New School deal had been put on hold, pending resolution of these questions.

Adam knew he had to do the analysis free of any brotherly influence. He was sure of his faculties for fairness, sure that he could reach the right decision without bending one way or the other on account of potential conflict. And that's all it was, he told himself, a potential conflict that he could remove through dispassionate and objective analysis. There would remain the appearance of conflict, but that could be handled by disclosure. He would tell Harry that the artist was his brother, using a footnote on the first page of his memorandum.

With a clarity and persuasiveness that met his highest standards, Adam concluded that the chunk of marble had been abandoned before the WPA came to occupy the building and, therefore, was owned by no one. The sculpture had not been produced by the project and, therefore, belonged to its maker and could be donated or even sold by him to the New School. The letter from Colonel Sommervell said that the sculptor would not take a dime of the $300 offered. The memorandum went to Harry Hopkins. With remarkable speed, Adam was summoned.

"Nice job you've done for us here, Adam. Neat, objective, legal analysis that wraps a very close call with persuasive ribbons of reason. The memo oozes confidence. Am I right?" Harry's face wore a quizzical, almost impertinent expression.

"Yes, indeed. It's the right result." Adam sensed something untoward, something hard to pin down that was beginning to erode the cocksure message he had just confirmed.

"Let me put you a case. You're the umpire in the final inning of the seventh game of the World Series, played in Boston. The Yankees are one run up, Boston's leading hitter's at the plate, bases loaded, full count. The pitch is possibly low and possibly outside. But, some saw it as a strike. It was a close call. Which is exactly how you see it, calling a strike. Got any problem with that?"

"None at all. Fair call. Game over. Yankees win. Where are you going with this, if I may ask?"

"Here's where I'm going. In the game wrap-up, after the crowd has quieted down, the announcer discloses that the Yankee pitcher is your twin brother. Then what happens?"

"But I disclosed all this in the footnote on the first page," Adam said, as heat spread across his neck and ears.

"Yea. Like telling the senior umpire with the hope he keeps it to himself. You haven't answered my question."

"All hell breaks loose?" Adam felt ripples of shame running up and down his back. His face began to burn with embarrassment.

"That's it in a nutshell. We can't have all hell break loose over this sculpture. However plausible, even persuasive, your legal analysis may be — and I grant you the memorandum persuades me as a matter of law and would satisfy the customs of most people — we live in a fish-bowl where public perceptions of what's right become as important, and sometimes even more important, than underlying correctness, particularly when, as in all matters involving the WPA, there are determined enemies looking for any chink in our armor, however tiny. In this case, I propose a pragmatic approach. Let me run it by you."

Adam thought he deserved to be tossed out of the office. Instead, his boss was going to run a solution by him. Not many bosses would take that tack. Of this Adam was sure.

"I propose to treat the sculpture as belonging to us. Knowing of the reputation of the New School for Social Research, I want to uphold the deal your brother made, allowing the art to be shown there. Our policy grants us the 'authority to place objects of art so produced in any building or park which is in whole or in part supported by taxes.' Since this institution, although private, is tax-exempt and therefore supported by taxes, we are permitted to place our sculpture there. I propose that we do just that, retaining ownership and relieving the New School of any payment obligation. Benno gets all important recognition as the artist. No cash but kudos galore. What do you think?"

Adam nodded vigorously. Had he been the boss' dog, he would have licked Harry's feet, toe after toe.

———◆———

The Freudian Psychoanalytic Society had formed a chapter in the United States. The meeting this year was set in New York City, where it would spread out over three long days. Perhaps not surprising given that the life blood of this young profession was a nearly endless process of talking, listening and interpreting. Rachel planned to attend. Among other things, it would give her a chance to see Benno, whom she last saw over six years earlier in her Manhattan home. She wrote him, suggesting dinner at the Waldorf, where the conference would be held and she would be staying. "Bring Violet, if she's free. I'd like to meet her." He agreed. But, since it was a rehearsal night for Violet, he went alone.

The Waldorf was not the sort of place he frequented. But, with help from the palace-like staff, smartly attired in brightly colored uniforms with shiny brass buttons, he found the house phone and reached Rachel. He stood by the elevator bank, watching the well-to-do come and go until she emerged. Exuberant as ever, she threw open her arms to him, wrapping him tight. He kissed her cheek, recognizing the same perfume she had always used when they gathered in her kitchen.

"We're going to the bar for a drink. I'll show you the way."

As he followed her, he racked his brain for the name of Rachel's perfume, the name of a flower, one that could easily slip away.

The bar was packed. Luckily, a couple were just leaving a table in the back as they approached. Benno nabbed it, holding a chair for Rachel.

"What are you staring at, Benno?"

"Everybody. They're mostly men, and they all look like shrinks. I bet there's something special about your profession. I mean, how it looks. Of course, I've only known you, but what I've seen in you must be a telltale, and I see it among these people. Am I right?"

"Of course you are. There are several hundred of us here, and to a man, and woman, they all use alcohol. But, what else runs through this crowd?"

Their drinks arrived: a martini on the rocks for Rachel; a draft beer for Benno. There were chips and a bowl of nuts on the table. Cashews, pecans and almonds, all far above what was affordable to Benno and Violet. He made short work of them and asked for more when the waitress came to take the order for a second round.

"That's a hard one. Beards, but a few are missing such protective covering. I'd say it's the intensity. I can't see a single casual conversation. They're leaning into each other, diving deep down in what's being said, taking it apart."

"That's good, Benno. Very good. I don't notice because I'm so accustomed. But you, coming into a room like this for the first time, you see something different. It's the observant artist in you, my friend. But enough of this. Tell me about your life. About Violet. And your job with the WPA. So, start talking. I promise to listen with intensity."

Benno talked and talked. Rachel led him through descriptions of Violet, her work and his. She always concentrated on the inanimate, whether thoughts, beliefs or feelings. Moving to one of the hotel restaurants, they resumed their respective roles. Whether it was the drinks or the wine, or the honed ability of Rachel to get into Benno's head, she plucked from him thoughts he'd never known were there. He talked about the sculpture, his feeling for Ekindu and the transporting moment he tried to capture. It reflected, alas, a sexual experience he could barely imagine for himself. And he talked of home.

"Yes, I miss Father, the one I knew as a child, before things turned and I lost him. I'd like to mend what's broken, yes I would, but not on his terms. Perhaps he thinks I changed. I didn't. He changed into an angry, vengeful person with no sympathy for those less fortunate. Have you seen him lately? How's he holding up?"

"We had tea together about a month ago. He's recovered from that horrible foreclosure. Got his old moxie back. I wish I knew how to bring him around. I'd try something if I knew what to try and knew that doing so wouldn't cause more harm than good."

"Isn't that your Hippocratic oath talking? But in your field, how can you possibly know? I don't think that rule should apply to shrinks. They'd never try anything."

"Interesting. You just might be right. But what would you suggest I try with Dan?"

"I'd start by asking him to think with you about what he's good at, and why. Because that will take you, right off, into the handling of his horses, his hogs and cattle, and his farmhands. And right there, if you get into the weeds with him, he'll start boasting about how he gets out of every animal, out of every farmhand, all one could possibly get and then some. And he'll explain it as his being creative and flexible, as treating each animal and each farmhand as different from all the rest, as needing special insight and handling. He'll talk of cutting them extra slack in the rope, where that's useful to get the most out of 'em."

"I see where you're headed with this. But if all you say he believes is true, why doesn't he use the same approach to handling you, and Adam?"

"That's the big question, isn't it! I wish I knew. But if anyone can find out, you're it. My hunch is simply that he sees us not as owned and controlled by him, like the animals and farmhands, but as being of and by him, a vital part of him, and, therefore, not needing or deserving to be cut even so much as an inch of slack. With his issue, its 'measure up or out you go.'"

"So, all you ask of him is to be treated as well as he treats his animals. Doesn't sound all that difficult, does it?" Rachel was laughing. She squeezed his hand until he joined her in appreciating the crazy joke.

They had finished strip steaks and baked potatoes when Rachel guided the conversation back to Violet, this time to discuss not her childhood in Dalhart or her acting career in New York, but their sex life.

"How did I know you'd get around to this?" Benno said, a woeful smile on his face.

"Because you know me. Because you remember how much time we invested in that birds and bees stuff, as you and Adam called it. I'm looking for a return on that investment, good, bad or whatever."

A waitress hurried past their table, sucking air behind her. The scent of Rachel's perfume was pulled along, announcing itself to Benno again, strongly, and with it the name of the flower.

"Tuber-rose! That's it," he announced, interrupting Rachel. He looked as pleased as if he had just deciphered the Rosetta Stone.

"You told me once you liked it. Do you still?" Benno heard a change in Rachel's voice. A softening. And, while she was still leaning forward, as shrinks do, the intensity was gone. Could it be, he wondered, seeing on Rachel's face what he thought might be a vulnerable expression.

"I do, very much. I wish Violet wore it."

Passing on dessert, they ordered coffee. Benno unburdened himself about life under the covers. He hadn't admitted to himself, and certainly not to Violet, how dissatisfied he was. "Perhaps dissatisfaction is too strong," Benno said. "I have orgasms and enjoy them."

"Yes, it's hard for a man not to enjoy an orgasm. So what's the problem?"

"It ought to be better. She says she's enjoying it, but I know she's not having an orgasm, and I can't seem to last long enough to give her one. Or perhaps it's not a matter of lasting, perhaps I just don't excite her enough. She won't talk about it, beyond saying she doesn't need to have orgasms to enjoy our time in bed. I say there's something missing, and she says no, there isn't. I try suggesting other things, but she seems to think the right way, the only way, is having sex with me on top, coming inside her. She won't try anything else. Doesn't want to. Don't get the wrong idea. We seldom talk. But when we do, we just repeat ourselves. I don't know what to do."

"I think Violet needs to talk with someone, a psychologist who can help her understand her physical needs and how the mind and body work together. It's tricky business for you, especially given your limited experience, to talk her into such a thing."

"Once, when we were getting close to the prospect of making love, she told me her mother saw it as mostly a duty to be performed, rather than something the woman got much pleasure from. Deep down, I suspect she retains this idea, and at some level may even believe it. Couldn't therapy pry this stuff out?"

"Yes, indeed."

The waitress presented the bill. Rachel insisted on paying. "It's a business expense. One I'm delighted to pay, Benno. Now, I want you to come up to my room for a minute or two. I have something to show you. Do you have time?"

Benno nodded. As they got up, he realized that, over the few minutes they had discussed his sex life with Violet, he had begun to look at Rachel as a woman — a very attractive woman. And thinking along these lines had aroused him. Of course, he knew, the whole idea of doing something with Rachel was absurd and out of the question. There was a disconnect between mind and body, and, looking down as if from afar, he found it funny.

They went up in the elevator to the 12th floor, and thence to Room 1237. Rachel unlocked the door and ushered Benno in. She then shut the door, locked it and took Benno in her arms, leaving him no time to even consider avoiding her lips, which she quickly pressed to his.

"Don't think too much about this, Benno. I knew you felt aroused. I felt it too. We are going to make love now. Stand there, by the bed, while I remove your clothes."

Rachel was feeling a deep anticipatory emotion. Benno was experiencing what she felt. Afterwards, Benno realized he had been treated to something marvelous by a very experienced woman.

"Is what you did with me a part of your training?" Benno asked. He was sitting on the edge of the bed, trying to take into his brain, rationally, what he'd just experienced through his brain, physically. "This may sound rude, but were you faking it, for my benefit?"

Rachel had washed up and returned to sit next to him.

"No and no, emphatically no. You gave me all that I experienced and it was great, as you could tell. I know you're going to return to your apartment and wonder about this evening, about how to think of it. So, let me answer that question before you ask it. What we just did is akin to eating a wonderful meal, a sumptuous, delicious meal to be enjoyed with the highest level of pleasure. And with utterly no guilt. And, as far as feasting again, I offer you now the right to return, and enjoy, so long as you leave all guilt behind. We will do this again. I don't know when, or for that matter, where, but we will because we are, at bottom, free agents, able to enjoy each other when the spirit moves. Now, it's time for you to get your clothes back on and return to your apartment."

Rachel put on a nightgown. She accompanied Benno to the door. With warmth, they kissed goodbye. The door shut and he made his way to the elevator.

16

———◆———

MARIAH LOST HER MOTHER TO a stroke in the Spring of 1935, just weeks before graduating from Newton. It was like a tsunami rising without warning from a placid sea to wreak havoc on the nearby coastline.

As a graduation present, her parents had planned a family tour of Europe. By this maneuver, they hoped to turn Mariah's head, or was it her heart — they were never sure — away from the Kingfish. Out of family loyalty, and because she really did like the idea of traveling throughout Europe, Mariah had postponed her planned return to New Orleans and the senator until the end of September. Her parents also thought putting some time and distance between their daughter and Adam might help halt the drift in their relationship, which seemed not in either's interest.

Despite her mother's death, both Father and daughter decided not to abandon the tour. They were abroad when, on September 8, Huey Long was gunned down in the State Capitol. Mariah read about it in the Italian papers. Hit in the abdomen at four feet by a handgun wielded by a Dr. Carl Weiss, Long died two days later in the hospital.

A great and growing sadness overtook Mariah, dampening the remainder of the tour. Adding to her distress was the absence in her Father's attitude of any concern over the senator's death or the slightest hint of vicarious sadness or empathy or even understanding of what Mariah was experiencing. In fact, as she could see plainly enough, her Father was overjoyed with the end of the senator, believing the senator had enthralled her, that her devotion to the idea of wealth redistribution, having been seeded in her mind by him, would now wither and die from lack of nourishment. Little by little she turned away from her Father. It was a slow process, fraught with conflicting emotions, which made her moody and increasingly harsh with her Father. She exercised her abundant capacity to hurt as her affection, and even sufferance, diminished to the vanishing point.

They wound up the tour in London, staying at the Savoy because it was cheek-by-jowl to the D'Oyly Carte Theater, only a five minute walk to the British Museum, and offered elegant dining at tables overlooking the Thames. It was directly opposite the Museum, in fact, that Mariah's Father perished, victim of American impatience and habit. Trying to dash across the Street to join Mariah in front of the Museum, he had gone against the light and looked the wrong way to check on traffic, an easy thing for an American to get wrong when trying to hurry across England's roads. The unlucky cabby slammed on the brakes, but nothing could have saved Mr. Massie, so sudden was his lunge and so direct his head's contact with the high-slung taxi.

Mariah's state of mind was chaotic. Her Father killed in front of her, following hard on the death of her mother. No one could expect to maintain the kind of level-headedness, the result-oriented thinking ahead, that Mariah began to exhibit. It was as if the double deaths of her parents were bloodless incidents to be handled through equally bloodless steps, taken without emotion but with much concentrated planning and execution. Mariah took hold and delivered a flawless performance, burdening no one with her own private anxieties, to the extent they existed, while organizing a series of events in Richmond that fulfilled even the highest levels of what society in the circle of her family expected. Mariah's parents were put to rest with exquisite taste and all the mourning appearances required. As Mariah knew, it was appearances that mattered, and she was a master at achieving all that Richmond expected with a large margin of safety.

As an only child, Mariah inherited her family's considerable wealth. She stayed in Richmond for the rest of the year and throughout 1936, trying to figure out what to do with herself. And the closely related question of what to do with her sudden wealth.

Mariah knew how to absorb a blow and move on. Even the deaths of her parents, occurring so close together, with the assassination of Huey Long sandwiched between, seemed not to disturb her equilibrium, despite having irrevocably changed her life. Her parents' closest friends, observing her through this period, could detect little, if any, grief. Some assumed she must be suppressing it, that it lurked somewhere inside, eating away like a cancer. Others said her veins were clogged with ice.

She continued an exchange of letters with Adam, who had journeyed to Richmond for her Father's funeral. Other than that sad and strangely formal occasion, which felt more like a financial closing than a human one, they had not seen one another since graduation in June of the preceding year. And even that visit had to be cut short due to WPA work.

Adam continued in conflict over Mariah. Despite his appreciation of her shortcomings, he remained attracted, both intellectually and physically. He thought he had plumbed the depths of her character and found, on balance, she was worth an endeavor to accept and love. In April, Mariah accepted Adam's suggestion to come to Washington for a couple of days. Senator Hugo L. Black, Chairman of a Special Committee to Investigate Lobbying Activities, was conducting hearings on April 8th, 10th and 14. The American Liberty League was to be the committee's focus that day. Adam had been assigned to attend, not only in regard to his boss' interest in the League, but in regard to his own familial connection to the Farmers Independence Council of America. In the run-up to the Presidential election, he thought Mariah, for her own reasons, might want to join him in the Senate Office Building.

She took the train from Richmond. Adam met her in Union Station and they walked to Capitol Hill, passing a circle of young oaks in front of the station. They looked newly planted. Mariah thought them an omen for something lasting and important that she might do with her wealth. Searching around, Adam found nearby a bronze plaque disclosing that the oaks were named "The President's Trees," and had been dedicated in 1934 by the Maryland State Society of the Daughters of the American Revolution.

"Someday they will be very large and beautiful, and offer shade to all who pass by, but no one will remember whose idea it was to plant them," Mariah said.

They caught most of the testimony given by Dr. E. V. Wilcox, Secretary and Treasurer of the Council, brought on board as a writer to prepare propaganda. Mr. Stanley F. Morse, the organizing force behind the Council, who appeared to be on loan from the League, had been asked to testify with Dr. Wilcox but declined, sending a last minute telegram to Chairman Black. With teeth bared, the chairman read it into the record:

> While the Farmers Independence Council has nothing to conceal that is contemptuous of your committee, my duty as executive vice president compels me to insist upon a formal subpoena before determining the proper action of the council.

The hearing exposed the Council as merely an extension of the League, using its office space and supplies, its office girls for multigraphing, and, of course, using Stanley Morse, who was designated by the League as its "consulting agricultural engineer" and who continued to draw salary from the League while working full-time for the Council. Although the Council was an arm of the League, this connection was kept secret from press and public. Neither its propaganda nor Dan Murdock's radio talks ever disclosed its tight link to the League, a deception that obviously was troublesome to the committee.

Wilcox had written for the Agriculture Department and also for the magazine *Country Gentleman.* He admitted that none of those involved with the Council were farmers. Its leaders were cattlemen like Dan Murdock and meat packers like the head of Cudahy Packing Co. Its resources were laughably thin, despite having taps into such non-farmer millionaires as Lammot du Pont.

When Stanley Morse finally appeared to testify, he was insistent in claiming that the Council was manned by dirt farmers. The chairman's questions shredded this claim. Morse claimed Eric Pierson Swenson to be one of the Council's "good farmer members." As the chairman pointed out, Mr. Swenson was President and Director of the Swenson-Texas Corporation, President and Director of the Swenson Land & Cattle Co., President and Director of Freeport-Texas Co., President and Director of the Freeport Sulphur Co., President and Director of the Freeport Sulphur Transportation Co., Chairman of the Board and Director of National City Bank, and Chairman of the Board and Director of National City Co. Morse was forced to acknowledge that Mr. Swenson was the Council's only "farm representation" in New York City. He was not exactly the sort of person AAA was designed to help.

By the time the Chairman got to Dan Murdock, Mr. Morse didn't even pretend.

"You're correct. Mr. Murdock is a cowman, first and foremost."

Adam took Mariah to dinner at the restaurant in the Hay Adams, the venerable hotel overlooking Lafayette Park and the White House. She thought him depressed.

The restaurant was full. They chose to wait in the bar and ordered drinks.

"Black's a good egg, don't you think?" Mariah said. Adam nodded, stirring the bourbon sour that had just arrived.

"Now, tell me, Adam, what's on your mind? You're strangely subdued." Mariah was never one to beat around the bush when directness could do the job faster.

"You still have that knack for reading people. Like Dr. Rachel but with religious rather than Freudian training. And I see from that silly grin that you love the game. Yes, the hearings hit me pretty hard. I told you about my evening with Father in New York last month. That was bad enough. But, now, this, a public hearing on Capitol Hill.

"Sitting there, you learned that my Father is the willing and perhaps, I say perhaps, unwitting tool of a bunch of eastern capitalists who hate FDR. Somehow they've bent his cowman's philosophy to serve their purposes. It's just a fact to you, inhaled without pain. But to me, it's triple strength embarrassment and humiliation. Father's philosophy, practiced by him alone, hurt no one. Indeed, in the minds of some Manhattanites, it was ennobling."

"No one outside the family," Mariah said. "From where I sit, I see hurt inflicted on his children."

"Ok, ok. From where I sit, you're pleased with yourself, again. Now, I was in mid-thought. Yea. Look, he's being paid to beam his extreme philosophy across the land on the air waves. Probably not in dollars, mind you. I'm sure of that. But something worse, the grandeur of associating with these eastern swells. And his passion, his conviction and his elegant way with words will persuade thousands, perhaps millions, causing harm to innocent people, to the country. Worse, the Council is such a pipsqueak that the big shots give it crumbs, while Father pours his heart into the radio talks. What's he think he'll get out of this? Become a great man and get an invitation to their clubs? It makes me sick with shame."

"Strange, what a difference blood lines can make. I was the same way about my parents. Still am in the sense of not knowing how to deal with their wealth, and embarrassed to have inherited it. Are all children embarrassed by their parents? Of course not. But you and I, a sample of two, cast a long shadow, don't we?"

Mariah stayed overnight in Adam's apartment. The perimeter fence around his desires seemed intact. He took the couch, giving Mariah his bed. They kissed good night before she disappeared into the bathroom with kit in hand. Her effort to find his lips was deflected by a swift dodge, as if he had known what was coming. They made contact cheek to cheek.

Deciding against sheets, he lay down on his back and pulled a blanket up around him, hands bent puppy-dog fashion on his chest. A night light softly illuminated the way from bathroom to bedroom or couch. She emerged from the bathroom in a transparent nightgown reaching the floor. The bathroom light illuminated her body. Except for a string of pearls around her neck, Adam could see she was naked. He could trace the contours of her body, checking against memory. Neither shape nor allure had changed. She headed for the bedroom. On reaching the door, she turned back, as if remembering something she had meant to do. She went back to the bathroom, turned off the light and then walked slowly toward the couch. She stood over him, unbuttoned the nightgown and, letting it drop from her shoulders, bent at the waist until her breasts were level with his eyes.

"Kiss me," she whispered, imperious.

"I won't, Mariah. Despite how attractive I find you at this moment. At almost every moment, in fact. I am practiced in resisting. I won't succumb."

Mariah broke down, sobbing with no sign of ceasing in sight. Picking up her nightgown to drape around her shoulders, she sat down on the couch, head in hands.

"This is different, Mariah. From other times, I mean, when I have resisted. You've been sarcastic, risen above the apparent turn-down, moved on with no emotion. What's going on?"

"You're not going to like this. And neither am I. But I can't go on with the lie. I've been deceiving you from our first days together. I put you down as old faithful — the one I could deceive with ease, the one I could come back to and marry, no questions asked, no suspicions raised. Since we met there have been other men. Many of them. Our relationships have overlapped with yours. Collecting men is like a drug. I do it not so much for the sex, although that's partly it. The bigger part, far bigger, is the thrill I get from successful seduction. I'm a slave to it, an addict."

For a long time, silence filled the room. Adam just stared at her. His mind racing, he recalled the shock of her pregnancy and of his accidental discovery of her miscarriage, a detail she was keeping to herself. Now this.

"When did this 'addiction' as you call it begin?" Adam was looking straight ahead in near darkness, and so was Mariah.

"Oh, long ago. A young Richmond kid of 18 was my first victim. It didn't take long to coerce him to want me, in fact, in those early days post-puberty, just a few pats and squeezes, or even a certain smile, combined with a slow encircling lick of the lips, would do the trick. From then on I collected males as FDR collected stamps. From college on, the challenge grew as my need for the rewards of being adored grew. That's the way with drugs — dosage growth becomes essential just to keep the high."

"Where is your used car lot?"

"Look, they just moved on, either because their infatuation faded or my need for a new conquest required that I end the affair. Often they suffered. Sometimes, I did. You often called me a control freak, and you were right, but without knowing the whole story. I don't think I know how to rid myself of the addiction, but I know, having confessed, I will have to give up on you."

17

———

Triple-a plowed under has closed in May, leaving Violet with just *The Madrigal Singers* for work and support. It was October. She had gotten four tickets to the opening of *It Can't Happen Here*. Her plan was to have both Adam and Mariah join them. This way, Adam would be restrained from trying to continue their small flirtation, which she told herself whenever the question arose in her head, was all that it was. Of course, there was more in her head than that. His advance and her willingness were upsetting. She felt ashamed from many angles. Adam read between the lines of her letter. Independently, before the confessional, he had thought it was about time Mariah met his brother and the actress from Texas, imagining a gathering of the two couples in New York. Now, although things were different between them, he wanted their friendship to continue, if possible. At least he would not be the one to untie it.

He called Benno and booked a spot on his couch for the night. They made a plan. Mariah would stay at the Waldorf. They would meet for drinks at the Algonquin, on West 44th Street, then walk eleven blocks north to the Adelphi Theater. Afterwards, they would take the subway to Chinatown and dine at Yat Bun Sing on Mott Street.

Adam hadn't seen Violet since sleeping over in Benno's apartment after his meeting with Hallie. He'd often imagined Violet and as often thought to write her, expressing his feelings. But it never happened. In part, because he hadn't plumbed the depths of his feelings enough to describe them. In part, because he thought it a slippery slope. And in time, as the frisson of that evening began to wear off, he realized why. He would have to square things with his brother. Each time he had the urge to reach out to Violet, he felt the weight of Benno restraining him. As for Mariah, they hadn't been in touch since her visit in April. He dreaded the call to Richmond that he had to make.

"Hello, Mariah. Adam here. How you doing?"

"Well, well, if it isn't the 'Casper Milquetoast' of the west, the Manhattan man who neutered himself to collar his emotions. I've been waiting for your call of apology for humiliating me."

"Mariah, that's ridiculous. Don't toy with me. It's not funny, after that confession. If anyone deserves an apology, it's me. But that's not why I called. And by the way, I hope you remember how that night ended. I wrapped you in my blanket because you were cold, sitting there shivering. I led you to my bed so we both could catch up on sleep. I wanted to discuss the whole thing over breakfast, but you had vanished by the time I woke up."

"What would you have said had I stayed?"

"That I can understand how many men there have been. I have always found you immensely attractive, as I did that night. That in your presence the merest touch can lead me to want more. That you're much more controlled than I. More controlling, too. And purposeful. And, hearing your story, I think I can understand, although I remain shocked. You're the first seduction slave I've known. None of this dovetails well. And so, you were right, I'm not going to renew."

"Interesting. But you know I'm not the pleading type. If not to apologize, why are you calling?"

"Oh, come off it, won't you. I called because I'd like our friendship to continue. I have a proposal for getting you together with my brother Benno, and his Violet. If you'll stop pretending, I'll explain it."

After hearing him out, Mariah said, "Count me in. Waldorf's fine. You'll see to the booking. By the way, I never read Lewis' book. Should I?"

"He adapted it for the stage at Hallie Flanagan's urging. You see, he wasn't interested in writing a play for only one production. Hallie promised him at least 20 productions in something like 16 cities; some like

New York would have two productions. What's more, she promised they would all open on the same night. That's October 27ᵗʰ, the night we're going to see it."

"I take it the play's message is Fascism can even reach our shores, that Hitler types are not confined to Germany."

"Exactly. He and his ideas are a danger to the whole world. Some have suggested he had your mentor in mind when he wrote the novel. Or Father Coughlin, but …."

"Or some crazy cowman from Manhattan. Hey, no jokes about the Kingfish or else I fight dirty."

The tone in Mariah's voice had changed. Lower, tender yet peremptory. Adam realized she wasn't totally immune to grief. Just selective. And, for Huey, the wound hadn't healed.

"Ok. About travel. I'll train up to DC, meet you at the Station and we can go on together. With the election so close, they'll be plenty to talk about. I hear Maine's favoring Landon. And you know that old saw: As Maine goes, so goes the nation."

"I doubt either of us knows a thing about Maine. Ring me when you have the train schedule worked out."

———◆———

Benno and Violet arrived first. Neither had ever been inside this French Renaissance structure on 44ᵗʰ Street, east of Sixth Avenue, frequented by so many leading lights of the theatrical and literary life of the city. Hotel Algonquin served as headquarters for the Round Table, the Thanatopsis and Literary Inside Straight Clubs and the Forty-Fourth Street Chowder and Marching Club. They learned these things from a prone-to-banter waiter, who, with self-important air, speaking as he might to dirt farmers fresh from the corn belt, boasted of them as he set down drinks with a bowl of nuts.

The train was late. When Adam and Mariah reached the Algonquin, there was just time for perfunctory introductions and a quick drink. The unctuous waiter was on hand to rush their order. He returned in remarkable speed. Setting down the drinks, he inquired where they were going.

"The Adelphi, to see the opening of *It Can't Happen Here,*" Violet said, appreciative of the waiter's interest.

"You'll be wanting a taxi," he said. "Allow me to alert the concierge."

Adam had only heard of this hotel but was quick to catch its pretensions. Waving off the waiter, he said, "No need. We're walking. And the bill, if you please."

The crowd outside the theater was still growing as the two couples arrived at 54th Street, between Sixth and Seventh Avenues. It was Federal Theater's big moment. Its chance to etch in the country's brain the notion of a national theater. As he watched the Adelphi filling up, Adam imagined this scene repeated that night in twenty other theaters across the land. Feeling a tinge of prideful ownership, he said, "Wow. A night to savor!"

They shuffled in, funneling down to a single line in front of the smartly uniformed clerk tearing off ticket stubs. The crowd was excited, the house packed. Hundreds of people were standing in back of the last aisle. From the moment the curtain rose, there was an uncommon quality of attentive listening in the audience, a silent, concentrated energy radiating from people swept up in the drama. The essential question Sinclair Lewis was about to pose on multiple stages that night was whether a nation of Babbitts could muster the passion for freedom required to resist the power of Fascism.

The Playbill described the *Place: The United States of America*; and the *Time: Very soon — or Never*. Among many riveting characters they met on stage, not soon to be forgotten, were Buzz Windrip, Senator, nominee for President from the Corporative Party, Doremus Jessup, editor and owner of the Ft. Beulah Daily Informer, in the small city of Beulah, Vermont, and his daughter, Mary Greenhill.

There were many curtain calls. Finally, the playwright appeared to take a bow. The audience demanded a speech. Looking at his watch, Lewis said, "I've been making a speech since 8:45."

The couples exited the theater and went by subway to Chinatown and their restaurant, Yat Bun Sing, picking up beer on the way since the restaurant offered no liquor. It did offer, as specialties of the house, subgum chow mein (meat, Chinese vegetables with fried noodles), gai young yuen war (chicken bird's nest soup), and egg rolls filled with various meats or vegetables. Soon their round table was covered with these dishes, together with various sauces, glasses for the beer, hot tea and chopsticks of unspoiled bamboo. It was always a marvel to Benno how swiftly an order in a Chinese restaurant was filled. Could it be a character trait among Chinese or something else?

"Red, as you call him, Adam, looked pleased, walking out of the Adelphi," Violet said, once they had settled around a corner table. "Twenty-one performances — a royalty of $50 per — so he made $1,050 tonight. And I hear lines are forming for advance sales."

"Well, he should be smiling," Adam said. "There's an interesting story about that 'royalty' you mentioned. Heard it from Francis Bosworth, Hallie Flanagan's Bureau Director. He was a drama teacher at Columbia. Had gotten to know Eleanor Roosevelt earlier, as a reporter covering Albany. Hallie had tried to hire him. He refused on the basis of horror stories about the Theater Project. Then he got a call from Mrs. Roosevelt inviting him to tea at her Village apartment on 11th Street. He went and who do you think was sitting there with Mrs. Roosevelt when he entered her apartment? Hallie, of course. And the President's wife pressed Bosworth to join. He explained all the problems he had heard about — no chairs, no desks, little money to get anything done, etc., even censorship; and Hallie confirmed it all. Bosworth then asked Hallie, 'and when these problems arise, what do you do about it?'

"And, then, proceeding as if he had signed on, Mrs. Roosevelt answered for Hallie:

"Mr. Bosworth, there's a doorbell at 1600 Pennsylvania Avenue. All you have to do is come and ring it and tell me about it.'"

"You were telling us about the royalty," Mariah said, with a touch of impatience.

"Ah, yes, I'm coming to that. Federal Theater wanted to produce modern plays. They had over 160 playwrights needing work in the City alone. But Procurement wouldn't allow the payment of royalties. Slippery slope problem. If playwrights could get royalties, then a sergeant making a funny little thing on a gun that made it a better gun would be entitled to royalties and a patent. And, so, the Government just couldn't do it."

"Well, I'm told it's absolutely impossible to run a modern theater without royalties," said Violet.

"Exactly. A collision course. Well, last Summer, Flanagan and Bosworth were down in DC, staying in the Hotel Powhatan. They were having a beer in the bar. Bosworth was just saying 'we're licked' when Hallie noticed Jim Landis across the way. She identified him as her husband's roommate at Harvard. And, now, he was Chairman of the Securities and Exchange Commission. She sent Bosworth across the room to ask him to join them for a minute. It was after midnight. They had more beer. Landis listened to the whole story. And, then, he said, 'Well, now, you know I was law clerk to Mr. Justice Brandeis and he's still in the city. He works here and I've seen him lately, the last couple of days. Let me call him up at the Court tomorrow morning. He'll solve your problem if anyone can. The best way is not to do it over the phone but in person.'

"So they got word to come to the Supreme Court at 11 AM, and go to Brandeis' chambers. They went up there and Jim Landis introduced them and Hallie explained the whole thing. Brandeis thought it over for a while and then finally he said, 'Now you know what you want to do is to be able to pay playwrights for their plays, and they have agreed to $50 a week, including Shaw, O'Neill and so forth.' And he said, 'That seems like a very good bargain.'

"Hallie said, 'Well, of course it's a good bargain. It's a wonderful bargain but how can we get around the Government?'

"'Well,' he said, 'because you're talking about royalties. Why don't you rent the plays for $50 a week?'

"They went back to Procurement and said, 'We don't want royalties. We've just been talking to Justice Brandeis. We don't want royalties. All we want to do is rent the plays.'

"The Procurement man said 'Well, why didn't you say that in the first place?'"

"What fun," said Violet.

"Yea, that's why I like hanging around with bureaucrats," Mariah added. "They've always got one or two good 'war stories' to offset the tedium."

Mariah said she had initially been moved by the play, but in the end, felt used because she couldn't imagine even the possibility of ever being threatened in America.

"That's remarkable, coming from one intimately familiar with how easily the Kingfish conquered Louisiana, subduing its people with roads and bridges," Adam said. "I think I mentioned that Lewis had your friend Huey very much in mind when he wrote the book." Downing a second beer, he grinned, ear to ear.

Mariah looked daggers at Adam, but only for a split second, hoping the others hadn't noticed.

"My dear fellow, that's absurd. The book was modeled on Hitler's take-over of Germany through democratic means. Every reader knows that Lewis' wife, Dorothy Thompson, a reporter stationed in Berlin, conceived the idea. One wonders, however, why the play was scheduled to open tonight, just two weeks from the election. Already, Landon's election crew is claiming the play an object lesson in what could happen if that budding dictator, the incumbent, were re-elected."

"Father, for certain, would join in broadcasting that message," Benno said. "He thinks FDR became a dictator within his first hundred days and since then has simply been using the reins of power to entrench himself in the White House and destroy the enemy."

"So, Mariah believes it can't happen here," said Adam. "Do you agree, Violet?"

"I see our people as highly susceptible to nonsense that comes wrapped in cellophane and offered by big men in fancy cars. It happened in Dalhart. My daddy was sucked in by snake-oil salesmen promising endless profits from the plow. So, yes. Fascism could, as the poem says, 'come on little cat feet' and when we woke up to the loss of freedom, it'd be too late."

"Nicely put," said Benno. "I've seen it again and again in the submissive eyes of men on the street, waiting for soup or lined up for city blocks just for the chance at a WPA job. Like beaten dogs shivering in the cold, willing, despite a thousand years of experience, to believe anything, accept anything, do anything for the man who feeds them. Could it happen? Yes. Will it happen? Not so long as Mr. and Mrs. Roosevelt hold the keys to 1600."

"You're not suggesting it could happen with Landon, are you?" Mariah said, her voice tinged with incredulity.

"Not at all. In fact, Benno and I took the trouble to read the platforms of both parties, and to read the acceptance speeches. A lot of moonshine, of course. Falsetto voices straining for emotion. Nothing like the world we live in or the one we can realistically expect to see down the road, whoever wins. But the thing that struck us was the similarity of the basic goals sought by the parties. Benno, you know them better than I."

"Right. The big differences seem to be in the ways and means of accomplishing these things. The Republicans accept our present economic arrangements as cast in stone. With hammer and chisel, they propose to work around the edges. The Democrats want to toss out the old order, stem, branch, root and all, and bring in something new."

Adam joined in. "I like your last point. FDR's speech was all about political equality being meaningless in the face of economic inequality. But I don't see the similarity you do. Here, for example, is a flier we've been examining at the WPA. I'm surprised you haven't had it thrust into your hand, Violet. You'll see it's issued by something called the American Artists Landon-Knox Clubs, a division of the RNC. One has to admire the humor of the thing, although I doubt its draftsmen were trying to be funny. If one enrolls in a Landon-Knox Club and sends 25 cents to the RNC, one receives a copy of the official campaign song *Win With Landon.* Then, the flier goes on, 'SING IT —PLAY IT — SWING IT — and DO IT!' And here, let me read you their big selling point:

> To the hundreds of thousands of American artists we can state emphatically that more than **PROMISE** of recognition for cultural artistry lies in the election of Alf M. Landon to the Presidency, for in him we find a man fitted by an unsheltered life to understand the problems of the average man. His home is mellowed by music — that of his gracious wife — an accomplished harpist.

Mariah's eyes flashed like red lights on the floor of the Senate. "Adam, your hero found the spirit of his message, its heart and soul, by going south to Louisiana, and there, picking up the Kingfish tune. Economic inequality has become FDR's foe; redistributive justice his solution. A clearer statement of Huey Long's crusade could not be found, unless one looked in *Every Man A King.*

"Didn't you write some of that stuff?" Benno said.

"I helped with the book over the Summer of '33. Mostly around the edges. You know, line editing and things like that. It was Huey's biography and his voice."

"Was it fun, working for a man like that?" Benno asked, sounding skeptical.

"Call it what you will. Adam says I was bewitched. But helping him was magnificent. A great privilege. All around him were converted members of his band, each with the zeal of newly discovered faith. I was no exception."

Adam couldn't resist piling on. "Hallelujah, it's all true. He became the center of her cosmos."

Tension covered the table. Mariah set her jaw, scowling at Adam. "For the love of Heaven. Go lay an egg."

Violet broke in. "When I said 'moonshine' I was thinking especially of this 'economic inequality' thing. What the candidates say is eloquent and noble. But, for us, the question is do they have any practical reality? Something we can put in our stomachs or sleep under? Take to the bank and spend? I'm a fan of the President, but I fear he's shining moon-beams in our eyes."

They carried on in similar vein throughout dinner, each a Democrat, each a supporter of the President, yet each for a different reason and with a different interpretation of the great man's words and intentions. The subject of love and relationships never came up.

Had they been able to read from Chapter 30 of *Every Man a King*, they would have been impressed at Long's insightful argument:

I foresaw the depression in 1929. In letters reproduced in this volume, I had predicted all of the consequences many years before they occurred.

The wealth of the land was being tied up in the hands of a very few men. The people were not buying because they had nothing with which to buy. The big business interests were not selling, because there was nobody they could sell to.

One percent of the people could not eat any more than any other one per cent; they could not live in any more houses than any other one per cent. So, in 1929, when the fortune-holders of America grew powerful enough that one per cent of the people owned nearly everything, ninety-nine per cent of the people owned practically nothing, not even enough to pay their debts, a collapse was at hand.

God Almighty had warned against this condition. Thomas Jefferson, Andrew Jackson, Daniel Webster, Theodore Roosevelt, William Jennings Bryan and every religious leader known to this earth had declaimed against it. So it was no new matter, as it was termed, when I propounded the line of thought with the first crash of 1929, that the eventful day had arrived when accumulation at the top by the few had produced stagnation by which the vast multitude of the people were impoverished at the bottom.

———•———

But when one man must have more houses to live in than ninety-nine other people; when one man decides he must own more foodstuff than any other ninety-nine people own; when one man decides he must have more goods to wear for himself and family than any other ninety-nine people, then the condition results that instead of one hundred people sharing the things that are on earth for one hundred people, that one man, through his gluttonous greed, takes over ninety-nine parts for himself and leaves one part for the ninety-nine.

18

RESPONDING TO THE INSTINCTS AND strong interests of the boss, the WPA's public relations department had become a well-oiled machine, as good at promoting accomplishments as averting disasters. There were constant opportunities to do both. Adam heard of a day-long conference PR was planning in June to dangle before the press some of the artists Federal One was supporting. The idea was to counter the mumblings that, in growing volume, were being heard on the Hill about wasting taxpayer money on art. PR circulated a staff bulletin inviting submission of suitable names to roll out. Adam immediately thought of Benno and Violet. Given his boss' warnings about appearances, he quickly dropped the idea of sponsoring his brother. Violet was another matter. Writing a glowing recommendation, he put her name in the hopper.

She was selected. Adam offered her his apartment for the night before the conference, so she wouldn't have to get up at an impossibly early hour to be in Washington when the event began. She accepted. Neither of them mentioned the incident in her apartment following the opening of *Triple A Plowed Under,* although it was very much on each of their minds as the conference date approached.

Violet arrived in Union Station in time for a late dinner. She saw Adam waiting at the gate. Greeting him, she dropped her suitcase for the welcoming embrace she had anticipated with care. Her only contact with Adam would be her lips touching his cheek, ever so briefly. Adam too had rehearsed the moment, and for him it would dovetail exactly with her plan. Despite the turmoil each of them felt as they embraced, neither plan fell apart. Picking up her suitcase, Adam hailed a cab and took her to a bistro near his apartment in Adams Morgan.

Violet had been briefed by PR over what seemed endless telephone calls.

"Your PR people leave no stone unturned, do they. Rather than relaxing me, I think all this prep work has made me more self-conscious. They want me to play up the 'soup kitchen to stage' angle. You'll succeed if you make the audience weep, one of them told me. Yes, really. Stop shaking your head."

"Ok. There's no accounting for the zeal of these New Deal PR types. Let's finish up this wine. It's late and you need time to dream, if that's your assignment. By the way, I should warn you, it's a hot, humid night and my flat's not air conditioned."

"The paper said it's supposed to rain buckets," Violet said.

Adam directed Violet to his bedroom. He planned to sleep on the couch. The windows in both rooms were open wide to catch what little breeze there was. The air was still and sullen.

"What can I get you before we turn in?" Adam said, after each had finished bedtime ablutions.

"I'd take a nice cold glass of milk, if that's possible," Violet said. "Otherwise, I'm all set."

He poured two small glasses of milk, draining the bottle. They clicked glasses, standing in front of the refrigerator.

"Here's to tomorrow's performance," Adam said.

A rainstorm hit soon after they were asleep, accompanied by thunder, lightning and plenty of wind. It caused the drawn shade to flap wildly and drove the rain into the bedroom, wetting the sheet that lightly covered Violet, who had chosen, because of the heat, to wear only her panties to bed.

She got up and headed into the rain to raise the shade out of the way and close the window. She was still fumbling with the shade when Adam came up behind her. He too was clad only in underpants. Each time the shade flew up, the street light etched Violet's body in dark and light. It was too much for Adam. He put his arms around her now thoroughly wet body and, squeezing, pulled her to him. He moved his hands up to cup her breasts. The shade continued to flap and the rain to splatter against them both. He slowly turned her around to face him. And there they clung, oblivious of the shade's racket or the wind and rain inside or the lightning and thunder outside, their bodies touching everywhere and all at once, in what seemed a timeless moment of lust.

When the storms, both inside and out, had abated, Violet knew, and knew she would never forget, feelings that sprang to life with Adam that night but had been missing with Benno for so long. Why it happened was beyond her ability to fathom. She hadn't fallen in love with Adam. She knew him much more through Benno in a vicarious way than face to face. His passion and vulnerability in dealing with his Father had engaged her emotionally and those tender feelings turned to passion in her apartment. And, then, in Adam's apartment, had ignited to achieve an entirely new result. She thought of Shamhat. Of Enkidu. Of his expression on the sculpture. Was this what Shamhat felt? Every time? The how of it puzzled her. Was it technique? None of this could she ask Adam to explore with her. Too personal and embarrassing for Benno. And equally for her. Impossible.

All Adam knew was that he had enjoyed the night and the company but there could be no repeat performances. His relationship with Violet was fraught with huge difficulties and risks. His attraction to her had buried itself in lust and escaped control, but only because of external events, or acts of god as some might describe them. Nothing like that would happen again. This he promised himself. And, then, in the morning, before they both left for the WPA offices, he exchanged promises along the same lines with Violet. For this was a subject they could discuss, and needed to discuss, together.

———◆———

After *Spending to Save* came out in 1936, Harry Hopkins found it hard to free up Adam to do anything other than write in the boss' style whenever the boss needed his ideas put into words. In contributing to the book's success, Adam had proved himself. Word got around. Others in the Administrator's office had projects for Adam, and Harry, during those rare moments when he tried to think like a manager, wanted Adam to spread his wings. Generally, though, Adam's book of assignments from the boss crushed such thoughts. He was so attuned to his boss that he could anticipate his needs, think as he thought and write as he would have wished to write. Increasingly, Harry Hopkins believed the projects he assigned to Adam could only be done by him.

One morning, in the Fall of 1936, Harry summoned Adam at 7:00 am to discuss a new project. On arrival, ahead of his boss, Adam found the office filled with last night's stale air, a sodden mix of burnt toast, coffee, tobacco and the sweat of New Dealers toiling past midnight to rid the country of poverty. They needed small excuse to put in all-nighters. Boasting rights rather than billable hours were their currency, with the number of night-time hours logged a widely accepted measure of their work's importance.

Adam was taking it all in when his boss arrived. His face, always lean, seemed more so this morning, skin taut across high cheekbones, angling down like an axe to his chin, where, Adam saw, some stubble had escaped his normally meticulous razor. The angular aspect of Harry Hopkins' face was exaggerated by large ears and the wide brim of the light brown felt hat he always wore. The man was a repetition of V's, looking down from his hatchet face to the narrow button down collar, narrow overhand knotted stripe tie, vest and single buttoned dark suit coat.

"Looks like a late night," Adam said as his boss ducked around the desk to plop down in his swivel chair.

"A night devoted to the campaign. We were honored, no, actually we were amazed, by Farley's interest and FDR's too. Honestly, they wanted to know how we thought FDR should handle all the venom coming from left and right. From Huey Long's followers, Father Coughlin and

Dr. Townsend, to Landon and that traitor, Al Smith. They're getting set for a major speech in Madison Square Garden on October 31. Oh, it was a wing-dinger of a night on the phone."

Adam had never seen his boss so pleased with himself. Sleep or no sleep, he was revved up.

"Don't look, but I must have developed a cauliflower ear. Why was it so much fun? Because he took our advice. And what was that advice? We urged him to apologize for nothing. Tell them that for four years he struck a balance between the liberty of citizens to do as they please and the needs of all citizens, of society in general. Tell them he believes in individualism up to the point where the individualist starts to operate at the expense of society. Tell them that never in history have the forces of business and financial monopoly been so united against one candidate as they stand today against him. They are united in their hate for him. Remind them of that. Then tell them that he welcomes their hatred. That, in his first administration, the forces of selfishness and lust for power met their match. Tell them that in his second administration, these forces will meet their master. Oh, it was a grand evening."

Adam didn't know what to say. On such occasions he had the sound instinct to say nothing. Now, despite being thrilled by his boss' sharing these disclosures and by the message they conveyed, one with which he wholeheartedly agreed, he kept silent. Of course, these ideas had little to do with the WPA's mission. But, as Adam long ago recognized, Hopkins was a man of many parts, the source of his genius, and of FDR's trust and affection.

"Well, here I am, reporting as requested. What'll it be today?"

"Have you noticed how hard our leaders are working to keep the WPA out of this campaign? Sure, last night we laid hands on FDR's message, but he won't boast about what we are doing and I know enough not to try to sell him on that idea, despite our accomplishments. We are the focus of all this baloney about Communism. You saw Hearst's rag claiming, in a front page editorial, that Moscow had ordered Communists to work on FDR's campaign!

"So, I need you to write a general purpose speech in defense of our work, looking at our white-collar projects and particularly at the women we hire. The jokes about our construction work, that our initials stand for "We Piddle Around" or "We Poke Along," have faded in the face of our solid record. Even the newly minted "boondoggle," which caught on last year after those Alderman hearings in New York. You remember I refused to apologize for our research projects. And I won't do it now. How absurd to demand of professionally trained scientists or artists that they be given picks and shovels to repair streets. It's dumb people who criticize because they don't understand, and that's what's going on around this country, God damn it!"

"Timing?" Adam asked, putting away his yellow pad, which by office protocol had to accompany anyone summoned to the boss' office.

"I have no date for this speech, but one could be set at any time. Design it for me or Florence to present at any and all occasions. In the meantime, I'll squirrel it away."

"I'll try to have it in a week to ten days. There are a few other things on my plate."

Adam rose to leave.

"A final thought. Be sure you talk about how many women we've hired. Close to 300,000 at last count. How important job opportunities for women are. And work in that story about Iturbi."

Adam had sat down. He looked perplexed.

"Yea, I bet you read about this hero's critique of women musicians."

"You mean Jose Iturbi, the famous conductor?"

"That's the one. He announced that women are physically limited from attaining the musical standard of men and limited temperamentally besides. This absurdity was answered by Antonia Brico, conductor of the New York Women's Symphony Orchestra. She demanded of Iturbi and the other male leaders of orchestras around the world a simple blindfold test. When auditions are held for orchestra positions, she wanted judges to sit behind curtains and select the players by ear with gender unknown. She pointed to the fact that in our big orchestras, women play only on the harp. But not in the WPA's Federal Symphony Orchestra, where artists are rated without prejudice. Next time you're in New York, go to hear the WPA Theater of Music. You'll see a woman concert master, Carmela Ippolito, fiddling away in the first violin's chair."

Adam was not as well informed about the woman's story as Hopkins assumed. But that was typical of the boss. He always, cavalierly, dismissed gaps in Adam's knowledge, saying that it was basic to a lawyer's tool kit that he be able swiftly to master new subjects. After all, this is what litigators do every day, and if they could do it, so could any trained lawyer.

Adam surprised himself by putting together a draft in just five days. It sat on his desk unedited for another three while he attended to other projects. And then he gave it a hard edit.

Adam turned the draft over to Harry Hopkins and Florence Kerr, his Assistant Administrator. Each accused him of writing in the voice of the other. Each followed that crack with praise. Were Adam a cat, that purring sound might well have been heard at the White House.

———◆———

When the Seventy-fifth Congress assembled in January, 1937, more than 75% of the membership in both House and Senate were Democratic. FDR stood at the highest pinnacle of political power ever seen in American history, at least in times of peace. What these facts meant for the New Deal's relief program was not clear, but Harry Hopkins was worried. Deep down, he knew FDR was no Keynesian.

Frances Perkins had reported on Keynes' impression of the President, and the President's impression of Keynes, right after their unsuccessful meeting in the White House in May, 1934. FDR told her, "he left a whole rigamarole of figures. He must be a mathematician rather than a political economist." Keynes countered by admitting to her some disillusionment. With regret, he told her that he had "supposed the President more literate, economically speaking."

And then there were the powerful influences of family, Groton and Harvard, which considered deficit financing an iniquity and balanced budgets the true moral pathway. Harry saw these forces pushed aside to make way for the first One Hundred Days. But he knew they had not been swept away entirely. In December, with signs of recovery appearing in the data (but not in the work force, where some 15 to 20 percent remained unemployed), FDR concluded he had turned the country around. Now it had the wind at its back. With Treasury Secretary Morgenthau cheering him on, he would not only reduce spending already authorized for the current fiscal year, ending June 30, but reduce it much more in fiscal 1938, a drastic cut big enough to balance the budget.

Harry Hopkins was appalled by the President's decision. He had fought it, but his gifts at persuasion ran aground on the President's soaring self-confidence. At his weekly staff meeting, with Adam taking notes, Harry said, "Boys, our work's cut out for us. The President smells recovery around the corner. Wants to restore 'home economics' to the country. It'll be ugly no matter what. Best I can do is ask for $1.5 billion."

"Why Harry, there will be blood in the streets," Aubrey Williams said. "That's less than a third of what we got two years ago. You must find some way to turn him around."

"Don't think I don't understand. Here's how bad it is. You all know Marriner Eccles — that great Mormon, great banker, great fed chairman. Well, the President met with him earlier this month to get his blessing. Eccles was blunt in rejecting FDR's plan. He said plain enough that if you reduce Government spending before restoring full employment you will abort recovery. He put it all in a memorandum. And word got around. In whispers, New Dealers were quoting the Fed Chairman's opinion: 'Any serious attempt to achieve a balanced budget in 1938 will not only fail but put the country into an economic tailspin.' Eccles was fearless. He even debunked FDR's repeated use, in public speeches, of the popular analogy between family debt and national debt. Look, boys, if Eccles can't turn him, don't expect Hopkins to succeed."

In fact, Hopkins had to mount a full-court press just to get the $1.5 billion. So vigorous was his campaign that many new enemies appeared on Capitol Hill to join those already dead set against his agency. When Senator James Byrnes of South Carolina asked Hopkins if he could get along with only $1 billion, he replied sharply, "I can, but the unemployed couldn't."

Upon learning that the House had passed the appropriations bill, Adam rushed into the boss' office.

Harry was facing away from his desk, deep in telephone conversation with his wife, Barbara, who had been diagnosed with breast cancer earlier that year. Sensing Adam had important news, he wheeled around, putting down the receiver after promising his wife to call back.

"Ok, let's have it," Harry said.

"Good news, Harry. The House gave you the 1.5. What's more, you won the battle over 'earmarking.' WPA can spend the money in broad categories, with discretion given to FDR and you."

"Terrific news. Is that all?"

"Yea, all the good news. The House stuck a sentence in the bill cutting your salary from $12 to $10."

"No fucking way. The hatred of these heroes knows no bounds. How petty can you get? You know why, don't you. It's not the 1.5 that's eating them; it's that I took away the earmarks, the pork they feast on."

"With earmarks, the bigger the WPA's appropriation, the bigger their feast. I get it."

———◆———

As word of the Hopkins plan to cut the WPA budget escaped, workers throughout the country, but especially in New York City, revolted. As layoff notices went out, they took to the streets. On May 27th, 7,000 from the WPA arts units in the City staged a one-day strike. Benno and Violet hadn't kept up with the news. That strike was a wake-up call.

"I want to get involved," Violet said, as they read what had happened. "They're charging Adam's boss with bad faith. For goodness sakes, Benno, you should call him on this one."

"If you're right, I think it's your turn to call Adam. But this is hard to believe about the man Adam worships. What sort of bad faith?"

"Apparently Hopkins, in support of cutting his budget, claimed that Government economists estimated at least 500,000 of the WPA workers being laid off would find work. Of course, nothing of the sort is happening. Please call your brother. I just can't do it."

Benno chose not to make the call. This time he saw vividly the conflict he would be dumping in Adam's lap. Violet took the lead in contacting fellow workers and preparing to protest. When the $1.5 billion appropriation became law, Harold Stein, administrator for the four Federal arts projects in the city, sent dismissal notices to 1,709 Theater Project workers and another 1,139 to those in other arts projects. She and Benno were among those dismissed. They also were among the 600 WPA artists, writers and musicians who imprisoned Harold Stein in his office on the third floor of 235 East 42nd Street, where the offices for arts projects were located. Violet agreed to join the strike strategy committee. It demanded appeals board review. The idea was to permit dismissal only if a worker had no need of WPA work.

The demands were rejected by senior staff in Washington. The committee refused to release Mr. Stein, who rejected police escort out of the building for fear of causing a riot. The demonstration grew in intensity, fueled by an ill-timed announcement by Lieutenant Colonel Somervell, the City's WPA Administrator, with jurisdiction over 169,000 workers on construction and white collar projects, that 34,000 of them would be dropped by October 15.

Over Violet's objection, and that of two others, the committee demanded Mr. Stein telephone Mayor La Guardia for help. The Mayor couldn't be found. Air in the crowded building became stifling. Two women were overcome and taken to Metropolitan Hospital.

Violet continued to beg Benno to contact Adam. In turn, he insisted she make the call.

"You're a member of the committee. It's ok for you to call in that capacity. As his brother, it's not ok for me. He'll go through the roof. Why in the world won't you do it?"

Explaining nothing, Violet remained adamant. As the situation deteriorated through the night, Benno finally picked up the phone. Adam was in his office and took the call. He listened carefully to Benno's description of conditions in the office and his argument for appeals board review. When Benno had finished, he said, "It's crazy down here, too. Thanks for calling. I'll see what can be done."

Through the night, triangular negotiations continued among the committee, Mr. Stein, and senior WPA officials in Washington. At 8 AM, the siege was lifted, allowing Mr. Stein to go home. He had agreed with the workers that the methods of dismissal had been "unsound." The strikers continued to hold the offices until late in the afternoon, when Washington officials promised appointment of an outside board to consider their problems. Some of the committee cheered the victory. The more skeptical ones kept their doubts to themselves. Count Benno and Violet in that camp. They returned to their apartment, downbeat and exhausted. The settlement was Rube Goldberg at his best. They had no idea what, if anything, Adam had contributed to the outcome. His tidy mind, Benno observed, could easily have rebelled.

They showered and slept. Over coffee the next morning, Benno said, "After an initial surge of excitement, I grew discouraged. I know you did too. Why? I think the problem is we're not just fighting Harry Hopkins. In fact, from all that Adam has told me, Hopkins has been a fierce fighter for us. The problem is bigger, much bigger than the WPA. It's the President and Congress. They're so exhausted by their own compassion and generosity that they're willing to bet enough's been done. They've been seduced into believing that a rising tide of private industry will lift all boats."

"I don't believe it, but there's not much we can do," Violet said. "I bet my last dime that last night was a Pyrrhic victory that lifts not a single lifeboat."

"Yea, what can we the people do?"

———◆———

With deliberate irony, President Roosevelt called the committee "un-American." He was not alone in thinking so. Harry Hopkins and his entire staff at the WPA held the same opinion.

On May 26, 1938, by Resolution 282, the House of Representatives created the Special Committee to Investigate Un-American Activities and Propaganda in the United States. At the time, the Democrats enjoyed fabulous majorities in the House of 244 and in the Senate of 58. The Speaker named Martin Dies, a Texas Democrat, Chairman. There were four other Democrats and two Republicans.

The incentive for creating this committee, known generally as the Dies Committee, was to inquire into the ramifications of Nazi activities in America. In the Spring, indictments in a German spy trial were handed down after months of investigation by the FBI. In addition, in April, a riot broke out between American Legionnaires and members of the German-American Bund. During the debate over Resolution 282, Martin Dies declared with passionate hyperbole that the American Nazi movement had 480,000 members and that the President was in danger of being assassinated.

Despite the narrow focus intended, the Dies Committee's authority was much broader, encompassing "un-American propaganda activities in the United States" and "subversive and un-American propaganda" instigated from here or abroad that "attacks the principle or form of Government as guaranteed by our Constitution."

Martin Dies was an odd choice. He enjoyed great popularity among many of the Fascist and quasi-Nazi groups that were supposed to be the committee's chief target for investigation. He had been the author of several bills designed to deport aliens and drastically restrict immigration. His bills were distributed by the likes of the "Order of 76," a New York anti-Semitic and pro-Nazi society. At an early June meeting of the American Patriots, a New York super-patriotic society, a speaker declared Dies to be head of "a good committee," one that "we American Patriots need not fear."

Hearings began in August. Only one day was devoted to testimony related to Fascist, Nazi and super-patriotic activities. Following this cursory examination, the committee's attention swung swiftly to communism, where it remained throughout 1938. A report of its investigation was submitted to the House on January 3, 1939. Chairman Dies sought one million dollars in funding to continue the committee's work by undertaking a full-dress investigation of the WPA. He expressed determination to rid the Government of such "subverters" as Harry Hopkins, Harold Ickes, Frances Perkins and other "communists and fellow travelers."

How did Sinclair Lewis know, in 1935, when he wrote his book, and then, a year later when he doubled down by adapting *It Can't Happen Here* for the stage, that in 1938 it would happen here, in the chamber of the most representative body in the country, the House of Representatives? How did he know that basic democratic principles would be cast aside by the Dies Committee in relentless pursuit of communistic wisps of its members' over-wrought imaginations?

Investigating committees operate as quasi-judicial bodies that are a law unto themselves. They have subpoena power and use it extensively. Witnesses who fail to appear in response to subpoena are cited for contempt. However, committees cannot be compelled to hear people who demand to testify. Their hearings follow few of the rules of evidence and procedure developed by the courts over centuries to assure essential fairness. They may hold secret sessions, hear witnesses *in camera*, and receive evidence in any manner they choose. They may hire investigators and other personnel. Persons accused by witnesses or members of the committee have no right to confront those making the accusations or to defend themselves. committees may alter their findings before giving them to the public so that what's made public in terms of both findings and testimony can be and often is altered from the full record, which has limited distribution to legislators. Finally, congressmen are immune from libel suits for statements made in the line of duty, however false they may be and whether knowingly made or not.

The Dies Committee's hearings were open to newspapermen alone. Characters were impugned and reputations destroyed by witnesses without even the knowledge of those being harmed. Opportunity to answer charges and weaken or destroy the credibility of these witnesses was denied. The first witness called in regard to communism set the stage for what was to come. He was Colonel John P. Frey of the American Federation of Labor (the AFL). He testified that the Committee for Industrial Organization (the CIO) was ruled by communists, that the leaders of nearly every union affiliated with the CIO were Moscow-dominated and that all of the central leaders of the CIO with the exception of John L. Lewis were likewise communistic. Colonel Frey named 280 CIO union officials, none of whom were allowed to appear before the committee, either for denial or corroboration. The committee paid no attention to the fact that the AFL and CIO were bitter rivals for the affection of workers.

The Dies Committee fattened the record by having testimony "read in" to the printed record with little or no attempt to establish its authenticity. Often such material was not even read to the committee, but furnished directly to the Printing Office for inclusion in the hearings. In the first volume of hearings alone, more than half the testimony (over 500 pages) had been "read in" with little or no questioning. This testimony named as "communist" 640 organizations, 483 newspapers and 280 labor organizers.

Despite being the paradigm of Washington's most inside insider, Harry Hopkins was slow to recognize the Dies Committee as a palpable source of danger to the WPA. As the committee began its hearings, four journalists, Frank R. Kent, Joseph Alsop, Robert Kintner and Arthur Krock each claimed Hopkins had said to a friend at one of New York's racetracks, in August, that "We shall tax and tax, and spend and spend, and elect and elect." It was surely a canard. Hopkins stated categorically that he had said no such thing. "I deny the whole works and the whole implication of it." But the phrase was too juicy to be forgotten. In late December, the President nominated Hopkins to his Cabinet as Secretary of Commerce. When Hopkins was called before the Senate Commerce Committee for confirmation hearings, the allegation became the subject of intense investigation. The anonymous, clandestine, mysterious witness was not revealed. The furor caused by this journalistic invention, without doubt, distracted Hopkins from the WPA work at hand, including a careful assessment of what the Dies Committee was undertaking. Although the entire arts program used less than three-fourths of one percent of the total WPA appropriation, Hopkins and his senior staff should have realized that the Dies Committee's intense focus on the Theater Project and the Writers Project was capable of adversely affecting not just those projects but the WPA overall. Instead, as they read, with increasing frequency, of the hearings, they thought it a Communist witch hunt, to be ridiculed at the water fountain or over a coffee break or between races at the track. The very effective capacity of the WPA's Information Division lay dormant.

In fact, the Dies Committee had mastered the art of creating propaganda through testimony and getting it transformed into news. Hallie Flanagan considered the committee an existential threat. Although muzzled by the WPA rule that only the agency's information division in Washington could answer press stories, she wrote Chairman Dies twice over the Summer, requesting the opportunity to put the work of the Theater Project on the record. Neither request was even acknowledged. The allegations presented to the Dies Committee, heedless of glaring questions of creditability, were scooped up by the press and presented to the public in hyperbolic form, leaving hard-to-erase marks on the public mind and the Theater Project's morale.

Adam first became involved with the Dies Committee hearings when, feeling ignored and desperate, Hallie Flanagan called him in September to ask for help.

"Dies means business, Adam. The threat is real. You've got to wake them up!"

Having followed in the papers the nearly daily output of the committee's propaganda machine, Adam was already alarmed. He went to the boss' office, where he found Harry Hopkins on the phone, speaking with the President about strategy for his confirmation hearing. Adam realized how difficult it was becoming for even a man of such large energy and intelligence, such ample capacity for bright peripheral vision in the field of politics, to tend to his knitting at the WPA. Emotionally speaking, Adam feared his boss, or at least a large part of him, had already decamped.

Hopkins waved Adam in with his left hand while stubbing out a butt with the right, phone held vise-like between chin and shoulder.

"Yes, yes. It must have been Max Gordon. No, a New York theatrical producer. He's backed off about the exact words. Now he just claims that's what I meant. Heywood Broun was there too. And Dan Arnstein. They'll testify if necessary. Don't worry. I'll handle it." Hopkins put down the phone, fixing Adam with his eyes.

Passion and hope, Adam thought to himself. They're what drives him. Hopeful passion; passionate hope. Whatever.

"Adam, I'm speaking to you. You're just the man I wanted to see. Expect a call from Hallie. She thinks I'm leaning on the shovel instead of using it against Dies. Thinks he's caught us with our pants down. I've asked her to pull a brief together, refuting every absurd charge Dies has ginned up. I'm assigning you to help her. If I recall correctly, you arrived with legal training. Couldn't have rubbed off so fast, even around this shop."

"Ok. Shouldn't we be pointing to have Hallie testify, once the brief is ready? I know she's eager to do combat with Dies and his fellow Fascists."

"Hey, watch that language. Who knows what a spook like that can do to a phone." Adam looked sheepish and confused. Was the boss joking?

"I'm sure you know what happened when my loose tongue began to wag at the racetrack." Hopkins was smiling as he rooted around in an almost empty pack of Lucky Strikes.

"As for Hallie testifying, that's for discussion. Some around here think she'd hurt her own cause. They think she's too honest and aggressive to handle the give and take of a hearing. We can't ask her suddenly to develop tact or guile. Wild horses aren't going to change her."

As Adam turned to leave, Hopkins said, "You might get legal involved. They can help."

The brief was completed by the beginning of December. On the first page, it summarized the committee's findings, drawn from testimony:

1. That plays produced by the Theater Project are "communistic, subversive and un-American."
2. That its audiences are communistic.
3. That its employees are communistic.
4. That it is dominated by the Workers' Alliance, City Projects Council and Supervisors' Council, all subsidiaries of the Communist Party.

On Sunday, December 4, Adam joined Hallie for a meeting called by Ellen S. Woodard, Assistant Administrator of the WPA for Women's and Professional Projects. Emmet Lavery and Theodore Mauntz, who had worked with Hallie on the brief, were present. So, too, was Henry Alsberg, head of the Federal Writers' Project, and David K. Niles, Hopkins' deputy from the Information Division. The committee had scheduled a hearing the next day. Hallie believed the meeting had been called to go over the brief and help Hallie and Henry prepare their testimony. So did Adam.

To shocked silence, David Niles announced that Ellen Woodard would appear for the WPA, representing the interests of both projects.

Hallie was the first to recover her composure.

"Henry and I have been silenced since these hearings began in August, unable to defend our projects against the malice and slander spewed forth by Dies. For reasons I don't understand, the formidable resources of the WPA's PR group were never tapped to come to our defense. But we were promised our day in court. Tomorrow is that day. With all due respect to Ellen, she won't be able to answer technical questions. How could she? And she won't be able to defend our briefs because she hasn't been part of the large effort to write them or assemble supporting material. I submit David, you are making a huge mistake, for Theater, a life-threatening mistake. Does Harry support this?"

Before Niles could answer, Henry Alsberg began. Hallie's question was never answered. Adam hadn't a clue.

Henry spoke passionately, to the same effect. David was unmoved. It was not Adam's place to argue uninvited, although had he been asked, he would have urged that Hallie and Henry be permitted to defend their own programs. Ellen Woodward, he thought, was a step away from almost all the facts surrounding the committee's claims, in truth a very big step that could not help but dilute and weaken the defense.

The next day, at 10 AM, Chairman Dies reconvened his committee and swore in Ellen Woodward. Adam was on hand to listen and report back to his boss. His report would begin with a brief sketch of the chairman, the rangy Texan with cowboy drawl and a big, black cigar.

Mrs. Woodward stated that she was appearing because she was the WPA official in charge of Federal One, the division housing the Writers and Theater Projects. Asked if she intended to put Hallie Flanagan on the stand at a later time, she said she had no such intention.

Adam grew increasingly chagrined as Mrs. Woodward accepted the high level of hostility present among committee members and, single-handedly, raised it throughout the day by being confrontational, ornery and defensive. Asked if she was familiar in detail with the work of the two projects in New York, she replied: "I am telling you what I know to the extent that any administrator could who has a nationwide program, and I repeat that we select the best people, the best qualified people that we can for this work."

Shown two letters on WPA stationery signed in her name by what appeared to be her signature, she was asked if, in fact, the signatures were hers. She replied that one appeared not to be her signature and one appeared to be her signature, but in each case she couldn't be sure. Neither letter was significant.

The chairman said, "Now, Mrs. Woodward, here you have admitted that you cannot even testify to your own signatures, and yet you undertake to degrade witnesses who have appeared before this committee and make the charge that this committee has handled this matter in an un-American way."

At one point she demanded to know if any of the committee members had actually read the plays being criticized. Congressman Starnes of Alabama responded. "We were appointed to ask questions and to investigate, not to be investigated." He demanded and received an apology.

Adam watched with distress as the committee grew in its conviction that Mrs. Woodward was trying to deny access to Hallie Flanagan and Henry Alsberg. Although Mrs. Woodward claimed to the committee that she could answer all its questions concerning the two projects, it became increasingly obvious that she couldn't or wouldn't. She was so evasive in her answers as to kindle growing suspicion.

Returning for the afternoon session, Mrs. Woodward brought Hallie Flanagan and Henry Alsberg with her. When asked by the chairman if she wanted to read the next statement on the Theater or have Mrs. Flanagan read it, she exhibited hurt feelings by replying that "it seems to be the consensus of opinion of the committee that you think that I am not a competent person to testify for my division." "Ouch" Adam muttered to himself.

It was "Ouch" again just before the day's session ended. The chairman had said that in the morning the committee would continue with Mrs. Woodward and then hear from Mr. Alsberg and Mrs. Flanagan. Mrs. Woodward replied, "The point the chairman was making is that my testimony that I am giving is not satisfactory to the committee, and the fact that I asked to testify as the responsible head of this division does not meet with the approval of the committee; is that true?"

Adam thought she was creating an ugly scene, one that would damage the WPA. Showing a restraint that surprised him, the chairman declared that Mrs. Woodward's gratuitous statement "evidences some animus."

Later, Mrs. Woodward stepped down and Hallie Flanagan took the stand. In departing, Mrs. Woodward repeatedly said she did not believe the committee had "reflected on her competency as a witness," despite having earlier claimed precisely that. And the chairman, in excusing her, adopted a parental tone in saying he understood that she couldn't have personal knowledge of many facts being sought by the committee. Adam thought both statements a contrived coda to a remarkably bad show for the WPA.

Harry kept shaking his head over Adam's report, obviously chagrined.

"You're upset, but by what part of my report?" Adam said.

"Oh, hellfire. That I allowed myself to be talked into using Woodward as our sword and shield. Don't say it. I know what you would have advised. Now, to Hallie and Henry."

Adam felt good in being able to report that both had distinguished themselves. Although the thrust and parry of the exchanges was a solemn affair, occasional bursts of humor would break the tension. Here's the best example. Congressman Starnes read from an article Hallie had authored for the *Theater Arts Monthly* in which she said that the ambition of workers' theaters to remake the social structure without the help of money was invested with "a certain Marlowesque madness." This exchange followed:

Mr. STARNES. You are quoting from this Marlowe. Is he a Communist?

Mrs. FLANAGAN. I am very sorry. I was quoting from Christopher Marlowe.

Mr. STARNES. Tell us who Marlowe is, so we can get the proper reference, because that is all that we want to do.

Mrs. FLANAGAN. Put in the record that he was the greatest dramatist in the period of Shakespeare, immediately preceding Shakespeare.

Harry roared. "That's as funny as anything I've ever heard coming from the Hill. Priceless! Should be front page news: 'Congressman discovers Marlowe not a Communist.'

What happened next?"

"Hallie was patient. Impressively so. She withstood mind-numbing efforts to undermine her powerful rebuttal. But, neither she nor Henry was able to erase from most of the committee the beliefs they had carried into the hearing room."

The danger to the Theater Project, in particular, was manifest, Adam told Harry. "This exchange between Dies and Hallie, towards the end of the session, will give you the picture:

> The CHAIRMAN. Then this Federal Theater is a very powerful vehicle of expression, isn't it, and of propaganda, because, as you say, it reaches 25,000,000 people. It therefore can be used or abused.
>
> Mrs. FLANAGAN. Yes.
>
> The CHAIRMAN. With serious consequences, can it not?
>
> Mrs. FLANAGAN. Yes, sir."

By Act of Congress on June 30, 1939, the Theater Project, alone among WPA undertakings, was killed. Adam explained it to Benno and Violet over the phone the following day.

"Look, we know that despite overwhelming Democratic majorities in both Houses, a strong reactionary trend began last year. Good people were knocked out of Congress. Times were getting better. People were losing the specter of the Depression and thinking in terms of their own pockets. So you see, we were getting a little more selfish again. A large part of the Congress campaigned on the promise to cut relief funds, cut WPA, get rid of Hopkins, etcetera. Even FDR had tacked right. But the Congressmen lambasting WPA didn't want to kill the whole thing. They had WPA projects in their backyard, whether a school, or a bridge or surveying or what have you. But they looked at the arts projects, and particularly the Theater Project, which was not only highly visible but, as Dies had shown, highly vulnerable as well, given its reach through language and ideas. Federal One was the only nation-wide project launched by the WPA. All others were strictly local and had powerful local support."

"That's the big difference, isn't it," Benno said.

"Did Hallie quit the fight after Dies finished with her?" Violet said.

"Hardly. In the Spring, the House Appropriations Committee debated a $1.8 billion bill to continue WPA's work. In reporting it out, the committee included a specific ban against the use of Federal funds for theater projects. Hallie had been ordered by Ellen Woodward and David Niles to lay low and do nothing. They assured her they were handling it. When she learned what was in the committee report, she went to see Hopkins at Commerce. He said, "It's your baby. Fight for it." That was all she needed. She didn't go and check with Woodward or Niles. She just started fighting. The issue had moved to the Senate. She lobbied like mad, visiting most of the senators. The Senate passed the bill and reversed the House on the ban. It proved a Pyrrhic victory. The bill went to joint conference of the Senate and House Committees. Giving up funding for the Theater Project was the Senate's last trade to get the bill approved. Despite a late start in her lobbying efforts, Hallie had almost won and probably would have if she had not been restrained by senior staff in Washington. You see, they had, early on, decided against making a fight of it. Harry wasn't on site to protect her. The President issued a statement condemning what he called 'discrimination of the worst type.' Of course, he had no choice but to sign. Defending the jobs of 8,000 employees in theater projects had to be weighed against the chance of throwing two and a half million WPA relief workers out of work."

19

WITH HIS BOSS GONE, AND the Theater Project dead and buried, Adam felt much of the joy he had found at the WPA vanish. It was time for him to move on, perhaps in Washington, perhaps in New York City, but certainly not in Manhattan, Kansas, where his Father's "Viking of the Plains" philosophy had grown more virulent with age and continuing setbacks in his fight against the New Deal.

Benno asked Adam if his experience at the WPA had changed him. Adam said, "I don't know. I met a lot of different people. You know, I think it probably made me a kinder, more considerate human being. Because I became aware of the other half, the different levels, the different problems of society. It made me aware of Government, aware of the possibilities of what it can do. And, frankly, what it can't do. It made me a little more tolerant all around."

Adam's relationship with Mariah continued in limbo. Whether it would advance or end was impossible for either of them to say. Adam had recovered from the shock of learning Mariah was, as she put it, a serial seducer. In time, he saw the addiction as just a funny quirk, an odd expression of the need for control that Mariah exhibited at every turn. They leaned into each other just enough to make other relationships, which each had tried, short-lived. They saw one another just enough to keep the tendrils entwined, their lives braided, but only in part and never enough. Adam knew the frisson he felt with Violet was, at least in part, an embrace of the things he admired in her and couldn't find in Mariah. If Benno weren't in the picture, he could imagine falling in love with her, or just loving her, even marrying and raising a family with her, with or without the "falling in" part. But for Benno, he could foresee something deep and lasting with her. Not the passion that could overtake him with Mariah. More like fresh-baked bread than Jersey-made ice cream. Eat it every day and never get sick of it. But Benno was around, with a life of his own to live, and for the moment at least he was sharing it, in innocence and gladness, with Violet. Adam told himself to relegate his relations with Violet, and the frisson they caused, to that remote place where "flings" go to be remembered as one grows old.

Adam knew someday his would die and he would be called upon to write the obituary. Could he respond with the expected cart full of half-truths, and even a few outright lies thrown in, to celebrate a man he could never comprehend and, as time passed, grew to despise?

Mariah struggled with her family's wealth, unable to give it away in service to her political goal and unwilling to spend it on herself. Her sights remained set on marriage to Adam. She came to understand that her drive to capture him had pushed him farther away, freezing their physical relationship for what, at times, seemed an eternity.

Benno and Violet remained together, trying to make it in their chosen fields in New York City. They loved one another, and knew each other, far better than most young couples who reach the altar. But the Depression's impact on their lives, though not exactly the same, discouraged them from putting marriage at the head of the list of needs, desires and ambitions each had assembled.

Violet's guilt over her night with Adam grew with time's passage and the continued obstacles in achieving in Benno's bed what she thought was her due. Finally, the burden became too heavy to bear alone. In exploring what had and had not happened during intercourse one night, Violet alluded to the wonders she had once experienced. When Benno asked her to explain, the whole story came pouring out.

When she had finished, Benno tried to comfort her with a touch of humor.

"You know, Violet, I don't mind too much. Adam was always the first to get on base as we grew up."

Violet looked hard at Benno, laughed softly and, then, began to cry.

"It was a fling for both of us," she said between sobs. "Nothing lasting, I can assure you. But for me this fling will always be remembered as joy wrapped in tragedy. Joy from the extraordinary orgasm I had during intercourse — the first and only one so far. Tragedy because of what we've been trying so hard to do, and not succeeding, despite our love, while here I go with a one night stand and it happens — gloriously — without trying at all. It should have happened with you, my love. Only with you."

"Life can be unfair. Things work out. I love you, Violet. They will. I promise."

Although symmetry might have been served had Benno told Violet about his night with Rachel, for many reasons, he did not.

The Theater Project became something of a metaphor for life, as the twins and the two women in their lives experienced it. Hard work, luck, skill, whatever, can lead to brilliant success, while at the same time carrying the germ of its own demise, precisely because it achieved so much. The pendulum swings. One excess breeds another. Consider, for example, Isaiah Bernstein and his Austrian cement plant, Huey Long or Dan Murdock. Or Harry Hopkins and the WPA. Or Hallie Flanagan and the Theater Project. Or, for the High Plains, the tractor and one-way plow. They didn't need to visit Rachel for these insights. Sir Isaac Newton captured them with his Third Law of Motion:

For every action there is an equal and opposite reaction.

And F. Scott Fitzgerald caught the idea in *The Great Gatsby:*

So we beat on, boats against the current, borne back ceaselessly into the past.

On January 10, 1939, a massive heart attack felled Dan Murdock over his typewriter, where a fiery screed was taking shape for broadcast the following week.

Dan's sense of invulnerability was not so sure as to persuade him to ignore commonplace precautions in case of emergency. Finding him, head resting heavily on the keys, the housekeeper called Adam, as Dan had instructed her to do.

The funeral was scheduled a week later. Given their Father's avoidance of organized religion in favor of a God at once more personal and abstract than found in a church, and his swerve toward pantheism, despite never using the term to describe his beliefs, Adam and Benno decided to set the venue in Wyandot's largest barn. They hoped to find enough space heaters if the collective body heat of mourners was inadequate. Of course, the barn's wiring wasn't designed for such things.

On hearing the news of Dan's death, Mariah informed Adam that she would attend, whether he invited her to travel with him or not.

"Why would you want to travel all that way for someone you never even met?" Adam said.

"You dumbest of dumb bunnies, it's you I will make the trip for. I want to help you get through it, help you prepare the eulogy and ..... Oh, so many reasons. And, if you don't like it, I'll be there anyway, ready when you change your mind. You'll recall I've had some practice in handling the death of one's parents."

About the same time, Benno told Violet. "I hope you can arrange to come with me."

When Rachel learned of Dan's death, she called Benno, pledging to help in any way she could.

"There are going to be lots of things to arrange that can best be done from town, and many that must be done before you get here. I expect you to call on me."

Before taking the train to Manhattan, Adam and Benno spent much time on the phone, helping each other digest their Father's ending, so sudden and unexpected that it took time to accept, and then only with

difficulty. He had always been there, a looming presence, looking criti-
cally over their shoulders. It would take almost magical thinking to realize he had vanished.

"Can you see yourself returning to run the farm?" Benno said.

"I've had a job I love. Now that I'm leaving the WPA, I expect to
practice law. Just because we inherit the farm doesn't mean we have to
be there to manage things, day to day. But how about you? You could
run Wyandot with your left hand and sculpt with the right. And I could
help on the business and legal side. You know, things that could be done
at a distance."

"As usual, Adam, you're way ahead of me. I'll think it over. We'll have
plenty of time to talk on the train."

Rachel had misgivings over the boys' pick of venue. When they
arrived in Manhattan, accompanied by Mariah and Violet, Rachel
immediately sought them out in Dan's house. Sitting around the kitchen
table with a pot of coffee, she explained her problem.

"I understand the idea. I think one of you told me once that your
Father loved the kingdom of beasts more than mankind. And since
neither of you attend church, holding the service there doesn't exactly
spring to mind. But here's the point. Unless you believe Dan will be
hovering over the mourners to catch every word, this funeral service,
like all others, is designed not for the dead, but for the living, offering
them a chance to mourn over a death, yes, but to remember and rejoice
in a life too. This process is best done where it's expected to be done,
where it's most familiar. And comfortable. That, my dear friends, is the
First Presbyterian Church on Leavenworth, where, I'm told, your mother
spent her Sunday mornings. Now, please, for the sake of the living in this
town, those who loved your quirky Father, move the service to that holy
place."

The couples listened in silence. They understood. And left quickly
for the church.

Dan's lawyer, Harold Simpson, was named executor in the Will. The
morning after they arrived, Adam and Benno met Harold in his office.

"Do take a seat. Like most things about your Father, there is nothing ordinary about this document. It starts with modest bequests, in the nature of termination fees, to Wyandot employees. It then directs the sale of Wyandot "forthwith," proceeds to be combined with Dan's liquid assets and held in trust by me, as trustee.

"What?" cried Adam. "That can't be."

News of their Father's decision to sell his beloved farm rather than directing its continued operation through ownership by one or both of his sons was a real shocker. It took minutes for the boys to accept what Harold had read to them.

"The terms of the trust are singular and, at first blush, perplexing," Harold explained. "The trustee is directed to invest and reinvest the corpus and all income therefrom for maximum return over an initial fifteen-year period during which no distributions are to be made. On the fifteenth anniversary, all of your issue then living become beneficiaries, receiving trust income until the youngest reaches the age of 25, when the corpus is to be distributed to all of them in equal shares and the trust dissolved."

"I hope you can tell us what's going on, Harold. Is Father bent on getting us to the altar or what?" Adam said. He was not amused.

"Hold on, Adam," Benno said softly. "We need to know more."

Harold continued.

"If neither of you have issue living on the tenth anniversary, the trustee is directed, in the very particular words crafted by your Father, 'to convey the corpus, including accumulated income, to a political policy-oriented advocacy organization whose purpose and demonstrated record, in the opinion of the trustee, after a pluperfect investigation and study, best exemplifies my corn-fed, cowman's philosophy.'"

"Oh, my God," said Adam. "At times I thought it was all a game with him. But now, his dead hand reaches out to squash us non-believers. His politics is no game. He's playing for keeps, even if it looks mean spirited and vindictive."

"Harold, can you give us a leg up on this thing? You must have some idea of Father's plan," said Benno.

"He believed it would take only a generation for his politics to sweep away the big Government types, like Teddy and FDR. He was convinced that in the space of, say, two decades, all children, even yours — no, as he put it — especially yours, would embrace his views on the role of Government."

"Ingenious," Benno said. "At once he's cut us off and not cut us off, assuming we have offspring."

"Ingenious, yes. But is it legal?" Adam said. "There must be some basis for a challenge. How about it, Harold."

"You're a lawyer, Adam. You know I can't help on that one. I wrote the Will, representing your Father, and now I serve his estate. The thing may be quirky, that I'll grant you. But it's not illegal. You'd be wasting your time."

Adam fumed. Back at Humboldt, reluctantly they disclosed Dan's directives to the two Misses, as Rachel had dubbed them.

"It's unbelievable," said Mariah. "Those detailed plans for the farm you spent so long developing on the train — tossed out the window. Gone."

"It's the power of the pen," said Violet. "But why didn't your Father talk these things over with you? I find that strange."

"Yea, held in a dead hand that's trying to reach far into the future," Adam said, bitterness now bubbling out, unrestrained. "I can't eulogize this man. I won't do it. Benno, if you have the stomach, the podium or whatever it's called in a church is all yours."

"Father liked facing us head-on in politics, but on deeply personal stuff, seldom if at all," said Benno.

"You're right. Only once, when he almost lost Wyandot, and then only because he believed his right thinking and goodness saved him and wanted to tell us about it."

Mariah had stood up and was roaming around the living room, looking frustrated and impatient.

"Adam, I've never seen you look so steamed," she said. "Whatever we're trying to accomplish, let's get to it."

No one in the room was willing to touch the Will's monetary reward for having babies. It hung, like a thunderhead, above them.

"Mariah, we've been just trying to understand Father's intentions," Benno said, "I think were almost finished with that. As for the service, I will try to pull some thoughts together. Why don't we all get some rest? Tomorrow we're going to need all the energy we can muster."

"Almost?" Adam said, looking quizzical.

"Yea. Before we retire, I wanted to share something important about the Will. At least to me. I interpret it as expressing Father's forgiveness of my career choice. Going forward, I'm treated exactly like Adam. Of course, neither of us is treated all that well, but that's only because of Father's opinion about the politics we share. He invests confidence in the offspring of a sculptor every bit as much as he does in those of a lawyer."

Violet was smiling. "Bravo, Benno. I can see from Adam's face he's about to pounce, so hang on tight."

"Benno, whether Violet approves or not, that's wishful thinking."

"Go lay an egg, Adam. It's my story, not yours."

The service was scheduled for 11 AM. There would be a reception at Dan's home afterwards. Aside from the minister, only two speakers were on the program, which included three hymns selected by Violet and Mariah, the only ones among the foursome who had attended regular church services growing up. At Adam's insistence, they would side-step Christ.

Poring over the First Presbyterian hymnal, Violet proposed three themes, with a hymn for each. Mariah suggested patriotism. Violet came up with nature. And, without much struggle, they agreed on optimism and faith for the third.

Bill White would speak first. Benno would follow. The minister yielded to Adam's request for what he called a "short-form" funeral service, having not a clue as to exactly what he meant beyond shrinking the formalities as much as doctrine and church rules would tolerate, and avoiding references to Christ.

By custom, the citizens of Manhattan came early to events clothed in sadness. To grieve the loss of Dan Murdock, they had almost filled the pews by 10:45 AM.

"Looks like a really big crowd," Violet whispered to Mariah, as they stood just outside the church door, waiting to be called by the ushers. The thought of how many Dalhartians her daddy would attract for his funeral flickered across her mind." "Who knows?" she answered, "but nothing like this. For that matter, who knows how many Dalhartians are still there?"

The first hymn was *Lord of All Hopefulness*, based on an Irish folk tune. Bill White followed, speaking briefly. He highlighted his long friendship with Dan and, for the most part, ignored Dan's politics and their disagreements. His one reference to the subject contained a stunning disclosure. "My friendship and devotion to the whole man — stockman, farmer, sportsman, philosopher, patriot and poet — always got in the way of honest discourse on our political differences, eye to eye. To be completely honest with this lovable fiery fundamentalist, I had to take refuge in the typewriter and postal service."

The congregation sang *For the Beauty of the Earth* with a deep reverence that Mariah thought could only be achieved by a farming community.

Then it was Benno's turn.

"Father was many things to many people. As you heard from Bill White, those who knew him well, who understood his eccentricities and singular attachments, who accepted him for the unique human being he was, loved him very much. I wish we could hear from the animals he nurtured: the hogs and sheep, the cattle and horses, and the cocker spaniels, for I'm sure they would praise him to the heavens, probably in the tongues of angels, for, were they to start talking, that's the quality of voice Father would have expected to hear.

"Father had more cow-sense and horse-sense than common sense. But so what. No one's perfect. Father was no dilettante. Everything he did, he did with enthusiasm — no, more than that, passion — and to a depth that eventually became mastery.

"Father could enthrall us in outings to experience nature. Especially joyful were our fishing trips to Cedar Creek in the hill pastures north of Wyandot, where its clear water, alternately swift flowing and pooled, meanders through shady forest. Following its course with a two-ounce rod, a Number 12 barbless fly and mesmerizing talk, he could turn the creek into the most promising trout stream in Colorado and transform lowly chub into majestic rainbow trout.

"Father's love for his Bluestem Hills was as ceaseless as the tides. It is customary at a funeral service to read passages from the Bible. We thought it more fitting, for Father's service, to read what he had to say about those Hills.

It's hard to describe the Bluestem Hills to anyone who has never known and loved them. They have none of the rich, flaming beauty of the forested New England mountains; none of the austere majesty of the Rockies. Rather, they are Mother Nature's round, undulating breasts, soft and warm in the sunshine, restfully inviting and rich in the promise of nurture.

There is always a breeze blowing there — cooling, refreshing, and strong enough to blow the cobwebs from a tired man's brain. There are sumac bushes and buckbrush to be found on top, but trees grow only in the dividing ravines, where little runs are fed by springs from the hills, and there the cattle find shade and water.

And, too, there is the seasonal procession of wild flowers: evening primroses, Canterbury bells, the dainty pink ball of perfume we call the sensitive rose, indigo flowers, the brilliant Indian paint brush — and dozens of others. And in the Fall, of course, the goldenrod, the wild aster and the purple Kansas gayfeather."

"Father was deeply serious about politics, a subject on which he lavished as much, and since the advent of FDR, even more, energy and time than he spent on Wyandot. As many of you are aware, his politics and that of his sons have been polar opposites, a fact that caused him untold anguish. And for Adam and me, it was no picnic.

"I have tried not to judge him in his role as spokesman for the right extreme of the Republican Party, expanded through radio broadcasts. Because I couldn't imagine it to be true, I concluded that Father wasn't the man he thought he was. I cut him a slack rope, hoping that in time, awareness of the disparity between who he thought he was and who he truly was would become clear. I now see how wrong I was. Overlooking his claim to be able to run through raindrops without getting wet, Father was exactly who he thought he was, true to himself, an original. Whether one agreed with him or not, one had to respect Father's integrity in actually being all that he seemed to be, nothing more and nothing less. Even the directives of his Will are of a piece with his beliefs and the expression of them in the life he led. Since those directives reach into the future to engage Adam and me in ways important to each of us, I think Father might have expected this eulogy to end with a bit of forward thinking.

"Uncertainties abound. In love as in politics; in friendships and families as in peace and war; in Manhattan, Kansas as in the other Manhattan; and in Washington, the seat of our Government, our prospects are ill-defined precisely because, unlike Father, we don't even know where on the stream of life we float or the how and why of being there. In the matter of exerting control over our lives, I believe Father hoped to accomplish after death what he could not accomplish in a lifetime. If that was his hope, it was doomed to crash on the rocks of reality. To be sure, we are Father's sons. And, as the orchardists say, apples typically don't fall far from the tree. But in the case of Father's twins, they fell far from the tree — much farther, indeed, than from each other."

"These thoughts bring to mind a statement Abraham Lincoln made in a hometown speech he gave in 1858. It captures with Lincolnian brevity exactly how Adam and I, and for that matter how Mariah and Violet, the women who came with us for today's service, feel as we try to peer into the future:

If we could first know where we are and whither we are tending, we could better judge what to do, and how to do it."

The service concluded with a full-throated rendition of *My Country 'Tis of Thee.*

THE END

SELECTED BIBLIOGRAPHY

Boats against the Current is a work of fiction, a product of my imagination exercised within a framework of American history from 1910 to 1938. Books relied upon to align the narrative with the enormous body of scholarship include, in alphabetical order,

Henry H. Adams' *Harry Hopkins: A Biography*

Alan Brinkley's *Huey Long, Father Coughlin & the Great Depression*

John Brooks' *Once in Golconda*

Arthur E. Burns and Edward A. Williams' *Federal Work, Security, and Relief Programs*

Papers of Dan Casement on file with the Kansas State University Library

Searle F. Charles' *Minister of Relief: Harry Hopkins and the Depression*

David Damrosch's *The Buried Book: the Loss and Rediscovery of the Great Epic of Gilgamesh*

Kenneth S. Davis' *Morning in Kansas*

Kenneth S. Davis' *FDR: The New Deal Years 1933-1937*

Morris Dickstein's *Dancing in the Dark: A Cultural History of the Great Depression*

Timothy Egan's *The Big Burn: Teddy Roosevelt & the Fire that Saved America*

Timothy Egan's *The Worst Hard Time*

Lehman Engel's *This Bright Day: An Autobiography*

Hallie Flanagan's *Arena: the Story of the Federal Theater*

The Autobiography of William Allen White, Sally Foreman Griffith, ed.

Harry Hopkins' *Spending to Save*

June Hopkins' *Harry Hopkins, Sudden Hero, Brash Reformer*

David M. Kennedy's *Freedom From Fear*

Paul A. Kurzman's *Harry Hopkins and the New Deal*

Sinclair Lewis' *It Can't Happen Here*

Huey Long's *Every Man a King, The WPA Guide to New York City*

George Mason University Library -- Oral History of the Federal Theater
Project of the WPA on file

Down & Out in the Great Depression, Robert S. McElvaine, ed.

Robert S. McElvaine's *The Great Depression*

George T. McJimsey's *Harry Hopkins: Ally of the Poor and Defender of Democracy*

Milton Meltzer's *Violins & Shovels: the WPA Arts Project*

John D. Millett's *The Works Progress Administration in New York City*

Stephen Mitchell's *Gilgamesh*

The National Archives

Clifford Odets' *Waiting for Lefty and Other Plays, New York Panorama: a Comprehensive View of the Metropolis*

Donald R. Ornduff's *Casement of Juniata*

Government and the Arts in Thirties America, Roy Rosenzweig, ed.

Arthur Schlesinger's *The Age of Roosevelt: Volumes I, II and III*

Gilbert Seldes' *The Years of the Locust*

Robert Sherwood's *Roosevelt and Hopkins, An Intimate History*

John Steinbeck's *The Grapes of Wrath*

Nick Taylor's *American-Made — the Enduring Legacy of the WPA*

Studs Terkel's *Hard Times*

T.H. Watkins' *The Hungry Years*

Nathanael West's *Miss Lonelyhearts & the Day of the Locust*

William Allen White's *Boys Then and Now*

William Allen White's *Forty Years on Main Street*

William Allen White's *Politics: The Citizen's Business,*

William Allen White's *What It's All About*

Marguerite Yourcenar's *Memoirs of Hadrian*

ACKNOWLEDGMENTS

WHILE A WORK OF FICTION, *Boats Against the Current* is my attempt to capture historical truths about the period in which the novel is set. There are a great many influences operating on one trying to write fiction in this way, too many to recount here. Instead, I wish to heap praise on Librarians as a noble calling and, in particular, those committed practitioners of this profession without whose help this book could not have been written. I refer to the Librarians at Kansas State University in Manhattan, Kansas, George Mason University in Fairfax, Virginia and the National Archives in Washington, D.C. I spent many days in the temples of history managed by these Librarians, benefiting from their dedicated and knowledgeable help, offered freely and with enthusiasm for my project.

I was extraordinarily fortunate to have a number of friends volunteer to read and critique early drafts of the manuscript. Their comments were thorough and incisive. And valuable in many different ways. I tried hard to address them in subsequent re-drafts, but never with a feeling I had succeeded entirely. I suppose a sense of falling short comes with the territory. These highly perceptive readers included George Carey, Susan Dooley, John K. Doyle, Bob Kerrey, Marianne Szegedymaszak, Franny Taliaferro, Hugh Van Dusen, Alice and Joseph Vining and Marie Winn. To all, I'm ceaselessly grateful.

No acknowledgment regarding the time-consuming process of writing a novel would be fair or complete without reference to Karen Shepard, whose always wise insights guided me through successive rewrites, and my wife, Clara, whose steady support found expression in the many meals she invented and then prepared alone and the other shared chores of living in which I fell short, all without complaint.

ABOUT THE AUTHOR

A graduate of Princeton University and Harvard Law School, Bevis Longstreth is a retired partner with the law firm Debevoise & Plimpton. He practiced in the firm's New York office for twenty years until President Ronald Reagan appointed him the sixtieth commissioner of the Securities and Exchange Commission in 1981.

In 1984, he retired from the SEC and returned to Debevoise, where he practiced corporate, finance, banking, and securities law until 1993.

A former adjunct professor at Columbia University Law School, he has been a frequent speaker on various securities and corporate law topics and has served on several banking, investment, and finance committees.

A periodic blogger for the *Huffington Post*, he has written two other historical novels, *Spindle and Bow* and *Return of the Shade,* as well as a book on law reform entitled *Modern Investment Management and the Prudent Man Rule.*

For more information, please visit www.bevislongstreth.com.

www.ingramcontent.com/pod-product-compliance
Lightning Source LLC
Chambersburg PA
CBHW072025020726
47501CB00006B/1953